D1033988

PRAISE FOR *SCARLET ODYSSEY*

"Rwizi says he based his unique science fiction and worldly tale on myths and stories he heard growing up in Swaziland . . . Because Rwizi combines technology, science fiction, and myth, the novel is like a video game filled with action and tension . . . Rwizi delivers a fast-paced story with vivid images of sub-Saharan Africa, lacing Salo's epic journey with flash, violence, drama, and a love story."

—Authorlink

"Rwizi's debut is noteworthy for its African-inspired setting."

—*Library Journal*

"It's a thrilling, fanciful debut, crammed full of imaginative world building and excellent dialogue."

—RevolutionSF

"Raised in Swaziland and Zimbabwe but now residing in South Africa, C. T. Rwizi is a remarkable new talent. He deftly juggles five very different protagonists; establishes a vast yet intricate new magical system unlike anything else I've ever seen; and unfolds stories scattered across the distant past, the chaotic present, and in entirely different planes of existence."

—Tor.com

"A promising new series by a promising new author."

—Fantasy Literature

"*Scarlet Odyssey* is an intricate and intense magical journey. This is lengthy and quite involved, with many characters and perspectives, so it could appeal to fans of the Lord of the Rings and Game of Thrones series."

—Young Adult Books Central

"At a time when we all need a little entertainment in our lives to distract from the reality of our world comes a book unlike any other."

—Fangirlish

"*Scarlet Odyssey* is an epic in every sense of the word. Almost six hundred pages of tightly woven plot, world building that keeps expanding with every chapter, a wide cast of characters, and an intricate magic system; this African-inspired fantasy has something in it for everyone."

—Bookshelves and Paperbacks

REQUIEM MOON

ALSO BY C. T. RWIZI

The Scarlet Odyssey Series

Scarlet Odyssey

REQUIEM MOON

C. T. RWIZI

Text copyright © 2021 by C. T. Rwizi
All rights reserved.

Published by 47North, Seattle

www.apub.com

Amazon, the Amazon logo, and 47North are trademarks of Amazon.com, Inc., or its affiliates.

ISBN-13: 9781542027236 (hardcover)
ISBN-10: 1542027233 (hardcover)

ISBN-13: 9781542022569 (paperback)
ISBN-10: 1542022568 (paperback)

Cover design by Shasti O'Leary Soudant

Printed in the United States of America

First Edition

For Busie

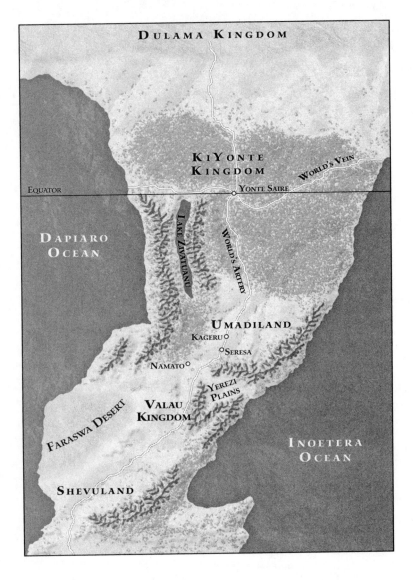

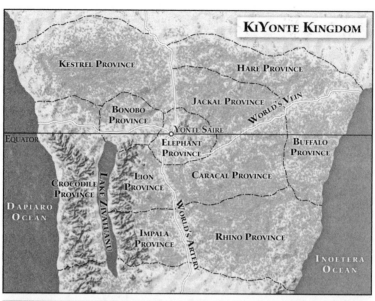

KIYONTE KINGDOM

KESTREL PROVINCE

HARE PROVINCE

JACKAL PROVINCE

WORLD'S VEIN

BONOBO PROVINCE

YONTE SAIRE

EQUATOR

ELEPHANT PROVINCE

BUFFALO PROVINCE

CARACAL PROVINCE

LION PROVINCE

CROCODILE PROVINCE

LAKE ZIVATUANU

DAPIARO OCEAN

WORLD'S ARTERY

IMPALA PROVINCE

RHINO PROVINCE

INOETERA OCEAN

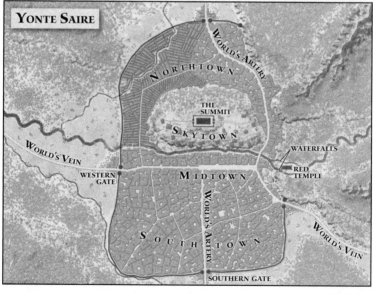

YONTE SAIRE

WORLD'S ARTERY

NORTHTOWN

THE SUMMIT

SKYTOWN

WORLD'S VEIN

WATERFALLS

RED TEMPLE

WESTERN GATE

MIDTOWN

WORLD'S ARTERY

SOUTHTOWN

WORLD'S VEIN

SOUTHERN GATE

DRAMATIS PERSONAE

Kingdom of the Yontai

MUSALODI (SALO), a young mystic

ILAPARA, his friend, a mercenary

TUKSAAD (TUK), his friend, an atmech from the Empire of Light

ALINATA, an Asazi

ISA ANDAIYE SAIRE, a king

JOMO SAIRE, her herald

THE ENCHANTRESS, a mysterious woman

KAMALI, a Jasiri warrior

OBE SAAI, a Sentinel, nephew of the Crocodile

ELEA SAAI, his mother, sister to the Crocodile

DINO SATO, a Sentinel, son of the Impala

IJIRO KATUMBILI, a Sentinel, son of the Bonobo

ODARI, a Sentinel

KITO, a Sentinel

RUMA SATO, a steward

AMIDI, a priest of Engai

TULIZA, his daughter

IKWE IWE, an ambassador of the Valau Kingdom

MWENEMZUZI SAIRE, a merchant prince

Mosi Akili, a mystic at the House of Forms
Ewa Akili, a mystic at the House of Forms
Anika Akili, an inquisitor of the city guard
Ayana, a prisoner
Fanaka, a prisoner

The Seven High Mystics of the Shirika

The Arc, high priest of the Red Temple
The Fractal, chancellor of the House of Forms
The Prism, curator of the Pattern Archives
The Spiral, supreme justice of the House of Law
The Torus, director of the House of Silos
The Trigon, grand artificer of the House of Axles
The Helix, high physician of the House of Life

The Ten Headmen

The Crocodile
The Bonobo
The Kestrel
The Impala
The Lion
The Rhino
The Buffalo
The Caracal
The Hare
The Jackal

Yerezi Plains

VaSiningwe, chief of Khaya-Siningwe
Mujioseri (Jio), his son, a ranger
Masiburai (Sibu), his son, a ranger
Aba Deitari (Aba D), his brother, a general
Aba Akuri, his brother-in-law, a ranger
Ama Lira, his wife, a teacher
Montari (Monti), a young boy (deceased)
Aneniko (Niko), a ranger
Nimara, an Asazi
Irediti, queen of the Yerezi Plains

Umadiland

The Maidservant, a mystic and a warlord's disciple
The Dark Sun, a warlord

Elsewhere

Prophet, an associate of the Enchantress
The Adversary, an enemy of the gods
Engai, a Primeval Spirit of the undercity

The Four Great Lights

AMA VAZIISHE, THE MOTHER, moon goddess and source of Red magic
ISINISO, VERITY, a deity of the white sun
ISHUNGU, VALOR, a deity of the yellow sun
VIGILANCE, a deity of the New Year's Comet

PROLOGUE: THE ORPHAN

With her mind, the Adversary reaches through a breach in the Veil between worlds and coalesces as a shadow at the banks of an underground lake. There she waits until the spirit who resides in the lake emerges from the waters to face her.

She has lost count of the number of times they have faced each other, she and the spirit, though each time, they have danced the same dance, sung the same song.

"Show me," she says, as she always says.

A shield of crimson rage swirls around her like a diaphanous cocoon. When the spirit attempts to overwhelm her with sorrow and claim her soul with its tentacled limbs, the shield holds fast, thwarting the spirit before it can touch her. The Adversary has never lost this battle of wills.

"You can never mourn them all," the spirit says, as it always says. *"Even you, who has lived for so long. They are more numerous than the sands of a desert, their tears more plentiful than the waters of this lake. You must accept the truth and let go. Embrace nothingness and know peace."*

"Show me," she says again, her rage giving strength to her shield.

The spirit is a featureless monstrosity, an abstract vision of twisting darkness, yet she feels its cold gaze watching her, assessing her, trying to find a weakness to exploit. She doesn't yield.

"As you wish," it finally says, and then, as always, it summons a memory from the lake, one of a multitude that dwells in these waters of despair, letting her see through the eyes of yet another hapless soul.

Today the memory belongs to a nameless orphan who never had a chance, whose story is to the Adversary like each and every story entombed in this lake: the strongest indictment of heaven and those who would hoard its glories for themselves.

Here is the orphan now, at the onset of the memory, hungry and abandoned somewhere off the perimeter of a large camp of sufferers. The storehouses could have been opened to nourish his people throughout the drought, but hunger is a weapon of war, and the warring factions of his land have used it to devastating effect.

The cracked earth stretches on for miles before his emaciated legs, interspersed here and there by tumbleweeds and animal carcasses. The soil is dry and parched and hungry, and the lone sun beats down upon it without mercy, scorching off every last whiff of moisture until there's nothing left but heat and death. Soon his bones will join the others littering the landscape, but this will not be enough. The earth's hunger will claim many others still.

He does not know where his mother is. The last he saw of her, they carried her away on a stretcher. He only remembers how cold she got during the night, how he tried to shake her awake but found her stiff and unresponsive. When they came to take her away, he curled up in the corner of the tent. No one noticed him there, or if they did, they were too busy to care. And when his mother didn't come back, he wandered away.

There's no food in the camp. No water either. Everyone is gaunt and hungry, and all the children have distended bellies. They are ghosts haunting the world with their dying breaths, and so is he.

Above him the vultures are circling, waiting patiently. He sits down, or maybe he falls. He can't walk anymore, and when he cries, his eyes remain dry.

The earth calls to him. Soon he gives in to its pull, and as he breathes his last, he remembers the day his mother sang him to sleep when it rained and thundered and he was scared. His last thought. The vultures descend.

He is four years old.

A nameless, forgotten victim of an unjust universe, but today the Adversary remembers him, and she mourns him.

And then she vows to destroy heaven on his behalf.

PART 1

MUSALODI

*

JOMO

*

ILAPARA

Witchwood:

Contrary to popular belief, witchwood is not a species of tree. Rather, the term refers to the final stage of alchemical transmutation brought about by the introduction of raw essence into living plant tissue. Indeed, any tree can become witchwood should it develop an affinity with essence and become infested.

Witchwood in the wild: Umadi people have mastered the art of trapping the spirits of tronic beasts within witchwood charms for temporary possession.

From On Arcane Materials, *an encyclopedia published by the House of Forms*

1: Musalodi

On the Way to Skytown

Yonte Saire. The Jungle City. The world's beating heart. No longer a fable but a vivid truth sprawling before Salo's eyes. Surreal. Intimidating. A place that seems designed to say: *You are not worthy to walk these streets.*

Behind him the two suns are golden orbs slowly dipping toward a mountainous horizon. Beneath him Mukuni the leopard totem rocks gently as his giant paws pad along the redbrick road, entering the city through the western gates. Riding ahead is the mounted guardsman assigned to show the group to their place of lodging somewhere called Skytown. Salo leaves the task of navigating to the totem while he soaks in his new surroundings in silent awe.

At first, he sees the beautiful, for that is what his eyes are meant to see.

The domes and terraced structures—bamboo, stone, glass—reaching high above the ground and into the jungle's canopy, mingling with luxurious gardens that brim with flowering plants and trees.

The gilded statues lining the roadways, monuments to this or that hero standing in silent testimony to the riches of the KiYonte Kingdom.

The elegant carriages trundling on the roads, most drawn by identical-looking zebroids, some without roofs and others closed like shells, curtained windows hinting at the comfort within.

As he rides past a building with flowery awnings—a store, perhaps—two pretty girls adorned with golden bangles and colorful cloths exit through the door, giggling. Tattoos run down their necks in thin lines and patterns. For a moment, Salo is mesmerized by their carefree laughter. Then he notices the old man in a gray tunic following meekly behind, burdened with what he assumes must be their shopping bags. The man has metalloid hornlike appendages curling out of his temples. *Tensors.*

He is Faraswa, and not the only one in this city.

In fact, the more Salo pays attention, the more conspicuous the Faraswa workers swarming Yonte Saire become, and whatever envy he felt earlier shrivels up and dies in his chest.

Faraswa are everywhere. Sweeping dung off the roads and shoveling it onto carts. Pruning trees in the endless gardens. Following quietly behind their well-dressed masters. Silent shadows no one seems to notice.

Salo looks to his right flank at Tuksaad, riding on his massive horned abada while Alinata holds on to his back from behind.

By the little smile on his handsome face, one would think the young man is only mildly amused, but his eyes have lightened to an almost startling shade of blue, which Salo has learned means he's excited. Pretty eyes, Salo would say, but they betray Tuk's every emotion to anyone who's learned to read them. Perhaps that was the intent of his makers.

"You've been here before, haven't you?" Salo asks, and Tuk nods.

"I passed through Yonte Saire on my way south. Stayed for a few weeks. Couldn't stay longer because I was running out of coin. As you'll soon find out, this place can be terribly expensive."

"Reckon there'll be slaves wherever they're putting us?"

The light in Tuk's eyes grows dimmer, his irises changing to the color of storm clouds. "Perhaps you'll be relieved to know that the Faraswa here are not so much slaves as second-class citizens. Not ideal, admittedly, but things are not nearly as bad as you think."

On Salo's left flank, Ilapara's ears have pricked. She's watching Tuk with hawkish intensity from her saddle on Ingacha, a red kudu buck of the Valau woodlands. As usual, the crimson veil on her head is wound tightly enough to keep her hair concealed. "How is a second-class citizen different from a slave? They're both exploited groups."

"True, but you can't buy or sell a Faraswa servant," Tuk explains. "You can't—technically—mistreat them. You're required to pay them for their work. That sort of thing. They aren't considered part of the KiYonte tribe, however, so they don't enjoy as many rights as true citizens. They can't open businesses or buy property, for example, and you'll never find Faraswa children in schools. Manual labor is often the best employment they can find."

"So they can leave if they want to?" Ilapara says.

"But why would they want to leave?" Tuk says, his voice carrying a trace of bitterness. "You've seen what can happen to them out there. This place is tame in comparison, and when you have no good options, you learn to take peace wherever you can find it."

Salo recalls the day he met both Tuksaad and Ilapara. It was the same day a Faraswa boy stole his purse while he was wandering the sordid streets of Seresa. He raced after the boy, shouting for him to stop, until he found himself in the town's meat market, surrounded by Faraswa people in cages. Later, he would watch from a distance as a wagon carrying many of those same people—people he'd tried to save—went up in flames of moonfire.

It was the third-worst day of his life.

The second worst was the day he killed his own mother.

And the worst was when Monti died in his arms after the Maidservant attacked his kraal and killed him with her foul spirits, launching Salo on the journey that would lead him to this moment.

The Maidservant.

Thinking about her fills Salo with a torrent of conflicting emotions. Sometimes he wishes he'd killed her while she was vulnerable. Mostly, he prays he never has to see her again.

They take a left off the World's Vein, which probably continues east, intersecting with the Artery before heading toward the waterfall. From this vantage point the waterfall is concealed by the city's canopy of foliage, but its low-pitched roar is omnipresent.

The city's colossus comes into full view minutes later as they follow the mounted guard across an arched bridge over a river. The gilded statue gleams in the late-afternoon sunlight at the top of a flat-topped hill, crowning the domed palaces built upon the slopes beneath it.

"Welcome to Skytown. Home of the richest folk in all the jungles of the Yontai, including the king." Tuk shakes his head, his eyes recovering their bright hue as he gazes at the palaces arrayed before them. "I still can't believe you leased a residence here."

Salo can hardly believe it either. "Let's not raise our hopes just yet," he cautions. "I know practically nothing of the arrangements made here on my behalf. We could be headed for the stalls of a stable for all I know."

"I don't care," Ilapara says. "At this point a floor and a roof over my head will be good enough. So long as this journey ends."

Alinata, the Asazi who has been silently observant all this time, decides to speak. "You should have more faith in your queen, Musalodi. Do you honestly think she would send her chosen pilgrim to sleep in a stable?"

Salo looks over at Alinata, where she seems perfectly comfortable in the saddle behind Tuk. Her hazel eyes stare back in defiance.

He still doesn't trust her, despite her help fending off the Maidservant. For one thing, the queen sent her to watch him, which in itself raises many questions. And for another, he keeps getting the feeling she knows things she's not telling him. Things about his mission here.

"I wouldn't presume to know her intentions, Alinata," Salo says. "Perhaps, as her apprentice, you could shed some light?"

Seeing through his ploy, she looks toward the looming colossus. "How about we start with a history lesson. Do you know how the eleven KiYonte clans came to be?"

Ilapara clucks her tongue in annoyance and mutters, "Why are Asazi always so evasive?"

"On the contrary," Alinata says, "I am doing Salo a favor. The tensions in this kingdom have always stemmed from the way their clans are divided. Understanding this will be key to navigating any political pitfalls he may encounter here."

"But *why* would he need to navigate any 'political pitfalls' at all?" Ilapara says, a frown twisting her face. "He's here for the Red Temple, isn't he? Or is he here for something else?"

The suspicion in her voice fills Salo with guilt for withholding key truths about his role in this city, that his pilgrimage is little more than a convenient disguise. "The report I read before coming here briefly discussed the KiYonte clan tattoos," he says, changing the subject. "Apparently they're the result of an ancient spell of Blood craft that infects every KiYonte child with the markings of his or her father's clan. The official account is that they simply appeared one day as a gift from the moon, but someone had to have cast the spell."

"And someone did," Alinata says, the excitement in her voice telling Salo this is a topic of interest to her. "Legend has it that eleven common men who sought to become princes pledged themselves in worship to a secretive cabal of mystics that lived around these parts, long before this city was even a city. To demonstrate their devotion, they offered up a close relative each as a burnt offering to the cabal."

Salo grimaces, feeling sickened.

"That's disgusting," Ilapara says.

"It gets better," Alinata goes on. "It is said that a great pyre of ten thousand trees was built for the offerings and that the smoke from its flames billowed to every corner of the Yontai for weeks. The mystics were so pleased with the sacrifices they cast a spell that would grant each of the eleven men his own princedom, sealed in blood. The whole tribe gained permanent marks that day, forever sorted into different clans, forced to bow to one of the eleven princes. The marks—and the clans they wrought—remain to this day. So does the cabal, although you'd be wise not to repeat that where you can be overheard."

"Why am I not surprised?" Ilapara says. "I doubt there's a single evil in the world that can't be traced back to power-hungry men. And why did they have to make it so patriarchal? Why not give the child its mother's mark? She's the one who has to carry it around in her womb for seven moons."

"They wanted to control everything," Tuk says. "It's not really surprising they skewed the system so they'd control biology too." He lets out a morose sigh. "You know, I heard a similar tale about the marks when I was here last. I just hope the truth isn't nearly as terrible as the legend."

"When magic is involved," Ilapara says, "the truth is usually worse."

Salo wishes he could disagree, but experience with violent magic has made him wiser. "What confuses me is why the Saires were elevated above the other clans," he says. "All kings of the Yontai have come from the Saire clan, have they not?"

"The first Saire king offered up the strongest sacrifice of them all," Alinata replies. "The other men are said to have given their brothers, sisters, nephews, or nieces to the flames. But the Saire king offered up his beloved firstborn son." Alinata's gaze returns to the colossus on the hill. "See that handsome fellow standing over there? That's supposed to be him. The son on whose ashes a dynasty was built."

"At least he got commemorated," Salo remarks. "If the stories are true, there should be ten other statues up there with him."

"Or," Ilapara says, "there should be no statues at all, because the marks are evil and should never have existed."

The road winding up Skytown is paved in obsidian flagstones, though they glitter like they were sprinkled with flecks of gold. And the palaces on this hill . . . Salo didn't know homes could look like this, like sculptures to be lived in. Any of them would make the royal palace in the Queen's Kraal look like a clumsy mud hut.

Halfway up the hill the mounted guardsman stops in front of a pair of imposing wrought iron gates. A spearman in a yellow tunic is standing sentry on the other side; upon seeing them, he opens the gates and stands at rigid attention while the mounted guardsman leads the way down a tree-lined drive.

A palace is waiting for them at the end of the drive, along with a welcoming party. Salo trades incredulous looks with the others as they arrive. *This* is where they'll be staying?

"Welcome, welcome," says the portly gentleman at the head of the party. His smile is so pleasant that for a second Salo wonders if they've met before.

"Oh my, look at these handsome beasts." Perhaps despite himself, the man's enthusiasm falters a little as he eyes Mukuni. "How absolutely gorgeous," he says with forced cheer.

Salo pulls out his best KiYonte, which he knows is thickly accented and not quite at home on his tongue. "Be at ease, Red-kin. The beasts are under my control. They won't harm anyone not trying to harm them."

"That's good to know," the man says. "And please feel free to come down from there. You're all so high my neck hurts just looking up at you."

With his job done, the mounted guardsman bids them goodbye and departs. As Salo dismounts Mukuni, the portly gentleman approaches with his hands clasped together respectfully. He looks too young to be middle aged, yet his temples are as gray as his simple boubou.

"Honored Emissary Siningwe," he says. "It is an honor to finally meet you."

A handshake, firm but brief. Salo almost winces at the ill-fitting and overly grandiose title.

"Allow me to introduce myself formally," the man says. "I am Ruma Sato of the Sato clan—that's the impala of the south—and I will be your steward until you decide otherwise. Just so you know, I have served as steward for many pilgrims and diplomats on this hill. Oh, but listen to me prattle on when you must be exhausted." His curious eyes wander to Tuksaad and Alinata, then to Ilapara. Once again, the smile on his face grows a little fixed, probably because of the spear in her hand. "Will your . . . companions be staying with you?"

"Will that be a problem?" Salo says.

"Oh no, not at all. There's more than enough space in this residence. Please, come meet your other servants. We've all been looking forward to your arrival."

About a dozen people are standing in a neat line beneath the shade of the palace's arching entrance. Most are Faraswa, which immediately gives Salo indigestion. He decides to shelve any questions for now. No need to be rude.

He forces himself to look cheerful and shakes hands with all thirteen servants, the whole time wondering why anyone on earth would need so many servants in the first place.

"This is your house, honored emissary," Ruma says afterward. "Please, come in. The stablemen will see to your beasts."

Without giving them a chance to respond, he glides into the "house"—and really, to call this place a house is to call a Tuanu waterbird a boat or a redhawk a bird. An injustice.

"A quick tour, shall we?" Ruma says as he breezes past a winding staircase in the high-ceilinged foyer, or what might be the foyer. Salo isn't sure. The building is a garden married to a palace of bamboo and dark stonework, so open and airy he can hardly tell where the interior ends and the outside begins.

The steward takes them through a maze of archways, courtyards, and rooms with tiled floors and tapestries whose warm colors flow effortlessly throughout the palace. Ornamental spears and swords decorate the walls, while patterns make their home on nearly everything, from the fretwork doors and window screens to the throw pillows tossed on every seat. The bathing chambers have stone baths large enough for uroko bulls to drown in. The smallest bedchamber Ruma shows them is something Queen Irediti would envy; the largest is something she might kill for. Ornate glass crystals hang like flowers from the ceilings, each with little splinters of enchanted witchwood frozen at their hearts. The diffuse light they give off is something stolen from a sunset.

So many enchantments buzzing in this place, so many sorcerous contrivances working silently.

When they pass a mechanical-looking table with a complex arrangement of keys and crystals, Salo pauses to investigate, putting his hand out to sense the magical energies present around the artifact. The cosmic shards singed onto his skin appear as he leans further into his arcane senses; invisible when dormant, the shards come to life as thin metallic patterns running from elbow to fingertip on either arm, glowing crimson with the moon's essence. A single ring running parallel to the patterns encircles each forearm, betraying that he is only recently awoken and hasn't had the chance to grow his power.

"What's this?" he whispers to Tuk when he fails to discern the nature of the artifact. All he senses is a distortion of space suggesting the presence of Void craft.

"It's a mirrorgraph," Tuk replies, and at Salo's blank stare he adds, "It sends written messages to other devices just like it throughout the kingdom. Every home on this hill probably has one."

"That's incredible," Salo remarks.

They move on, catching up to the steward.

"Until recently," he says, finally coming to a stop in the foyer where they began the tour, "this residence housed a pilgrim of the Halusha tribe. When we heard you'd be joining us, we had to refurnish the whole place. The Halusha have . . . unconventional tastes in decor, you see. Lots of hides and dead animals." Ruma shudders visibly. "Anyway, everything you see here is brand new."

Even Alinata fails to hide her amazement. How much did all of this cost? "It's all very nice, Bwana Ruma—" Salo begins.

"Please, Ruma is fine, honored. I am a servant in this house."

"And yet my culture demands I show you respect as my elder, Bwana Ruma."

The steward's eyes crinkle in the corners. "As you wish, honored."

"Thank you. I was saying that I am pleased with everything, but it looks like a lot of work to maintain."

"Oh, but you mustn't worry. The other servants and I will see to such things. You won't have to lift a finger."

"About those servants," Salo says, finally getting to his real question. "Are they really servants or . . . I guess I'm wondering if they *want* to be here."

"Ah, I see." Ruma's lips seem to twitch. "In preparing this house for you, I tried to ensure there would be nothing your people would find offensive. There are no exploited workers here, only servants who are grateful for the employment opportunity. They will be paid well, I assure you."

Salo flicks his tongue into the gap between his teeth. He wouldn't want to take away lucrative employment from people who need it, but . . . they shouldn't *have to* need it, should they? This shouldn't be the best they can get. *But what are you going to do about it? Have them dismissed? That would only make their lives worse.* "I appreciate your thoughtfulness," he says.

Ruma beams. "It's my pleasure to serve. Before I leave you be, I'm to inform you of your invitation to the New Year's Feast at the Summit tomorrow night. This will be your first opportunity to present yourself before the prince regent, and he will be expecting your presence now that you're here. I know a clothier well versed in the dressing traditions of the southern tribes. Shall I arrange for him to visit tomorrow morning?"

Salo frowns. He looks at Tuk and sees his confusion reflected in the young man's yellowish eyes. Ilapara looks like she's missed something too. Alinata, though—her sudden retreat behind an expressionless mask tells Salo that she knows something.

"Prince regent?" he says to Ruma. "I don't understand. What happened to the king?"

Ruma's smile freezes on his face and slowly melts into dismay. "You . . . but how have you not heard?"

"I've been traveling these last few weeks. What have I not heard?"

"Well . . ." Ruma adjusts his boubou, looking like he'd rather talk about anything else in the world. "His Majesty . . . passed away a few weeks ago. It was a sad, sad day for all of us."

His lips say *passed away*, but his body screams *crime and treason*. Whatever killed Mweneugo Saire clearly wasn't natural.

Why wasn't I warned? Salo wonders. All the emissary told him that day in the kraal's council house was that there were troubling political winds stirring in the north and the queen wanted to know more. She said nothing about a murderous coup.

Maybe because they knew I'd have never agreed to come if she'd told me.

"I'm sorry to hear that," he says, choosing his words carefully. "What happened?"

"Oh, I can't speculate, honored emissary. All I know is what the palace told us, and that is what I have told you. But we mustn't linger on such morbid topics; you must be famished after your long journey." Ruma considers them. "You know, you're much younger than I expected."

"I'm recently awakened," Salo explains, deciding to let his questions go for now.

"Even so. It's most impressive that you acquired your station at your age. All right, I'll stop chattering now. This is your house. Feel free to freshen up. Dinner will be served in the back garden shortly. Should you need anything, every servant here, myself included, is at your disposal. Do you have any questions?"

"None right now, Bwana Ruma. Thank you very much."

"I live to serve." The steward bows and glides away.

Ilapara waits until he's out of earshot before turning to Salo with suspicion in her eyes. "The KiYonte king is dead? What on Meza have we walked into here?"

"Maybe Alinata can tell us," Salo says, glaring at the Asazi. "You knew, didn't you. You knew and you didn't warn me."

"I was under orders not to." She doesn't even bother denying it.

"Why the devil not?"

"I'm sensing a pattern here," Tuk remarks. "First, she doesn't warn us about the Maidservant, and now she says nothing about this. One would almost think she's willfully trying to get us killed."

"Treachery is an Asazi's natural state," Ilapara says, which makes Alinata seethe with displeasure.

"It was better for your reaction to the news to be genuine," she says to Salo, then glances down the hall. "There may be spies among your servants. Even the steward might be a spy, and it's possible he understands Sirezi, so we must watch what we say in this house."

Silence echoes off the walls of the foyer for a few seconds. Ilapara folds her arms and shifts her glare from Alinata to Salo. "I think you owe us an explanation about what's going on here. You clearly haven't told us everything."

"I'm sure he had his reasons," Tuk says, though he regards Salo with doubt. "Nonetheless, I do find it curious that the steward kept calling him the KiYonte word for *emissary*. So did the Jasiri at the city gates, now that I think of it. That's not a regular title for pilgrims."

"*That's* what the word means?" Ilapara says, visibly alarmed. "Emissary? I thought it was just a title of respect or something. Are you an emissary, Salo? As in appointed-by-the-queen-and-everything emissary?"

Salo lets out a weary sigh. Not long ago his life revolved around his workshop back in Khaya-Siningwe. He may not have been wholly content—what with being an outsider among his people for his unmanlike affinity with the magical arts—but his days were quiet and his work kept him occupied. Monti was always nearby, ready to make him laugh. He had a friend in Nimara, and even in Niko. He would have shed no tears had life continued as it always had.

Then a witch attacked his kraal, killing Monti and sending Salo off on a journey that has led him here, thousands of miles away from the lands of his people, in a city with deadly secrets and treachery.

"I need a bath," he says to his suspicious companions. "I need a change of clothes and food. I also sense that the stable hands are having trouble with our four-legged friends outside. Let me handle that, and I'll tell you everything I know. Sounds good?"

Like a proper coward, he flees the foyer without giving them a chance to answer.

2: Jomo

The Red Temple

"Mother's grace, young Herald."

"Blessings, Herald."

"Stand strong, my child."

As he makes his way along the vaulted walkways of the Red Temple, Jomo Saire tries to look friendly and confident but ends up with a grimace. "Yes, yes, thank you, Saire-kin. Mother's grace upon you too."

Feeling his throat constrict, he tugs at the high collar of his royal-blue robe and continues to limp past the gaggle of people looking up to him like he's their personal savior, his leg brace squeaking with every step. In his bid to walk faster, he leans deeper into his cane with one clammy hand while the other clutches at the scepter of his office. He imagines he probably looks ridiculous, but he doesn't care. Not so long as he gets away.

Look how mature I've become, Mama, he thinks. *Just like you always wanted.*

He's sick of how he can't walk anywhere in this damned citadel without people wishing him well. And it's not because of the well-wishes, exactly, but the suffocating hope he senses beneath them. Hope in him, the king's herald, who goes down to the city every day to get things done, because he must be getting things done, right? He must be finding a way to save the people of his clan from looming genocide, right?

They never ask, never pressure him, but Jomo can see the desperation in their eyes. He can hear their silent pleas whenever they look at him. *How far? Time is running out. Save us! Save our people!*

I don't know what the devil I'm doing! he wants to tell them. *I was never meant for this job! My brother was the mature one, the one Mama was grooming for an important role in the king's court. Not me! Find another savior.* But he never utters these words.

The Ruby Paragon hovering above the temple citadel has just flashed seven times across the dusky skies of Yonte Saire when he reaches the king's private quarters. Two spearmen in the aerosteel and green tunics of the King's Sentinels are posted at the door. In unison they beat their chests once with their fists to acknowledge him. He nods, opening his mouth, but suffers a momentary lapse in memory.

One of the two Sentinels, a young man with narrow, shifty-looking eyes like those of a snake, has markings of the Kestrel on his neck. A friendly clan, the kestrels. The elephants have always gotten along with them, and Jomo is on good terms with their headman. The other Sentinel is an admittedly good-looking guy with an affable charm about him. Pity he's a member of the jackal clan, whose headman has all but allied himself with the devil-spawn usurper Kola Saai.

Jomo looks away from the young jackal and addresses his more agreeable comrade. "Kito, is it?"

"Uh . . . no." The snake-eyed kestrel shares a visibly amused glance with the other Sentinel. "I'm Odari, Herald."

"Huh. I could have sworn you were Kito. Any relation, perhaps?"

"None whatsoever, Herald."

"Well, you look alike."

The kestrel's lips quirk like he wants to smile, but he says nothing. Jomo narrows his eyes. "Something funny?"

"Herald, perhaps if you took another look at Kito, you'd change your mind about our likeness." Odari jerks his head toward his comrade. "He's standing right over there."

Jomo slides his gaze over, his cheeks burning with embarrassment. They really do look nothing alike. While Odari is bulky and embodies the kind of man you'd cross the street just to avoid at night, Kito is slim and carries himself with a princely grace.

What is this, the third or fourth time Jomo has made such a mistake in less than a week? A herald who can't even remember the names of the guards watching over his king.

"I'll be sure to get it right next time," he says with as dignified a tone as he can manage. "Right now, I need to see the king."

A snide glimmer of judgment shines in Odari's eyes, but he keeps his expression neutral. "Of course, Herald." He steps aside. "You may enter."

Smug little bastards, Jomo thinks as he steps through the door. He really should know their names by now, but he's never really liked the Sentinels, so he hasn't bothered getting to know any of them better. Besides, it makes his skin crawl to think that they're only loyal to the king because of a six-year-long curse. Who knows what they secretly think?

Kola Saai was once a Sentinel, and he went on to butcher the entire royal family.

No. Jomo wouldn't trust any of those assholes with a single hair on his head, let alone his life. Which is why he resents the fact that they are currently the only thing deterring genocidal militias from launching attacks on his people. Lose the Sentinels, and it'll be open season on the elephant clan.

"I'm not certain I understand how this will help, Your Majesty," comes an older male voice from within the king's living room just down the hallway. "But I will approach him as you've commanded."

Jomo enters to find King Isa sitting with a prominent Saire merchant, both overdressed for such a modestly appointed room. Jomo recognizes the merchant as Mwenemzuzi Saire, the owner of the continent's largest transport company and an old boor the late king and herald had to tolerate because of his financial clout. *What the devil is he doing here?*

Isa briefly looks up to make eye contact with Jomo but returns to her conversation with the merchant prince without acknowledging him.

"You are a persuasive man, Bwana Mzuzi," she says. "You possess a forceful presence that commands attention and respect, and you speak many languages. It is why I have chosen you for this task. Reach out to him. Persuade him. It is important I know just how far he can be pushed."

She rises to her feet to signal that the conversation is over.

Mzuzi does the same, though his bushy eyebrows gather in a way that suggests he's not happy with whatever task Isa has assigned him. "As you wish, Your Majesty." His face sours further when he looks over at Jomo. "Your Highness."

Jomo matches his clipped voice. "Bwana Mzuzi."

"Bwana Mzuzi was just leaving," Isa interjects.

Mzuzi maintains the staring contest for a while longer, then finally bows to the king. "Your Majesty."

Jomo sneers at his back until he exits. "Commands attention and respect? More like contempt and revulsion."

With a sigh, Isa sits back down and begins to knead the muscles of her long neck. "We need him on our side, but he doesn't trust us yet. He thinks we're children playing adult games." She laughs. "He's right."

For a moment Jomo lets himself study the young king. The many golden chains her father used to wear now grace her shoulders, cascading over her rose-colored strapless gown like she was born to wear them. Today she has combed out her hair into a bouffant mass adorned with gilded threads, and she's shadowed her eyes and glossed her lips with metallic face paints that bring out the amber hue of her irises.

She and Jomo weren't close before the night of the Royal Massacre. He thought her aloof and somewhat icy, a spoiled princess who believed herself better than everyone else. Now he understands she was probably just bored. The brains inside that girl's head . . . most people in the palace probably seemed like dull-witted idiots to her. And to think she wanted *him* to take the mask-crown when it turned out they were the only two surviving members of the royal family.

Him, the guy who has to check every morning that he hasn't worn his shirts and tunics back to front.

Thank the Mother he had the sense to know better than to accept.

"What was that meeting about?" he says as he lowers himself onto the couch facing her. He tries not to flinch in pain from the stiffness in his left leg. "And who were you talking about?"

She makes a dismissive motion. "Just testing the waters. It might not pan out. We'll see."

Jomo almost growls in annoyance. "Keeping secrets from me now, are we? Making major decisions without consulting me? Your herald? First, you agree to marry the Crocodile, which, I'll say again, have you lost your mind? And now you won't tell me why you're giving mysterious commands to merchant princes in your private chambers. I know you're the king, but I'm no use as your herald if I don't know what's going on in that head of yours." Jomo takes a breath. He needs to get a grip. "Your Majesty," he adds rather belatedly.

Isa's hand stops massaging her neck, and she looks at Jomo like she's only just realizing that he's upset. She winces. "I'm sorry, cousin. I'm still trying to find my way. I don't want to raise your hopes just yet."

"But we're in this together," Jomo complains. "Crushing my hopes should be the least of your worries. I can handle disappointment. I can't handle being in the dark about what you're thinking."

"I know, and I'll tell you everything. Just . . . give me a little more time to find my footing, all right?"

He sniffs. "I guess I can give you the space you need. But Isa, I don't want you to feel you have to shoulder this burden alone. I'm here for you. Not just as your herald but as your cousin. As your friend."

Her amber eyes glitter with affection. "How did the negotiations go? I heard you had fun toying with the guests."

Before he answers, Jomo leans on his cane and moves to push himself up to his feet, but Isa motions for him to keep seated.

"Don't worry; I'll get it for you."

"You don't have to," he protests mildly. "I'm not an invalid."

"You're most assuredly not," Isa says. "But I am the king, so you have to do what I tell you."

Isa is already pouring him a glass of golden Valau rum by the sideboard in the room. She keeps that bottle there specifically for his use and has never once discouraged his drinking, even though he knows he should probably ease up. His fondness for alcohol was always a point of contention with his parents and older brother. In the end, his fondness for alcohol was what saved his wretched life.

She hands him the glass, and he takes a sip, closing his eyes to savor the familiar burn and the subsequent warmth in his chest. He isn't sure he can forgive her for going behind his back and agreeing to marry that slimeball Kola Saai. But it's her choice, and she's asked him to negotiate her bride-price, which he has to do as her only living male relative.

Doesn't mean he can't be spiteful about it.

Earlier he had to suffer through a formal negotiation with the Crocodile's rabid dog of a brother, an older uncle, and a neutral mediator. The whole time he had to restrain himself from leaping off his chair and biting into their faces. *Vile excuses for human beings.*

"I made them sit in the sun," he says. "Told them I wouldn't speak to them until the spirits of my slain kin were appeased. When they offered me ten pieces of regular gold, I took offense and left. Told them they better come with moongold next time."

"Jomo . . . ," Isa says with a slightly reproving tone, though the light in her eyes betrays her amusement.

"Don't worry. They'll be back. They must have known I wasn't going to make it easy for them."

"True, but I hope you don't make it too difficult. The wedding needs to happen sooner or later."

How about never? Jomo thinks. "We still have time. Right now, I'm more worried about the next Mkutano. Should nothing change, we'll be losing the Sentinels by vote soon. The Kestrel and the Lion are allies, so I guess we have their votes. The Impala was a friend of my mother's, so maybe I can leverage that into something. He's in the city, so I'll be visiting him tomorrow to see if we can come to some sort of agreement. But that's it, and it's not enough."

Jomo knows the next Mkutano will be at the Summit on the afternoon of the full moon in two weeks. As things stand, the Jackal, the Bonobo, the Buffalo, the Hare, the Rhino, and the Caracal will all be voting with the Crocodile to disband the Sentinels, thus stripping away the last layer of protection insulating the elephant clan from the forces of genocide. Jomo understands that Isa's wedding to the Crocodile is meant to be insurance against such an eventuality, but he's not convinced the bastard would lift a finger to stop the killings.

Isa squints, likely performing the political calculus in her mind. "The Rhino and the Buffalo have never been our enemies. Is there nothing we can offer to win them over?"

"I sent them both mirrorgrams requesting to meet after the New Year's Feast, and they both declined." Jomo relaxes into the couch. The rum is already beginning to numb his sorrows. "What hope do I have of winning them over if they won't even let me through the door?"

"We need leverage," Isa says, staring intently into the middle distance. "We need to entice or force them to the table to negotiate. Even if I marry Kola Saai, we can't lose the Sentinels."

"I'm working on it," Jomo says. He stares into his glass, wondering how much he should tell her. Then he sees the hypocrisy of keeping secrets, given how he was just coming down on her for doing exactly that. "Actually, I'll be attending the New Year's Feast tomorrow. And before you complain, no, I'm not going there to cause a scene or take a piss on Kola Saai's bed. Although . . ."

Isa's eyes narrow with suspicion. "Jomo?"

He waves her concern away. "Contrary to popular opinion, I'm not a complete idiot. I sent a message to one of the Faraswa maids still working at the palace, and I asked her to discreetly extract an item from my mother's study."

"An item?"

"Yes," Jomo says, deliberately reticent. "Hidden well enough that I doubt the Crocodile's people found it. With luck, this . . . item will give us the leverage we need."

Isa maintains her scrutinizing gaze. "I hope you don't get the maid in trouble, Jomo. If even one Faraswa servant is caught doing our bidding, the rest might be put in danger."

"I asked her to be careful."

Isa keeps watching him, and under that gaze he begins to doubt himself. But she sighs and says, "I trust your judgment." Then a smirk animates her face. "I also trust that you will behave yourself, cousin. No sneaking into any chambers and urinating on the beds."

"Understood, Your Majesty."

"Good. In the meantime, we need to take some pressure off our people. Anti-Saire rhetoric is too prominent in the kingdom's collective consciousness right now. We need to dilute it and muddy the discourse. If the public is talking about other things, they're not talking about killing us."

Jomo frowns. "Is that why you agreed to marry the Crocodile? To get people talking about something else?"

"In part," she admits, tilting her head. "At the least it means we keep Kola Saai thinking he'll get what he wants without escalating matters. And the longer we draw out the wedding rites and preparations, the more time we buy."

"I still don't like it," Jomo says. "Honestly, Isa, the idea of you with that reptile makes me physically ill."

"That's why you're the perfect man to negotiate my bride-price." Isa's eyes flash with malice. "Who knows. By the time you're done with the crocodiles, maybe we'll have enough coin to appease the mobs thirsting for our blood."

Jomo looks down at his glass and sees that it's almost empty. He goes ahead and drains it, then places the glass on the table in front of him with a loud thunk. "What does the high priest think about all this?"

Isa looks away, something cryptic entering her voice. "He supports whatever decision I make."

"I see." Jomo doesn't understand her relationship with the high mystic, not really, and he's not sure he wants to. Frankly, the old man scares the devil out of him. What are the concerns of puny humans to those who can call lightning down from the sky and kill ten men with a single look?

The Mother must have been smoking something cosmically potent when she decided it was a good idea to put mystics and ordinary people on the same world.

Jomo runs a finger over his heart and quietly apologizes for his blasphemy.

"I hope you know what you're doing," he says to Isa. "But you have my support. I'll do whatever it takes to help you, even if I don't understand."

"I appreciate that, Jomo. And speaking of things you could do for me . . ." Isa casually gets up from her couch and drifts over to the windows, where she stares down at the city sprawling beneath the temple's twin waterfalls. Backlit by the daylight, she is a graceful silhouette, a vision of poise and calm Jomo finds himself envying.

"I keep having this dream," she says. "I'm some sort of god climbing a ladder, and with each rung I climb, I become more powerful. But the power is never enough, so I have to keep climbing. On and on without end."

Jomo furrows his brow, remaining silent.

"I know how crazy it sounds," Isa says.

"Hey, no judgment from me, cousin. I have weird dreams all the time."

She turns back to face him. "I need you to set up a meeting with the leaders of the undercity," she says. "The independent mystics, the Faraswa Collective, the apostate sanctuaries. I have thought about it and believe they could be valuable allies."

Jomo considers his cousin, waiting for her to burst into laughter and tell him she's joking. She doesn't. "Okay," he says, drawing out the word. "I don't see how it would help, but I'll meet with them if that's what you want."

She smiles a little. "*I* will be meeting with them, cousin."

"You want them to come here?" he says, confused. "You do know what *apostate* means, right?"

"I'll meet them where they are. In the undercity."

Jomo's mouth falls open. He closes it. He opens it again with a fierce protest on his tongue, but Isa preempts him with a raised hand.

"Not many people know what I look like. I barely ever left the palace. If I wore the clothes of a common woman and painted my face a little heavier than usual, I could walk the streets of Northtown, and no one would recognize me. I can pose as my own handmaiden if necessary." She gives him a look halfway between imploring and resolute. "It's time I got back out into the city. As my herald, I need you to make it happen."

Jomo thinks about getting up and pouring himself more rum. Instead he wipes the sweat off his forehead and says, "Well. Shit."

3: Ilapara

Ilapara once spied the inside of a Shevu prince's wheelhouse when it stopped over in Kageru and was floored to see so much plushness crammed into such a confined space, the carpets of leopard skin, the furnishings of silver and tronic ivory. She thought it the height of luxury.

Now she dips herself into a scented stone bath so large she has to tread water to stay afloat at its deepest end. Soapsuds float on the surface while hidden contraptions work to cycle and clean the water, reheating it to just the perfect shade of warm before spewing it back into the pool through serpentine brass pipes arrayed at the edge of the bath.

Her first instinct is to wallow in the water and let its scents carry her away into a dreamless sleep, but she doesn't allow herself to linger. She finds a brush, scrubs the journey off her skin, washes out her hair. Then she towels herself off and leaves.

Twilight has blanketed the city when she arrives at the dinner table out in the trellised garden behind the residence. She's the first one there. A lazy sheen of golden light plays on the silverware arranged on the table, cast by the many glowing crystals shining within and without the residence.

More lights sparkle up at her from the city below and from the citadel above the waterfalls. A view fit for a king, but as she takes a seat by the table, she lets her eyes take it all in with as much dispassion as she can summon. This place might *feel* like a fanciful dream, but she knows that dreams can quickly mutate into nightmares.

An obsequious servant comes to ask if she'd like something to drink; she declines. Alinata shows up a minute later, freshly bathed and smiling at some hidden joke. She always carries this deliberately enigmatic look in her eye, like she wants you to know she knows something you don't, and it makes Ilapara want to bite something. Typical Asazi.

Like Ilapara, she has wrapped herself in one of the plentiful khangas the servants left folded neatly in almost every wardrobe in the palace, though the Asazi has slung hers around her neck in a way that makes it look like an actual garment rather than a long piece of cloth tucked in at the chest. It's also clear she chose hers carefully—a silky pale gray with swirling black patterns reminiscent of those ravens of hers. Ilapara just picked up the first one she found, which happened to be mostly red.

The Asazi settles herself across the table without a word, but she makes a show out of peering under the table, at the spear resting next to Ilapara's sandaled feet.

"Something to say?" Ilapara asks.

"Me?" Alinata says. "Oh no. Nothing at all."

The servant returns, and she accepts a glass of citrus juice from his tray. She sips it like she belongs in this garden. Closes her eyes in bliss as it goes down her throat. Then that look returns to her face. "You and I are not so different, you know."

And there it is. "I highly doubt that," Ilapara says.

"In our own ways, we both fight to protect what we care about."

"I'm a mercenary. I fight for coin. You're an assassin. You spy and kill to advance your master's political ambitions."

A flash of annoyance briefly tarnishes the Asazi's smug look. "So you uprooted your life in Umadiland," she says, "fought your way up to the world's equator, just for coin? Either you're lying to yourself or you're being deliberately obtuse."

"I'm here because I got mixed up in something I still don't understand," Ilapara says. "I didn't choose this. I didn't want it. And the only reason I'm still here is the promise of coin."

"I watched you in Seresa. You could have walked away from Salo at any time. But you didn't. And I specifically remember how you were willing to sacrifice yourself for him shortly before the Umadi witch attacked. Was that also for coin?"

"I don't lack honor," Ilapara says, trying not to grit her teeth. She won't let this girl get under her skin.

"Neither do I," Alinata says. "Contrary to what you think you know about us Asazi."

"I know all I need to know about your kind."

The Asazi takes a sip of her juice, then places the glass on the table. "Let me guess. Your test scores were atrocious, so you were rejected from your kraal's grammar school, forever barred from joining the Asazi. The girls who made it were cruel to you, made fun of you, called you dumb. So you got angry and turned to the man's path as a way of showing them just how much you didn't need them. In fact, you're still trying to show them, hence your presence here. How am I doing so far?"

I am not my emotions. I am not my emotions. "You know *nothing* about me."

The Asazi leans forward, eyes hard as the red steel circlet on her head. "The way you feel right now? That's exactly how I feel every time you look at me like you know everything about me. I get it. You don't like me. You don't trust me. That's fine. But if you stop acting like you know who I am and what I'm about, when really, you don't, I'll pay you the same courtesy. Why don't we get to know each other first and reserve the judgment for later?"

Ilapara bites back a retort as Salo and Tuk emerge from the palace, both wearing colorful khangas wrapped around their waists. Salo has the toned physique of a cowherd, which she's seen many times given his rather Yerezi tendency to wear little more than a loincloth, but Tuk . . . the guy looks like he was chiseled from stone.

When they get to the table, Tuk grins like a fool at Ilapara and points. "Your hair!"

She tries not to bristle. "What about it?"

"You've been hiding *that* under your headscarf this whole time? It's amazing!"

"I wasn't *hiding* it." She can't help tousling the crimson dreadlocks falling all the way down to the small of her back. "You both smell like flowers, by the way."

Salo chuckles as he takes the seat next to hers. "Your hair's nice, Ilapara. And you smell like flowers yourself."

"It becomes you," Alinata says while Tuk seats himself next to her. "I'm almost tempted to start growing out my own hair."

No spite in those words, but Ilapara finds them hard to believe. "All right, fine. Thanks, all of you. Now enough about my hair. You owe us answers, Salo."

Salo fiddles with his reflective spectacles. "Food first."

As if on cue, a servant comes with a pitcher of soapy water and a pewter bowl to wash their hands. Three more servants follow bearing a dozen different platters of stews, cold vegetable relishes, ugali, and sourdough flatbread. Yet another brings a ewer of palm wine. Ilapara's mouth waters at the aroma, and she silently agrees that food first is a good idea. They all proceed to feast and drink quietly, too hungry to do anything else but enjoy the sumptuous meal. The KiYonte people evidently know their way around a kitchen.

"So I spoke to the groundsmen for a few minutes after Salo got the animals settled," Tuk says as he dishes himself his third helping of stew and flatbread. "They told me some interesting things. It turns out the king didn't just pass away, as the steward suggested."

For a man on the shorter side, Tuk consumes an awful lot of food. He's the only one who went for seconds, and now thirds.

"No surprise there," Salo says as he sticks a toothpick into his mouth and relaxes into his chair. "It was obvious from the look on his face that something suspicious is afoot."

"Try something diabolical," Tuk says, then gets a mistrustful look on his face, searching the gardens around them. "How freely can we speak out here? Alinata mentioned spies."

"We should be fine so long as we keep our voices down," Salo says. "I don't sense anyone else within earshot. Although . . ." Salo suddenly acquires the same wary look. "Maybe we should speak *very* softly just to be safe."

Across the table, Tuk lowers his voice almost to a whisper. "So apparently, the king and his entire family were butchered in one night as they slept, and the Royal Guard is rumored to have done it."

While Salo breathes out a curse, Ilapara gapes. "The Royal Guard? You mean to tell us that the same men who were charged with protecting the royal family are the ones who turned around and"—she looks around for prying ears—"*butchered* them? Why?"

"No clue," Tuk says, covering his mouth so he can speak while he chews, "but that's what I was told. Also, at least one of the princesses survived and is now hiding in the Red Temple, or something? Meanwhile, the ten headmen elected the leader of the crocodile clan as prince regent, ostensibly to restore order." Tuk shakes his head as he looks out at the city. "You know, there are usually signs long before such things happen. Tension on the streets. Civil unrest. But that's not at all what I sensed when I was here not long ago. Funny how fast things can change." He looks back, his eyes turning dusky, like the skies. "You know what bugs me, though?"

"What?" Salo and Ilapara both say.

"Why would the Shirika let this happen? They've always protected the Saire monarchy. What kind of momentous shift would make them abandon centuries of tradition?"

"But *what* are the Shirika exactly?" Ilapara asks. "I know they're mystics, but what role do they play in all of this?"

Alinata finally slides into the conversation. "Remember the secretive cabal of mystics I mentioned earlier?"

"The ones who cast the tattoo curse?" Ilapara says. "Yeah. Hard to forget."

"Well, their descendants became the mystic caste. They bow to no totem and inherit a visually distinct mark. Only members of this caste can ever awaken as mystics, and the Shirika are the seven most powerful mystics in the kingdom at any given moment. Tuk is right when he says they've always supported the Saire clan. As for why they suddenly changed their stance . . ." Alinata lets her voice drift off as her eyes bore into Salo like she expects him to finish her thought.

He stares at the platters of food in front of him. "I suppose that's one of the things I'm here to find out."

"Come again?" Ilapara says.

Leaning forward and folding his arms on the table in a rather nervous fashion, he says, "The truth, Ilapara, and you, Tuksaad, is that I was sent here as an emissary by the queen to gather information on the current happenings of this city. It's also possible that at some point the queen will expect me to . . . take action, and don't ask me what action because I don't know. I guess I didn't tell you because . . . well, I feared that if you knew, you might decide not to come with me."

Ilapara waits for him to tell her he has misspoken, but the guilty look remains on his face. "You're actually serious," she remarks, and he gives a solemn nod.

"So you're not walking the Bloodway?" Tuk asks, scratching the stubble on his face. His forehead is creased with the same confusion Ilapara feels, and his eyes are a sickly shade of yellow she hasn't seen on him before. At least not where Salo is concerned. Is that disappointment? Betrayal? Ilapara certainly didn't think Salo could be so good at keeping secrets.

"Oh no, I'm definitely walking the Bloodway," he says. "But my pilgrimage is secondary to my true purpose. At least, that's what I was told. It's supposed to be a cover so I can stay in the city without attracting too much scrutiny."

Tuk keeps scratching his face, though his eyes lighten ever so slightly. "But how is it a cover? Your title as emissary isn't exactly a secret."

"I'm wondering the same thing," Ilapara says, trying hard to restrain her annoyance and reserve her judgment. Because apparently, she has a problem with judging people too quickly.

When Salo seems to flounder for an answer, Alinata throws him a withering look. "Pilgrimages tend to be planned several comets in advance," she explains. "A pilgrim will therefore carry the benefit of the doubt that his presence in the city, even so soon after the king's death, isn't a calculated decision but a mere coincidence. He can claim that he was always going to be here, and no one will be able to dispute or disprove that claim."

"But why does it matter?" Ilapara says. "With the king dying so mysteriously, I'm certain every tribe will be sending someone to figure out exactly what the devil is going on here."

"The optics always matter in this city," Alinata says with a hard edge in her voice. "A diplomat who's obviously here to gather intelligence will be easily brushed aside. But a diplomat who's also a pilgrim carries a certain authority that can't be denied. Convention will force the powers that be to acknowledge and even accommodate him."

Ilapara looks at Salo, and he seems to shrink into himself. She knows there are women of the Asazi who are trained from a young age in the arts of manipulation and persuasion, to speak with honeyed tongues. To bend the wills of those around them. Such a woman is who Ilapara would have expected the queen to send thousands of miles away, to the most powerful city in all the Redlands, as her emissary.

Not this timid, soft-spoken young man.

"Why you, Salo?" Ilapara says, because it makes absolutely no sense. "Why you specifically? And why would you *ever* agree to this?"

He gives a sad smile. "I was told I'm dispensable. No other Yerezi mystic could leave the Plains indefinitely. And the queen promised that if I did her bidding, she'd get one of her apprentices to awaken and serve my clan. After a decade without a mystic, and with the attack on my kraal . . ." He lifts a shoulder in a defeated shrug. "I didn't really have a choice."

"I thought *you* were set to be clan mystic when you returned."

"That's not going to happen, Ilapara."

She feels her eyes getting narrower. "Exactly how long do you intend to stay here?"

"I don't know. Probably until whatever's happening is resolved and the queen no longer requires my presence in the city. Maybe longer."

"Indefinitely, then."

Salo appears to gulp. "Yes."

Feeling boxed in, Ilapara gets up from the table and starts to pace. She would shout, but she restrains the urge in case there are spies listening—and dear Ama, now she understands the need to worry about spies. She stops with her hands on her waist. "Why didn't you tell us, Salo? I thought you'd be in and out of the Red Temple, and then we'd be riding back south. I had a life. Now I find out you're planning on staying to 'take action'? After what looks like a bloody coup? Are you mad?"

"I know," Salo says. "I know, and I'm sorry. Look. Can you sit down? You're really intimidating when you stand like that."

Slowly, Ilapara lets her hands slide off her waist and forces herself to comply.

"I'm sorry," Salo says again, addressing her and Tuk. "Not telling you was selfish of me. And I won't hold it against you if you decide to leave, though I'd really like you to stay. But if you decide to leave, I'll still stand by the promises I made to you. I'll pay you, Ilapara, for getting me here. And Tuk, my blessing is yours, though I'll need some time to prepare. Blessing a person isn't like blessing an animal. There's a whole mental ritual involved."

"I'm in no rush," Tuk says. "Let's get you through the New Year's Feast; then we'll talk."

"So . . . you're staying?"

Tuk grins crookedly, dimples on full display, eyes flicking to a light shade of green. "I told you the day we met, Salo. It would be foolish of me to let you out of my sight. You won't be getting rid of me anytime soon."

Relief takes some of the tension off Salo's shoulders, but he is uncertain as he looks over at Ilapara. "I'd pay you on a continuous basis if you stayed," he offers. "I have access to a money vault in the city; judging by this place, you'll have as much coin as you want, and my offer to bless you still stands."

For a moment Ilapara wonders if she hasn't misread him all along. Maybe he *was* trained in manipulation. Maybe his perceived naivete and softheartedness are simply aspects of his unique brand of persuasion. Maybe that's how he ropes people in and holds on to them, why she can't let herself break free.

She doubts she would have lingered this long or gone so far for anyone else. She's always been an independent spirit. A solitary creature. She had friends back in Khaya-Sikhozi, an uncle who doted on her. Yet in the end, she had no problems leaving them to find her own way in a foreign land.

But ever since she met this boy, she's felt compelled to follow.

"Do you believe in fate?" he asked her as they laid their eyes on the city for the first time.

Ilapara has never believed in fate and doesn't believe in it now, but being around Salo often feels to her like being in a river, pulled by unseen currents toward *something*.

That troubles her. And excites her.

The massive ruby hanging above the distant temple catches her attention as it flashes seven times. "A blessing is a big commitment," she says.

"It can be undone, if that's what you're worried about," Salo says. "I know it wouldn't be the usual way of things, but I've broken so many conventions already. What's a few more?"

"I'll think about it," she says, the next best thing to a flat rejection.

He takes the hint and turns to the Asazi. "And you?"

Her eyes dart to Tuk and then to Ilapara like she's trying to make sense of the question. "Me?"

"Yes, you," Salo says. "How much can I rely on you?" Alinata raises a pair of affronted eyebrows, but he lifts a hand to cut off her protest. "I'm not asking you to take my blessing or work for me, Si Alinata—perish the thought. But you *are* enjoying my hospitality, are you not? Where would you be if I hadn't asked you to join us? Probably perched in those trees over there, watching us enjoy this feast."

Tuk smirks and covers his mouth. "Eating bugs and carrion for dinner."

Alinata probably kicks him beneath the table, because he yelps and starts choking on the flatbread he was chewing. She pushes a glass of water in his direction before turning to Salo with a clench of her jaw. "You may rely on me wherever our objectives are aligned."

Salo's mouth quivers at one corner. "And where would they not be aligned, Si Asazi?"

"I'll be sure to let you know should we ever come to such a point."

They stare at each other, the tension thick. Salo ends the moment with a sigh and a resigned shake of the head. "I suppose you'll tell me what you want to tell me. Just do me a favor, will you? Be kind in your reports to AmaYerezi. I don't need her thinking any worse of me."

"I'm sure you have nothing to worry about," the Asazi says, though Ilapara would swear she sees a shadow crossing the girl's face.

But Salo nods and lets the matter go, so Ilapara holds her peace.

4: Musalodi

Skytown

Bright and early on his first day in the city, Salo navigates the many halls of his new residence in search of the steward. A part of him keeps expecting one of the servants to leap out of a closet and tell him that this was all just a big mistake, that he doesn't actually belong here and could he please leave. Instead, the servants he encounters are overly deferential and won't look him in the eye.

He finally finds Ruma in what he thinks is the drawing room, relaying instructions to a Faraswa maid. Ruma promptly dismisses her when he spots Salo standing by the arched door. Like the other servants, he's never in anything more colorful than simple gray, though the embroidery on his current tunic appears quite involved.

"Bwana Ruma," Salo says in greeting.

The steward clasps his hands together respectfully. "Honored Emissary Siningwe. I hope everything thus far has been to your satisfaction."

"I think I'd have to die and walk the Infinite Path to get anything better than this."

Ruma eases into his smile as it becomes less synthetic. "I'm glad to hear that. And please, let me know if there's anything I can do to improve your stay."

"Actually, there is," Salo says, moving farther into the drawing room. "I intend to complete my pilgrimage in the near future, and I wanted to check with you about visiting the Red Temple. Especially given the . . . how to put it, the rumors I've heard. Would I be acting inappropriately if I showed up at the gates unannounced?"

Ruma's cheerful mood seems to wilt. "I know almost nothing about mystical matters, honored emissary. All I know is that the temple has been closed to visitors for the last few weeks. Some sort of arcane barrier went up, and I'm told it won't let outsiders through. Perhaps the mystics at the House of Forms could tell you more?"

Deflection. Salo blinks at the steward, wondering why the man is so afraid of discussing what's going on.

He might be a spy, is what Alinata said. But working for who? *Maybe I should just ask.*

Salo resists that last thought. "The House of Forms," he says pensively. "That's the kingdom's academy of magic, is it not?"

"Indeed," Ruma says, clearly relieved by the change of subject. "Would you like to pay them a visit? They're always happy to receive pilgrims. In fact, visiting the academy is usually one of the first things a pilgrim does upon arrival. I could message ahead and let them know to expect you."

"Perhaps I can do that this morning," Salo muses. "I assume you will message them with that interesting machine in the hallway. A mirrorgraph, is it?"

Ruma stands straighter, oozing pride in the machine. "That's a mirrorgraph, yes, and my extensive experience as a scribe means I can send and receive messages on your behalf with no trouble at all."

A spy, Salo thinks again. "That's good to know. I suppose you can go ahead and warn the academy I'll be on my way."

"Yes, honored." Instead of leaving, Ruma gives Salo a brief once-over, his lips tightening the slightest bit. "If I may be so bold as to ask, will you go dressed like that?"

Salo looks down at himself. He's barefoot, wearing one of the best white loincloths he packed for his use in the city. It's made of a high-grade, dirt-resistant Yerezi linen, the kind he'd normally reserve for special occasions. "I could wear my straw hat and blanket cloak if more formal dress is required. My sandals too, of course. I never leave those behind."

Ruma visibly cringes. "May I make a suggestion?"

"Go on."

"The New Year's Feast is tonight, and it would be, shall I say, prudent for you to look your utmost best. Yesterday I mentioned a reputable clothier; the timing isn't the best, but I could have him come over this afternoon to get you ready for the feast."

Salo's stomach curdles at the idea, and he shakes his head. "I'm sorry, Bwana Ruma, but I am Yerezi, here as a representative of my people and my queen. I will not dress in foreign garb."

"That is not at all what I meant to suggest, honored emissary. As a matter of fact, this particular clothier is acquainted with the dressing customs of your people. He will make sure you remain Yerezi in every way, only much more . . . becoming of your station. You are, after all, a mystic and, as you've said, the representative of your queen in this city. There must be absolutely no doubt about it when people look at you."

Why, though? Salo wants to ask. *Why can't it be enough for me to know what I am? Why must I inspire fear to be secure in my own power?*

"I suppose there's no harm in seeing what he has to offer," he says. "But the feast is tonight, and I might be out the whole day, so I'd have to meet him some other time. Next week, perhaps?"

Ruma presses his lips together, but he nods. "As you wish, honored. If there's nothing else, I will go ahead and send a message to the House of Forms."

"Thank you, Bwana Ruma."

The steward executes a polite bow and glides out through the archway.

Salo waits a few heartbeats before he says, "You can come in now, Alinata." She's wearing a rueful look when she shows herself. Salo scowls at her. "I thought we agreed on no lurking."

"I wasn't lurking," she says. "I just didn't want to interrupt."

"I'm sure," Salo says. "Anyway, as you likely overheard, I'll be visiting the academy later this morning. Will you be coming?"

She seems to think about it. "I'll go with you to the feast, but I'd rather do something else on my first day in the city. You don't mind, do you?"

"So long as you're not *lurking*, I'm fine with however you choose to spend your time."

"Understood." She looks him over, a hint of disapproval in her expression. "The steward wasn't wrong, you know. An emissary of the queen cannot run around looking like a common cowherd. That you weren't furnished with a new wardrobe before you left the Plains was a serious oversight."

"What else am I supposed to wear, Alinata? I can hardly don the regalia of an Ajaha, and I certainly won't be wearing Asazi beads."

"I guess not," she concedes. "But you are the son of a chief as well as a mystic. An unusual combination, but workable." She considers him again, a crafty look in her eye. "Yes, a nice pair of sandals, a new cloak, better linen, lots and lots of copper. Tell you what: since you're too busy, I'll visit the clothier for you. If I'll be standing next to you at this feast, I won't have you looking like you just came from milking the goats."

Salo stares at her, unamused. "Do what you will, but I reserve the right to reject anything I don't like."

"Of course."

"Then I guess I'll see you later." He starts to walk away but stops when she speaks.

"What are you going to do about the temple?" she says. "You'll need to get in at some point."

Salo doesn't need the reminder. Even if the political situation in the city resolved itself today, he wouldn't be able to return home until he completed his pilgrimage. Getting into that temple must be a priority. "I honestly don't know," he says. "I guess I'll do whatever it takes."

Alinata watches him like she has something more to say, then nods. "I'm sure you'll manage."

◆　◆　◆

An hour later he rides down Skytown with Ilapara and Tuk, following the same gold-flecked road they ascended yesterday. Sleek carriages pass them by along the way, some with open tops, carrying passengers decked in silvers, silks, furs, and peacock feathers.

Optics. Salo is beginning to acquire a new appreciation for that word.

"I don't think I'm comfortable with you entrusting your financial affairs to me," Tuk says shortly after they settle into a good rhythm down the road.

They mean to leave him at the city's financial institution while Salo and Ilapara proceed to the House of Forms southeast of town. Earlier Ilapara pursed her lips as Salo handed Tuk his queen's medallion and asked him to visit the money vault on his behalf.

"How do you know I won't take your money and run away?" Tuk says.

He has returned to wearing black—a sleeveless dashiki, pants, and boots, all of it black. Combined with his jet-black hair and the sable coat of his tronic mount, those garments make him look rather grim. Not at all the charming young man Salo has come to know.

Ilapara has also returned to her crimson robe and veil—the same ones she wore all the way from Umadiland, though she had them washed and dried overnight. Still, her lack of clothing is one of the main reasons Salo wants the money issue dealt with soon, so he can pay her and encourage her to stay.

"Because I don't think money is what motivates you," he tells Tuk. "And it's not really *my* money. It belongs to the Yerezi crown. Truth be told, I barely understand the concept, so it's hard for me to care about it."

While Ilapara shakes her head, Tuk looks over from his horned mount, yellow eyes uncertain, seeking reassurance.

"I trust you," Salo tells him. "Trusting you has kept me alive so far. Besides, you understand money. If you handle this for me, you'll be taking one more item off my long list of things to worry about."

Tuk keeps eyeing Salo for a moment longer, then chuckles at the road ahead. "I'll try not to be tempted. Too much."

"I doubt you'll be tempted even a little," Salo says.

"You're either a fool or the world's best judge of character," Ilapara remarks, sounding resigned.

A spectacle greets them as they reach the main arched bridge to Midtown. First, they see a grand carriage rolling toward them, escorted by two pairs of nervous-looking outriders wearing green tunics and aerosteel armor. Then they hear people shouting angrily behind the carriage. When it finally rolls past, giving them a better view of the source of this commotion, Salo feels a chill spreading across his skin.

Following at a casual jog not far behind the carriage is a gang of rowdy youths. They appear to be shouting insults at the carriage and brandishing machetes in threat to whoever is inside. When Salo draws level with them, they give his sharp-toothed totem a wide berth but otherwise ignore him and the others, continuing their slow pursuit of the carriage until it has crossed the bridge over to Skytown, where they stop and break into song.

"The reaping is nigh, Saire pig!" Salo hears one of them shout. "Your blood will paint the streets scarlet when we reap vengeance for your crimes! Rise, Wavunaji!"

He shares concerned looks with the others; then they ride on and leave the spectacle behind.

"You have all the ingredients of a catastrophe," Tuk says sometime later. "The Saires ruled over the other clans by the grace of the Shirika, and the other clans resented them for it. Now that grace has been withdrawn, they have no legion of their own, and the Royal Guard betrayed their king. That carriage had an elephant painted on its doors. Did you see it? I'm certain that's the royal seal."

Salo saw the seal but didn't make the connection. "Could that be the living Saire princess in there?"

"I doubt she'd risk her life so brazenly," Tuk says. "If I had to guess, that was an official acting on her behalf. Still. Armed gangs openly threatening a royal carriage? Bad."

"I think I'm beginning to understand the movement we saw along the World's Vein on our way here," Ilapara says in a grave voice. "Some people sense what's coming and are running for the hills. For the Saires, that means being closer to the city, where they think they'll be safer in numbers. For many others, it's as far from here as possible." She looks at Salo with worry reflected in the pools of her umber eyes. "Are you sure you can't just go back home?"

Despite the sense of dread now growing at the base of his spine, Salo shakes his head, elaborating no further.

Ilapara exhales. "I had to try."

They leave Tuk near Midworld Park, a grassy square not far from the meeting point of the World's Artery and the World's Vein. Imposing multistory buildings of glass and magically reinforced bamboo line each side of the square, and just beyond it, the two major roadways of the Redlands become one, running due east for a mile exactly along the world's equator.

On this wide strip of road, which signs refer to as the Midworld Confluence, the twin waterfalls and the Red Temple rise directly ahead, framed by a corridor of gilded bamboo towers and glass-paneled domes. Salo is amazed by how thickly traffic seethes along the roadway—lumbering carriers pulling multiple wagons, their gears powered by repurposed tronic mind stones; two-story wheelhouses drawn by massive beasts; carriages and mounted riders.

As they advance along the Confluence, the drone of the twin waterfalls rises to a thunderous roar so powerful it calls upon some instinctual part of Salo to prostrate himself. More, the cosmic shards hidden beneath his forearms begin to thrum uncomfortably with the power emanating from the temple. The sensation is quite like staring directly at the suns.

At the end of the Confluence, the road splits once more; the Artery veers left, where it should proceed into Northtown, crossing the river next to the waterfalls, while the Vein turns right, where it begins to climb up the city's southeastern hill, which rises somewhat adjacent to the waterfalls.

Salo and Ilapara ride along the Vein for a time, then branch off onto a narrower road lined by the strangest witchwood trees he has ever seen. Their pale boughs aren't barren like they're supposed to be; they're weighed down instead by red-petaled blossoms. The House of Forms is a staggered complex of domes built halfway up the hill, sprouting out of a grove of many such trees.

The guards are expecting them when they arrive at the arching entrance to the complex. Salo and Ilapara are directed to leave their mounts with the stable hands while they wait for their hosts to come and receive them.

A minute later, two men approach them along a stone path. Though they both bear the white, thin marks of the mystic caste on their necks, they are dressed quite dissimilarly. One is barefoot, though clearly not out of austerity, since his robe is crimson-and-gold silk and his breastplate aerosteel with intricate trimmings of moongold. A long blade is sheathed by his side, while brightly colored tattoos peek out from underneath his robe on his collar and forearms. His companion, on the other hand, is draped in the folds of a pristine white robe, wearing fine leather sandals on his feet and a circlet of moongold on his head, no weapons in sight.

Salo recognizes the first as the Jasiri who welcomed him at the city gates. Kamali, was it? His expression is coolly polite, his thick mane of dreadlocks tied behind his head, a well-groomed beard framing his strong jawline. His clean-shaven companion has a mischievous slant to his lips and a glint in his eye that Salo finds instantly discomfiting.

"We meet again, Emissary Siningwe," says the Jasiri. "Mother's grace this New Year's Eve, and welcome to the House of Forms."

It might be all the moongold the two men are wearing, but Salo could swear he senses power oozing off the Jasiri's tattoos. "Acolyte Kamali Jasiri of the Fractal," he says, offering a hand for a handshake. "A pleasant surprise to see you here."

"Please, honored emissary," the Jasiri says when the handshake is over. "Acolyte Kamali will suffice." He gestures at his companion. "And this is Acolyte Mosi Akili of the Spiral. We will be your hosts this morning."

"A pleasure to meet you, Emissary Siningwe," Mosi says with a slight bow of his head.

"Likewise," Salo says, and he goes on to introduce Ilapara, who continues to watch the two men with poorly concealed suspicion. Kamali pays her almost no attention. Mosi doesn't even look at her.

"Forgive me for asking," Salo says, "but these titles of yours, what do they mean exactly?"

Mosi's lips quiver at the corners like he's fighting back a snicker. Kamali appears to chasten him with a subtle glare.

"We're both acolytes of our respective covens, honored emissary," Kamali explains. "I am of the warrior class and am therefore Jasiri. Mosi belongs to the scholar class and is therefore Akili. Our artisans, healers, and technicians are Msani. Those who have yet to be assigned a class and coven are Kijana. And the high sorcerers to whom we pledge are Faro."

Understanding dawns on Salo. "I see. So the Fractal and the Spiral—these are your covens."

"As well as the titles taken up by the Faros at the head of each respective coven," Kamali says.

"Fascinating. You'll have to tell me more. I know next to nothing about your covens."

Mosi turns a stifled laugh into a brilliant smile. "The topic would easily fill a library, Emissary Siningwe, but we will do our best."

By the ripple of his temples, Kamali must be annoyed by his companion's condescension. "Why don't we begin with a tour of the premises?" he suggests and motions them down the same stone path from which they emerged. As they begin to walk, he says, "If you don't mind me saying so"—he shoots Mosi a rather pointed look—"your command of our tongue is impeccable. Quite unusual for an outsider. One would think you've lived in this city for many comets."

Salo notices the way Mosi rolls his eyes slightly. A snobbish ass, it seems, but Salo grew up with true masters of assness in the form of his two younger brothers, so he has a considerably high resistance to it.

"My grandmother was a great teacher," he says, keeping his voice friendly. "She almost always conversed with me in a foreign tongue. I learned quite a lot from her. Sadly, she passed on two comets ago."

"I'm sorry to hear that," Kamali says, sounding sincere. His companion, by comparison, is almost irreverent.

"Yes, that's very sad. Interesting, though. Can you imagine being instructed by your grandmother, Kamali?"

The Jasiri's light skin flushes with repressed emotion. Ilapara's face remains inscrutable, though Salo imagines she's fighting against the desire to use her spear right about now.

"Is it true that most Yerezi men are illiterate?" Mosi asks as they approach what looks like the academy's largest dome.

Adolescents in blue robes loiter all over the place, some reading books on the lawns or beneath the red-blossomed witchwood trees, others engaging in animated discussions by the fountains. Salo reckons these are the Kijana, the students who have yet to receive a class or be placed in a coven.

"Sadly, yes," he replies as courteously as he can. "Education is typically offered only to those girls who wish to become Asazi. It isn't useful to everyone else. We are a pastoral and agrarian people. I was a cowherd myself when I was younger."

"A cowherd," Mosi says. "Did you hear that, Kamali? How folksy."

"It was a simple life," Salo forges on. "Without many cares. I miss it, to be honest."

"Of course you do. Yonte Saire must be *overwhelming*."

"Like you wouldn't believe. I have a whole palace in Skytown and a view of the city from my massive bed. Overwhelming is an understatement."

Mosi's sneer loses its acidic edge, and his eyes spark with something dark. Salo almost fails to hold in a smirk. This isn't a hard game to play after all.

The Jasiri's face, on the other hand, transforms as he openly beams. "Hear that, Mosi? A whole palace in Skytown. Beats sharing a dormitory with two other grown men, doesn't it? And I bet his bed isn't lumpy either."

"My bed's not lumpy," Mosi growls. Then his sharp gaze pivots to Salo. "Speaking of which, is it true—"

"If you don't mind me asking, Emissary Siningwe," Kamali cuts in, "how old are you?"

They have come to a stop at the entrance to the grand dome, and Salo becomes aware of just how tall these men are. He's not used to looking up at people, being rather tall himself, but he has to look up at these two. And the power seething off the Jasiri's skin is not unlike that of a mind stone—like the energy of a contained tempest—seemingly emanating from the tattoos hidden beneath his robes. *Could he be hosting spirits on his own body?*

"I'll be seeing my nineteenth comet tonight," Salo says.

Kamali grins at his colleague. "Hear that, Mosi? Only eighteen and already the master of his own Axiom. Where were you when you were eighteen? Oh, wait, I remember. Still running around in blue."

"Please," Mosi scoffs. "Anyone can build an Axiom. It's the quality that counts."

"Why don't you be useful and go find out if we can drop in on a class? I'll explain the covens to our guest while we wait in the assembly hall."

Their gazes clash for a moment, icy determination versus pride and resentment. "Fine," Mosi says at last, then stalks away, his white robes billowing behind him.

"I apologize sincerely," Kamali says afterward. "Mosi is . . . well. That's how he is, really. I won't make excuses for him. He's actually the reason I insinuated myself into this tour. I didn't wish for you to develop a low opinion of us. We're not all like him."

Salo looks in Mosi's direction. "It's all right. I have experience dealing with his kind."

"Something we have in common, then." Kamali spares a glance for Ilapara and gestures into the building. "Shall we?"

Sunlight falls in brilliant shafts through the glass dome in the assembly hall, bouncing off the checkered floors to lend the place a rather stately ambience. A series of tapestries has been hung on the walls, each featuring a different mystic Seal throbbing with hypnotic power against a vermilion background.

Several pairs of students in orange robes are hurling spells of moon-fire, lightning, or ice at each other in the hall, sparks flying off into the air as the spells hit speedily conjured kinetic barriers and counterspells. The students all look about Salo's age, but they each boast two rings of power around their active cosmic shards, meaning they can already call upon twice as much raw essence as he can for their spells.

"This is the assembly hall," Kamali says as they stop a good distance away from the duels. "But we also use it as a sparring ground. These students are Msani preparing for their practical assessments early next year. Many will go on to serve the kingdom as arcane engineers and machinists."

Salo watches with envy as one of the students traps her sparring partner in a cage of moonfire, only for her opponent to thrust his hands outward and launch a freezing wave of Storm craft that dissipates the flames. He quickly retaliates with a bolt of red lightning that hurtles toward the other student, but she crosses her arms in front of her in time to create a shield of raw essence that absorbs the attack. Salo is shocked to see the move work; he wasn't aware that raw essence could be used defensively against lightning. He wasn't aware it could be used for anything at all.

As the students sling spell after spell at each other, it dawns on him just how incomplete his mystical education really is. First, he knows only two spells. Second, these students received formal training from a young age, while he illicitly cobbled together what he knows from his dead mother's tomes and writings. He might have survived confrontations with two deadly mystics on his way to the city, but he was lucky more than anything. If he had to face any of these students in battle, even the weakest among them, he would surely lose.

I have a long way to go, he thinks, morose.

"Don't they worry about hurting each other?" Ilapara asks Kamali as she watches the duels with a dubious eye. "Many of these spells look dangerous." She speaks in the Umadi tongue, since she's self-conscious about KiYonte, but from the way Kamali's eyes gleam, he understands her perfectly.

"There's an enchantment beneath the hall's floor that saps the power of any spell it deems lethal," he says. "We also have a team of the kingdom's best healers on standby in case of accidents."

"I suppose that works," Ilapara says, though there's lingering doubt in her voice.

Salo didn't know he was capable of reaching such depths of envy. "I wish I could have gone somewhere like this," he utters.

For some reason Kamali's eyebrows lift with surprise. He studies Salo, looking him over appraisingly. "But you are the master of your own Axiom, are you not?"

"I . . . am, I guess?" Salo says, not quite understanding the question.

"Come. Let me show you something." As they walk slowly along the curved wall, Salo keeps one eye on the dueling students.

Covens are made possible, Kamali goes on to explain, by the KiYonte ancestral talent, which circumvents the need for every aspiring mystic of the tribe to devise their own Axiom prior to meeting the redhawk. Instead, most KiYonte mystics bind themselves to one of a handful of the very best Axioms in the land, and the time saved allows for deeper levels of efficiency and specialization.

"The Seals you see on the walls represent each of the seven covens of the Shirika," Kamali says. "They're named after the general structures or behaviors of their Axioms, which we call the Forms. The Forms are the best Axioms of the orthodoxy at any given time, to which the rest of us must bind ourselves."

Kamali stops to consider one of the Seals, a fractal pattern that resolves into the image of a tree. Its branches each look like the whole tree, and the branches on the branches also look like the whole tree—on and on at progressively smaller scales. The arcane image reaches into Salo's mind to tell him of the one to whom this Seal belongs: a towering matron who wields power over blood and death.

"This one here is the Fractal of Hypnotism and Necromancy," Kamali says. "An Axiom of pure Blood craft mastered by Her Worship Talara Faro, chancellor of this academy. Hers is the best Axiom in the kingdom with a fractal macrostructure and therefore the one most worthy of the Form. This means she gets to rule over a coven, granting her acolytes use of her Axiom so they never have to go through the trouble of constructing one themselves. And most students here never do. Most of us spend our entire lives content with being beholden to another mystic, while you, young as you are, are already a master of your own Axiom." Kamali's lips move into a half smile. "Knowing this, do you still wish you were one of us?"

Some of what he said went over Salo's head, but the puzzle is beginning to make sense. *House of Forms. Kamali Jasiri of the Fractal. I understand now. Necromancy, though? That might explain the strange energy I sense around him.*

But it *does* make Salo feel a little better about himself, to know that these students and their flashy spells didn't actually go through the process of creating an Axiom. At least there's one area where he has an advantage.

He moves to study another Seal along the wall, this one a maze of lines that resolves into a pair of rapidly spinning intertwining coils of blood. The image tells Salo of a ruthless academic with immense power over living flesh. "What coven is this?" he says in fear and awe.

"That is the Helix of Healing," Kamali answers. "The only other Axiom of Blood craft currently active as a Form. Its master is the high physician of the House of Life."

"I see," Salo says, fascinated.

They do the same for the other Seals: the Arc of Lightning, the Prism of Illusion, the Trigon of Fire, the Torus of Earth, all of them speaking silently of terrifyingly powerful figures.

"And this must be Mosi's Spiral," Salo says, coming to a stop in front of a series of whorls that resolves into a devouring vortex. In that

Seal, Salo sees a fanged grin and the outline of a man who can change shape into a frightful creature of the night. "Void craft, I presume?"

Ilapara breaks her silence with a snort. "I wouldn't be surprised. He does seem like there could be something unpleasant hiding inside him. Maybe a bat or a snake."

Kamali gives an almost inaudible laugh. "Yes, this is the Void Spiral of Metamorphosis and Conjuration," he says. "Though Mosi hasn't risen high enough in his coven's hierarchy to become a metamorph. Perhaps he'll get there in a few comets, once he's completed his dissertation or designed a good spell or two."

Kamali eventually loses his patience with waiting for Mosi and decides to move on from the assembly hall without him. First, he takes Salo and Ilapara on a tour of the academy's impressive enchanting workshop, where they come across more students in orange robes working on identical orb-like artifacts mounted on stands. When Salo asks what those artifacts are, Kamali explains that they're cipher shells—reusable enchantable devices for charms of simple to moderate complexity.

"They're mostly novelties, but they can be useful if you know your way around charms," Kamali says. "Back when I was a Kijana, I had a friend enchant one to wake me up at the same time every morning. There's a store in Midtown that sells them if you're interested."

Salo quietly makes a mental note to visit this store.

They proceed to the alchemical laboratory, but a practice examination in progress discourages them from entering lest they disturb the students. Salo glimpses through the open door a large assortment of brass instruments and glass containers holding fluorescent liquids, and he feels a twinge of homesickness as he remembers Nimara's workshop in the kraal's bonehouse. She would have loved it here.

The academy's library is open to them, however, and Salo is greatly pleased when Kamali lets him know that all Bloodway pilgrims enjoy complimentary borrowing privileges they can use at any time during their stay in Yonte Saire.

"Do you have spells here?" he asks as he wanders down the aisles of bookshelves, each fully stocked with beautifully bound volumes. He once visited the library at the Queen's Kraal, and though it was larger, the opulent architecture here gives the place a more auspicious feel. And if he can borrow as many spell books as he wants, he can work on increasing his arcane repertoire.

Kamali shakes his head. "No spell books are kept in this library, unfortunately."

"Oh." Salo deflates, failing to hide his disappointment. He stops searching the shelves and eyes the Jasiri. "Where do you learn spells, then?"

"Every student here has limited access to the Pattern Archives in Midtown. That's really the only place you'll find spells around here. Foreigners can pay for access, but I'm told it's quite expensive."

A library at a magical academy without any spells? "Why set it up this way?" Salo asks. "Seems counterintuitive."

"To control who gets the spells, I suppose," Kamali says. "There are mystics who do not subscribe to the orthodox ways. We call them independents. They don't attend the academy or join our covens. As a result, we exclude them from our institutions and the benefits they provide, including the hard work and resources that go into spell crafting."

"Not ten minutes alone with our guest, and you're already blabbering about independents." As if from thin air, Mosi materializes next to them with a disapproving frown. "Why am I not surprised?"

Kamali's jaw throbs as he clenches his teeth. "I was simply answering a question."

"Whatever you say." Mosi's eyes sweep over to Salo. "We've been cleared to sit in on first-year Axiom Design Theory. That is, if you're up for it."

Salo is curious to see what's taught in their classrooms, but the idea of meeting more snotty mystics like Mosi isn't appealing. "I won't be intruding, will I?"

"Not at all," Mosi says. "Come, the class starts in a few minutes. And after that we will take you to the Pavilion of Discovery."

"That won't be necessary," Kamali says with a stern set to his brow. He had thawed during Mosi's absence, but now his gaze is frosty again.

"But it's tradition, my dear Kamali. Every visiting sorcerer passes through the Pavilion."

"Tradition does not make requirement."

"What is the Pavilion?" Ilapara asks in her first use of KiYonte.

Mosi looks over like he's offended that she would speak in his presence. "What do you know? A talking bodyguard."

"A valid question," Salo counters.

"It's nothing dangerous," Kamali says, glaring at his colleague. "It's simply where acolytes who have built Axioms test them against the Forms."

"Keeps them humble, if you ask me," Mosi says. "Shows them how far from perfection they've fallen."

Salo's heart slows inside his chest; his blood cools. "You wish to test my Axiom against the Forms? Why?"

"It's a silly tradition," Kamali says, flushing with embarrassment. "It's all very stupid. This whole tour is supposed to validate our high mystics, and therefore ourselves, by belittling you and proving that we're better. It's stupid. You don't have to do it."

Mosi gives what Salo would say is the most impressive eye roll in history. "You can be such a sanctimonious killjoy sometimes, Kamali. It's just healthy competition." He looks at Salo with a dare in his eyes. "What's the harm?"

Salo glances at Ilapara, who gives a subtle headshake, then at Kamali, whose face is pinched with discomfort. "I'll think about it," he says, earning a grin from Mosi.

"That's the spirit. Come on. The class is about to start."

5: Jomo

Skytown

"The prince will see you now, Herald."

Jomo stops fidgeting with his gilded scepter and rises to his feet, propping his weight onto his walking stick. His leg brace makes that infernal squeaking sound, and he just about manages to fend off a wince from the accompanying throb of pain. Back when the world was still kind to him, he'd have been sipping a drink somewhere nice right now, spending time with an even nicer girl. Now he can't ride down the motherdamned street without gangs threatening to hack him to pieces.

"If you would please follow me."

He runs through the words he came here to say as he follows the servant farther into the palace. A rather staid residence for Skytown, Jomo would say, almost rustic in its simplicity. Then again, Totomo Sato has never been known to be a complicated man.

Which is one of the reasons he's the first headman Jomo has decided to approach.

Obe Saai and Dino Sato are walking statues behind him, both in their pristine green tunics and aerosteel armor, like proper Sentinel bastards. They are of a size, the two boys, both as well muscled as they are stupid. Jomo understands why Isa insisted he come with Dino—this is his father's palace, so of course bringing him to the meeting makes sense. But why the Crocodile's nephew?

It's all Jomo can do not to reach for the knife sheathed by his side and slit the boy's throat to make him pay for his uncle's crimes.

Not that you could slit his throat if you tried, he thinks bitterly. *The bastard would probably gut you first.*

The servant leads them out into a sunny courtyard, where Prince Totomo Sato, headman of the impala clan of the south, is waiting for them.

Receiving them in his courtyard means he doesn't see them as threats, which is a good thing, but the fact that he has covered his face with the moongold mask of his office means he doesn't see them as friends either. Jomo suffers a spasm of disappointment, which he hides behind a tight smile.

A golden-furred monkey with curved horns of tronic bone is perched on the man's left shoulder. As soon as it spots Dino, it leaps to the floor and runs toward him, making shrill noises. Dino bends forward to pick it up with a huge grin and laughs when the beast immediately attempts to groom his short hair. "Looks like someone missed me."

The headman grunts. "Take that little rascal with you when you leave. I've endured enough of his foolery for a lifetime."

Dino ruffles the creature's fur. "He doesn't mean that, Tazu. He would weep if I stole you from him." Tazu seems to agree by the way it shrieks.

"Weep! Ha! I would throw a gala for the whole kingdom." The Impala's glowing eyes finally land on Jomo and Obe. "But where are my manners. I have guests."

Jomo executes a bow. "Your Highness."

"Our most esteemed herald," the Impala says, coming forward to shake his hand. "Mother's grace upon you this New Year's Eve."

"And upon you grace, Your Highness. Thank you for receiving me at such short notice."

"My pleasure."

Like Jomo, the man is somewhat on the plump side, though Jomo stands much taller, so people often call him heavyset rather than outright fat, which wouldn't be an entirely misleading description for the Impala. He doesn't appear to mind, though, seeing as he's wearing nothing but a khanga wrapped around his waist, leaving his bulging belly hanging bare for all to see.

His bovine mask rearranges itself to give him a serious expression, and he interlocks his hands in front of him. "My sincerest condolences for . . . well, for everything, really. Words cannot suffice, but for what they are worth, I am truly sorry for your loss. Your mother was a good woman and friend to me."

Another reason Jomo came here first. "I appreciate it, Your Highness."

"How is Her Majesty coping?"

"Better than I am, if you'll believe it."

"Oh, I believe it," the Impala says. "The young woman I saw at the last Mkutano was fire and brimstone. She is clearly her father's daughter."

"I would not argue with that assessment."

The Impala smiles; then his eyes drift back to Dino, who's still catching up with his beastly friend. "Hello, son."

Dino pries his attention from the creature and gives the headman a respectful nod. "Father."

"I see the Sentinels are treating you well. Come here and let me look at you." Dino does as he's told, and the Impala grips him by the shoulders, sizing him up. The young man is a giant next to his father. "My, but what are they feeding you boys these days? You're so big!"

They laugh and embrace. "It's good to see you, Father," Dino says.

At length the Impala returns his attention to Jomo and Obe, who've been watching the exchange in awkward silence. "Please, sit. I know this is no social call."

They sit on wicker chairs, and the servants offer them palm wine in gourds. After a sip of his drink, the headman leans back in his chair. "Forgive me for asking such an indelicate question, but, well, there's no other way to put it," he says. "How is it you survived on that terrible, terrible day?"

Jomo rubs a thumb along his scepter, fighting the sting in his eyes. *I'm still alive because I was drunk. I was drunk, and I passed out in a closet; then Isa and Obe found me there. I slept through the slaughter of my family.*

"I found a good place to hide and kept as quiet as I could," he says, ignoring the shame, the guilt. "Her Majesty found me when it was over." He almost flashes Obe a glare when the Sentinel stirs in his seat. The annoying little crocodile is one of the few people who know the truth.

"I see. And you don't fear for your life anymore?" The Impala lifts an open palm to show he's not making a threat. "I ask only because I wouldn't set foot out of the temple were I in your shoes."

Jomo shrugs. "What threat do I pose? The Crocodile would gain nothing from my death. Without me, he'd lose his only contact with the king. And I'm the one who'll be negotiating her bride-price, so he needs me alive."

Jomo should be more tactful, but he's not going to sit here and pretend that Kola Saai isn't the one who murdered his family. He will not insult their memory.

The courtyard is painfully silent. The Impala taps one hand on his lap as he regards Jomo, perhaps deciding whether to risk continuing with the conversation. "I see," he finally says. "You know, if Her Majesty has agreed to marry the Crocodile, *he* will be king. Unless you're telling me, as many have claimed, that the wedding won't be happening after all. That it is a simple ploy to buy time."

Jomo starts itching to reach for his gourd of wine, which he has yet to touch. "The mask-crown is our clan's only hope. The king knows this and will do everything in her power to hold on to it."

The Impala's metallic face settles into a neutral expression. "I assume you came here to ask something of me," he says.

"I did, Your Highness." Jomo glances at Obe and Dino before he continues, but neither gives him the encouragement he seeks. Whatever. He doesn't need them anyway. "As I'm sure you know, the Crocodile will call a vote to disband the King's Sentinels at the Mkutano in about twenty days. I'm here to ask . . . no. Your Highness, I'm here to *beg* for your assurance that you will vote against him. Without the Sentinels there'll be nothing to deter the slaughter of my people. Thousands will perish. I beg you not to let this happen."

A young servant in a flimsy garment is polishing the checkered floors nearby. She fails to notice when the Impala briefly leers at her stern. "You do realize that you could end this peacefully by giving the Crocodile what he wants, don't you?" The Impala picks up his gourd of wine. "It is foolish to resist him when the Shirika have shown that they are on his side."

"Not all of them," Jomo says firmly. "And if we give him the crown, we lose the Sentinels. What will stop the murderous gangs from going after us? They're sharpening their knives as we speak."

The Impala knocks back the rest of his wine and sighs. "What do you think of this, son? I assume you're here because you agree with them."

While his golden-haired friend clings to his shoulder, Dino Sato stands up with his gourd. He takes a sip and starts to pace, his forehead wrinkled like he's thinking hard.

"If I'm to speak to my father on this matter," he finally says, addressing Jomo, "I need to speak freely. I can't be bound by arcane oaths of loyalty."

Jomo shoots Obe a worried glance. *What is he doing?*

I don't know, seems to be Obe's answer.

"Uh . . . you are free to speak your mind," Jomo says. "By royal decree." He doesn't know how the Sentinel death bonds work, but he thinks explicit permission won't cause them to trigger.

Dino returns to pacing momentarily, then stops to face the headman. "Father. I say to the pits with the Sentinels. Disband them."

Pain lances through Jomo's left leg as he lurches in his chair. "You treacherous dog. What the devil do you think you're doing?"

"I'm sick of you, Jomo," Dino says. "I'm sick of Isa, and I am so motherdamned sick of that filthy reptile over there! Yes, I'm talking about you, Obe. You think I don't know what you've been doing with *Her Majesty* behind closed doors? You think I don't see the way you look at her?"

Jomo gapes at the two Sentinels, feeling like he's been tossed out of a rocking boat. "Dino, what are you talking about?"

Dino juts a finger at Obe. "Your cousin has been spreading her legs for that filth! They've been at it for weeks!"

"Moons, actually," Obe says, and Jomo struggles up to his feet, gripped by rage, his cane trembling beneath his right hand.

"Obe, you bastard."

"Isa and I—"

"You sick bastard!"

Obe raises his voice. "We were together long before any of this happened! And the only reason Dino is so pissed off is because he's jealous."

Dino laughs coldly. "Jealous? Ha!"

Nostrils flaring, Obe gets up and struts toward Dino but stops when the monkey perched on Dino's shoulder snarls threateningly, setting its ears on fire. The yellow flames lick upward, following the contours of its horns so that it looks like an evil spirit.

Obe glares from a safe distance. "You don't think I know? I've seen how *you* look at her. You hate that she chose me over you, and now thousands could die because of your petty grudge, you useless piece of shit."

Dino steps forward. "How dare you!"

"Boys, boys, boys!" The Impala finally comes between them, snickering and shaking his head like this is the most amusing thing. "Boys playing politics. This is what always happens." He puts an arm each around them and looks at his son. "Why fight over something you can get anywhere? You want girls? There are many girls here. You can have any of them. Why, you can have all of them if you can handle it."

Dino wrests himself free and storms out of the courtyard with his pet.

Jomo glares at him as he departs. "Don't come back to the temple! I'll tell the Arc so the barrier fries you if you try to pass through."

Dino is already gone and out of sight.

"Tell you what, young Herald." The Impala returns to his seat, calm and relaxed, while Obe stands in place like an idiot, fists clenched by his sides. Jomo feels just as foolish and can't even look the headman in the eye. *It's all gone to shit now, hasn't it.*

"I sympathize with your people, really, I do, but if I'm going to do something that might displease the Shirika, I'm going to need something in return."

Jomo lowers himself onto his chair. A part of him expected this, but he was hoping his mother's friendship with the headman would . . . would something. Anything. Certainly not this. "What do you propose?"

The Impala steeples his hands. "The crown has mining holdings in my province. This has always displeased me."

Bastard. "We have an equal share in the profits," Jomo reminds him.

"In *my* province."

"We put up the capital. Pay for the machinery, the mystics who oversee the work, the miners."

"In *my* province," the Impala repeats, "and you no longer have the power to defend your claim to these mines. I could easily take them.

Who would stop me? I am doing you a favor by making a trade: the mines, all the mines, all the shares, for my vote."

Jomo glowers at his scepter. Eventually, he shakes his head. It's stupid to ask, but he can't help it. "Why bother? If you can take them anyway, why make the trade?"

"I need it in writing, sealed by an Akili of the House of Law." The Impala grins. "That way, the Crocodile won't be able to steal them from me when he's king."

When he's king. Jomo snorts and finally reaches for his gourd of wine. He almost hopes it's poisoned. When he's downed every last drop, he wipes his mouth, grips his cane, gets up, and says, "I will consult with Her Majesty."

The Impala chuckles. "By all means. Just don't take too long. Time moves quickly these days."

Outside, Obe Saai follows him silently to their carriage. He looks like he wants to say something, but Jomo won't pry it out of him. Let the bastard stew.

"Your Highness . . ."

"What?"

Obe squares his shoulders. "Look, I know you have no cause to like me—"

"No shit."

"—but I love your cousin. I would die for her. I would never do anything to hurt her."

Jomo stops to face the Sentinel and shocks himself by what he says next. "I believe you."

Obe's face scrunches up like he was expecting a punch and got a pat on the back instead. "You do?"

"I need all the allies I can get right now," Jomo says, realizing only now just how true this is. "Whatever you and Isa do in private shouldn't cloud my judgment." He looks back at the Sato palace, and a vestigial twitch of anger from Dino's betrayal makes him scowl. "I never liked that asshole anyway."

Obe grunts. "Neither did I." He becomes thoughtful, like a man contemplating a risk, then extends an open hand. "Truce?"

Jomo looks at the hand, the hand of a crocodile, Kola Saai's own nephew. He'd have slapped it away in disgust before today. Now, though, he takes it. "Truce."

6: Ilapara

House of Forms

Ilapara feels three inches away from driving her spear straight into Mosi's gut, if only to watch his disdainful smirk die on his face. But suffering through an hour-long lecture on a subject she has absolutely no interest in, delivered in a tongue she's not comfortable with, helps numb some of her anger with boredom.

Salo gets seated at a desk among the blue-robed Kijana while she stands at the back of the class, observing silently. The class is preparing for an upcoming exam, it seems, so they keep their eyes forward for the most part, though a few lingering glances get thrown Salo's way.

He doesn't notice, or pretends not to. But Ilapara notices everything—*the smell of chalk and strong perfumes; a mechanical model of the heavens hanging from the ceiling, metallic little worlds whirling around two iridescent suns; the boy with vicious acne who keeps craning his neck to look at her; the instructor, a man in black robes, with deep-set eyes, a nasal voice, and the tendency to pace up and down the rows of desks—*

He answers the questions his students throw at him in a rather accommodating fashion, though most of his droning words fly right over Ilapara's head. She does pick up a few things here and there, however, some of them more disturbing than others . . .

". . . As I have said many times before, an Axiom will be viable if and only if it is the product of its creator's mind. You may share and emulate general macrostructures and frameworks, but the Axiom's specific architecture must be self-derived. How much sharing is too much? I can't say. But I can tell you that the Mother has no patience for intellectual thieves. Test her, and you will be fodder for your redhawk . . ."

". . . Though the strength of your shards, as manifested in the number of rings they present, dictates how much essence per unit time you can draw from the moon, the quality of your Axiom is far more integral to effortless spell casting. Why? Because your Axiom determines how much of this stream of essence becomes useful magical energy. Your shards might be as strong as the suns themselves, but with an inadequate Axiom, that power won't do you any good . . ."

". . . What is the relevance of Agony Mysticism to Axiom architecture? Why don't I throw that question right back to the class?" The instructor stops by Acne Boy's desk and raises an eyebrow at him. "Well? Can you answer the question, Kijana? Or is the Umadi bodyguard too much of a distraction?"

Ilapara takes no offense at being mistaken for an Umadi woman. After all, she's dressed like one, and it's a look she chose for herself.

"Agony Mysticism," the boy recites, shifting uncomfortably in his seat, "refers to the practice of seeking spiritual insights by subjecting oneself to intense agony. For reasons unknown, these insights have positive effects on the Axiom design process."

His answer must be satisfactory, because the instructor resumes pacing. "Axiom architecture is not merely an intellectual exercise, people. It is also emotional and physical. Intellect alone can get you a good Axiom, but an intimate knowledge of agony is indispensable to a great one. What are some of the common ways people go about achieving spiritual insights of agony? Examples, everyone."

They come quickly from all over the class:

"Scarification."

"Self-flagellation."

"Drinking bloodrose essence."

"Gonorrhea."

"Living in Northtown."

"Taking this class."

The instructor chuckles. "Charming."

"Disfiguring one's eyes," someone says, and a palpable silence grips the classroom. At first, everyone looks at Mosi, because he's the one who spoke those words; then their gazes slip to Salo and his reflective spectacles. Salo's hands ball into fists on his table.

The instructor seizes the opportunity to stop pretending he doesn't exist. "Perhaps our guest could help us," he says. "Honored emissary, what do *you* think is the absolute best way of achieving spiritual insights of agony?"

Salo's throat bobs, the silence stretching uncomfortably. When he finally opens his mouth, his voice sounds like it's coming from far away, and what he says chills Ilapara to the bone. "The worst agony you could inflict on yourself is to consciously and willingly inflict agony on someone you love. The trauma of knowing what you're doing, knowing that you're hurting this person, knowing that they know what you're doing, and yet doing it anyway . . . I cannot think of a worse pain."

Mosi can't hide his surprise, much like the rest of the class.

The instructor starts pacing again. "Our guest has touched on a salient point you all missed, Kijana, and it is this: guilt. Physical pain can be a powerful source of spiritual insight, but mental anguish, torment of the heart and soul, these, too, are a boon to practitioners of Red magic.

"Look at muti sacraments, for example, the most foul and base expression of the art. We don't know why they sometimes work, why even the nonawoken can use them, why they can augment the power of a mystic if performed beneath a Seal, et cetera. But there is little debate that guilt is an important factor in determining their success.

"The fleeting insights achieved at the moment of sacrifice, when you willingly and knowingly shed the blood of another human being, when you weep over the act, when it violates your soul—that agony is what gives the sacrifice its power. The greater the guilt, the greater the insight, the more powerful its effects. This is why a heartless man cannot perform an effective sacrifice, because the sacrificial act causes him no guilt and therefore provides him no insights."

The instructor stops by a window and stares at the red-leaved witchwood tree outside. "But I digress. This is not a discussion of muti killings, which I personally abhor. We are talking about spiritual insights of agony and their nontrivial though admittedly ill-defined effects on the Axiom design process." He glances at Salo with a knowing sparkle in his eyes, returning to his pacing. "And yet the point remains, my dear Kijana. Guilt is so potent that sacrificing a complete stranger can give you formidable insights that can translate well into the prose of your Axioms. But what more if you take the life of a loved one? How much stronger would the resulting insights be? I shudder to think of it. Next question."

The lecture is a worm burrowing into Ilapara's mind as they leave the domed hall. On their way to the city, Tuk called Salo's eyes synthetic, like his, and the look on Salo's face made it clear this was not a topic of discussion he'd welcome. And though she has caught unsettling glimpses of the eyes behind his spectacles, the faceted irises that seem to scatter light like optical prisms, she has kept her questions to herself.

Now she can't stop wondering if his current eyes are synthetic because he . . . *did* something to his natural eyes in his quest for magic. And if guilt is such a major component of Axiom design, what exactly is Salo guilty of?

By the tense look on his face, she can see that he's shaken. Mosi can probably see it, too, the snake.

"Did you enjoy the class, honored emissary?"

Salo takes time to chew on his words before he speaks them. "Your academy is impressive, honored acolyte. My classroom was an ancient thatched hut and my teacher a determined old woman. I would not trade them for the world, but I do envy what you have here. I look forward to visiting your libraries in the future."

The unexpectedly polite words seem to defang some of Mosi's malice, and for the first time since they met him, he acquires a semblance of humanity. "You are always welcome here." But his snideness returns, and he says, "Are you ready for the Pavilion of Discovery?"

Next to him, Kamali scowls. "Let it go, Mosi. For the Mother's sake, you're embarrassing us."

Mosi gives him an exasperated stare. "He's the first Yerezi sorcerer we've ever met. Aren't you a little curious how he compares to everyone else?"

Kamali has nothing to say to that, which Mosi appears to take as affirmation. They both look at Salo, one expectant, the other defeated. "It's your choice," Kamali says.

"Don't feel pressured," Ilapara says in Sirezi, their home language. "We could leave right now. I don't trust these people."

Salo considers her. She can tell he's curious—too curious, this boy—and it's why she knows he's already made up his mind.

"All right," he says to the KiYonte mystics. "Lead the way."

Ilapara tries not to sigh.

◆ ◆ ◆

The Pavilion of Discovery is a fancy round building of stone and stained glass, with a ribbed vault and an army of sullen-looking statues standing along the circular wall. Sunlight filtering in through the windows makes the statues shimmer like they're coated in flames—which . . . *Dear Ama, is that moongold? Are these statues made of moongold?*

Ilapara hisses out a curse. Just one of these statues would net her a fortune, and there are dozens of them. Moreover, they each bear large rubies inlaid in their foreheads like third eyes, as well as ornate moon-gold shapes resting in the palms of their outstretched hands. Ilapara recognizes some of these shapes as the Forms Kamali showed them back in the assembly hall. A fractal tree. A double helix. A prism. More.

I could buy a whole kingdom with the wealth in this place.

"These statues are what we call the Vicars of the Mother," Mosi explains as he leads them past a pair of armed guards, deeper into the Pavilion. "Most of the Forms they carry are dormant."

"What that means, Emissary Siningwe," Kamali elaborates, "is that there are no current Axioms using those particular Forms."

"None worth acknowledging, in any case," Mosi adds.

"I see." While Salo regards the statues with open wonder, Ilapara takes note of the guards standing sentry by the Pavilion's three other entrances, each of them holding spears of aerosteel. Curiously, there are also a number of Faraswa people in dull-gray robes bowing endlessly at the feet of some of the statues, muttering prayers.

She suffers an inward shiver of revulsion, wondering if they're being paid to do this. More likely they're being forced. Otherwise, why so many guards?

Upon closer inspection she notices that the seven statues carrying the active Forms have their heads slightly raised and eyes partially open, unlike the others. These statues are also the only ones with worshippers bowing at their feet. And there might be flames flickering inside those rubies on their foreheads, but she can't bring herself to look directly at them . . .

For some reason it feels too much like looking into the faces of dead gods.

A tingle moves down Ilapara's spine, and she feels the sudden urge to drag Salo out of here, but the enchanted look on his face tells her he wouldn't be amused if she did.

"So what happens when one of you makes a better Axiom than a high mystic?" he asks.

"In theory, they would unseat the Faro, and their Axiom would become the new Form," Mosi says, his eyes glittering like he finds the question amusing. "In practice, superseding an active Form is nigh on impossible, not to mention how foolish it would be to go after a living Faro's throne."

"Yes, I can see how that would be unwise," Salo responds.

A stone pedestal rises in the center of the chamber, right beneath a large, clear crystal hanging from the ceiling. Standing next to it is a young woman with long braids and white robes. She seems to be casting a spell on the stand, or on the thing resting on the stand—it looks to Ilapara like a smooth metal cube. Probably more moongold.

Veins of reddish-white light keep pulsing down the metallic patterns singed onto the young woman's arms, gathering in her splayed hands, which she's moving around the cube. She has a determined frown on her face as her eyes peruse the large sheet of paper hovering directly in front of her, held still in the air as if by invisible hands.

"How timely of you," Mosi says as they stop next to her. "We were just about to show our guest how the cube works."

"You'll have to wait your turn," the young woman says without looking away from the patterns on the floating sheet.

Mosi turns to Salo with a smirk. "This here is Ewa Akili of the Spiral—or at least, she *was* of the Spiral, until she built her own Axiom of Void craft. Now she's just Ewa Akili. Of course, she could return to our illustrious coven if she just admitted that her Axiom isn't much good."

"Shut it," says Ewa, though there isn't much of a bite to it. "You're just jealous I'll be a Faro before you don the black." She finally looks away from her sheet, keeping her glowing hands above the cube. Then she does a double take when she spots Kamali, and her heavily lined eyes snap back to Mosi with a question. "What's *he* doing here?"

By her tone of voice, one would think Kamali was diseased and contagious.

Kamali says nothing, though Ilapara sees his temples ripple.

"He's . . . helping me give our guest here a tour," Mosi says, his eyes brimming with an inside joke. "Emissary Siningwe hails all the way from the Yerezi Plains."

"Yerezi, huh?" She looks Salo over, her expression growing arch. "Now the outfit makes sense. Or the lack of one, rather. *Love* the staff. Do you shave your legs? Wait a minute . . . Yerezi? Don't your people have a thing against men doing magic?"

Ilapara grits her teeth, boiling with the desire to tell this girl off.

"You could say the tribe is changing stance," Salo says with an embarrassed smile. "I wouldn't be here otherwise. And no, I don't shave my legs. In fact, I'm not entirely hairless. You just have to look closer."

Ewa's eyes glisten suggestively. "Is that an invitation?"

"Are you quite done, Ewa?" Kamali interjects. "We don't have all day, you know."

She huffs and returns to her task. "If you'd ever transcoded an Axiom, you'd know it takes time." She flicks a wrist, and the hovering sheet flings itself around. "And shouldn't you be on gate duty or something?"

Kamali doesn't respond. "Come, honored emissary. We can take a seat while we wait."

He proceeds to lead Salo and Ilapara to one of the elaborate gold-leafed benches lined against the walls between the statues. Mosi remains with Ewa, and their giggles float behind them.

Ilapara chooses to remain standing while Salo and Kamali sit down on the same bench. Salo gets a slightly nauseous expression as he regards the bowing Faraswa.

"I've noticed from your manner of dress," Ilapara says to Kamali, "that you're a member of the esteemed Jasiri order."

The question softens Kamali's frown a little. "Yes, I am Jasiri."

"But Mosi and Ewa are not."

"No."

"Is that because they're from different covens?" *Is that why they treat you like garbage?*

Kamali is wise enough to intuit her silent question. "What coven we pledge to depends on which craft we are most comfortable with as Kijana. For me, that was the science of Blood craft, which was why I was assigned to the Fractal. As for my vocation, you have to understand that the mystic caste is not homogeneous, as many believe. There are families within the caste who can trace their lineages back to the first members of the Shirika, and there are families like mine, who have no legacies to speak of. Suffice it to say, mystics from the more ancient families are more likely to join the scholar rank, while mystics like me are more likely to become Jasiri."

He doesn't have to say more. The picture becomes crystal clear in Ilapara's mind; Ewa and Mosi are from the more ancient families, while Kamali is not. And for that reason, they look down on him. He's a grunt in their eyes. That's what the Jasiri are within the mystic caste, grunts.

Ilapara shakes her head. What kind of system puts warriors as renowned as the Jasiri at the bottom of its hierarchy? Stupid.

"I assume only members of the scholar rank—the Akili, is it?" Salo says, no longer gawking at the bowing Faraswa.

"Yes," Kamali confirms. "Akili are the scholars."

"So only the Akili can ever rise to the Shirika."

"That is the way of things, yes." After a beat, Kamali sighs, scratching his beard. "Look, you must understand, I take my vocation seriously, and I'm proud of it, but I'd rather be honest about why it was chosen for me than spin lies. That's just how I am."

"I understand," Salo says. "And thank you for being so candid, Acolyte Kamali. I imagine this tour would have been unpleasant had you not insinuated yourself into it, and just so you know, I don't think any less of your people because of Mosi and Ewa. People like them aren't exclusive to your tribe."

The Jasiri answers Salo's words with a smile, brief but full of genuine warmth.

"If you could come closer," Mosi shouts from the center of the Pavilion. "The cube is ready now."

When they return to the pedestal, Ewa is biting her nails nervously while Mosi regards her with fondness. "Ewa wishes to revive the Arrow of Void craft and become the eighth member of the Shirika," Mosi says. "Never mind that seven is considered a natural limit of sorts, as there are rarely more than seven living Faros at any given time."

"The limit is a myth," Ewa grits out.

"We'll find out soon enough, won't we?" Mosi says. "For the record, honored emissary, this will be her third attempt. Go ahead and activate the cube, Ewa."

Ewa stares at the cube like it'll transform into a grootslang at any moment and attack. Eventually she shakes her head and steps back from the pedestal. "You do it, Mosi."

"Are you sure?"

"Do it before I change my mind."

"As you wish." He steps forward and presses down on the cube, producing a loud, resonant click as it settles into a depression on the pedestal. Almost immediately the top folds in on itself to reveal a warped maze of light and little mirrors inside.

Ilapara looks away, disturbed. If the statues are dead gods, then this box holds the broken, twisted remains of their minds. The mirrors inside must rearrange themselves, because a powerful shaft of red light shoots out of the box and into the crystal above. Then gears start to crank loudly somewhere unseen, and Ilapara feels a rumble coming from the floors and rippling up her legs as if a great mechanical beast were coming to life beneath the Pavilion.

The crystal begins to spin as it drinks in light from below, gaining speed by the second. Then the light appears to *shatter* within the crystal's interior, splitting itself over and over again until what was clear becomes as scarlet as the giant ruby looming over the city. Ilapara has to force back a gasp when the light proceeds to burst out of the crystal in multiple shafts, bathing the chamber in crimson.

The Pavilion was beautiful before, but now it might as well be something from beyond this world. Like frightened sheep, the worshippers turn their reverence to the crystal, their bows and prayers growing more fervid.

"If you look at the positions of the beams," Mosi says, pointing at the focused shafts of light radiating from the spinning crystal, "you will note that each one hits a single Form exactly at its center. You will also note that some beams are brighter than others. There's a reason for that: the brighter the beam, the closer the Axiom has come to achieving that particular Form."

Ilapara sees that most of the beams aren't bright, at least compared to the shaft of light shooting up from the pedestal and into the spinning crystal. The beam hitting what looks like a series of arrows, however, is noticeably brighter than the others.

Mosi walks toward the statue holding this Form and points. "What Ewa wants is for the beam over here to be so bright it awakens its Vicar, just like the other awoken Vicars, whose Forms are currently active. If and only if that happens, the Form will be considered revived, and she will join the ranks of the Shirika as the new Arrow. She'll be sanctioned to establish her own coven, with her own acolytes groveling for her favor."

"That's incredible," Salo mutters. He adjusts his spectacles as he cranes his neck to look around the Pavilion. "How did you people manage to build such a thing?"

Ilapara was wondering the same thing.

"Some say we didn't," Kamali answers in his frank voice, and he shrugs when Mosi glares at him. "Just telling it like it is."

"Maybe you can tell me what it looks like?" Ewa says impatiently. She's hugging herself, standing with her eyes shut like she can't bear to look.

"It's shameful, Ewa," Mosi tells her. "Abysmal. I can barely see your beam."

Huffing in frustration, she opens her eyes, only for her shoulders to sag as she sees the beam resting on her chosen Form.

"Come on, Ewa," Mosi says, chuckling with amusement. "You made a massive improvement."

"Clearly not enough of one." She flicks a peeved finger, and the floating sheet flies into her hands. "At this rate I'll be ninety before I make it."

Mosi shakes his head. "You're such an overachiever."

"So what happens now?" Salo asks her. "Will you face the redhawk again with a different Axiom?"

Ewa snorts with derision. "Why would I do that when the Red Temple is right there?"

"The Red Temple is where they update their Axioms, honored emissary," Kamali explains. "The Mother accepts their changes through prayer and meditation."

How strange, Ilapara thinks, and she sees Salo opening his mouth like he wants to ask more questions on the topic, but maybe Mosi's and Ewa's rotten attitudes have put him off, because he simply says, "I see." Then, "If you don't mind me saying so, Acolyte Ewa, you have a very good kinetic Axiom there. I'm sure in time you'll figure out ways to improve it."

Ewa lifts an eyebrow. "How would you know?"

"I may have taken a peek at your designs," he says. "Your prose is impeccable, though I suspect your Axiom might be devoting resources to producing forms of Void craft you won't be using. I assume the Arrow is strictly a kinetic Axiom?"

Now she studies him with a suspicious frown. "It is."

"Then you might need to deepen your specifications of exactly what manner of Void craft you need at the onset, excluding all others. I see you handling variables of the temporal aspect of the Void, which shouldn't be necessary for a kinetic Axiom such as yours. This might be bloating up your prose and slowing down operations."

A thoughtful look crosses Ewa's face, and she appears on the verge of asking a question, but her pride visibly reasserts itself. She tilts her head, sharing a devious look with Mosi. "Well. Before I start taking your advice, how about we see how well you measure up yourself?"

Ilapara fails to keep her mouth shut. "You don't have to do this, Salo."

"I know," he says, replying in their tongue. "But maybe I need to. I feel . . . there's something here. I need to see what it is." To Mosi and Ewa he says, "We may proceed."

Ilapara is forced to wait anxiously with Kamali, Mosi, and Ewa while Salo infuses the cube with his Axiom. He stands by the pedestal, still as the moongold statues in the Pavilion, his staff in one hand, the other hovering over the cube and pulsing with light. Barely a minute passes before he looks at Mosi and says, "I'm done."

Mosi blinks. "Are you sure? That was quite fast for a whole Axiom."

Salo lifts his left arm, showing off the bracelet of red steel looped around his wrist, a serpent with large crystalline eyes. "This is my talisman. My Axiom is already transcoded and stored inside. Makes it faster, I guess."

Mosi's lips curl downward like he's impressed. "Interesting. Well, go ahead and push the cube down."

"Okay." Salo does as he's told, and nothing happens. He waits a whole minute, then another, then looks to Mosi with his brow creased up. "Did I do something wrong?"

Ilapara exchanges a nervous glance with Kamali. She actually hopes Salo did something wrong. Maybe that way they can get out of here sooner.

"Did you actually transcode an Axiom, honored emissary?" Mosi says as he walks over to inspect the cube.

"I did. I think so."

After bending forward and taking a look, Mosi shakes his head. "It doesn't look like you did, though. It's practically dead."

"Maybe it's broken," Kamali suggests, sounding hopeful, to which Ewa clucks her tongue contemptuously.

"Come now, Kamali. I just used the damned thing. If it isn't working for him, then he either didn't transcode correctly or . . . well, maybe his Axiom is just that bad."

"She might be onto something," Mosi says by the pedestal. "Can you actually cast any spells, honored emissary? Maybe nothing's happening because your Axiom is—"

Light. Pure and red like a flame stolen from the heart of a distant star. It fills the Pavilion as the dead gods along the walls all raise their heads and *open their eyes*.

And not just their eyes of moongold, but the ruby eyes on their foreheads, too, which ignite with the punishing brilliance of moonfire. Meanwhile, a powerful beam projects from the pedestal and into the spinning crystal above, which splits it once, twice, thrice, on and on, hitting *every* Form in the Pavilion with a bright shaft. Ilapara feels like the whole chamber has been set on fire.

And when the gods block out the windows by spreading their metal wings—*wings*, which she had not noticed before now—and when the moongold Forms resting on their hands begin to unfurl like dust in the wind, and when that dust begins to reassemble into a single structure beneath the central crystal, and when the Faraswa scream in terror and run for the exits, and when the guards can do nothing but watch with slackened jaws—when she witnesses all this unfold, Ilapara realizes, to her dismay, that her life in this city, that Salo's life in this city, is now in grave peril.

The structure that forms out of the dust is a ghostly cube, and it floats beneath the spinning crystal like it was always meant to be there. A long-lost piece of a puzzle finally found.

Mosi is the first to recover his speech. "What does this mean?"

"It's one of the great Axioms of old," Ewa whispers with awe.

Mosi shakes his head. "That can't be. The All Axioms were lost millennia ago."

"And yet this must be one of them," Ewa says. "It can't be anything else, Mosi."

Ilapara would swear the spinning crystal is now looking at them, seeing them, knowing them.

"But how?" Mosi whirls on Salo very abruptly, reverence and fear in his animated gaze. "You, cowherd of the Plains. How is it you carry this?"

Salo doesn't respond. He's looking into the crystal like he can see something inside. His head is tilted, his lips slightly parted. "It's a key," he murmurs. "The Axiom is a key! But to what?"

Mosi gives him a bewildered stare, but his expression becomes manic, and he points at Salo, looking at the frozen guards. "Seize him! Seize him at once! There are questions he must answer. The Faros must know of this."

Thus commanded by a mystic, the guards are quick to move forward with their spears, cutting Salo off from the exits. Ilapara maneuvers herself in front of him, calling upon her training to speed up her heart rate and flood her muscles with strength. Eight guards and three mystics might be impossible odds, but she'll be damned if she lets them take Salo without a fight.

"What's going on?" Salo says, at last awakening to the danger he has walked them into.

She pushes him back, her eyes on the enemy. Mosi yells at the guards to move faster. Ewa's cosmic shards are aglow. Ilapara doesn't like the look in her eyes, like she's waiting for an excuse to attack.

But it's Kamali who attacks first.

With a flare of his shards, the Jasiri summons a spirit that gives him the ghostly feline visage of a dingonek, complete with eyes burning with moonfire. He crosses the chamber in a blur of heat, so fast Ilapara barely has time to move with her spear in defense—so fast that she doesn't realize he's attacking the guards until he's decapitated two of them. Heads fly off their shoulders in gushes of blood. Tunics rip and chests implode. The Jasiri's single-edged blade sips blood like nothing Ilapara has seen, ending the eight guards before they've even screamed.

As the last guard falls, his partially severed head lolling to the side, the Jasiri lowers his dripping blade and relinquishes the spirit he invited to possess him.

Blood, shit, and terror all fill the air with their stench. Ilapara has seen death before, she has killed, but this . . . this is monstrous. She nudges Salo farther back, keeping her spear uselessly aimed at the Jasiri. In his horror, Salo doesn't resist.

From across the chamber, Mosi and Ewa stare at Kamali in shock. "What the devil have you done?" Mosi yells.

Kamali's voice comes out as a doleful whisper. "I'm sorry," he says. "But the high mystics can never learn of this."

"What are you talking about? Of course they must know!"

"I can't let that happen, Mosi."

Ewa's sheet of paper flutters to the ground as she runs for the nearest exit. With an inhuman roar, Kamali revives his dingonek spirit and flies across the chamber, cutting her off. In her desperation she launches a wall of shimmering force in his direction, but the Jasiri somersaults over it, landing in a crouch with feline grace.

She begins to scream but is cut off when Kamali blurs forward and hits her in the head with the hilt of his blade.

She crumples to the floor, unconscious. Then the Jasiri turns his burning face toward Mosi.

"I'll have your head for this!" Mosi tries to look assertive in his anger, but his hands tremble as the Jasiri walks toward him.

Behind Ilapara, Salo starts to lose his wits. "By Ama, he'll kill us. He'll kill us all, Ilapara!"

"Stay out of it," she tells him but doesn't lower her spear.

Gesturing with a glowing hand, Mosi conjures a terrible serpent from the Void, a spitting cobra many yards long with scales as black as pitch. It materializes in the Pavilion in a whirlwind of shadows, fangs dripping green acid that sizzles as it hits the floor. Mosi has it slither in front of him, putting it between himself and Kamali. "You're dead! Filthy baseborn Jasiri!"

The serpent launches two jets of green venom toward Kamali. But the warrior is the wind when he lunges forward, whipping his blade in an arc that cuts the serpent's head clean off its neck.

Mosi's back hits one of the moongold statues. "You can't do this! I'm an Akili! You'll die, you filthy—"

But Kamali has already leaped forward in a haze of fire, silencing his colleague with a punch to the face. Like Ewa, Mosi falls to the floor.

The flames around Kamali diminish once more as he stares down at Mosi's immobile form, his broad shoulders heaving as he breathes. "You must go."

Ilapara immediately grabs Salo's arm and starts dragging him away, sidestepping as much gore as she can. Halfway to the exit Salo resists her, the idiot, and looks back at Kamali.

"Why? Why would you do this? You butchered the guards! You're a murderer!"

Kamali Jasiri of the Fractal struck Ilapara as restrained, brutally honest, and perhaps a little diffident, but now his eyes are cold, without mercy. "My job is to protect this kingdom, and if *this* ever gets out"—he points at the ghostly cube beneath the crystal—"we will all be in jeopardy. *You* will be in jeopardy, Emissary Siningwe, if you're not already. Now go."

Ilapara prods Salo toward the exit, knowing that if the Jasiri changes his mind, they'll be dead in seconds. "We must leave."

She drags Salo away and doesn't look back.

7: Musalodi

Skytown

A boy dying in his trembling arms. One. A wagon burning along the World's Artery while the stench of rot swirled around him. Fifteen. And now, eight guards torn apart right in front of him, all in the space between two breaths.

As he flees the House of Forms with Ilapara, Salo tries to count the number of lives he has cut short with his negligence. He comes up with a total of twenty-four.

I am pestilence, walking death.

Ilapara keeps looking back as they trot down the academy's hill, then along the Confluence, and then across the city. It's midafternoon by the time they cross the bridge over to Skytown and its gold-flecked road. They ascend quickly and quietly, but as the gates to their residence come into view, Ilapara pulls on the reins of her buck, guiding him to the side of the road. Salo draws Mukuni to a stop too.

By the way she looks at him, he's not sure if she wants to punch him in the face or check him for injuries. "Are you all right?" she finally says.

"I think so."

"What the devil happened back there?"

He pinches the bridge of his nose, a flash of pain blooming behind his eyes, the herald of an incoming migraine. "I don't know."

"Not good enough," Ilapara says. "*Every* damned statue in that room moved. The whole place lit up, and I *know* you saw something. Spit it out."

Even now Salo can feel the Pavilion's call, the ancient power in its foundations drawing him in like a box of secrets lying within reach, just begging to be opened. Looking back now, a part of him knew it was a honeytrap, and yet he had to see what was inside.

His mouth feels dry, his words like grit. "When I looked into the crystal, I got this . . . feeling. Like the Axiom was a piece of a greater puzzle, or even a key . . . I don't know."

"A key to what, Salo?"

"Honestly, if I knew, I'd tell you."

That answer does little to lessen the lines on Ilapara's forehead, but the light of suspicion dims in her eyes. "Are you really going to stay here after this? There's no way the Jasiri will be able to hide what happened. The truth will come out; then what? You heard what he said. Your life will be in peril."

"I can't leave, Ilapara. I owe it to my clan to stay and see this through."

She shakes her head, giving him a strange look. "Who are you, really? Why is any of this happening?"

Salo stares back in silence.

"You don't even know, do you?" When he fails to respond, she sighs and prods Ingacha back into motion.

He draws up next to her as they make the rest of their way to their residence. "Alinata can't ever find out."

"Do I look stupid?"

"Of course not."

"Then don't treat me like I'm stupid. Now get a grip. Your hands are shaking."

◆　◆　◆

They find Tuk and Alinata lounging by the stone pool in the garden, drinking coconut water straight from the shells with reed straws.

The second Tuk sees them, his eyes, which were green as grass, sharpen to a suspicious hazel. "What is it? What has both of you looking like you've seen tikoloshe?"

"Nothing to worry about," Salo says as casually as he can. He moves to sit on the reclining chair next to Tuk, fishing out his pipe from his pouch. "Just some rude people at the academy. It seems KiYonte mystics have a high opinion of themselves."

"I could have warned you about that," Alinata remarks. "What else would you expect from a city that calls itself the 'world's beating heart'?"

While Tuk continues to watch him, Salo starts to fill the pipe's bowl with his last herbs of medicinal nsango, trying not to let his hands tremble too much. *Do they even have nsango in this city?* "The whole tour was supposed to make me see just how superior they are. I shouldn't have bothered."

Tuk remains watchful but doesn't push the matter. "That's a shame," he says, and then his eyes lighten again as they settle on Ilapara, who won't stop looking toward the perimeter walls like she expects the entire Shirika to fall upon them at any moment. "Take a seat, Ilapara," he says. "Put that spear down and your feet up. It's a beautiful day, and you're far too young to brood."

She shakes her head in a way that discourages any further discussion.

Noting the curious look developing in the Asazi's eyes, Salo tries to move the conversation elsewhere. "How did it go in the city, Tuk? I take it by your presence here the money wasn't enough of a temptation?"

"Ha! If anything, it was *too much* of a temptation. No way a fortune of that size isn't cursed. My hands would probably start putrefying if I started spending it. No thanks."

"Is it really that much?" Salo says, surprised.

"I'll show you the statements later. You shouldn't want for money for the next ten lifetimes."

Salo blows out a cloud of smoke, finding some modicum of relief as the pain behind his eyes begins to abate. "As far as I'm concerned, that money belongs to the crown. It's not really mine."

"Actually," Alinata says, stirring her drink, "that vault was opened to support pilgrimages and diplomatic missions in the city. So it *is* yours, technically, so long as you remain within the city."

"Then I'll only spend what I need."

"Which is the general idea, but you are allowed to spoil yourself. It is, after all, a fortune." She takes a long sip of her coconut water through her straw. "Speaking of which, make sure you wear everything I've laid out on your bed. Everything, Salo. It is important your introduction to Yonte Saire's high society goes without a hitch."

Salo groans inwardly at the reminder of tonight's feast.

"Does he really have to go?" Ilapara says, coming out of her silent brooding. "Can't he claim he's still recovering from his journey or something?"

"He can't miss it, I'm afraid," Alinata says.

"Why? Because you said so?"

"I have to go, Ilapara," Salo interjects, then frowns at the Asazi. "But what happened to me reserving the right to accept or reject your wardrobe suggestions?"

"I selected nothing objectionable," she says flatly. "I also went ahead and ordered more garments for you. They will be delivered here in the near future. All expenses charged to your vault, of course. And don't worry about size; I gave them a complete set of your old garments for reference."

Salo bristles at the invasion of his privacy. "You forget yourself. I never asked you to do that."

"And yet it needed to be done, and we both know you weren't going to do it yourself." Alinata meets his gaze without remorse. "You did ask me to help, didn't you? This is me helping."

Maybe you should help less, then, Salo almost says, but he decides he doesn't have the energy to quarrel right now. "Anyone else coming to the feast?"

Tuk makes a pained face. "I'd rather not go somewhere likely to be crawling with mystics. I tend to attract . . . unwanted attention."

Salo tilts his head. "You've had problems in the past?"

"A few times," Tuk says, his gaze growing distant. "A Blood mystic in Ima Jalama tried to dissect me so he could learn my secrets. I'd only just crossed the desert, and the Redlands were still new to me. He lured me to his villa on the pretext of showing me his collection of rare magical artifacts. Only reason I'm still alive is that my body purged his poisons faster than he expected. I woke up strapped to a table in his cellar with half my guts hanging out. The look on his face right before I broke free of my restraints . . . he was still wearing it when I took his head off."

Salo gapes, disturbed by how relaxed Tuk seems as he relates the tale. Like it's simply one of many.

"Nothing else that bad," Tuk says with a laugh, perhaps noticing everyone's quiet shock. "A few curious stares here and there, nothing I couldn't handle. In fact, I'm less concerned about my own safety than the questions you might attract to yourself by virtue of your proximity to me. I think staying home might make the night a little simpler, no?"

"I agree," Alinata says, and Salo feels a current of resentment for her unsolicited opinion, even though he happens to agree as well.

He looks up at Ilapara, still standing with her spear. "What about you? Are you coming?"

"I'd rather not play dress-up," she says. "I'll go as your guard. The Asazi can be your escort."

"The Asazi has many garments in her Voidspace," Alinata says. "We're nearly the same size. I'm sure one of them will meet your exacting standards. Needless to say, Salo will be judged by his company. We must be impeccable, without fault."

Ilapara looks away and says nothing, which to Salo means she's probably trying hard to keep her temper in check.

He reminds himself to make sure he pays her so she isn't tempted to just give up and leave. Not that he would blame her if she did. Rising to his feet, he says, "I think I should go get ready for the feast."

"Good idea," Alinata says as he walks off. "And make sure you get a haircut. One of the servants was hired specifically to help with your grooming. I've spoken to him, and he knows what's expected."

Salo considers rebuking her. Instead, he keeps walking.

The first thing he sees arranged on his bed when he enters his chamber confirms his worst fears.

Made of the finest crimson wool he has ever seen, bearing a prominent leopard motif in gold-colored thread, it might have made a beautiful Yerezi blanket cloak were it not for the fact that the motif printed onto it is *moving*.

Salo adjusts his spectacles and pads a little closer, thinking his eyes are perhaps deceiving him. But no. The golden leopard on that woolen cloth keeps roaring at him and licking its snout. Over and over again, like a moving painting.

"Alinata!"

Seconds pass while he marvels at the cloth; then he hears footsteps running up the stairs and approaching his chamber. The door opens, and Alinata's face peeks in. "Did you call me?"

He turns toward her, spreading the cloth for her benefit. "What the devil is *this*? Is this an *enchantment* on the wool? How is this even possible?"

She ventures farther in, folding her arms with a smug look on her face. "Remarkable, isn't it? I thought you'd appreciate this particular design. Moving prints are the new thing in the city, apparently."

"I can't possibly wear it," he says, still eyeing the cloth.

"But you know it's a good idea," she says, capitalizing on the hesitation in his voice. "You'd remain Yerezi while paying homage to a local trend and supporting local business. A good impression to make, no?"

He dismisses her, silently cursing himself for ever inviting her to stay. He should have remembered how persuasive Asazi can be.

In the end, he goes along with all of Alinata's suggestions. After he bathes, he sits on the balcony outside his chamber and allows the elderly Faraswa gentleman she spoke of to shear his hair off on the sides and trim it down a little on top.

Later, Tuk enters Salo's chamber to find him staring at his reflection in a mirror. The loincloth wrapped around his groin and thighs in the Yerezi style is white and finer than any linen he has ever known. Wristlets of copper gleam expensively on his arms, and his leather sandals, whose straps run up to his shins, are threaded with gold. He even wears the plain copper circlet Alinata placed on the bed, as well as the crimson blanket cloak with the moving leopard.

"I look ridiculous, don't I," he says, blinking at Tuk through their reflections. "Is it the circlet? Yerezi mystics wear them, so I thought I'd wear one, too, but maybe I should take it off? Is it too much?"

Tuk's eyes shine in the chamber's dim lighting, and there's something Salo can't place in his voice. "On the contrary, I'd say you finally look exactly like what you are."

"An idiot?"

"Someone with power."

Someone who can make statues move, a voice adds in Salo's mind. *Someone who can get people killed.* He nearly shudders. "So why the frown on your face?"

"That charm on your cloak." Tuk takes a few slow steps closer, his head tilting as he studies the blanket draped over Salo's shoulders. "I've seen many others like it before."

"You have?"

"Yes. Just never on this side of the Jalama." Tuk reaches out to feel the motif between his fingers. "How curious. Kind of looks like Mukuni, doesn't it? Even without the spines."

"Literally the only reason I'm wearing it," Salo confesses.

"It looks good on you," Tuk says. He appears to consider his next words. "So Ilapara filled me in on what happened. You all right?"

Salo stares at his reflection. The young man in the mirror looks like an impostor. "I'm terrified," he says. "There'll be members of the Shirika at this feast. I don't know what will happen."

"Maybe I should come with you."

"You made a good case for why you shouldn't."

"You don't have to go, you know. We could leave."

"If only." Salo looks away from the mirror and moves to pick up his witchwood staff, which he placed leaning against the wall next to his large bed. "It's time I get this night over with."

Alinata meets him in the foyer, and he quite literally stops breathing for a moment when he lays his eyes on her.

The train of her inky sheath dress swishes on the stairs as she descends. By its texture and shimmer, one might think it were made of black pearls. Chokers of red steel cascade down her slender neck, offering a striking contrast to the white stripe of paint running down the center of her face. A string of pale beads rests around her bald scalp like a crown.

Salo is instantly reminded that Alinata is the queen's favored apprentice and likely successor. And if the queen is the malaika of dusk in the flesh, then here stands the malaika of midnight.

"Oh, you are simply stunning," Ruma gushes. "Extraordinary. Sensational."

"Magnificent," Tuk adds in a snide imitation of the steward.

"You look wonderful, Alinata," Salo tells her, though it sounds inadequate to his ears.

She reaches the bottom of the stairs and takes him in with her eyes. "And you don't look too bad yourself. Hopefully you'll keep it that way."

"We should get going." Ilapara emerges from a corridor with her spear in hand, and Salo gapes for a second time.

"Ilapara . . . wow."

"And here I thought you didn't want to play dress-up," Tuk says, eyeing her up and down.

"The Asazi insisted," Ilapara grumbles, to which Alinata smirks.

"Looking at the results, I'm glad I did."

Ilapara is still wearing a veil like an Umadi woman, and her lips are painted black and her eyes ringed with kohl. But her bodice and the layered skirts of kitenge, which are shorter in the front while reaching the floor at the back, are something an Asazi might wear to a wedding.

"Can we go now?" she says. "Ideally before I trip and fall in these ridiculous skirts." She breezes past Salo and out the door, and he can't help the grin that visits his face.

He bids Tuk and Ruma goodbye and files out the door with Alinata, only to stop when Tuk shouts: "Wait!"

Tuk rushes up the stairs, then returns a minute later bearing the wooden case Salo was given back in Khaya-Siningwe to present to the king as a gift. "You wouldn't want to forget this."

Salo accepts the case with a sigh of relief. "Dear Ama, that's one disaster avoided. You're a lifesaver, Tuk."

The young man puts on a cheerful face, though his eyes don't seem as bright as usual tonight. "Just don't have too much fun without me."

"Believe me, Tuk. Fun is the last thing on my mind right now."

Since it would be highly undignified to be seen arriving on the back of a mount, or so Ruma says, the three get carried up to the King's Summit in a hired zebra-drawn carriage, complete with a coachman and pair of footmen. The ride is unreasonably smooth, the leather seats so comfortable a treacherous part of Salo enjoys himself too much.

"Keep your eyes open tonight," Alinata says along the way. She's sitting across from Salo with one leg crossed over the other. A hard gleam flickers across her eyes in the carriage's gloom. "This will be the regent's first major feast since his rise to power, so there'll be many people there trying to get the measure of him. It might be a good idea to talk to some of them." *Ask questions,* she says with her eyes. *Do your job.*

Pushing down a wave of pique, Salo looks out his window. Yellow crystal lamps mounted on tall posts along the road cast moving shadows into the coach. They arrive at the King's Summit amid a convoy of other carriages. The place is an extravagant medley of gold, glass domes, enchanted bamboo, sprawling lawns, and every blooming flower in the world. Salo quickly reaches a point where the grandeur feels cloying and oppressive, so he empties himself and lets the experience wash over him like water through a sieve.

An usher in a green caftan is waiting for them when their turn arrives to alight from the carriage. She leads them through a security checkpoint manned by a mystic in orange robes and legionnaires with marks of the crocodile. The mystic extends a glowing hand in their direction, palm spread open, and scans the trio with a reddish thread of light that rapidly snakes its way around them from their feet up to their heads before returning to her palm.

Salo is allowed to enter with his staff, but Ilapara, much to her chagrin, has to part with her spear, which she relinquishes to an unsympathetic guard.

"You can collect it when you leave," he tells her.

"How am I supposed to be a bodyguard now?" she hisses under her breath when the mystic finally waves them through.

"You were never going to make it in with your weapon, Ilapara," Salo tells her.

"How come you did?"

"They probably know I don't need my staff to be a threat."

"And I don't need a weapon at all," Alinata says, to which Ilapara makes a disgusted noise.

They follow the usher through the halls of the Summit, where collared lions lounge on plinths and murals of redhawks adorn the tiled floors and marble columns. Apparently, the prince regent will be welcoming important guests in the principal reception room before the feast begins, and Salo has been deemed important enough to warrant an invitation.

Taking note of how the hundreds of guests milling about the halls part for him and his little group like nervous cattle, he tries to walk as nonthreateningly as possible, but it doesn't help matters. Alinata chose his garments perhaps a little too well.

There's a spectacle unfolding in the vast reception room when they finally arrive. Salo barely notices the usher handing him over to a masked Jasiri; he quickly finds himself rapt, eyes wide and jaw slack like everyone else in the room.

The man at the center of attention—a rather old man, it seems—is standing before the throne, shouting at the crocodile-headed prince sitting upon it.

"I am not afraid of you, murderer. Filth. Hideous creature."

"Hideous?" the prince says, and his metallic mask moves in tandem with his words, exposing an arsenal of frightful teeth. "But my dear old man, you will never see a more handsome crocodile than the one in front of you. Isn't that so, my queen?" He leers at the woman sitting next to him, the one draped in glittering scarlet and violet and a veil of golden strands. "Am I not the most handsome crocodile in the world?" She looks down onto her lap demurely, which must satisfy the prince, seeing as he turns back to the old man and says, "See? I smile at her and she blushes. Such a lovely creature."

"Plunderer! Look at you sitting on the throne like you own it. You are no king! You're a thief! Spawn of the devil. May the Mother curse you for your crimes, usurper."

"Mother above," the prince says with a shudder, bringing a hand to one ear. "Must you be so loud? They can probably hear your fulminations all the way in Northtown. It's unbecoming of you, Bwana. Can someone get him a glass of water? Better yet, a cloth for the spittle. He's frothing at the mouth, and it turns my stomach."

"You think you can poison me, usurper?"

The prince lets out a long-suffering sigh. "Let's set a few things straight. First of all, I usurped *nothing*. I did no wrong. I played no part in the tragic events that took place here, and you can't prove otherwise. Second, I did not go out plundering or marauding or whatever it is you think I did. A crocodile lazes in the sun, Bwana. He waits for food to come to him. He does not go out hunting. All he need do is lunge and snap his jaws." The prince gnashes his hideous teeth together for effect.

"How dare—"

"Ahp ahp ahp. I'm not done yet. Third, I find you very, oh so incredibly tiresome, and even though I could easily have you killed, I will not stoop so low as to validate your infuriating existence by plotting your death. In fact, henceforth, I shall simply pretend you don't exist. Next!"

A pair of legionnaires advances on the old man, but he doesn't wait for them to manhandle him. He hawks a glob of phlegm onto the floor and storms away in a swirl of saffron robes. A servant materializes behind him to mop up his spit and promptly disappears.

"Why must he hound me on such a fine evening?" the prince moans to the throne room. "And I was in such a good mood."

He gets a smattering of tense laughter, and Salo shares speechless glances with Alinata and Ilapara.

"Honored emissary," says the masked Jasiri to whom the usher turned them over. Her eyeless mask is an unsettling depiction of a weeping skull, and her voice has a sullen, metallic edge to it. "You will be presented to the prince regent in a moment. If I could please have your gift."

"Of course." He hands over the wooden box, and she examines it with yet another mysterious Mirror spell, lights unfolding from her glowing shards and coiling around the box. After a few seconds, the lights dim, but she holds on to the box.

"Your guard will not follow you to the throne; she will wait for you here. Moreover, you will address the regent as Your Highness."

Salo glances at Ilapara, who shrugs. "Understood," he says to the Jasiri.

"Then follow me."

His heart begins to hammer against his rib cage, but he somehow manages to comply. It certainly helps to have Alinata quietly following two paces behind him. They might have disarmed his designated guard, but Alinata was right when she said she doesn't need weapons. Not when the power of their queen flows so strongly within her bones and red steel.

The Jasiri presents him to the prince on the throne as "Honored Emissary and Pilgrim Musalodi Siningwe of the Yerezi Plains," which makes Salo cringe a little inside. A curious hush descends upon the throne room at the mention of the Plains.

"Ah. This looks interesting. Approach, honored one."

Salo obeys. The man on the throne, dressed in green robes that pulse and shimmer with moving patterns, is somewhat short of stature. Two masked Jasiri stand silently nearby, both with sheathed blades.

Feeling his legs grow wobbly, Salo tightens the grip on his staff and tries to remind himself that he is born of copper; speaking to power should be nothing new to him.

"Greetings, Your Highness," he says, bowing his head. "I come to this city as a pilgrim, but also as an emissary of Her Majesty Queen Irediti of the Yerezi Plains, with the hopes of establishing closer relations between our two tribes. As a token of goodwill, I would like to present you with this gift"—he gestures at the Jasiri, who approaches the throne with the wooden box—"from my people to yours."

The Jasiri opens the box for the prince to see, and his crocodile head glows in the tremulous light escaping from within, but it isn't immediately clear if he's pleased with the gift or not. As the silence stretches, Salo begins to fear the worst; then the woman on the prince's right gasps aloud, bringing a bejeweled hand to her chest.

"What are they, exactly?" the prince asks her.

"A set of active redhawk scales," says the woman, and her gasps are echoed throughout the throne room. Salo can't really see her face because of the veil she wears, thin golden strands running down her face from a circlet encrusted with precious stones. Her silken voice carries a foreign accent. "An exquisite gift, Your Highness. Priceless."

The prince tilts his metallic crocodile head, taking another look at the glowing scales inside the box. "Are they now. Well then." He dismisses the Jasiri with a gesture. "We thank you, Honored Emissary . . . er . . ." He leans toward the woman in scarlet and violet, the mystery behind the veil of golden strands, and she whispers something into his ear. "Yes, yes. We thank you, Honored Emissary Siningwe, for this exquisite gift, and we welcome you to the Yontai and to this great city. We know there's currently an irregularity with the Red Temple, but we assure you it will be resolved soon, so please do not worry. We wish you a successful pilgrimage, and we hope that your presence here will foster closer ties between our two peoples."

Salo bows. "I appreciate your kind welcome, Your Highness."

"And we appreciate your appreciation, honored one. I hope you appreciate this."

"I do, Your Highness. Greatly."

"Good. We appreciate that."

"So. The Yontai's new sovereign is a comedian." Alinata swirls the black wine in her crystal glass. "How delightful."

Salo glances at the throne, where the prince regent is now receiving a Dulama merchant. "He's right there, you know," he cautions in a low voice. "And there might be people who understand our language here."

Alinata gives him a bored look. "I really doubt he cares what people say about him." She finishes up her wine, and a servant materializes as if from thin air to accept the glass. "Excuse me. I'll be right back."

Baffled, Salo watches her drift away. He tries to catch Ilapara's eye, but something else has seized her attention.

"Heads up, Salo."

He follows her gaze to the full-figured woman with a towering head wrap making her way toward them. Her scarlet robes, throbbing with moving fractals, wrap around her in a way that must have taken eons to get just right. A fractal moongold pendant draws attention to her ample chest, and a moongold mask covers the left half of her face.

People practically trip over each other to clear a path for her. "Emissary Siningwe," the woman says as she comes within conversational range.

Salo's heart almost blows a ventricle. The power radiating from her is frightening. If he didn't recognize her as a high mystic before, he certainly does now.

He bows his head and coaxes his tongue back to life. "Your Worship. It is an honor."

"I believe the honor is mine," she says. "I know how rare it is for sorcerers of your tribe to travel beyond your borders. In fact, if I recall correctly, you are the first Yerezi mystic to visit us in almost three decades."

Her voice is crisp, commanding. There are princes in the throne room, but here stands a god. "But where are my manners." She places a hand on her chest and bows her head. "Talara Faro at your service, otherwise known as the Fractal, and chancellor of the House of Forms. Allow me to be the first of the Shirika to welcome you to this city."

Desperate not to cause any offense, Salo bows again. "I thank you, Your Worship."

He catches sight of Alinata's glittering dress just as she exits the hall with a tall man in a red robe. *Is that another high mystic?*

"It's a rather interesting time to pay us a visit," says the high mystic in front of Salo. "We haven't been receiving many pilgrims of late."

He takes deliberate breaths to keep himself from losing consciousness. "My grandmother used to say that all times are interesting given the right perspective."

The Fractal shows her teeth behind her half mask. "Then your grandmother was a wise woman. Correct me if I'm wrong, honored, but male sorcerers are abominations to your people, are they not? Or has that changed?"

"The queen decided it was time to test the basis of that belief, Your Worship. You could say that I am the test."

"A queen is not easily convinced to test her long-held convictions," the Fractal says. "She must hold you in high regard."

"I think I may have simply benefited from being in the right place at the right time, Your Worship."

"Somehow I sense there is more to the story." The Fractal looks Salo over, eyes lingering on his staff. An icy ripple moves through his body. "In any case, I understand that you paid a visit to our academy this morning. What did you make of it?"

And that's when she throws the first mental punch, catching him completely off guard. Without even engaging her shards, she unleashes a torrent of hypnotic waves that burrow into his mind, seeking to untangle his psyche and extract the truths hidden within. A direct challenge.

In that second, Salo realizes that she knows something. She knows, and she wants to pry the truth out of him right here in the throne room. He almost gives in to her out of fear, but the greater fear sparked by the memory of Kamali's warning forces him to react. He might not have access to Blood craft at present, but that doesn't mean he's defenseless.

"I was impressed, Your Worship," he says. "I truly wish we had a place like your academy in my tribelands. And all the students there are incredibly learned." Beneath his calmly spoken words, Salo scrambles to weave a thin barrier of cipher prose around his mind—the best defense he can manage so quickly. The barrier takes form as a membrane of ciphers she'll have to break through if she wishes to continue.

It doesn't faze her. She launches a quiet decryption algorithm that immediately begins to unravel the membrane. And it's fast. Too fast. The Fractal flashes her absurdly white teeth as she senses his alarm. "But there must be something we're missing. If your people can produce fully fledged sorcerers as young as yourself, then you must know something we don't. Wouldn't you agree?"

Just as his membrane collapses, Salo conjures a second one using a different, slightly more complex architecture. She sets upon the barrier with her decryption spell, and it immediately begins to unravel.

"My circumstances are rather unique, Your Worship," he says. "Our mystics typically see at least twenty comets before they awaken." Sweat beads on his temples. It takes everything he has to keep his shards dormant. Every mystic in the room must know what's happening, but none are looking his way.

The Fractal has almost breached his second barrier.

His witchwood staff was built to enhance concentration, like a lens focusing scattered rays of sunlight onto a single point. He calls on its power to focus his thoughts; then he calls on his talisman, interfacing with its high-speed core.

The Fractal probably senses he's doing something because she hits him with a subtle confusion spell, akin to a slap on the face. With his focused mind, the spell slides off him like water on glass.

"Then you are truly one of a kind." The Fractal's forehead creases slightly as she pours more mental effort into her decryption. If she drew essence into her shards, she would shatter his defenses in seconds, but she holds off, maintaining the illusion for those without the power to see what's happening. "Color me impressed," she says.

"I thank you, Your Worship."

"Tell me, honored emissary. One of my acolytes gave you a tour of the academy. Do you remember him?"

The second barrier is now in tatters, but Salo is already building up a third, much stronger version. People are talking, laughing, and drinking wine around him, many oblivious to the battle being fought. "Acolyte Kamali? Yes, he was most obliging."

"A kind, impressionable young man, my Kamali. Very humble. Which is why I find it strange that he turned himself in for several counts of murder right after you left. Two other acolytes are in comas at the House of Life. He will face excommunication and death in the arena should he be found guilty. Curious, is it not?"

The second barrier shatters to pieces, and Salo almost stumbles in shock, almost leaves himself open to her probes, but his talisman completes the third barrier just in time for him to throw it around his mind before she can burst in. And this one won't be so easy for her to decrypt, seeing as it changes every heartbeat. She could probably break through if she wanted to, but not without calling on a much more obvious spell.

"That's terrible," Salo manages, genuinely horrified. "Is there something I can do?"

The high mystic isn't smiling anymore. Her probes retreat, though not without a few exploratory pokes. "You could start by telling me exactly what happened in the Pavilion of Discovery."

Salo glances at Ilapara, whose face gives nothing away. He worries the Fractal will attack her, too, so he readies himself mentally to come to her defense. "All was well when I left," he lies. "They'd just explained how the cube and crystal work."

"Did you use them?"

What did Kamali tell her? If their stories don't match, she'll know he's being dishonest. "I chose not to, Your Worship."

She studies him for a tense moment, and he turns his eyes away, thankful for his reflective spectacles.

"I see," she finally says. "Very well, honored emissary. Should you remember something else, anything else, please do not hesitate to find me. A good man's life is at stake." She leans closer and smiles, toothy like a feral jackal. "And by the way, you have just made yourself very interesting."

Salo gulps as he watches her swish away.

8: Jomo

King's Summit

Lights glare at him from outside his carriage as it rolls down the Summit's long drive. He adjusts the kufi hat sitting on his head and pulls on the collar of his embroidered golden shirt so he can breathe a little better. Then, for the hundredth time tonight, he closes his eyes and mutters a prayer to the moon.

Please let this go smoothly. Please let this one thing go my way.

He was never fond of the palace. He was a minor prince destined for obscurity, living in the inescapable shadow of princes more accomplished and important than he, both past and present. The palace's history felt suffocating to him, the pillars and domes seeming to mock him for his unworthiness. And yet, it was the only home he'd ever known.

Now the lights around the palace are like pins in his eyes, and the humid air feels thick and hostile, poisoned with the scent of blood. The blood of his family.

Oh, they washed the floors and the walls after the fact and replaced the stained rugs and drapery. He saw that much when he came to witness the headmen electing Kola Saai as regent. But he can still *smell* the blood, taste it at the back of his tongue, a metallic, harrowing smell that won't go away.

He opens his eyes when the carriage comes to a stop. His Sentinel escorts for tonight, Odari the kestrel and Kito the jackal—whose names Jomo has finally stopped confusing—are already waiting outside the door as it opens. With the aid of his cane, Jomo steps out into the humid air and winces at the onslaught of bright lights.

"What's he doing here?" he hears someone say not far away. "He wasn't invited."

Jomo blinks, and lo and behold, a guard with the marks and motifs of the Crocodile is scowling at him, blocking the carpeted entrance to the palace with his arms folded over his aerosteel breastplate. A few other recently arrived notables throw furtive glances in their direction.

"I am the king's herald," Jomo says with something close to a snarl. "I don't need an invitation."

The guard scoffs. "You are herald to an illegitimate king. You have no authority here."

"Her Majesty was crowned in the Red Temple by His Worship the Arc, who I'm sure is in the palace as we speak. Shall we summon him so he may address your concerns in person?"

The guard's smirk disappears, and he goes back to scowling. "You're not on the list," he says petulantly.

"And if I go through anyway? Will you attack me? My guards will have to come to my defense. What will you do then?" Jomo points at the Sentinel on his right. "This handsome fellow here is the Jackal's nephew. What do you think the headman will say when he finds out that you attacked his nephew on palace grounds, on the eve of a New Year, no less? I'm going through, crocodile. Try to stop me at your own peril."

Hatred flashes in the crocodile's eyes. "Your guards are slaves bound by foul magic, but don't you worry, Your Highness. That will be rectified soon." He bows with exaggerated deference and steps aside.

Fuming, Jomo proceeds into the palace, Odari and Kito following close behind. His anger goes straight into his stride and makes the squeak of his leg brace more pronounced. He ignores the stares he gathers from the guests milling about the hallways. *Let them stare. They will not cow me into silence or submission.*

But then the memories come, almost all at once, flashes of these same halls stained with blood, littered with bodies. His stride falters, then slows.

He was in a drunken haze, but he remembers. There were so many bodies, and dear Mother, the *smell*.

Both his parents were in their private apartments when they were found, his mother on the floor by her desk in her office, his father by the door, cut down trying to defend them both. His older brother had jumped from a balcony after being stabbed, breaking his leg in the fall and bleeding out before assistance could arrive.

He'd argued with them that morning. They'd been growing critical of his intemperate ways, especially where alcohol and young women of questionable reputations were concerned, and that morning over breakfast they'd come down on him with scathing rebukes.

"We've been lenient with you," his father had said. "We've always let you get your way because of your disability. But you've taken advantage of our love to become a debauched lowlife. They laugh about you on the streets! My own son."

"You could be so much more," his mother had said. She never raised her voice, that woman, never lost her composure or spoke unkindly, yet her words and the perpetual disappointment in her eyes had still found the soft bits of Jomo's heart and cut them into ribbons. "You could learn so much from your brother. We are so, so proud of him."

Sitting across the breakfast table, looking utterly disinterested, Jomo's brother had sighed. "I've tried, Mother. Nothing seems to stick. He's intent on drinking himself into an abyss . . ."

Later that day, and not for the first time, Jomo had gone out and drunk himself into a stupor just to spite them.

His cane trembles in his hand, the memories prickling the backs of his eyes. He still feels the sting of their criticism, the indignation at being targeted, but he didn't want them *gone*. Not like this. Oh, dear Mother, the smell.

"Your Highness? Are you all right?"

They have stopped walking. Impulsively, desperately, Jomo turns to Odari and Kito, seeing them through a film of moisture. "I need you to be honest with me," he says, hoarse. "Both of you. You're free to be absolutely truthful, no consequences, no bonds. I need to know what you really think of me."

The Sentinels exchange skeptical looks. "Honestly?" Odari says.

"No bonds," Jomo repeats. "Just the truth. Please."

Thoughtful silence, and then Odari straightens his posture as if to brace for the worst. "I think you're an ass, Your Highness."

Jomo nods, digesting this. After Dino's betrayal, he doesn't really expect the Sentinels to be loyal beyond their bonds. "Fair enough." He looks at Kito. "And you?"

"I'm not done yet," Odari says. "I think you're an ass and a bastard. You're self-important, you're arrogant, you care little for those you think are beneath you, which—and let's be honest—is pretty much everyone on earth."

"Wonderful."

"You're a hothead, you're impatient, and you drink too much."

"You're really going for it, aren't you."

"But I don't think you deserve any of the shit that's happened to you and your family, and I don't think your people deserve to be butchered like animals. So if I have to keep wearing this uniform to stop it from happening, that's fine with me."

Jomo blinks, genuinely surprised. "Wait, really?"

"Took the words right out of my mouth," Kito says, looking amused. "Even the part about you being an ass and a bastard. *Especially* that part, because man, you really are."

A begrudging smile moves Jomo's lips, and he finds that he no longer feels the prickle of emotions behind his eyes. "You're both enjoying this, aren't you? Calling me an ass."

"And a bastard," Odari reminds him. "Hey, you asked for the truth, and we gave it to you."

"You sure did. So how do I change your minds about me?"

Both young men seem taken aback by the question. They share another look, eyebrows raised.

"I'm serious," Jomo says. "I was horrible to my parents and brother the morning they were . . . how do I change? How do I become less like me and more like you guys?"

"You could start by seeing us as people, for one thing," Kito ventures.

"But I do see you as people. How else could I see you?"

"You see us as assets. You value what we offer you. But you don't really care about us as people. It took you weeks just to get our names right. How many other Sentinels do you know by name?"

A fair point. "I'm going to try to change that," he says. "And from here on out, I'd like you to speak your minds around me. Don't hold anything back. It's not an order; I'm asking you to do it."

The Sentinels regard him like they're trying to find the trap in his words.

"Don't make me beg."

"Fine," Odari says. "But if we're going to be honest with each other, maybe you can finally tell us what the devil made you decide that attending this feast was a good idea. What are we doing here, Your Highness? Is this just about showing everyone the size of your balls?"

Jomo chokes with a suppressed laugh. "I'd be lying if I said that didn't cross my mind. I can't have people thinking I'm afraid of leaving the temple. But no, I'm here to collect a few important personal effects and family heirlooms that got left behind. I'm allowed to do that, aren't I? This was my home, you know."

"We know," Kito says, pointedly. "We lived here too sometimes, remember? And we were here that night. We fought for our lives here, we bled here, and some of our brothers died here."

"I'd never forget," Jomo says. "You boys saved my life. My cousin's, too, and I'm grateful. Maybe I'm an ass, but I know we owe you an unpayable debt."

Kito winces, perhaps at the sincerity in Jomo's voice. "I wasn't suggesting—"

"It's fine, Kito. Hey, notice how quickly they redecorated?"

"Oh, we noticed." Odari makes a face as he looks around the refurnished halls. "It's similar enough that I can't tell *what's* different, but I know in my gut that *something* is different, and it's creeping me out."

"Eerie is what it is," Kito says, himself looking uneasy. "I'd hoped to never come back here."

"That makes two of us," Jomo says, "but I hardly had a choice. Speaking of which . . ." He pulls out a golden timepiece from a pocket, glancing at its ticking face. The Crocodile will be receiving guests in the reception room for another hour, perhaps; then the feast will begin. "A maid put my things in a box, and one of you will have to carry it. Let's go find her, shall we?"

"There you go again, being an ass," Odari remarks.

"Hey, if you walk with a cane, you get to be an ass sometimes. Now come on. We have a long night ahead of us."

Over a dozen Faraswa servants lost their lives during the Royal Massacre. Most of those who survived did not return to the palace, because they either were too injured to resume their posts or decided the employment wasn't worth the risk. Bibi Lishan, now the head cook, is one of the few who came back.

She's overseeing the bustling kitchens when Jomo finds her. He waves when he catches her eye, and a flash of guilt racks him at the sight of the long gash on her right cheek. It looks freshly healed.

"Bibi Lishan," Jomo says as he approaches her, speaking over the noise of clattering pots and kitchen utensils. Aromas of spices and cooking meats saturate the air.

"Your Highness," Lishan says with a bow. She wears a gray smock over her matronly figure, and her tensors are veiled beneath a white head wrap. Her voice is polite, her gaze downcast and to the side. "Mother's grace this New Year's Eve."

She seems a little distant, but Jomo doesn't blame her. With the recent shifts in power, loyalty and deference to a Saire prince might be considered dangerous. "It is good to see you," he says, "although I wish the circumstances were different. How have you been?"

"I've been well, Your Highness, considering. Are you perhaps here for the matter you discussed in your message?"

Straight to business. *She really wants me out of her kitchen, and fast.* "Yes, Bibi Lishan. Did you manage to salvage any of the things I mentioned?"

"Please come this way, Your Highness."

She ushers him deeper into the kitchens and into the large pantry, closing the door gently behind her. In here the din from the kitchens is muffled, and a lone crystal lamp casts a weak glow over her dark skin, her crimson eyes seeming to acquire a disconcerting glow.

"Your Highness," she says in a quiet, almost conspiratorial voice, "about the . . . item you asked me to retrieve from your mother's study—may her soul find peace on the Infinite Path—I tried not to get caught, but I couldn't hide it from her."

Jomo's limbs lock in place, his heart lurching in his chest. "From *her*? From who, Bibi Lishan?"

"The Crocodile's sister, Your Highness. It seems she anticipated exactly what you asked me to do and caught me in the act. I'm sorry. I had no choice but to hand it over."

"Mother damn me to hell."

Lishan appears to hesitate. "Your Highness, that's not all. She knew you'd come for it tonight, and she told me to tell you to meet her in the tangerine orchard. She said to come alone."

"The tangerine orchard? Are you shitting me?"

"That's what she said, Your Highness."

Jomo curses again. Of all the ways this night could have gone, this is among the worst. "You're not in any trouble, are you?"

"The lady understands I was simply following orders I could not refuse, Your Highness."

"I see." At least that's one less thing for him to feel guilty about. "Well then. I guess I'd better go walk into whatever trap she has set for me."

Lishan carefully avoids making a comment on that front. "The other items you requested are in the box over there." She points at the box of unvarnished wood sitting on the pantry floor, right next to a pile of sacks filled to bursting with corn flour.

Jomo stares at the box, considering, then shakes his head. "Those things were only meant to be a cover for what I actually wanted. I'm not a sentimental person. I have no use for them now."

"I understand, Your Highness. If there's nothing else, I must return to my duties now."

"Of course, of course. I'm sorry for keeping you." His eyes wander to her facial scar, and a realization strikes him: *This is probably the longest conversation I've had with this woman.* She has worked in the palace kitchens since before he was born, he grew up eating food her hands had prepared, and this is the first time she has become a person to him. *Because I needed her. Because she was an asset. I really am an ass.* "And thank you, Bibi Lishan," he says. "For everything. For what it's worth, I'm sorry you and your people got caught up in our politics. You deserved none of this."

Concern briefly shows in her eyes, but in times like these, the powerless must always be wary of what they say. And to whom. "Wellwishes for the New Year, Your Highness. You and your cousin both. May the Mother watch your steps."

Jomo is beginning to doubt that the Mother cares to watch over him, that he even deserves her attention in the first place, but he nods and accepts the well-wishes. "And may she watch yours, Bibi Lishan."

◆ ◆ ◆

Against Odari's and Kito's insistence, Jomo walks alone down the steps to the palace's tangerine orchard, a grove of trees growing north of the main palace complex.

He knows that the choice to meet there can't be a coincidence, for it was within that grove, when he was a boy of six, that a baby ninki nanka leaped out of the branches and sank its fangs into his left leg, injecting so much venom with its bite not even the Akili at the House of Life could fully purge it from his system. That they saved his life, let alone his leg, was nothing short of a miracle, or so Jomo was told.

How the reptile got there in the first place, no one could say. Jomo's brother once told him an assassin had put it there, but it had bitten the wrong person. Another time he told him it had been sent by the Mother to punish Jomo for being a naughty child.

Jomo barely remembers the ordeal, but anyone who knows anything about him also knows that he *never* goes to the motherdamned tangerine orchard.

The gardens where the feast will take place later tonight are a hive of activity. Servants are bustling about arranging dinnerware in precise configurations, casting shadows whenever they walk past the dim lamps sitting on every table. Jomo circumvents these gardens on his way to the orchard, scowling as the trees come into view just ahead, each awash with pale-green bioluminescence.

Leg brace squeaking with each step, he follows a paved pathway through the trees to the circular marble fountain at the center of the orchard. He finds a graceful older woman sitting by the water wearing a patterned gown with a plunging neckline and a matching, intricately arranged head wrap. She appears to be alone.

Elea Saai, older sister of the Crocodile and mother of the Sentinel Obe Saai.

He's seen her before at feasts and other palace functions. He might have even seen her speak to his mother once, but he's never given her much thought. Jomo approaches the woman with as confident a gait as he can manage, only to stiffen when he spots the journal sitting next to her, bound in familiar green leather.

The hint of a smile moves her mildly painted lips. "Herald. I wondered if you would come."

Jomo studies her openly, trying to see what machination might be in play here, what he might be missing. "An interesting choice of venue, Bibi Elea."

"I know of your history with this orchard and wished to test your resolve. I like to know the character of a man before I treat with him."

"Treat with me?" Jomo chuckles. "How about we skip the games and get to the part where you have me assassinated. But before you do it, at least tell me how you'll spin the story. What lies will you tell of my murder, Bibi Elea? That I tripped and fell? Or maybe I choked on my own spit?"

The woman lifts an eyebrow. "You think I lured you here to kill you?"

"Yes. That's usually the intent behind luring. And let's face it: this would hardly be the first time your kind dispensed with mine."

If she takes offense, she doesn't show it. "I wish you no harm, Your Highness. Neither does my brother, believe it or not. He may be many things—ambitious, ruthless, an opportunist—but not a murderer. He doesn't have the stomach for it."

"Tell that to the ashes of my family."

Elea Saai looks down at the hands intertwined on her lap. "I did not expect I could change your mind. But that's not why we're here, is it?" She proceeds to pick up the green journal by her side, lifting it up for Jomo's benefit. "We're here to discuss your mother's rather delightful trove of scandalous secrets."

Jomo has to subdue the impulse to lunge forward and grab the book. He watches helplessly as Elea Saai begins to turn the pages, a lacquered fingernail running over the meticulously written script.

"I knew she had eyes everywhere, but dear Mother, did I severely underestimate her reach. Some of the secrets in here would tear this kingdom apart. You'd have never known it from looking at her, so unassuming, so prim, but your mother possessed a singular view into our kingdom's rotten underbelly." Elea Saai lifts her sharp gaze from the journal. "I respected her before; now I admire her."

Jomo's eyes dart from the woman's face to the book in her hands. He silently prays she won't toss it into the water. "You lured me here. I came. What now?"

"A good question. What now? What to do with this?" She taunts him by shaking the journal. Her expression remains even, though a shrewd glimmer reflects in her eyes. "I could run to my brother and show him the book. He'd be pleased. Of course, the Faraswa woman you employed to unearth it for you would lose her job, and you would be no better off than you started."

Jomo feels his temples rippling, his patience coming apart at the seams. "I assume you have a counteroffer."

"I do." Elea Saai extends the book toward him, the golden bangle on her wrist shimmering in the orchard's greenish glow. "I could simply give this to you and forget I ever saw it."

He was willing to snatch the journal from her just a second ago. Now Jomo stares at it like it might bite his fingers off if he reached forward. "In return for what?"

"I expect only one thing, Herald: that you use it well. In the right hands the knowledge in these pages would be an invaluable weapon. I'd hate to see it go to waste."

A grin breaks on Jomo's face. "You must think me a damned fool. What could you possibly gain from such an arrangement?"

"Maybe I'm a glutton for chaos," she says. "Maybe I like to throw pebbles into well-oiled machines and watch how they break. Maybe I have my own reasons, Bwana Jomo. A man dying of thirst does not ask why he has been offered water to drink. He simply takes it and says thank you."

"Unless, of course, he suspects the water is poisoned," Jomo says. "For all I know, you could have laced that journal with lies."

"I made a few edits, to be sure, but only to remove information that would compromise me personally. Everything else is intact. You know your mother's writing, don't you? You can confirm this for yourself."

Take it. Take it, you idiot. Jomo continues to stare at the journal.

With a disappointed sigh, Elea Saai begins to retract her hand.

"Wait." Jomo finally steps forward to accept the unexpected boon.

"A wise decision," she says as she hands it over. While he weighs it in his hands, still trying to see what he's missing, she stands up and starts to leave, then stops some several yards away. "Well-wishes for the New Year, my dear Herald. Use my gift well. I expect to be entertained."

Then she disappears into the glowing trees, leaving Jomo alone by the fountain, wondering what the devil has just happened.

9: Ilapara

King's Summit

The high mystic's departure leaves Ilapara feeling like she's walked through a cloud of static. All around her, dignitaries in brocades and enchanted silks continue to chitchat and drink as though all is well, but light-headedness and the tingle in her bones let her know she has just survived a brush with death.

She tries to modulate the alarm out of her voice. "What just happened?"

"There was an incident after we left the academy," Salo says, not quite meeting her eyes. "One of our hosts was arrested for murder. Can you believe it?"

Even now he continues to pretend. And he might have convinced her were his grip not so tight around his staff.

It all becomes a little too much. To be so far from anything familiar, in this heavily perfumed bastion of treachery and excess, and then to have to stand here and pretend and lie.

This is not who I am.

Ilapara's vertigo mutates into a sensation so suffocating she feels it will crush her windpipe. The throne room spins, and the lights seem to merge, becoming too bright, the laughter like thorns inside her ears.

She vaguely registers Alinata reappearing next to her with a concerned look on her face. "What was that about?"

"Her Worship the Fractal was just introducing herself," Salo continues to lie. "What about you? Was that another Faro I saw you talking to?"

"Don't change the subject, Salo."

Too bright. Too loud. A sensory overload. *What is this?* "I need air," Ilapara says. "Excuse me."

She doesn't linger long enough to hear their replies. She moves through the sea of perfumes and bright lights, nearly tripping into a servant bearing a tray loaded with crystal glasses.

She has faced reavers and giant snakes and watched the life extinguished from a warlord's disciple impaled upon her spear. She would never consider herself a coward. And yet all she can think about right now is running.

Running far away from this place and never turning back.

She emerges onto a marble-columned gallery with a view of a sprawling lawn dotted with palm trees and ponds. The colossus rises beyond the trees, lit by powerful lanterns at its base so that it forms a ghostly outline against the night sky. Too humid, still too bright, but being out in the open helps loosen the vise around her neck.

When she was a young girl, her uncle used to tell her that the New Year's Comet sometimes whisked children away from the earth and took them to better worlds. She'd watch the heavens in wait every New Year's Eve, wondering what it would feel like to be sucked into the comet's wake and taken elsewhere. Perhaps she would fit in better there. Perhaps the people there would understand her and let her figure out who she is for herself, not try to mold her into something she isn't.

Several New Year's Eves later, several thousands of miles away, and she finds herself looking up at the heavens, remembering her uncle's story with the same yearning she felt as a girl.

"I hope you find your place in the world," he said to her when she left their kraal.

I still don't know who I am, she thinks now, *but I know this isn't it. I didn't leave home to play games with high mystics and watch Jasiri butcher innocents.*

She takes a deep breath, and as calm returns to her veins, she begins to feel silly. *Dear Ama, why am I being so emotional? Did that high mystic cast a spell on me?*

She recovers control of herself when she notices she's not alone on the gallery. A tall, somewhat heavyset young man is standing next to a pillar not far away, nursing a glass of rum in one hand, the other clutching the head of a cane. A gilded contraption clinging to his left leg catches the light from a nearby crystal lamp. His face is stubbled, and tattoos slither down his neck. By the high-quality sheen of his golden brocades, Ilapara surmises he must be someone important.

A certain haggardness lingers in his puffy eyes, but he smiles when their gazes meet, lifting his glass in greeting. He is interested, that much is obvious, and Ilapara might have encouraged his interest on another night. She certainly finds him intriguing enough.

But she's not here to make friends.

With a polite nod, she leaves the stranger out on the gallery, staring out into a view of lawns and palm trees with nothing but his rum to keep him company.

Salo and Alinata are in the middle of a hushed argument when Ilapara rejoins them back in the principal reception room.

"What did I miss?" she says.

They both look at her, Salo's spectacles reflecting the room's bright lights, Alinata with obvious suspicion. "Are you all right?" Salo says.

"I felt a little dizzy, but I'm fine now."

"You felt that way because apparently the high mystic tried to get into Salo's head," Alinata says accusingly, "and the spells pressed against your unprotected mind."

Ilapara's eyes fling wide open, and she barely manages to keep her voice down. *"What?"*

"It's no big deal," Salo hisses. "She saw nothing. It's fine. Let's talk about something else. Please."

"Why on Meza would she do such a thing?" Alinata demands. "What did you do to provoke her, Salo?"

"Nothing," he says defensively.

The Asazi's eyes narrow.

"Emissary Siningwe," says a husky, thickly accented voice, and the three turn around and find themselves face to face with a bald, spindly woman so encumbered by colorful chokers, face piercings, and bangles it's a wonder she can still move about. Her mud-cloth robe bears the face of an immensely corpulent man. A shorter woman dressed similarly stands next to her, and a giant in gilded armor lurks behind them. Ilapara pegs them as Valau by their manner of dress.

"Allow me to introduce myself," the woman says. "I am Ambassador Ikwe Iwe of the Valau Kingdom, Third Incarnation of the True Priest-King." She proceeds to introduce the other woman as her wife and the large man as their guard.

Ilapara is mildly surprised to learn that the ambassador has a wife, especially considering the highly polygynous culture of the Valau people. As far as she knows, most if not all Valau women are married off at the earliest opportunity. Could that be why she chose to live in Yonte Saire? After all, the city and the Yontai in general are known for their tolerance where matters of love and marriage are concerned.

"A pleasure to make your acquaintances," Salo says.

"The pleasure is mine," the ambassador says, a full set of crooked, yellow teeth on display. "It's not every day one gets to witness a high sorcerer being denied what she wants so publicly. You've made quite an impression to those of us with eyes."

Salo glances nervously at Alinata. "That was not my intention, honored ambassador."

"But you mustn't be startled, honored emissary. Such duels aren't uncommon in this city. And rare as it is, you're not the first to successfully resist a Faro. I hear doing so is actually the best way to earn their respect. I'm sure you'll find that you now have the Shirika's ear, should you want it."

As well as their eyes, Ilapara thinks, and she prays to Ama that Salo doesn't find a way of making things worse.

"Forgive me if this is an inappropriate question," he says. "But when you say 'Incarnation of the Priest-King,' does that mean he's speaking through you right now?"

By the slight spasm that tarnishes Alinata's smile, Ilapara figures this is not a proper question to ask.

The ambassador doesn't seem to mind, though. "I merged my soul with His Holiness through the gift of our ancestors, and when necessary, he can speak through me, see with my eyes, feel with my senses. But it is I, Ikwe Iwe, who stands before you now."

"Apologies if I caused offense," Salo says belatedly.

"None was taken, honored emissary. It is perfectly natural to want to know exactly whom you're speaking with."

Thankfully, Salo steers the conversation into neutral waters, asking harmless questions about the Valau Kingdom and doing a good job of appearing interested in the answers. Ilapara even relaxes a little, letting her thoughts drift away from their voices and her gaze roam the throne room in search of the odd stranger she met outside.

She doesn't see him. Eventually, the prince regent marches out with his consort and the nine other headmen, apparently to a more exclusive meeting. Meanwhile the rest of the guests are directed to start making their way to the vast gardens outside, where the feast will take place.

The tables are arranged in front of a two-tiered stage, with more tables set on both the lower and upper tiers—an obvious place of honor, as whoever will be seated there will be in an elevated position relative to the others. Ilapara, Salo, and Alinata get seated together with the ambassador and her retinue at a table not even ten yards away from the stage.

The Shirika begin to trickle in soon after. They seat themselves at the tables on the higher tier of the stage, their arrival quiet and without fanfare, in stark contrast to the prince regent, who marches in minutes later with his consort and the other nine headmen to loud cheers, ululations, and music.

A spirited dance performance begins as soon as they settle down on the lower tier of the stage, beneath the Shirika. Then an army of servants bustles about with endless platters of foods both familiar and odd. Meats, relishes, flatbreads, yams, soups, sour milks, porridge—the food piles up on Ilapara's table, more food than the six of them could eat in days, weeks perhaps. Palm wine overflows from the pitchers, and the guests freely indulge, gorging themselves, their tongues growing loose, the air becoming charged with feverish excitement as the seconds tick toward the end of the old year and the arrival of the new one.

"Have you been to many of these gatherings, honored ambassador?" Salo says, beginning to take advantage of the noisy acoustics to extract information from the ambassador.

"More than I can count," she replies with a flash of yellow teeth, "though none as exciting as this one."

"Oh? What's so special about tonight?"

"Besides the obvious? Why, tonight is the night we all find out what manner of king the Crocodile intends to be. I hear he has an announcement to make."

Salo chews slowly on his roasted buffalo and swallows. "You truly believe he's to be the next king?"

"Of course," the ambassador says, appearing surprised by this question. "The Shirika have all but distanced themselves from the matter of succession. All he has to do now is deal with the *other* king, and that will be that."

Ilapara's ears prick, and she pays closer attention. "What other king, honored ambassador?" Salo asks.

"But how can you not know?" she says. "I speak of the king hiding in the Red Temple."

"You mean the Saire princess?"

"*Former* princess. She was crowned shortly after that nasty business with her family. A young girl, too, barely your age. Hasn't left the temple since her coronation, hence the regent still being a regent, not a king." The ambassador leans forward with a crooked grin and whispers, "Because he can't get to her."

Unconsciously, Ilapara looks around, half expecting a squad of Jasiri to emerge from beneath the tables and clap them all in chains. The ambassador's wife scowls with disapproval but remains silent.

Salo is careful with his next words. "I assume Her Majesty's . . . inaccessibility has something to do with this barrier I've heard about? The one around the temple. I ask only because I'll need to enter the temple to complete my pilgrimage."

Ambassador Iwe gives a throaty laugh. "Less the barrier and more the person who summoned it. Rumor has it the high priest was the one who saved the princess and whisked her away on the night of the you-know-what."

Ilapara wonders which of the seven Faros up on the stage is the high priest. When she lifts her gaze, she sees that the Fractal is laughing at something the dreadlocked man next to her has said. Beneath them, the regent's consort is swaying in her seat to the music, a goblet of wine in hand, the only rose among the ten masked princes.

"Confounding, is it not?" the ambassador says, her eyes fixed on the regent. "This kingdom has always been a stabilizing force across the Redlands. Always predictable. I would part with much coin to know what changed."

The feast progresses as the night wears on, the temple's ruby flashing in the distance to mark each passing hour. Just before Heaven's Intermission—the last twenty-one minutes of the day—the music simmers down to a steady, tense drumbeat, and the guests fall silent in anticipation of the night's main event.

All eyes watch as the prince regent rises to his feet and comes down from the stage, the dancers singing his praises as they move to flank him.

"A great power once rose to rule much of the world beyond the Redlands," he shouts, "long before this city's first brick was laid." His arresting voice booms across the crowded gardens. The expression on his reptilian face is one of hunger. "It was an empire unlike any the world had ever known, whose spirit was conquest and whose heartbeat was glory. We call ourselves children of the Mother, but I tell you, the kings of this empire were her vicars."

The Crocodile begins to pace with his hands folded behind him. He has captured the whole garden's attention now. "Do I speak of the foe beyond the Dapiaro, those feckless sun worshippers who call themselves the Empire of Light? Or perhaps I speak of our lost cousins beyond the Jalama Desert, the former slaves of this so-called Empire, who know not the true ways of the Mother?"

He stops and faces his audience with a chuckle, his crocodile teeth glistening in the lights from the crystals strewed about the gardens. "Not at all, my blood-kin. I would not speak to you of things so trivial on such a glorious night. I speak of something much more ancient, much, much greater, a force whose reach knew no bounds when the Mother's vicars yet walked the earth. My blood-kin, I speak to you of the Ascendancy."

A surprised murmur spreads across the garden. The Crocodile silences it with his resonant voice. "The well read among you will know more about it than I do; after all, I was raised a warrior, not a scholar. You may know its history, the names of its kings, the cities they built, the kingdoms they conquered. You may know all sorts of things I do not.

"And yet, despite my lack of knowledge, the Mother has chosen me, humble warrior that I am, to tell you a secret that will shock even the most educated among you, a secret that made me tremble when it was told to me."

Here the drums fall to a low rattle, the sound of a thousand wildebok galloping in the distance, an electric current in Ilapara's veins.

"Listen close," the Crocodile says, a chilling whisper that reaches every ear present. "The Ascendancy lives to this very day. It never died."

Ambassador Iwe laughs quietly. Everyone else at the table remains still, captivated by the regent. Ilapara was fleeing across the Umadi savannas when she first learned of the Ascendancy. Tuksaad painted an incredible picture of it, and she thought his words little more than a far-fetched myth of something ancient and distant. A fable. Surely nothing she'd ever need to deal with in real life.

Yet here is a prince, standing before the Shirika, speaking of the Ascendancy as not only real but *alive*.

"It's true," the Crocodile continues in the ringing silence. "Its heart still beats, and its blood still flows. Ask any of the Wise Ones behind me, and they will tell you. They have always known this secret and have been waiting for the rest of us to catch up."

No one sitting on the highest tier of the stage objects, which seems to affirm the Crocodile's claims.

He spreads his arms, raising his voice. "*But where is it?* you might ask. *Show us this mighty empire so we may see it for ourselves.*" Once again, the Crocodile laughs, the harsh laugh of a reptilian king assured of his throne. "Well, here is my answer, my blood-kin: you are living in it!"

Silence.

"Historians will tell you that the Ascendancy fell over a thousand comets ago, that all its lords perished when the cowardly sun worshippers stormed their cities and razed their palaces to the ground. But those are lies conjured deliberately to disguise the truth. Indeed, many did perish, but many others survived, and just as the Mother seems to disappear from the skies when she rises with her jealous brothers, the lords of the Ascendancy concealed their survival to fool the sun worshippers, and when their deception was complete, they retreated to this continent in the dead of night."

The Crocodile's glowing eyes flare as he points to the very ground he stands on. "Yes, my blood-kin, they came here, to these lands we call the Redlands, and they quietly assimilated themselves into the scattered tribes who lived here at the time, noble people who worshipped the Mother in their own unique ways. They learned from each other, they became one with each other, and together, my blood-kin, they became us. *We* are the heirs of the Ascendancy, each of us here, be you KiYonte, Dulama, Valau, Shevu, Senga, Inoi, Halusha, Tuanu, Yerezi—we all carry a piece of the Ascendancy in our blood."

The regent lets the drums do the talking for a moment as he scans the stunned crowd. "But what, pray tell, have we done with this glorious legacy? What have we done with the gifts given to us by the Mother? Have we lived up to them? Have we strived to be worthy of them?" He shakes his head, long teeth bared. "No, we have not. Instead, we have squabbled and fought and killed each other needlessly. We have contented ourselves with squalor and tyranny and tribal warfare, and we let ourselves forget our own past. We have shamed the Mother, my blood-kin. We have shamed her."

Out of the corner of her eye, Ilapara spots a masked dancer leading a bleating goat toward the prince regent.

"Well, no more!" the prince shouts. "The Mother is sick of watching us squander our wealth. Sick, I tell you. And how do I know? Because she put me here! Because I'm standing here, making this speech! If she was satisfied with the way of things, she would have given you tidings of peace and contentment this New Year's Eve. But she gave you me, and I do not bring contentment. No, my blood-kin. I bring change. I bring fire!"

He extends his right hand, and a dancer rushes to hand him a long knife. While two other dancers wrestle the goat into submission at his feet, the prince looks toward the east and makes an oath.

"On the night of this new moon, as the New Year begins and we welcome the Star of Vigilance to our skies, I honor our ancestors with this sacrifice, and I honor the Mother, who guides them into the Infinite Path. I vow in their presence that the Ascendancy shall return, stronger and more glorious, right here in the Redlands, where it belongs. I vow, this new moon, that all of us, all tribes of this continent, shall be united, that we shall rise to claim our legacy, for this is the Mother's will. I vow this before the divine Shirika, before the heavens, and before you, my blood-kin!"

They call it a comet, but Ilapara knows that the Star of Vigilance behaves not like any other comet in the heavens. For one thing, it does not orbit the suns but the earth. For another, its appearance and subsequent disappearance are sudden, and it remains visible to the naked eye for roughly twenty-one minutes—disappearing into the horizon at the end of the Intermission, as the clocks tick into the first minute of the New Year.

A powerful wave of blue light washes over the garden as the comet finally appears. Everyone present knows what to expect, but there are still audible gasps. Ilapara almost gasps herself at her first glimpse; either her vision has drastically improved since last year, or the comet appears much larger tonight than she has ever seen it, a white-blue fireball shining with the brightness of a small sun, cutting across the heavens at an astonishing speed.

A scream wrests her gaze from the comet just as an arrow sails through the air over her table toward the headman.

"Death to Kola Saai!"

She turns to look, and to her shock she sees that a figure in sack-cloth garments has leaped onto one of the tables. In his hands is a bow with a second steel-tipped arrow ready to fly. The guests seated at the table scramble away. One of them, an older lady in a green boubou, topples back in her chair with a shriek.

"Death to the crocodiles!" he shouts and has just enough time to release his arrow before a guard slams into him from behind.

The arrow flies through the air. The headman goes down. More screams. Commotion. Ilapara holds her breath as the dancers crowd around him. But then she sees him stir and watches as he cautiously gets up. "I'm fine!" he says to the guests. "I'm fine! Everyone relax! The assassin has failed."

Another scream, this time coming from the stage. The regent's consort points at the masked prince on the first tier sitting motionless with an arrow sticking out of his chest. The other princes around him are panicking.

"The Kestrel!" someone shouts. "The Kestrel has been murdered!"

"Death to the crocodiles!" shouts the assassin, now struggling beneath the weight of three armed guards.

"He's a Saire!" shouts one of the guests. "The Saires have murdered the Kestrel!"

Some of the guests are already rushing for the exits. Salo is stiff and slack jawed, the Asazi is an emotionless mask, and the ambassador seems delighted.

"That's it. We're leaving," Ilapara says and grabs Salo by the arm for the second time today. He doesn't resist her. He bids the ambassador a stunted goodbye and picks up his staff, and together they flee across the gardens. The Asazi follows quietly.

Ilapara retrieves her spear while the others wait for their carriage to arrive. The tidal wave of guests trying to flee the palace flows around her, a ghostly exodus beneath the eerie light of the New Year's Comet. The legionnaires guarding the exit don't try to stop them.

Salo is biting his nails when she catches up to him and Alinata. They're careful not to speak as they wait, the trundling of carriages and the murmur of voices filling the silence.

Then an old man in saffron robes emerges from the fleeing crowds and approaches them. "You there," he says to Salo, speaking in thickly accented Sirezi. "You're the Yerezi mystic, are you not?"

Salo lowers his visibly shaking hand and regards the man with caution. "I am. How may I help you, Aaku?"

The old man has a pinched face and bags beneath his protuberant eyes. Ilapara recognizes him as the man who shouted at the Crocodile in the throne room. He ventures closer, looking determined. "You know what you just witnessed, don't you, honored emissary? The treachery that is already being blamed on my people even before the victim's blood has cooled? Tell me you saw it."

Salo glances at Ilapara; she shakes her head in warning. "I saw it," he says, and the old man takes another step closer.

"And you heard the Crocodile's plans for the Redlands, did you not?"

"I did, Aaku."

"And what do you think?"

Salo takes a moment to answer. "They are concerning plans."

"Concerning?" the old man spits. "They are murderous! He will murder anyone who resists him, just as he will murder my people!"

"I . . . I'm sorry to hear that."

Another step closer. "That's it? You're sorry? Tens of thousands of my people could die, and you're sorry? A great lot of good that will do."

Salo watches the man. "I don't know what you want from me, Aaku."

"What I want is help! My people have no one in this city. We're all fattened calves waiting to die, and no one wants to touch us. I don't expect you to save us. Just answer me this: Can we come knocking on your door when the rest of the world forsakes us? Or will you turn us away like everyone else?"

Their carriage finally arrives. A coachman opens the door and waits.

"We should go," Ilapara says. Alinata takes the lead by stepping inside, but Salo foolishly stays put.

"To be honest," he says to the old man, "I don't think I'd be able to do much for you, but if there is something I can do, then I'll do it."

Ilapara curses beneath her breath. *Idiot, idiot, idiot.*

"Thank you, honored Yerezi." The old man rushes forward to shake Salo's free hand. "Thank you, thank you. May the Mother shower you with grace."

Inside the carriage, Ilapara frowns at Salo, wondering what the devil came over him, that he would make such dangerous, open-ended promises. "What have you agreed to?" she says. "Do you even know?"

He looks out his window, the comet's blue light illuminating one side of his face and reflecting on his spectacles. "Such beauty, and yet such horror," he whispers. Only after the carriage has rolled out of the palace grounds does he finally answer her question.

"I don't know what I agreed to, Ilapara," he says, shaking his head. "I don't think there's a single thing I know right now."

And isn't that just great?

Interlude:
The Widow

At the shores of an underground lake, the Adversary stands before a spirit of seething blackness and utters a habitual request.

"Show me," she says.

The spirit reaches for her with its black tendrils, trying to fill her with consuming sorrow, but the shield of rage boiling around her keeps her safe from its grasp.

"You can never mourn them all," it says, its voice a cold echo in the vast cavern. *"They are like the darkness between the stars, their sorrows deeper than the abyss from which you came. Accept this, and you shall know the peace of nothingness."*

"Show me," she says again, and just like she knows it will, the spirit reluctantly complies, releasing a new memory from the lake of suffering for the Adversary to live through.

Today, as the memory subsumes her, she becomes a childless widow who paid the price for being weak and defenseless, a victim of injustice whose name was lost many ages ago.

She was widowed early on in life, and though she has lived to a ripe old age, she has drifted through most of it like a ghost, waiting for her body to catch up to her soul, which died with her husband all those years ago. She has watched from the periphery as the other women in her village raised children and then grandchildren. She has spent her nights in a cold, lonely bed and her days in a cold, lonely house.

At least until a little girl wanders into her kitchen one morning, with a smile bright as the moons. In her the widow finds a friend, and the girl a friend in the widow, and their days become a little lighter, a little happier. But the girl is sickly, and when the long winter comes and goes, it takes her with it, leaving the widow's kitchen empty once more.

They call her a witch.

They. The people of her village.

They say she killed the little girl out of spite, childless and jealous crone that she is. This is not the first time she's been accused of such a thing. There have been whispers about her for as long as she remembers. *That old hag who lives down the street,* they say. But she's never let it bother her.

Here she is now, tied to a stake. They hurl insults at her, curse her for her wickedness. They do not know, nor will they ever know, that the widow was the girl's only friend. That when the girl died, she took away the light she had given back to the widow, and that the widow mourned her—mourns her still, with every breath.

And as the flames begin to lick at her feet, the villagers cheering at her screams, no one notices the wooden figurine held tightly in her right hand. The girl's last gift to her.

When the fires are doused, the ashes are scattered, and the village never speaks of her again.

She is forgotten, a nameless victim of a most treacherous universe, but today the Adversary remembers her, and then she makes her solemn vow: Heaven will fall.

PART 2

ISA
*
MUSALODI
*
THE ENCHANTRESS

Moongold:

The most valuable material known to the peoples of the Redlands, moongold is a naturally occurring ore of essence-transfigured gold. It is also the best-known material for process-ing arcane ciphers, requiring only the smallest of slivers to host entire enchantments. The lack of a cheaper alternative has kept magical artifacts largely in the hands of the extremely wealthy.

From On Arcane Materials, *an encyclopedia published by the House of Forms*

10: Isa

The Red Temple

The girl in the mirror wears a patterned sundress of modest quality, and her braided hair is hidden beneath a head wrap of emerald brocade. Around her right wrist is a single bangle of tronic ivory, procured illicitly from an undercity enchanter. The weak charm of hypnotic Blood craft it holds was designed to make its wearer a little less interesting to the eye. Combined with her simple manner of dress, she would be dismissed on the streets of Yonte Saire as an ordinary Southtown woman or the maid of a wealthy Skytown household.

Only those who know her well would recognize her as the princess who is now king.

Leaning on his cane behind her dressing table, Jomo scowls at her reflection. "I can't believe you're still going through with this. It's even more dangerous out there after what happened. You're being reckless."

Isa Andaiye Saire considers herself in the mirror, a hand toying with the single beaded necklace resting on her shoulders. It's a welcome change from the heavy golden chains she must wear as king. A disguise, and yet it brings her closer to the truth of things, for beneath the moongold mask-crown is a girl pretending to be something she is not.

"Any response from the Kestrel's family?" she asks, which only deepens the furrows on Jomo's face.

"His heir won't even talk to me. Damned fool believes the stories the crocodiles are spinning. I mean, you'd have to be a fool to believe them, right? A Saire assassin somehow makes it past *all* the guards at the feast, all the motherdamned Jasiri, except he botches the job and winds up killing our clan's strongest ally? How is that not an obvious setup? They murdered his father in front of the world, and he's eating right out of their palms!"

A headman assassinated at the New Year's Feast. Isa knew her enemies were ruthless, but her understanding of ruthlessness was clearly limited in scope. Was she not planning the guest list and menu for this feast not that long ago? It all seemed so mundane to her at the time.

You will have to die, Your Majesty. You will have to play games.

Isa wills away the tremor in her hands and turns her attention to the cosmetics sitting on the dressing table. She begins by adorning her eyes with a modest coat of bronze eye shadow, then her cheeks with little dots of white face paint, finishing off with a vertical white line running down her lips—a rather common look for a woman of the city. "Perhaps his grief has clouded his judgment," she says, lifting her chin to admire her work. "But we can't afford to lose his clan's support. We were already at a disadvantage before this. We need to find a way to convince him of our innocence."

Jomo grunts. "If you figure out how to do that, let me know."

She slides her gaze to his reflection and notices that his eyes are especially bloodshot this morning. For hours after he returned from the feast three nights ago, all he did was sit on a bench outside his chambers and stare into space. Isa had to pry out the cause of his shock from the Sentinels who'd escorted him to the Summit.

Odari, a kestrel himself, couldn't even look her in the eye, and she could sense him wondering if she was behind his headman's death, even if the arrow had been meant for someone else.

As if losing Dino wasn't bad enough.

"This assassin, do we know for sure that he was a Saire?"

"I didn't get a good look, but the people who did say his mark was ours."

"Well, whoever he is, he had inside help. He wouldn't have made it onto palace grounds otherwise, let alone within striking distance." Isa stares into the mirror, the skeleton of an idea beginning to take shape in her mind. "If there was some way for us to interrogate him . . ."

"If they haven't executed him already," Jomo says.

She turns in her seat to face him. "You know, this doesn't have to be a complete loss for us."

The look in his eye is skeptical. "How so?"

"You monitor the movements of the headmen, don't you?"

"Yes?" he says with a doubtful inflection.

"Well, tell me this. How many headmen have left the city in the last three days?"

Jomo answers off the top of his head. "Only the new Kestrel, the Jackal, the Buffalo, and obviously the Crocodile are still around. The others returned to their provinces the day after the feast."

Isa almost smiles. "Think about it, cousin. The headmen typically linger in the city for at least two weeks after the New Year. Do you know why?"

Jomo sighs like he's humoring her. "Because they have to be present in person for the year's first Mkutano at the Meeting Place by the Summit."

"Yes, a Mkutano that must be held on a full moon," Isa says. "Usually the first full moon of the year, two weeks after the feast. But not necessarily."

"I'm not sure I see where you're going with this."

"The headmen ran, Jomo. The new Kestrel might be convinced we're responsible for his father's death, but the others aren't so blinded by grief that they can't see the truth. They saw what happened for the brazen power grab it was, and they ran, fearing they might be next. My guess is they won't be keen on coming back to the city for a long time."

The light of understanding sparks in Jomo's eyes as he begins to follow her logic. "So you're thinking I could use this to postpone the Mkutano."

"Summon an informal gathering with the headmen or their representatives and suggest the Summit Mkutano be moved to the second full moon, six weeks from now. There's precedent for this, and as much as they might want to disband the Sentinels, they'll probably be too worried about their safety to reject you."

"The second full moon?" Jomo rubs his chin in thought. "That would be the Requiem Moon."

"We'd get one more month of protection," Isa says. "One more month to figure out a way out of this mess."

"I'd take it, but I'd need a good pretext for proposing the delay. We can't be too obvious."

"Say you think there should be a full investigation into the killing before any formal gathering of the princes," Isa suggests. "Something along those lines."

Jomo contemplates her for a moment. "You know what? This might actually work. I'll get right on it."

"Good," Isa says, turning back to the mirror for one last inspection of her face paints. "In the meantime, I have a meeting I must attend in the city." She rises from her seat and walks to pick up the shoulder bag sitting on her bed.

"For the record, I object to this," Jomo says. "I'd rather I went on your behalf. That's my job as your herald."

"You already have too many things on your plate as it is. You need help, and I can't trust anyone else with this."

"What I *need* is for you to be safe, Isa."

"And I *will* be safe. Your arrangements have seen to that." She walks close enough to take his hand in hers and looks up into his doubtful eyes, rimmed with more sorrow than a man his age should know. He has made her his only reason to remain in this world, a view she will have to change someday soon. "Our enemies will stop at nothing. You see that, don't you? It won't be enough to simply match their determination. We must go where they would hesitate, act where they would second-guess themselves. That is the only way out of this."

"But it doesn't mean putting yourself in danger," he pleads.

"I'll be careful. I promise."

His wide shoulders heave as he takes a deep breath, an argument on the tip of his tongue, but the fight leaves him when he exhales. "As you wish, Your Majesty. But if you're not back by dusk, I'll tear the city apart until I find you."

"I'd almost pay to see that." She squeezes his hand. "You mustn't worry, cousin. I won't let you down."

He escorts her out to the temple's large forecourt, where two Sentinels are waiting by an unmarked carriage. Both young men are out of their uniforms today, dressed in civilian dashikis and trousers, but Isa immediately notices the single-edged blades fastened to their hips.

Altogether the Sentinels look like a pair of hired thugs.

Isa barely contains an exasperated sigh. "The point was to blend in," she complains to Jomo in a low voice. "How am I supposed to do so with those two following me around? The bangle's enchantment will be useless."

"Absolutely nonnegotiable." Jomo doesn't bother lowering his voice. "It's either this or a full company of armed Sentinels. Your choice."

"I thought I was king."

"You are, Your Majesty," Jomo says. "But you trusted me to make arrangements for your safety, and that is what I have done. Besides, I made sure to include your 'friend.' Unless . . ." He studies the side of her face. "What's this? Do I sense trouble in paradise?"

"Shut up. They can hear us," she says.

One of the Sentinels by the carriage is Ijiro Katumbili, sixth son of the Bonobo and the youngest Sentinel in the trusted circle of advisers and guardians Isa has built. The other is Obe Saai.

Since they both know her well, the sorcery of her bangle fails to work on them. Isa attempts a smile as they both incline their heads respectfully. Things have been awkward with Obe since she accepted his uncle's marriage proposal, even more so after Dino's betrayal. *She* has been awkward with Obe and has actively avoided him because she can't bear to look into his eyes and face her guilt.

Because sooner or later, she'll have to break his heart in more ways than one.

"I hope you'll remember I'm meant to be a simple handmaiden," she tells the Sentinels. "From here on out, keep away from any titles or honorifics that could give me away."

"Understood," Obe says.

"Of course, Your Majesty," Ijiro says, then shows embarrassment. "I mean, yes, no honorifics."

"You may call me Andaiye. Handmaiden Andaiye if you must be formal."

She bids Jomo goodbye and steps into the carriage while Obe holds the door open for her. Before he closes it, Obe leans in, looking like he's wondering how to phrase a question. Finally, he says, "May I ride with you, Andaiye?"

She'd rather he sit up front with Ijiro and the coachman so she can keep avoiding him. "Of course," she replies.

After unfastening his weapon and setting it on the floor, Obe ducks beneath the frame and sits across from her in the enclosed space, close enough that she can smell his musk-scented bath soap. A second later they hear the crack of a whip, and the axles beneath them begin to turn as the carriage lurches into motion.

A driveway of pebbles leads out of the forecourt and toward the citadel gates, framed by rows of witchwood trees. Then a long bridge spans the river that feeds the southern waterfall. Winged malaikas stand on either side of the road, fashioned from stained copper. They cast shadows within the carriage's interior as it rolls along. Isa keeps her gaze out the window.

"You look wonderful," Obe says.

She closes her eyes, not wanting to see the expression on his face. "Please. Don't make me say it."

"I'd never force you to do anything you don't want to."

"Then stop staring at me like that."

"Like how?"

She opens her eyes, irrational anger taking hold of her. "Like I made the suns come up! Or the jungles bloom with flowers!"

"You mean, like you're everything I could ever want in this universe and more? You'll have to gouge out my eyes to get me to stop."

"Obe, I'm marrying your uncle. You know that, right?"

He looks away, scratching his nose. "Still doesn't change the way I feel about you."

"You like the idea of me," Isa says. "A romanticized version I couldn't possibly live up to. I know I encouraged it, and yes, maybe I enjoyed having you put me on a pedestal, but I'm not that person. I'm not who you think I am."

They reach the end of the bridge, where the last two copper malaikas hold metal rods sheathed in intimidating clouds of red static—the only visible sign of the active barrier protecting the citadel from unwelcome visitors. The statues let the carriage pass unharmed.

"You think me simple and naive," Obe says. "And maybe that's true to an extent, but I've seen the woman in front of me, and I think I have a pretty good idea of who she is."

"Then you're better off than me, because I don't."

He leans forward, looking into her eyes with an intensity that raises the temperature in the carriage. His nose is slightly crooked. The last time it was broken, it was on the night he defended her from the maddened guards butchering her family. "Then let me help you figure it out."

She sighs, feeling her self-control slipping away. "Obe, let's not. Please. You're not making this easy."

He glances at her lips, then lifts his gaze until he's looking into her eyes again. Isa has to remind herself to breathe as a slow smile takes over his face, like he can see his effect on her. "As you wish," he says, then leans back into his seat and looks out the window.

They say nothing more until the carriage stops along a road hemming the southern edge of the crowded Northtown market square. Thick air and a thousand different scents attack all at once as soon as Isa steps outside. Ijiro rejoins them while she tries not to be overwhelmed by the bustling crowds. She knows that the city's wheelhouse terminal is nearby, and the market is a melting pot of vendors, shoppers, and travelers passing through the city.

"Where's this meeting again?" Ijiro says.

"Healer Majii's clinic," Isa replies, partly distracted. "You don't happen to know where it is, do you? I was going to ask for directions."

"Then it's a good thing we're here," Obe says while he secures his weapon back onto his belt. "Come. It's this way."

"Hang on." A racket deeper in the market square has drawn Isa's eye, and she catches a few words from a man standing on a crate, shouting at the crowd gathered around him. She frowns, trying to get a better look. "What's going on over there?"

Obe follows her gaze. "An orator. And with such a crowd, there can only be one thing he's preaching about. We must not linger here."

"Long have we toiled beneath their heavy hand," the orator shouts, "consigned to scraps while they feed like fat cockroaches on the fruits of our labors. For centuries, the Saires have ruled over us like masters, taking the best portions of the kingdom for themselves while leaving the dregs for the rest of us. But no more! The Mother has delivered judgment unto our oppressors, and their king is dead!"

The cheers that erupt from the gathered crowd chill Isa to the marrow. She almost covers her neck to hide her marks.

"You have a meeting, handmaiden," Obe says, taking her arm in a steady grip. "We must go at once."

She lets him pull her away, but the orator's hateful words chase her like the lashes of a burning whip.

As they enter a narrow alley, Isa forces the shock out of her system with a heavy breath. She knew there were militias organizing themselves to attack her people once the Sentinels were no longer bound to protect them, but she didn't anticipate that even civilians, the ordinary men and women on the streets, were being poisoned against them so aggressively.

"The orators have been getting worse," Ijiro says, sounding regretful. "There's one speaking every day now."

They come to a stop next to a staircase leading down to an open door. "What he was saying . . ." Isa looks at the Sentinels, trying to find something to keep her grounded. "Is this how most people feel about my clan?"

Obe doesn't flinch from her gaze, but his words offer little comfort. "I wouldn't say most," he says. "But the orators have been effective at stirring hatreds over the last few weeks."

"We have to stop them."

Obe's eyes glisten with sympathy. "I don't know if we can."

"Then my people are already dead."

Neither Sentinel has any arguments to the contrary.

"We must proceed," Obe says and gestures down the staircase.

She should not expect him to reassure her. She should not expect him, or anyone else for that matter, to fight her battles for her. She should simply learn to stop underestimating her enemy.

The orator is still shouting in the market square. She can hear his voice if she pays close enough attention.

She lifts the skirt of her dress and descends the staircase.

The open door leads down to yet another staircase, this one descending to a dimly lit corridor—quite what Isa expects of the undercity, all things considered. Past this corridor, however, a vibrant subterranean cosmopolis unfurls before her like the petals of a flower, defying her assumptions of what could feasibly exist underground.

They enter a vaulted chamber crammed with shops and market stalls. Constellations of crystal lights provide enough illumination to approximate daylight. Arched entryways all around the chamber lead into more corridors, and people weave in and out like ants. Many are Faraswa. Many others don't have clan marks.

Obe doesn't miss a step as he leads the way through the bustle into one of the corridors. Isa follows, taking a moment to peer onto a nearby vendor's smoldering grill. Though she fails to identify the meats roasting on the gridiron, she notes how smoke from the fire curls up toward the grates near the ceiling above, as though being sucked in by an unseen force.

There are other fires and other food vendors, and the mingling scents of spice, cooked plantain, and roasting meat are not entirely unpleasant.

"You clearly know your way around," Isa comments to Obe.

"There's a shebeen my friends and I frequent when we get time off. The owners are Shevu. They sell this really great ginger beer, and it's dirt cheap."

"A shebeen?" Isa gives him a slantwise look. "But you don't drink."

He shrugs slightly. "I mostly come for the company. And to make sure the boys don't get into too much trouble."

Flanking Isa on her other side, Ijiro takes in their surroundings with obvious interest. "I've never been down here," he remarks.

"That's because you're too young," Obe tells him. "The older boys are expressly forbidden from bringing first years to the undercity."

"Ha! Then it's a good thing I won't be a first year for much longer," Ijiro says. "It's a new year, remember?"

"I notice a large foreign presence," Isa says after they pass two men wearing silken, tightly wrapped headcloths, speaking with each other in an exotic tongue. Neither man has any mark on his neck. Earlier they passed a woman with many rings embedded in her lips. "Do they all live here?"

"Immigrants often can't afford to live anywhere else," Obe says. "Not when they first arrive, at least."

"It's so . . . colorful."

Obe grunts in agreement. "I've heard every tribe of the Redlands is represented down here. Not sure how true that is, but I know there are many good places to get food if you're hungry."

"But don't they worry about ninki nankas?" Ijiro asks, looking puzzled. "I honestly thought we'd have seen one by now."

"You've listened to too many myths," Obe answers. "Ninki nankas stick to the lower levels, and only the foolish or those with something to hide ever go down there."

"But how deep does the undercity go?" Ijiro asks.

"I don't think anyone knows."

"Oh, someone knows," Isa says. "They just haven't shared the secret."

Obe gives her a dubious glance. "I've heard the tunnels in the lowest levels are flooded with water. Not to mention crawling with voracious beasts. I'm not sure anyone who goes that deep ever makes it back."

"People have made it back," Isa says. "Look at all these lights. The automatic ventilation. The plumbing. What do you think powers it?"

"I don't know," Obe says. "The same thing that powers the rest of the city, I guess?"

"No. Actually, the magic down here is said to come from a Primeval Spirit named Engai, who supposedly resides somewhere deep beneath Yonte Saire. I've read that brave souls sometimes venture down with crystals to meet this spirit; if they succeed, they return with their crystals filled with Engai's power and become heroes of the undercity. Here, look."

Isa stops when they come across an image of a fig tree carved onto a wall, lines radiating away from the trunk like rays of light. "See this?" she says, pointing at the engraving in excitement. "This is a depiction of Engai. I've read that these images are engraved everywhere in the undercity."

Folding his arms, Obe studies the image with a skeptical look. "I guess I've seen it before, but you mustn't believe every undercity myth you read, you know. I can't tell you how many I've heard, and I'm pretty sure none of them are true."

Isa sighs and starts walking again. The Sentinels jog to catch up.

"I didn't mean to condescend," Obe says.

"It's fine." The excitement Isa felt has petered out. "You're probably right anyway."

In the awkward silence, Ijiro clears his throat. "But isn't the tree some apostate god or something? My father believes all apostates should be wiped from existence."

Isa glances at him, noting the faraway look in his eye. "I'm sorry, Ijiro, but your father is wrong."

His response is to look down at his walking feet. When Isa took him to the Meeting Place by the Sea during the last Mkutano, she sensed how terrified he was of his father. The Bonobo even sneered down at him, and when the meeting was over, Ijiro refused to go and greet the man. Still, she understands how he might not take well to being told his father is wrong.

"The clinic is through that door over there," Obe says, dispelling yet another uncomfortable silence.

Ijiro leaps at the change of subject. "Yes. Let us proceed."

◆ ◆ ◆

The clinic's antechamber is a waiting room. Several people are seated on benches lined against the whitewashed walls—women with babies nursing at the breast, an elderly couple, a man with his leg set in a protective cast. They regard Isa and her companions through glazed eyes. But a woman with a rose in her hair, sitting behind a simple wooden table, welcomes them with a bright smile.

"Welcome to Healer Majii's clinic," she says. "Are you here for an appointment?"

Isa moves close enough to the table to speak in a low voice. "In a sense. We are here on behalf of Her Majesty the King. The herald set up a meeting with Healer Majii for this morning; he should be expecting us."

Any thoughts or emotions that pass through the receptionist remain hidden beneath a flawless mask of politeness. "Ah, yes. He mentioned you'd be coming. But he's in surgery right now, and he might be tied up for the next half hour. Would you be interested in a tour of the clinic while you wait?"

"That would be lovely, yes."

"I'll be right back."

Isa and the others wait silently while the receptionist disappears down a hallway leading deeper into the clinic. The offer of a tour is a good sign; it means Healer Majii won't be immune to financial advances.

"I have a plan to help my people," Isa said to the Arc not long ago, in the privacy of his chambers. "But I need your advice."

"I hope you have not forgotten your priorities, Your Majesty," he said. "It's important that you focus on convincing our 'friend' to help us."

"I haven't forgotten, but my people are in desperate need of allies right now."

The high mystic was holding a pipe. He blew smoke from his nostrils as he watched her, then nodded. "Go on."

"There are groups in the warrens I can rally to our cause," she said. "If I can tap into their grievances and anger, perhaps I can convince them to join us by giving them a stake in the fight."

It disgusts her deep down that she must orchestrate such manipulations, but she knows she can't let her conscience get in the way of duty.

The receptionist returns with a younger man in tow. A long olive-colored robe clings to his thin shoulders, and white neck tattoos mark him as a member of the mystic caste. But since he's down here, he must be unaffiliated with the House of Forms and its covens. He has a youthful face and kind eyes, which puts Isa at ease.

He introduces himself as Healer Azizi, and Isa introduces herself as Andaiye, handmaiden of the king. He seems to accept this at face value.

He is deferential as he shows her around the clinic. Isa counts ten different healers performing various procedures on patients in old but spotlessly clean rooms, their arms throbbing with magic. There are probably more healers behind the doors he leaves closed.

In one room they enter, a female mystic is in the midst of healing a little Faraswa boy's fractured arm while his mother watches worriedly. Azizi explains that the arm will be set in a plaster cast after the spells are completed.

Isa raises an eyebrow. That would make the second plaster cast she's seen since walking in here.

Her brother Ayo once broke an arm so badly the bones were sticking out. An Akili from the House of Life came to the palace and mended the injury within minutes, no cast needed. Ayo was running around being a nuisance again that same day.

"How much do you charge your patients for treatment, honored healer?" she asks once they leave the operation room.

"We charge them nothing. Our services here are free." Azizi walks with a self-assured posture, his hands clasped behind him. Obe and Ijiro are silent shadows following close by.

"And you treat anyone who walks through the door?" Isa asks. "Even foreigners?"

"Our policy is to turn no one away, Handmaiden Andaiye," Azizi replies, perhaps deliberately drawing a stark contrast to the House of Life, which will ignore anyone without a mark on their neck, even to the point of letting them die on their doorstep—unless, of course, they can pay.

"Then how do you afford to keep running?"

"Mostly we receive generous endowments from the Faraswa Collective. The many nonconformist sanctuaries of the undercity also make regular donations."

"I see," Isa says, intrigued. She knows the Collective is the main reason the Faraswa people continue to thrive in the kingdom despite being denied basic rights, such as access to the House of Life and its smaller branches. The idea behind the Collective is that every Faraswa individual of able body finds work, earns wages, and contributes most of those wages to a common fund, which is then used to ensure that every member of the community is provided for. A sort of informal government, one could say, except without the betrayals and blood-thirsty politics.

She shouldn't be surprised that the Collective would be the largest benefactor of the independent community. It's quite ingenious when she thinks about it, how the undercity is a symbiotic ecosystem. It's also rather unfortunate that this is the only way the Faraswa can survive despite being important contributors to the kingdom's economy.

What does it say about me that I am only now discovering this? Would I even be here were it not for my desperation? Would I have come had I not needed to play games with these poor people?

Eerily, Azizi appears to read her changing mood. "Once upon a time the Crown was our biggest benefactor," he says rather delicately, "though it has been a while since the last donation. We hope your presence here represents a shift in the way of things."

A not quite subtle overture, if politely delivered. "I believe it does, Healer Azizi. And I commend you for your good work. The kingdom owes you all a great debt."

His eyes shine with doubt, but he nods. Then he looks down the corridor, where the receptionist is gesturing at him. "Healer Majii is ready to see you. Please follow me."

◆ ◆ ◆

They enter another room, where the lights are dimmer than usual. Perhaps it is a designated meeting room, as there is nothing else inside but chairs and a long table.

Three individuals are seated on one side of the table, facing the door. They have obviously staged themselves for effect.

In the center: a graceful elderly man with white marks on his neck and a full head of grizzled, neatly combed hair. To his right, a Faraswa woman in a pearl-colored veil. And to his left, a rake-thin man with a thick beard, a pronounced widow's peak, and a brooding presence about him. A steel pendant in the shape of a fig tree dangles from a chain around his neck.

Healer Azizi performs the introductions.

"Handmaiden Andaiye, I present to you Healer Majii, who leads our clinic and is master of our coven. Next to him is Bibi Berane, the current chairwoman of the Faraswa Collective. And the man on the left is Bwana Amidi, a priest in the Sanctuary of the Dazzling Light. My elders, I present to you Handmaiden Andaiye, here on behalf of Her Majesty the King."

Isa inclines her head, as befits the role she's playing. "An honor to meet you, my elders. Her Majesty wished to come speak with you in person, but current circumstances necessitate that she remains in the Red Temple. So she sent me in her stead, with a message of goodwill to you and the people you represent."

Healer Majii's eyes move between Ijiro and Obe, who have taken up posts on either side of the closed door. "A crocodile and a bonobo," he mutters and looks back at Isa. "Sentinels, I presume? They look awfully tense for the escorts of a mere servant." When she doesn't answer, his lips curl upward on one side. "A rather interesting time to visit the undercity, Your Majesty."

Azizi's eyes bulge for a moment, and Isa winces at having been caught so easily. "I apologize for the deception," she says, in part to Azizi. "Anonymity is the only way I can move about these days."

"We understand," Healer Majii says. "And rest assured, your visit will not be spoken of beyond these walls. We are all taking a big risk by being here."

"I appreciate your discretion."

"Then perhaps we should arrive at the point of your visit, in the interest of keeping it short." Majii gestures at the lone chair across the table. "Please, take a seat."

As she moves to settle down, a question gives her pause. She thought she'd be meeting with the leaders of three different groups, but now she's not so sure. "Forgive me, Healer Majii," she says, "but do you speak for everyone here?"

Catching on to her concern, Bibi Berane replies, "The independent mystics of this city have always been good to the Faraswa people, Your Majesty. We look to them for leadership and trust Healer Majii's judgment implicitly."

"The same goes for us," Bwana Amidi says.

Isa nods as she regards the apostate priest. She knows the Dazzling Light is another name for the Primeval Spirit Engai, whose power supposedly sustains the undercity. If this man is a priest of Engai, then he's probably an influential figure. "And do you speak for all the apostates of the undercity, Bwana Amidi?" Isa asks.

He was already glowering—a glower seems to be his default expression—but now the furrows on his gaunt face deepen. "The term is *nonconformist*. *Apostate* is a word used to dismiss and persecute us."

"I didn't wish to cause offense."

"Bwana Amidi is a well-regarded member of the nonconformist community," Majii says diplomatically. "He does not lead them, per se, but his word carries much weight."

Amidi nods in agreement. "And I defer to Healer Majii's judgment."

In other words, Isa surmises, *go through him to get to us.*

"I see." She brings her fingers together on the table and begins the speech she prepared. "Well, as you probably all know, my family was slaughtered not long ago, and the usurper Kola Saai now sits on the throne as regent—"

"Allow me to make things simple for you, Your Majesty," Majii interrupts. "And I mean no disrespect, but your time is precious, and so is ours. You have come here to seek our help in the troubles that have befallen your people, correct?"

Isa blinks. It's been a while since someone interrupted her. "I seek allies in the fight against a would-be tyrant and butcher of innocents."

"Which brings us to the question at the heart of this meeting, the why of things. To wit, *why* would we help you? Why should we choose a side in this war, when your enemy appears to enjoy the full support of the orthodoxy and most of the headmen?"

The forwardness is unexpected, but Isa keeps her voice steady. "First of all, your assertion that the orthodoxy is united behind him is erroneous, seeing as I was crowned in the Red Temple by the high priest himself. Secondly, the regent's success would inflict on this kingdom a campaign of conquest bloodier than anything we have ever seen.

Countless lives across the continent would be lost, all to feed one man's greed. Surely you see why he must be stopped."

"What I see, Your Majesty, is why *you* would want to stop him, and I see why our support might aid you in your quest. But those are *your* whys. I still don't see an answer to ours, so I'll ask you again: *Why* should we involve ourselves in your war against the regent?"

A test. Everyone in this room knows how easy it would be for her to offer inordinate sums of money in exchange for their support. Perhaps that's what they expect.

"If you are intent on dealing with the leaders of the undercity, then you must handle them deftly. Appeal to things they hold most sacred."

"I won't make the mistake of offering you money," Isa says, following the Arc's guidance. "I see how your clinics might benefit from more funding, and I fully intend to make a contribution regardless of the outcome of this meeting. But I realize that money isn't why your communities continue to thrive despite the many adversities you face every day. You thrive because you believe in each other. And if I want you to join my fight, I must first make you believe in me. That is why I'm here, my dear elders. Help me see what I can do to make my fight *our* fight."

All three elders register surprise, though at varying degrees. "Well spoken," says Bwana Amidi, the surly nonconformist. "But how can we trust you? You have sought us out only because it is convenient for you to do so. No Saire royal has ever set foot down here."

"My father was a patron of the Sibyl Underground. He came to consult with her on several occasions."

"That is true," Healer Majii concedes.

"Bah." Amidi waves a dismissive hand. "He cared only for what she could do for him."

"And yet," Majii says, "she was safer because of it. Consider what happened shortly after his death."

Amidi's scowl and the silence from the others pique Isa's interest. "What do you mean? What happened?"

"The sibyl and all those in her sanctuary were purged, Your Majesty," Majii explains in a solemn voice.

"I'm sorry," Isa says, confused. "Purged?"

"He means butchered like diseased dogs," Amidi spits, and Bibi Berane shakes her head in sorrow and disgust.

"There were many of my people in that sanctuary," she says. "Some of them good friends."

"That's . . . that's horrifying," Isa remarks. "Who would do such a thing?"

"Who else?" Amidi says in a growling voice. "That's how the orthodoxy keeps us in check. Swift and brutal attacks on our sanctuaries when they become too successful, and the courts never bring those responsible to justice."

"I . . . didn't know."

"How could you? Saire kings have always turned a blind eye to our plight."

"Amidi . . . ," Majii cautions.

"But it's true!"

"My father—" Isa begins.

"Yes, yes, he protected the Sibyl Underground for his own personal gain, but what did he do to stop the arbitrary persecution of nonconformists in this city? Nothing."

Majii tries to intervene again. "But even you must concede there were no purges during his reign."

"Perhaps, but to be a nonconformist has always meant you can be mugged, beaten, raped, and killed with impunity, and he did nothing to change that."

"What if I pledged to be different?" Isa says.

Amidi seems to calm down for a moment but still shakes his head. "The Shirika have not recognized your authority. They don't have to listen to anything you say. How would you stop them?"

"Let me worry about the Shirika, but I can pledge here and now that in exchange for your help, and upon my enemy's defeat, you will know all the rights and protections known by every other citizen of this kingdom. I extend the same offer to the Faraswa people. You've been here for centuries, yet you're still treated as foreigners. That will change."

Silence casts a shadow over the room. Bibi Berane is the first to dispel it. "What do you propose?"

"Full citizenship for your people," Isa says. "The right to own land, establish businesses, send your children to school, petition the courts. If a citizen can do it, you, too, shall be able to do it."

"Lofty promises," Bibi Berane says, "yet you ask us to take you at your word, which is asking a lot. And to be frank, Your Majesty, I do not see a path to success for you. The powers arrayed against your people are simply too great."

"I would not be sitting here if there was no way forward. And yes, I'm asking you to trust me, and I'll make any vow of blood or sign any contract if it will help me convince you. Kola Saai's success will mean the continuation of the status quo. Help me defeat him, however, and you can change your lives—the lives of your people—for the better."

Bibi Berane and Bwana Amidi exchange a glance; then together they look to the man sitting between them.

"And what of the independents?" Healer Majii says. "What would we stand to gain from allying ourselves with you?"

"*The Faraswa have longed to become full citizens of the kingdom for centuries. The apostates wish to practice their beliefs in peace. And only one thing will win you the support of the independents, Your Majesty, and it is this: spells.*"

Isa words her reply carefully. "As I wandered the halls of your clinic, Healer Majii, I saw that you use plaster casts to mend broken bones.

While I'm sure it works, eventually, I wonder why you use such slow methods when mystics of the House of Life can mend the same injuries within minutes."

Healer Majii smiles without humor. "The House of Life is the best medical institution on the continent, Your Majesty. They enjoy unrestrained access to the Pattern Archives and its dedicated teams of spell wrights. We, on the other hand, lack such resources and must make do with what's available. But our patients are always grateful for what we do for them."

"I'm sure they are," Isa says. "And believe me, I, too, am grateful for the work you do." She leans forward, looking the mystic directly in the eye. "Healer Majii, what if I told you I could acquire a large cache of spells from the Pattern Archives for you? Would that be enough to win you over to my cause?"

The man gulps visibly. "We've tried. We've hired foreign mystics, at great cost, to enter the Archives and memorize spells and bring them to us, with very limited success. The orthodoxy is extremely good at cutting us out of their institutions."

"Give me a list. I will have your spells the next time I come here."

"Have our friend steal the spells for you," the Arc said with a contemplative shine to his eyes when she sought his counsel. "Perhaps this is a good time to bring him into the fold after all."

At the time Isa was about to take a sip of tea from a cup. She paused midway, wondering if she'd made a mistake coming to the high mystic. "I'm not certain I can convince him to do such a thing. I was thinking of hiring as many foreign mystics as I could and paying their way into the Archives."

"I have something you can offer him," the Arc said. "Something he will not be able to resist. Mystics of his tribe are also clever and resourceful. Given what he's already achieved, he won't be any different." The Arc looked at her, a hard certainty in his unbending gaze. "Offer him this gift, and you won't have to hire anyone else."

Back in the undercity clinic, Healer Majii looks over Isa's shoulder at Healer Azizi. "Bring me a pen and a notepad."

With a silent nod, the younger mystic complies.

"I suppose this will be an opportunity for us to see the worth of your words," Majii says to Isa. "Bring us the spells, and you shall have our support."

11: Musalodi

Skytown

Salo rests the handle of his little screwdriver on his lips and peers at Tuk from behind the mahogany desk of his study. The individual in question is reclining on the upholstered lounge chair by the glazed doors that lead to the gardens outside, frowning intently at the puzzle polygon in his hands. He's wearing a cloth with salmon patterns around his hips, and his bare feet are tapping idly on the chair.

It has not escaped Salo's attention that Tuk is an extremely well-put-together young man. But he sees the way he looks at Alinata and has decided not to let himself admire him too much lest he compromise their budding friendship with unrequited affections. Salo knows better than to go down that road again.

And he was succeeding, at least until a few days ago, on the night of the New Year's Feast, when he returned from the Summit to find that Tuk had shaved off his beard and trimmed his long hair, a look that made his dimples more prominent and took years off his face.

Years. Salo had pegged him as at least five years older than himself, but now he's not so sure. He thinks they might actually be the same age.

"Having second thoughts?" he says.

Tuk keeps frowning at the polygon as he twists its many segments this way and that. "No. Why?"

"You seem troubled."

"It's nothing."

"Nothing you want to talk about, you mean."

"Nothing you should worry about," Tuk says. The polygon makes a sound like little gears each time its segments twist against each other. "I was just thinking about how fast things have changed in Yonte Saire. It's not the place I visited when I was here last."

"Did something happen yesterday?" Salo asks. Tuk left the residence yesterday for a solo trip to the city. He was a bit downcast when he returned.

"Not really. How's your enchanting going?"

Salo looks down at the disassembled cipher shells, screws, and little crystals strewed all over his desk, which he was working on before Tuk walked into the study and distracted him. "It's going, I guess," he says, to which Tuk smirks.

"Really? That's surprising, considering how you've been staring at me the whole time I've been here."

Heat crawls up Salo's neck. He wasn't aware he was being that obvious. "I've been wondering how old you are," he says, deciding to finally come out with the question he's been thinking about all morning. "Just wasn't sure how to ask."

Tuk stops twisting the polygon, his hands falling to his sides. He blinks at the ceiling several times and sighs. "It's the haircut, isn't it?"

"And the shave."

"I look ridiculous, don't I?"

"I'm sure you know exactly how you look, Tuksaad. You don't need me to stroke your ego."

Dimples appear on Tuk's cheeks. "Is that your way of saying I'm handsome?"

"Is that your way of evading my question?"

Tuk becomes serious again, turning his gaze back toward the ceiling. "You wouldn't believe me if I told you."

"Try me."

Pale green-yellow eyes slant toward the table. Salo has learned that Tuk can't lie without his eyes subtly shifting color. He has to look away, but even that betrays him.

"How old are you, really?" Salo says. "You don't have to tell me if you don't want to, but I'm curious."

"Biologically? Intellectually? I feel . . . I don't know." Tuk fails to maintain eye contact and returns to his polygon. "Anything between seventeen and twenty-two."

"That's a fairly large range."

"That's how old I *feel*. But I'm actually . . ." His throat bobs. "I was made about seven comets ago." When Salo says nothing, Tuk risks a tentative glance, only to roll his eyes. "Close your mouth. A bat could fly in there, and you wouldn't notice."

"So let me see if I heard you correctly: you're *seven* years old?"

Tuk sits up with an exasperated sound and sets his polygon aside. "I prefer not to think of myself that way. Yes, my memories might go back only seven comets, but I came to life with the spirit of a teenage boy and all the knowledge and emotional intelligence appropriate for a teenage boy. I even went through adolescence." Tuk raises an eyebrow. "Since we've met, have I ever given you the impression that I'm a child?"

"I guess not," Salo says, then points, his lips curling up at one corner. "Though you *were* just playing with a toy."

"Oh, for Ama's sake. This isn't a toy. I've never played with toys." Tuk's sulky glare would be a lot more convincing if his bright-green eyes didn't twinkle so much. When Salo tilts his head back and laughs, Tuk gives up the pretense and laughs too. "Hey, toys can be a good way to relieve stress. Now get back to work and finish up whatever you're doing. You're supposed to bless me, remember?"

The reminder helps Salo get his laughter back under control. It's not that he doesn't want to give Tuk his blessing; he does, and he's spent many hours in meditation since the New Year to prepare himself for it. He's just nervous that he'll mess up somehow.

"What are you working on, anyway?" Tuk says.

Returning to what he was doing before Tuk walked in, Salo picks up a little disk of tronic ivory and carefully fits it into an appropriate slot at the back of a circular golden pendant.

"Trying and failing to perform my first enchantment," Salo says as he inspects his handiwork. "You know, when I first saw these things, I wondered why they weren't more popular. Turns out they're ridiculously difficult to enchant."

The pendant is one of several cipher shells he bought from a Midtown store during a shopping trip to the city center. He'd been curious about cipher shells since he'd seen them at the academy, but given how Kamali dismissed them as novelties, he wasn't expecting to find much in the Midtown store beyond eye-catching trinkets of little to no practical use.

And they were certainly eye catching, made of precious metals and fashioned into various shapes and sizes. Some were in the form of jewelry, others arranged on the polished counters, waiting to be the centerpiece on a side table.

He was wondering what he could actually do with one if he bought it when the shop clerk showed him a demo shell in the form of a golden ornamental orb that had been enchanted with layers of Void craft. Together the charms worked to remotely animate a large swarm of mechanical golden skimmer flies that zipped around the orb in aesthetically satisfying patterns.

There were other enchanted shells on display. A pendant for cooling the wearer's skin. An orb to sweeten the air around it. And most impressive, a shell that could capture and preserve one image from the world and store it, displaying it as a mirage at the push of a lever.

Salo would have bought all the demo shells, had the clerk allowed it, but apparently the House of Axles forbids private citizens from selling enchanted artifacts, so he could only purchase empty shells and the necessary parts to make them work.

A pity that they just won't obey him. "I have an efficient Axiom that can handle tough spells," he complains. "But my mind can only go so far. It's almost impossible for me to transcode spells onto a cipher core so small without prose overwrite."

"Have you tried using your talisman?" Tuk asks.

"I'm about to do that right now. I fed it the automatic barrier spell I used when we fought off the Maidservant. If I succeed, this pendant will make its wearer especially difficult to hit."

"Useful," Tuk remarks.

Salo grins. "My thinking exactly."

He goes ahead and draws essence into his shards, preparing to conduct it into his talisman. Tuk's watchful eyes reflect the red glow of Salo's magic while the steel serpent looped around his left wrist lifts its head, its crystal eyes flashing with light. With his thoughts he directs it to look at the golden pendant nestled in the palm of his other hand and then commands it to release the spell he fed it into the pendant's cipher core.

For several seconds, the serpent's eyes flash rapidly, faster and faster, until they're shooting out steady white beams at the cipher shell. But then the beams sputter and fail, and the shell releases a painful shock that forces Salo to drop it onto the table like it's on fire.

"Damn it!" he cries, shaking his electrified fingers.

Across the room, Tuk's eyes are an almost incandescent green. "What happened?"

"Failure," Salo says a bit testily. He sighs, slumping into his chair. "If even my talisman isn't strong enough, how does anyone manage to enchant these things? Or anything at all?"

Tuk's eyes maintain their amused hue. "Now you know why they call them novelties. A real pity, given how much you spent on them."

"Well, I'm not giving up," Salo says. He sits up, clapping his hands together. "Are you ready for your blessing?"

Tuk holds his gaze. "If you're ready."

"I made a promise to you, and I intend to keep it. Let's do this."

"Then wait here. I'll be right back." Beaming from ear to ear, Tuk dashes out of the study before returning a minute later with a bemused Ilapara and Alinata in tow.

"First, an audience to witness my transcendence." Both young women roll their eyes as Tuk rubs his hands together with palpable excitement. "So what happens now? Do I kneel, or something?"

Alinata folds her arms. "Typically, an Ajaha must partake in a dance prior to receiving his mystic's blessing. There's usually a whole ceremony to commemorate it."

"You'd have to wear hide and cover your face with clay," Ilapara says, eyes full of glee. "Slaughter a goat for Salo. Sing his praises and impress him with your strength. Make him feel like the most special mystic in the whole world."

"And yet we shall skip that part so as to not make an already awkward situation more awkward," Salo cuts in.

"Are you sure, Salo?" Tuk says. "I can dance, if you want."

"You will not." Salo points a finger in warning. "Not if you still want my blessing."

While the others giggle at his expense, he strides toward the glazed doors, opens them, and steps outside. He takes several breaths of the warm, garden-scented air before he turns around and holds his hands out. "All right, Tuk. Give me your arms."

Tuk's body is blood and sinew, but his bones were reinforced with several different metals, some of which Salo has no names for. The metals also weave into his heart and lungs in fine threads and gather around a powerful node in his cerebrum—what Salo assumes is his tronic mind stone.

Given his rather unusual anatomy, blessing him should be a decidedly onerous task, and yet, when they grip each other's forearms, Salo's ancestral blessing flows with no resistance from his glowing shards and into Tuk's bones, infusing them with morsels of arcane power. They both gasp, wide eyes staring into each other.

The power keeps flowing. On and on without end. Salo tries to wrest his arms free—too much power and Tuk will die—but Tuk's system holds him like a lodestone to iron, continuing to absorb his strength, sending it along the metal threads that weave throughout his body. With a surreal sense of horror, Salo can do nothing as the power converges upon the cerebral node.

And breaches it. The exact moment is as fleeting as the day's first sunray, but for Salo it seems to stretch and comes with a flood of revelations as Tuk's mind stone yields its secrets to him.

His soul was lifted from a boy who lived and died a long time ago. His body was designed down to the last hair follicle to be an exact replica of the dead boy, from the dimples on his cheeks to the mole on his left big toe. His mind was bound with nefarious spells that twist around his being like fetters—*broken* fetters.

They no longer bind him, but Salo sees their lingering ghosts. Spells meant to rob him of courage. Spells to make him meek, insecure, and subservient. Spells to make him worshipful of his masters regardless of their treatment of him. Many, many other such spells, each one designed to control, dominate, enslave, each one broken.

The mind stone drinks and drinks, growing brighter to Salo's vision, until a surge of static ripples down Tuk's body and shocks them both, flinging them away from each other. Salo lands on his back several feet away, the sky spinning above him.

"Are you all right?" he hears Ilapara say. He blinks, and her worried face comes into focus, hovering nearby.

"He's out," comes Alinata's tense voice. "You held him for too long, Salo."

Ilapara helps him sit up, and he sees the Asazi kneeling next to Tuk's convulsing form. His eyes are wide open and yet strangely empty. His limbs are rigid, and he won't stop shaking.

No. "I tried to pull away, but I couldn't."

"You have to take it back," Alinata says, her voice urgent.

Tuk's body stills, drool seeping out from his mouth, eyes unblinking.

"Salo, take back your blessing, or we'll lose him!"

Ilapara tries to help Salo up, but his muscles give out. *What have I done?*

Suddenly Tuk starts to laugh, and Alinata draws back from him like she thinks he might become a tikoloshe.

"I'm fine, everyone," he says. "It'll take something a lot bigger to kill me."

Pure relief. Salo tries to get up again, but his legs won't cooperate, so he ends up on all fours. "Alinata is right, Tuk. I have to take the blessing back."

Tuk groans and rolls onto his side. His expression is halfway between a grimace and a grin. "I'll be fine. Trust me."

"You could have died," Alinata admonishes him. "You could still die. That's too much power for someone without shards." She redirects her glare toward Salo. "And you. How could you be so reckless?"

"I don't know what happened, all right?" Salo says weakly. "His anatomy is . . . I can't even describe it."

"No need to worry, Alinata," Tuk says. "I've survived a lot worse."

"How's transcendence, Tuk?" Ilapara asks in a mildly mocking tone. "Is it everything you hoped for and more?"

"I've never felt better in my life." Tuk groans again, lifting a hand to pinch the bridge of his nose. "It's like you're in my head, Salo."

"That's the tether he forged between the two of you," Alinata explains. "Honestly, I'm surprised you're both still breathing after how long he held you. Don't attempt telepathic communication until the tether has settled."

"Wait." Tuk lifts his head, evidently surprised. "We'll be able to communicate telepathically?"

"Your psyches are now partially entangled, which is why you can draw from his power." Alinata raises an eyebrow at him. "Didn't you know what you were getting yourself into? Did Salo explain nothing at all?"

"Not that part." Tuk's questioning eyes find Salo, the look on his face suggesting he might vomit. "You can read my mind now?"

"Of course not," Salo says. "You'd have to consciously subvocalize something and mean for me to hear it, otherwise I won't."

"Well, that's a relief. No offense, Salo, but I like my thoughts private, you know?"

"And my own mind is loud enough as it is," Salo says. "Speaking of which, I think it'd be best to put some physical distance between us until the mental bond has settled. You feel like a hammer inside my head right now." This time Salo stays on his feet when Ilapara helps him up. "Maybe I should get around to contacting the queen. Ama knows I've avoided it long enough. You guys can watch him, right? Let me know if anything changes."

Alinata shakes her head. "Ilapara can stay. This blessing could kill him at any moment. I have better things to do than watch you both being foolish."

"I don't mind," Ilapara says. "I can't explain why, but watching him like this is mildly entertaining."

Still sprawled on the ground, Tuk says, "Send Her Majesty my regards, Salo."

"I'm sure she'll be pleased." At the threshold to the study, Salo pauses to glance one more time at Tuk. He tries and fails to envision the person Tuk might have been when he was still bound by his fetters. The young man Salo has come to know is confident and brave and wouldn't let anyone cow him into submission.

Who were your masters? Salo wonders. *What did they do to you, and how on earth did you break your chains?*

Minutes later, he sits on his large bed in his chamber and scowls at the red steel medallion resting in the palm of his hand. The mystic Seal carved onto its shiny faces tricks his eyes into seeing a pair of kaleidoscopic suns sinking into a distant horizon. He was still on his way here when he last spoke to the queen, the day after surviving an attack from one of the Dark Sun's disciples. He wasn't keen on speaking to her then, and he's not keen on speaking to her now, but he knows he can't put it off forever.

Obeying his command, his serpent talisman awakens on his left wrist and transcends distance, seeking out the mystic who cast the Seal on the medallion. Not a second later, it forms a link with another talisman far away—

Then the world blurs, and Salo finds himself standing in a golden grassy plain just before dusk: the false mental construct the queen created to host their entangled minds. Here the full moon has just risen, swollen and bright like an immense globe of blood, and the suns are prismatic spheres dipping toward the western edge of the plain. A part of him remains aware of his real surroundings: the birds chirping outside his chamber, the rich smell of freshly cut grass floating in through the open patio door.

Queen Irediti appears in front of him once more as a shapely silhouette of golden-red light, like the last kiss of dusk on a full moon. Salo has appeared simply as he is.

He bows. "Irediti Ariishe. Ama's blessings this New Year."

"Hello, Musalodi. A blessed New Year to you as well. I trust you arrived safely."

"I arrived almost a week ago, Your Majesty." *Not that you don't already know, what with the spy you sent to watch me.* "I thought it best to wait until the celebrations at the Queen's Kraal were over before I contacted you. I didn't want to interrupt you at an inconvenient time."

Whatever she makes of this partially true excuse, the silhouette doesn't give it away. "Do you have something to report?"

"I do, Your Majesty."

Salo proceeds to relate what happened at the feast on the night of the New Year, including Kola Saai's troubling speech and the accidental assassination that followed it. He also tells her everything he learned from Ambassador Ikwe Iwe, but he leaves out the old man who accosted him outside the palace, though he suspects Alinata has already told her everything.

"In summary, Your Majesty, I believe Kola Saai intends to launch a military campaign to conquer all the Redlands and rule the continent as emperor. As for the assassination, I'm not sure what to make of it."

The queen seems thoughtful. "A prince making big promises at a feast. Perhaps harmless bluster."

"My impression was that he really believes what he said, Your Majesty. And worse, I believe the Shirika agree with him."

"Belief and agreement are still a far cry from mobilizing."

"He can't mobilize right now. He's still consolidating power, and there seems to be some disagreement within the Shirika. But the general consensus is that the regent will ascend to the throne sooner or later; then it'll just be a matter of persuading the other headmen to follow his lead, which won't be difficult if the Shirika back his ambitions."

"So what is your assessment of the danger he poses?"

Salo considers the question. *Are you really asking for my opinion or driving me into a corner?* "I'm no military strategist, Your Majesty, but together the KiYonte legions are by far the largest and most organized military force in the Redlands. They could probably launch simultaneous campaigns north and south of the Yontai and still be unstoppable.

And with the warriors of the Jasiri fighting on their side, I doubt that even our cavalry could stand against them."

The silhouette paces momentarily, then comes to a stop. "As I see it, we have two choices. The first: We could seek to form defensive alliances with the other tribes south of the Yontai. But let us take a look at our options, shall we?

"We could approach the Umadi warlords, who certainly possess the numbers to mount an effective defense. Except that they despise each other so much they would sooner bow to the Yontai than cede any influence to each other. To think those brutes would start cooperating because we asked nicely would be overly optimistic. Any alliance with them would be fraught with treachery.

"We could approach the Valau, who don't breathe unless their so-called priest-king tells them to, which, mind you, might have been convenient for us in this situation. But the man is a gluttonous swine who has shown contempt for military confrontations, preferring to use gold and assassination to solve his problems and surrender if he can't.

"That leaves us the Qotoba, who are seafarers with no standing military; the Muomi, many of whom are mindless cannibals; the Shevu, who are so distant they might as well live on a different continent; and a dozen other tribes too small to be worth considering."

I'm being herded into a corner. "That doesn't sound promising, Your Majesty."

"No, it does not. Which is why we must consider the second choice: to make sure that we never need an alliance in the first place."

Inside his bedchamber, Salo's heart begins to race. "You mean . . . stopping the Crocodile before he's even started."

"Precisely."

"I'm not sure I know how we could do that."

"I don't expect you to. At least, not yet. We need more information. Your best move at this point is to seek out his enemies. Find out what they know. Find out what they're planning. Information is a weapon, Musalodi, one we sorely lack. That's why I sent you there."

I'm not trained for this! I'm no spy! "I . . . I'll do my best, Your Majesty."

"I understand my Asazi is now living with you; I had not planned for her to linger in the city for long, but perhaps this is for the best. Listen to her advice. Be discreet, and don't take unnecessary risks."

"Understood, Your Majesty."

"Good. I'll be expecting news of your progress."

The queen's silhouette begins to turn away.

"Your Majesty, if I may beg a favor of you."

She stops. "Go ahead."

"If it's not too much trouble, would you please let my family know I'm all right? I'd hate for them to worry."

A pause. "I will send word." Then she disappears into the eternal dusk, leaving Salo to emerge from the construct with a migraine throbbing beneath his right temple.

I will lose my head here, he thinks.

He shudders when a knock raps against his door.

"Who is it?"

"It's me," says Ilapara's muffled voice. "You need to come outside right now."

Instinctively, Salo concentrates on the new tether in his mind. It's still unsettled and uncomfortably energetic but otherwise stable. "Is it Tuk?"

"No, Tuk is fine. It's the old man from the Summit. He's shouting for you at the gates."

With a groan Salo lets his back flop onto his bed. "What the devil does he want now?"

"I don't know," Ilapara says from the other side of the door. "He says he won't leave until he speaks to you."

"I'll be out in a minute." Closing his eyes, Salo takes a moment to let his heartbeat slow down. "Is this a punishment?" he whispers to the ceiling. "Did you bring me here to kill me?"

Shockingly, the ceiling doesn't respond. He slowly rises and goes to see what the fuss is about.

◆ ◆ ◆

"We will not leave!"

The guard at the gates has his arms folded bullishly in front of him, staring at the old man behind the wrought iron bars with stony indifference. "Move along, Bwana. There's nothing for you here."

"We will not leave until we speak to your master!" The old man's protuberant eyes bulge even more as he spots Salo walking down the drive with Ilapara. "Honored emissary!" he says in Sirezi. "You must speak to us at once!"

"I'm coming, I'm coming," Salo mutters under his breath. He comes to a stop in front of the gates seconds later. "What's the problem, Aaku? What can I do for you this morning?"

"You must let us in!"

The man has come with a harried-looking family of five, all Saires by the elephant markings on their necks. He stands apart from them in his lordly indigo robes and an almost manic look in his eye.

"He's been shouting for you for the past half hour," the guard says without taking his gaze off the visitors. "Would you like them removed, honored?"

"No, no. That won't be necessary. Just open the—"

"Wait," Ilapara interrupts. Then whispers, "Find out what they want first."

"I can hardly speak to him with a gate between us, Ilapara. That would be rude."

"Need I remind you this gate could be watched? What message would it send if you let the man who publicly insulted the regent walk through it just days later?"

Salo blinks. "I didn't think about that."

She gives him a look that says, *I know.*

Turning back to the old man, Salo says, "Forgive me, Aaku, but I don't think I caught your name the other night."

"My name is irrelevant, but this family is in imminent danger. You must grant them asylum immediately."

Salo glances at the family for a second time. A middle-aged man with a receding hairline, his portly wife, and three young children. They've brought bags filled with stuff to the point of bursting. "I don't understand, Aaku," Salo says to the old man.

"You have diplomatic privileges. By law, this residence is a privileged area. No one can enter without your express permission, not even the Shirika. You must grant this family asylum immediately. If you do not, they will be murdered on the streets."

Baffled, Salo turns to Ilapara, who offers no wisdom beyond shaking her head. "Aaku, I'm sure you could ask the city guard for protection."

"Ha! I might as well kill them myself."

"The King's Sentinels, then. They are barracked in this city and sworn to protect your people, are they not?"

"But for how much longer?"

Salo pushes his tongue into the gap between his teeth as he considers his options. He likes none of them. "You're putting me in a compromising position, Red-kin."

"Ah, I see." The old man nods like he's proved his suspicions. "So you lied to me that night. You're just like the rest of them."

Suddenly the situation becomes clear to Salo. "Is this your way of testing my word?" He shakes his head in disgust. "If this family had no one else to turn to, I would take them in; my culture would oblige me to do so. But I won't be coerced into making a political statement just to prove myself to you. I didn't come here to make enemies, Aaku. I understand your fears, but I won't needlessly jeopardize my mission here."

"So you'll just stand by and watch them slaughter us like pigs? *Tch.* And here I thought you Yerezi had some decency."

"How about this, Aaku. I will, today, in fact, as soon as this conversation is over, express your concerns to the Shirika. I will ask for their reassurance that they will not allow blood to flow on the streets. Should they refuse, and should the Sentinels cease to exist, I will grant asylum to whoever seeks it, if I even have the power to do such a thing."

"You do," the old man insists.

"Then I will do so after the proper ways have failed. That is a promise."

The old man's bitter expression remains fixed for a moment longer. "That is acceptable," he says at last. "Thank you once again, honored emissary. You are most kind."

On their way back to the palace, Ilapara gives Salo a peeved look. "Why must you keep making these dangerous promises? You *really* shouldn't be involving yourself in this matter."

"What else was I supposed to tell him? I can't just do nothing."

"Yes, you can. Doing nothing is easy. You just *do nothing*. I mean, how will you even talk to the Shirika? And what if they try to read your mind again?"

Salo shivers at the reminder. "I'll try approaching one of them. Not the Fractal. Someone else. Maybe Ruma will have a suggestion. And speaking of which. You know, if you took my blessing, you'd be completely protected from any unsolicited mental invasion."

"Salo . . ."

"Sorry. Forget I said anything. How's Tuk?"

Ilapara looks somewhat grateful at the change of subject. "He's enjoying his transcendence in the pool." As they come to the end of the drive, her face contorts with an unasked question.

"What is it?" Salo nudges.

"How does it . . . feel, exactly?"

They stop at the front door, facing each other. "To take a blessing?"

"No, to give one. Can you tell where Tuk is right now? What he's doing? What he's thinking?"

Is that what she's worried about? "Not really," Salo says. "Like I said before, I can't know his thoughts or anything like that, but I can sense if he's in danger or if he needs my help or how far he is. He can also sense the same things about me, and we can talk to each other from a distance. It's still strange right now, but it's something I could get used to."

"I see." Ilapara recedes into her own thoughts as they enter the residence, and Salo decides not to push her any further.

Ruma Sato comes knocking on his door barely a half hour later. "His Worship the Spiral has agreed to meet you this afternoon," he announces, sounding mightily pleased with himself. "He's the supreme justice of the House of Law, in case you've forgotten."

Supreme justice? *Sounds like a big deal.* "He agreed to meet me *today*?"

"Yes, honored. I must say, such a quick response from a high mystic is rather unusual. He must hold you in high regard." Ruma leaves that statement hanging like a fishhook with a fat worm writhing on its end.

Salo doesn't bite. "We've never met, so I wouldn't know."

"I see. Well, the lady Alinata asked me to remind you to make use of your new wardrobe. I went ahead and asked a servant to prepare your outfit while you bathe."

A growl builds up in Salo's throat, but he swallows it down. "Thank you, Bwana Ruma."

Indeed, when he returns from the bathing chamber, pristine white linens, brand-new copper jewelry, and enchanted fabrics are waiting for him on the bed. Today his blanket cloak is a rich crimson wool with slowly spinning geometric outlines etched in metallic colors. Salo tries hard to convince himself that he hates it all as he puts on each of the items selected for him.

He doesn't quite succeed.

◆ ◆ ◆

He takes a rented carriage down to Skytown with Ilapara, and as they walk across Midworld Park, she crouches to pick up a stray piece of paper blowing with the wind.

"These are everywhere." She knits her eyebrows in distaste as she reads it, then hands the flyer over. "Here."

Salo takes his eyes off the winged statue standing on a stepped pedestal of the landscaped park. Visually striking multistoried structures of stone and bamboo rise on all sides of the park, all of them glazed.

Depicted on the leaflet is a grotesque elephant-cockroach abomination. Salo shivers with dread as he reads the words beneath the image out loud: "Rise, Wavunaji. Exterminate the Pests. Purge the Land. Reap Your Vengeance."

"It doesn't take a genius to figure out what that means," Ilapara says.

"No, it does not, unfortunately." Salo folds the leaflet, deciding to keep it. Perhaps it'll be ammunition.

An intimidating air of authority assaults them as soon as they enter the House of Law, a place of cold glass, harsh lighting, and morose statues that seem to watch and listen in. Stiff-necked, unsmiling people in black garments pass each other like strangers in the hallways. Salo gulps as a masked Jasiri welcomes them and leads them up a winding staircase to the Spiral's office.

So this is what the largest bureaucracy in the Redlands looks like, Salo thinks, and he decides that he doesn't envy it at all.

The Spiral's office is itself a microcosm of the entire building: grand and ornate to the point where visitors can never feel comfortable. The tusk of a grootslang is the centerpiece on one wall. The plush skin of a leopard sprawls beneath the low table in the corner, which has dusky leather armchairs surrounding it. Salo even detects subtle spells of intimidation Blood craft woven into the walls, though he finds them rather easy to shut out.

He glances at Ilapara. Her face is professionally impassive as usual, but she's probably feeling the effects of the spells. Perhaps he shouldn't have brought her.

"Welcome, honored emissary," says the man who greets them at the door. "It's a pleasure."

Long dreadlocks frame his angular face. Black robes hang smartly around his lanky frame. Salo's a little taller, but the man's presence dominates the air around him. And those startlingly long canines of his . . . are actually fangs.

Real, actual fangs in his mouth.

Salo shakes the man's hand. They share pleasantries; he invites Salo to sit on the chair in front of his imposing mahogany desk, offers him a drink, pours himself a glass of strong-smelling liquor when Salo politely declines, sits on the large leather chair on the other side of the desk.

Gives Ilapara an appraising glance.

She doesn't flinch by her chosen post near the door. A life-size skeletal warrior stands next to her, carved in obsidian stone.

The Spiral flashes his fangs at Salo. "Let us dispense with the 'Your Worships' and the 'honored emissaries,' shall we? I'm sure we both know what we are and need not keep reminding ourselves."

"As you wish," Salo says with a forced chuckle. He wonders why this man needs intimidation spells. He's terribly frightening as he is.

"You were at the feast on the New Year's, were you not? Nasty business, how it ended." The Spiral speaks with a lazy, confident drawl that carries the subtle undertone of mockery. The voice of a man used to speaking to people he knows are beneath him.

"A sad day indeed," Salo says, consciously choosing not to express any politically charged opinion. "May the deceased find peace on the Infinite Path."

"I hope you haven't been disenchanted by what you witnessed. Our city is normally an exemplar of peace and progress, but we are going through a difficult time. I remain optimistic, however, that order shall soon be restored."

Not if you help a would-be emperor become king, Salo thinks. "That's reassuring to hear."

"So." The Spiral lifts his glass and takes a languid sip, his gaze never leaving Salo. "To what do I owe the pleasure of your visit?"

Salo has to work not to swallow. "I'm not sure how you'll take this, but I'm actually here on behalf of a tribesman of yours."

"Oh?"

"Yes. He came to my gates earlier this morning with a family of five, asking that I grant them asylum—the family, that is. They're Saires who fear persecution given the current political climate."

The Spiral nods. "And what was your response?"

"I told them to seek protection from the King's Sentinels, but I couldn't just turn them away, so I promised I'd speak to the Shirika on their behalf. I may be a foreigner, but since they came to my gates, I can't help feeling somewhat responsible for them. I thought it would be wise to bring them to your attention."

"I see." The Spiral takes another sip from his glass. "You may consider us notified. Was there something else I could help you with?"

Salo blinks at the man. "Uh . . . will you take any action on the matter?"

"What action do you propose?"

"Well, for starters, if you reassured the Saire people that you won't let violence erupt as they fear—"

"The House of Law cannot give such assurances."

"I don't understand. I've seen leaflets threatening the Saires in no uncertain terms." Salo unfolds the leaflet in his hand and places it on the table for the Faro to see. "Their fears are not unfounded. If you just told them that you won't let them—"

"Perhaps I misspoke." The Spiral doesn't even look at the leaflet. "We cannot give such assurances because we wouldn't stop interclan violence if it came about."

Salo feels like the world has tilted wrongly beneath him. "Why not?"

The Spiral is definitely a Void mystic. Salo can almost feel the Void's chill emanating from across the table like air from a frostbox. "The House of Law is a judiciary; we study the laws, and we judge those who break them, but we do not enforce them. That is not our job." He steeples his bejeweled fingers. "Surely you must know this."

"Forgive me," Salo says carefully, "but I thought I was speaking to you in your capacity as a member of the Shirika."

The Spiral strokes his well-groomed stubble. "It is tempting to view us as a distinct entity, isn't it? A single body that decides everything together. But that is not the case at all. We each work separately in the running of those institutions best left to the kingdom's mystics. As the supreme justice of the House of Law, I oversee the kingdom's judicial system on behalf of the Mother. The chancellor of the House of Forms, whom I believe you met"—the Spiral shows his fangs in a knowing smile—"is responsible for the kingdom's libraries and institutions of education, including the city's academy of magic.

"Likewise, the high physician of the House of Life oversees all matters of health in the kingdom, the director of the House of Silos oversees all things botanical, and so on. But none of us have the mandate to perform law enforcement or, for that matter, to meddle in the political affairs of the sovereign and the headmen."

Do you really expect me to believe this? Salo wants to say. *You propped up the Saire monarchy for centuries! And now you're supporting the Saai coup!* The words hang in the room unsaid, like looming storm clouds. The Spiral's mocking eyes shine like he's waiting for Salo to speak them, like he *wants* Salo to speak them. "But what about the Jasiri order? Will they do nothing as well?"

"The Jasiri are bound by the same constraints that bind me and the other high mystics. Their duty is to protect the kingdom against all magical threats. That is not the same as general law enforcement, which is the responsibility of the king's herald and the city guard."

I bet you could remove those constraints if you wanted to. Salo tries to remain calm, but he hears the desperation in his own voice. "Your kingdom is on the verge of bloody ethnic cleansing, if not outright genocide. I saw empty villages on my way here. Does this not concern you?"

"It concerns me greatly," the Spiral says, "and the House of Law will punish any who partake in criminal activity. What we won't do, however, is stand in their way. As I have said, that role is for the herald, who controls the city guard and its investigative branch."

Salo sinks back into his chair. So much bureaucracy created to give people excuses to do nothing. "I understand your point," he says, "but you do realize that one word from you would stop the violence before it even starts, don't you? You wouldn't even have to do anything, only speak out against it."

"Which would constitute meddling in the political affairs of the sovereign and the headmen."

"This is a humanitarian affair."

"A political humanitarian affair. Speaking out either way would carry significant political ramifications. Look, your sympathy is admirable, but our role as mystics in society is simply to protect the Mother's interests across the kingdom. We do not go any further than that, for that would be in violation of the sacred principles of free will and self-determination. The Mother's children ought to be free to live as they please. If they wish to butcher each other on the streets, then that is up to them, so long as they know that they will face justice when we mete it out."

Understanding dawns on Salo. "Punishment, not prevention."

"We are merely following the Mother's direction. Does she stay the murderer's hand? Still the swindler's tongue? No. Crime is a power all people are free to wield should they choose to. But their souls will face judgment before the Mother and her servants when all is said and done. Such is the natural way of things."

The Spiral's office has a grand view of Midworld Park and Skytown's glimmering slopes. A coal-feathered bird perches on the windowsill outside.

Knowing he will get nothing else here, Salo extends his hand across the table. "It's been a pleasure, Your Worship."

The Spiral takes the hand. "Likewise, honored emissary."

Salo remains bewildered as he exits the House of Law. Then he starts to get angry. His stride along the sidewalk is so brisk Ilapara has to jog a little to keep up with him.

"Useless," he fumes, not caring if anyone hears him. "Utterly useless. You have these *hugely* powerful mystics, yet they won't lift a finger to stop the genocide brewing right under their noses."

Ilapara says nothing, frowning hard at the pavement ahead.

"They think they're above the concerns of regular people," Salo continues. "Did you hear how he likened himself to Ama? Ridiculous. As if she would ever condone such callousness."

"Every tribe has its own interpretation of Ama's will, Salo," Ilapara offers.

"Well, it's the wrong interpretation if it calls for sitting on their hands while people prepare to butcher each other like animals." Salo is so busy glaring at Ilapara he doesn't notice the broad-shouldered young man walking toward him until they bump into each other.

His enchanted cloak disarranges itself, and something metallic clanks onto the ground.

"I apologize sincerely." The young man quickly bends forward to pick up the fallen object and hands it over without looking Salo in the eye. "I believe you dropped this."

The item is a small cube of steel giving off a strange but subtle resonance. Salo inspects it in the sunlight for a second before sliding his gaze back to the stranger. "This isn't mine."

"I'm sure you dropped it," the stranger says. "I think it fell out of your pocket. Again, please accept my apologies."

"I have no pockets," Salo says, but the man has already joined the flow of people walking along the pavement.

"What the devil was that about?" Ilapara says off to the side.

"I don't know." Turning his suspicious gaze back onto the cube, Salo concentrates on the almost imperceptible source of energy emanating from its heart, where a fragment of moongold is likely embedded. To his surprise, the string of ciphers contained therein do not describe an enchantment but a message.

I can help you get into the Red Temple, the ciphers read. *Meet me by the water lily pond in the botanical gardens tomorrow at high noon. Come alone.*

"What is it?" Ilapara says, more worried this time.

"Something I've been looking for," he says, deliberately cryptic. Feeling much better, he palms the cube and resumes his walk down the pavement. "Come on. I believe you wanted to see more of the city and spend some of that money I'm paying you."

12: The Enchantress

Skytown

A prince barges into the Enchantress's boudoir and begins to pace behind her gilded dresser with his hands on his waist, his mood irritable. Finally, he stops and glowers at her back.

"I'm tired of wondering," he declares. "Just tell me if you had something to do with it."

Calmly, the Enchantress picks up a glass atomizer from her dresser and sprays her neck with its delicate attar. Once, her beauty was the only measure by which her worth was judged. She was beautiful to look at and therefore worthy to exist.

A whore. A plaything. Beauty was her curse.

When she finally took the reins of her life, she was tempted to cast off the curse and make herself anew. Scar her face, perhaps, so that no one would ever desire her again.

So that they would fear her instead.

Then she thought better of it. She would keep her beauty, she decided, and if she must be a whore, she would embrace the role proudly, for who knows better than a whore the things that lurk in the shadows of a man's heart? Who better to exploit them? To be a whore is to know the night, where the coldest truths of the universe shine brightly in the sky.

She sets the atomizer down and turns in her seat to face the prince. "Perhaps it would help if you told me what exactly you're upset about," she says.

"Don't treat me like a fool," he barks.

"Then you should stop acting like one," she replies.

His scowl deepens, meaning to intimidate. The Enchantress rises to her feet and stalks toward him, letting his eyes drink her in, from the crimson jewel around her neck to the train of her sheer indigo-and-cerise gown. She senses his skin warming as she draws nearer. He shivers when she slowly brings one arm to rest over his shoulder, raising the other to run a finger along the line of his stubbled jaw. His eyes briefly close, perhaps despite himself, as he savors the sensation.

"You're so handsome when you're angry," she says.

"Only when I'm angry?"

She taps his nose. "Especially when you're angry."

"You went too far," he says, though the heat in his voice is already melting into the husky growl of desire. "How will the other headmen trust me now? They all secretly think I did it."

"Hush." The Enchantress puts a gentle finger over his lips. "You're blameless. Innocent. You know nothing."

The perfume she's wearing today is a subtle but potent blend of allure and suggestion. Most people beyond the Redlands would be inoculated against the influences of such a simple concoction. The people here, however, powerful though their sorcery may be, have yet to encounter Higher magic at its smallest, most insidious scales.

Not even the high mystics are immune.

"Never again, understood?" the prince says. "You don't do anything of this magnitude without consulting with me first."

She draws back just a little so she can consider his face. "But my prince. I have admitted to nothing."

His eyelids droop in an exasperated look.

"It's true. And besides, whoever did this, for whatever reason they did it, the result was positive for us, no? Your enemy lost a valuable ally. A gift we must enjoy."

"At what cost? I will lose support if I look like a ruthless tyrant."

"You did nothing wrong, and that's the truth. Even the Shirika know this, and everyone else will take their cues from the gods."

She could have chosen any of the other princes for her purposes, but she saw in this one someone who wasn't content to simply walk in the footsteps of his forefathers; here was a prince who wished to surpass them and build his own legacy. So far he hasn't disappointed.

He licks his lips, eyes glassy. "I know one way you could ease my worries."

"Do you, now."

She lets him slide a hand down her back, lets him kiss her neck and inhale her scent, lets him inflate his desire until she can almost feel it burning with the heat of an inferno. They inch toward her bed; then she pushes him onto the silken bedclothes. He falls onto his back, his hungry eyes looking up at her expectantly.

She smirks. He was meant to be a mere instrument, a piece on a game board; she didn't expect it would be so thrilling to see him come undone. "As much fun as this would be, I have an important guest I must entertain."

Looking incredulous, he watches her move back to her dresser, where she sits back down and puts on her circlet of gold and precious stones.

"More important than your husband?"

"No," she says. "But entertaining my husband is a pleasure I must leave for last."

He shudders visibly, collapsing onto the bed with a pained groan. "What must I do until then?"

The Enchantress looks herself over one last time in the mirror and is satisfied. At the doors to her chamber, she says to the prince, "Content yourself with thoughts of me, dear husband, and the coming night."

Then she leaves the poor man alone on her bed, consumed with desire.

◆ ◆ ◆

In another time, somewhere far, far away, where the powerful claim domin-ion not over land but over the heavens themselves, the duke and duchess of the Two Suns Eclipsing appear to have everything they could possibly want: youth, power, money, beauty. Yet their palaces of shining gold and silver offer them no joy, for the duke and duchess despair over their inability to conceive a child.

They try everything they know to try. Potions filled with liquefied sun to enhance fertility. Rituals of dance and starlight. Lavish offerings to gilded temples where the suns stand incarnated as pillars of infinite brilliance. They pay fortunes to renowned physicians, priests, and solar alchemists. They even seek a blessing from the empress, which she grants, for the duke and duchess are both scions of powerful houses, and their lines must continue.

But the duke's seed does not take, and despair grips them tighter within its clutches. Soon it drags them to the edge of desperation, that hopeless chasm where the restraints of pride and principle begin to break at their links, making what was once forbidden permitted, deadening the palate so that what was once distasteful becomes tolerable.

At this precipice, the duke and duchess of the Two Suns Eclipsing agree, in the blackest hour of night, to try one last thing, a decision that brings them to a less affluent district of their city and the doorstep of a dark priest.

The man has a kindly disposition, wears robes the color of ivory and a shock of hair as gray as a winter sky, yet he is a dark priest, since his power comes not from the suns but from that other *light in the heavens.*

The cursed light. The angry, bloodshot, vengeful light whose essence can be corrupted by the foulness of the underworld.

They should never cross paths with such a man. Indeed, as lords of the suns they should spit at his feet and curse his name, as they have cursed others like him in the past. But the duke and duchess visit him anyway, under the cover of night, their faces veiled behind anonymous golden masks so that no one can ever know they were there.

As for the priest, he is neither perturbed nor impressed by their appearance, for they are not his first such guests. He has helped many other lords and ladies who would shun him in the light of day. It is why they know to seek him out. He has a whispered reputation.

"We heard that you could help us," the duke says. "We wish to conceive a child."

"We'll pay whatever you want," pleads his wife. "Whatever the cost. Just help us. Please."

In a land far away, in a different time, the priest is moved by their entreaty and agrees to help them.

◆ ◆ ◆

The Enchantress is waiting in the palace's Ruby Drawing Room when a servant escorts Her Worship the Prism through the doors.

Now here's someone who knows how to make a lasting impression, the Enchantress thinks as she rises to receive her guest. Statuesque and stunning, the high mystic wears a form-hugging gown that does little to hide her unblemished dark skin. A golden head wrap crowns her, and subtle face paints adorn her cheeks and eyelids. Her irradiated irises hold permanent spells of illusion so they appear to contain flickering flames.

While the other Faros take pleasure in the fear they inspire in others, often molding their appearances to intimidate, the Prism molds hers to dazzle and beguile, and even the Enchantress is forced to control her reaction lest she become too taken by the woman.

"Your Worship," she says with a bow. "I'm honored."

"The honor is mine, Your Highness." The Faro looks and speaks like a young woman, but her aura of wisdom seems to bend the gravity around her. "Thank you for seeing me at such short notice."

They settle down on couches with cherry-colored velvet upholstery, facing each other, and continue to exchange pleasantries over spiced tea. For a high mystic, the Prism proves surprisingly adept at idle chatter, which the Enchantress has found not to be true for her colleagues.

Of course, she could simply be trying to charm me.

When the Enchantress first approached the high mystics with offers of superior enchanting technologies, the Prism was resistant to the idea at first. Even when the other Faros leaped at the opportunity, she remained skeptical. The Enchantress doesn't doubt her presence here means she wants something; she just can't guess what.

"You mentioned in your message you had something you wished to discuss," the Enchantress eventually says.

In addition to the couches, the drawing room's reddish theme manifests itself in the artworks on the walls and the patterns on the Dulama carpets. Ornaments of silver and gold provide contrast. An ornate glass table is the centerpiece. The high mystic rests her porcelain teacup on that table, her movements deliberate, controlled.

"I did," she says. "And it concerns the schematics you delivered to the House of Axles."

"You mean the designs for ciphermetric machines," the Enchantress ventures. In the end, these designs were what convinced the high mystics to work with her. The Trigon, who leads the House of Axles as grand artificer, practically salivated at the leap in enchanting technology the machine promised.

"Indeed," the Prism confirms. "The House of Axles made several prototypes from the schematics, one of which ended up with us at the Pattern Archives. We meant only to study it, see for ourselves that the machine was truly as powerful as you claimed." She pauses, like she's about to divulge an uncomfortable secret. "I must say, I was doubtful at first, but that one little machine has increased our productivity by an order of magnitude."

The Enchantress takes her time to digest this. She knows that the Pattern Archives, which the Prism leads as curator, are home to the continent's most gifted team of spell wrights. Mystics from across the Redlands pay exorbitant sums of money to enter the Archives and peruse its libraries of well-crafted spells.

What the Enchantress doesn't know is how the Prism and her people were able to adapt a sophisticated artifact of Higher technology to work with spells of Lower Red magic so quickly. In a matter of weeks. She thought it would have taken a year at least.

"I'm not sure I understand," the Enchantress admits. "Do you mean to tell me you have *already* used the machine in your work with spells at the Archives?"

"Yes, that's precisely what I mean," the Prism says. "Each of our spells has until recently taken years to develop and years more to refine, even with dozens of the most talented scholars working in the Archives. With that one machine, however, we were able to double, triple, and in some cases quadruple the efficiency of our entire collection—all in just two weeks. We were even able to develop a benchmark for testing spells without casting them, a trick we previously thought too resource intensive to be possible. Your machine has challenged many of our preconceptions."

The Enchantress almost smiles. If the so-called uncivilized folk of the hinterlands are seen appropriating advanced technologies at such breakneck speeds, combining them with their powerful sorceries, they will be a threat not even the most pacific lords of the Empire's court will be able to ignore. She can already hear the drums of war beating.

"How curious," she says in a measured voice. "I wasn't aware the schematics were so easy to adapt to Lower . . . excuse me, to axiomatic ciphers."

"They were not, but I had the best minds working on it." Amusement shows in the Prism's enchanted eyes. "You need not correct yourself, Your Highness. I'm aware your people refer to our magic as Lower and yours as Higher, but the principles underpinning them are ultimately the same. They are, after all, both Red."

"The terms *Higher* and *Lower* simply describe the nature of the scripts, Your Worship. Nothing more. We call axiomatics low level simply because they are closer to the true nature of the source than the script we use. Your script is actually more powerful where spellcraft is concerned."

"Except yours permits greater sophistication with enchantments."

"That is my understanding," the Enchantress says, treading carefully. She knows they're reaching the marrow of the conversation and senses opportunity in the air. "It's better suited to influence events at a small scale, which makes the script well adapted for complex enchantments."

"I think there's room for such a script in our spellcraft," the Prism says. "Metaformics, is it?"

"Yes, that is the common name for the script."

"We have often struggled with subtlety, you see. Any competent Fire mystic of my tribe could easily conjure a flame that can consume an enemy in seconds. A more powerful mystic might raze a building to the ground with the wave of a hand. But what if she wished to increase the ambient temperature by a tenth of a degree? What if she wished to target and destroy a single cancerous cell? We know how to do things that can make the masses tremble with fear, but finesse is an art we've yet to master."

"An interesting perspective," the Enchantress says in a placid voice, then nudges the conversation along yet again. "I assume you're here to make a request."

Lifting her head, the Prism brings her fingers together. "Actually, what I'm here to do is find out what you want in return for your help."

The Enchantress opens her mouth, then closes it again. Upon seeing this, the high mystic gives a half smile.

"I may look young," she says, "but I've lived a long time, and I tire of playing games. Let us not play games with each other, Your Highness. Let's speak plainly."

The irony. A woman who wears illusions for eyes demanding honesty and candidness. *Alas,* the Enchantress thinks, *I am not quite finished playing games with you.*

She knits her fingers together, mirroring the high mystic's posture. "All right," she says, hardening her tone just a little. "In the spirit of being frank, perhaps you could tell me why my husband has yet to be crowned king when I thought we were all in agreement on the direction we would take. Why do I find myself adrift, lost in intrigues and murders, my husband about to marry another woman to secure his crown, when you gave your word it would be his by now?"

"If we work together," her accomplice said when they first conspired, "it will strictly be between you and me, and they need not know that you have betrayed them. I will take the blame, and you will appear as confused by my actions as they are."

The Prism thins her lips and glances at the ticking timepiece on the wall. "A minor disagreement," she says, the irritation plain in her voice. "A senile old man trying to show that he's still relevant. Do not worry; the Arc's tantrum will not persist for much longer. He will return to the fold, and your husband will be king."

"I'm relieved to hear that. The palace grows more dangerous by the day, as you witnessed on the New Year's. I would rather the matter of succession be resolved sooner rather than later."

"As would I, Your Highness, but I fear we've digressed. We're here to talk about the academic resources you can provide so I may learn and master metaformic script and what you would want in return."

The Enchantress decides that she likes this woman. "I suppose there is something I'm curious about," she hedges. "A certain volume I heard was hidden somewhere in this city. If it has a name, it cannot be spoken, nor can the writings within it be remembered. Would you know where I might find it?"

The high mystic barely reacts, but her next words are frosty and spoken with a sharpness that brings the Enchantress to the edge of her seat. "I know the tome you speak of. Rest assured it is not in the Archives, and even if I told you where it is, you could never go there, and even if somehow you did, you would never return."

She did not expect that particular tome would ever be within her reach, but the Enchantress finds the Prism's abrupt change in demeanor interesting all the same. "How tragic."

The Prism appears to hesitate, an oddity for someone of such power. "Is there nothing else I could offer you in exchange for your help?"

For a sweet second, the Enchantress savors the feeling of holding power over a Faro, but only for a second. She knows it is not wise to test someone who could kill her by blinking her eyes. "I will give you the resources you need free of charge, Your Worship. We're working toward the same goal, after all. But if there are Jasiri in your coven whom you can spare, the palace would welcome them."

The high mystic nods. "I'll see what I can do."

The Enchantress offers up her loveliest smile. "Then we're in agreement. Shall we share some more tea to celebrate?"

◆　◆　◆

The next matter she attends to leads her to the kitchens. The cooks and maids scurry out of her path as she walks among them.

One particular cook flinches and drops her bowl of batter as soon as she spots her. The room goes silent, but all the other cooks continue to work, concentrating on their present tasks, not daring to glance in her direction.

The Enchantress wears an expression of concern and friendliness. "I'm sorry. I didn't mean to startle you."

"It's no fault of yours, Your Highness," the cook rushes to say. She bends to pick up the fallen bowl. The whisk is still lodged within the batter. Her hands are trembling. "How may I be of service?"

"May we speak in private? I'd like to discuss the menu for this evening."

"O-of course, Your Highness," the cook stammers.

Outside the kitchens, the cook won't stop wiping her hands on her apron. Her tensors are hidden beneath a white head wrap; they thrum with a mysterious latent energy the Enchantress's metaformic jewel has identified as being specific to the Faraswa people. The Enchantress has yet to determine the nature of this energy, and though she'd like nothing more than to study it further, that's not why she's here.

"I wanted to catch up with an old friend," she says, watching the cook closely. "See how you're doing given the recent changes. We haven't had a chance to talk since I arrived."

Like water bursting through a crack in a dam, the cook's face twists with anger, though her hands continue to tremble. "We are *not* friends, Your Highness."

Just as I suspected. The Enchantress sighs. "Don't be so dramatic. Is your new house not to your liking?"

"You lied to me," the cook whispers, shaking with rage. "You said the guards would fall asleep. You said it would be a simple heist, nothing more. Instead they went mad and killed everyone! I almost died."

"And yet here you are." The Enchantress studies the long scar running down the cook's right cheek. "Fine work, that scar. A good idea too. It would have looked suspicious had you escaped unscathed. Did it hurt when you carved it onto your own face?" The cook simply glares, unable to defend herself, and the Enchantress leans closer. "We're bound to each other, you and me, our fates intertwined like vines. If I go down, so will you; then who will look after all those beautiful grandchildren of yours? And what of your people? When the world learns that it was you who helped throw the kingdom into disarray, what do you think would become of them? You should ask yourself these questions before you let your misguided conscience get the better of you."

Tears gather in the cook's eyes, hatred shining through like twin torches. "You don't have to worry, Your Highness. I know my place. I'll keep my mouth shut."

The Enchantress wonders about that, not quite convinced. She hates loose ends. *It would be so easy to be rid of you, so why haven't I already?*

"We all have to make sacrifices for the things we want," she says. "Remember that as you sleep in your lovely new home." When she sees someone approaching out of the corner of her eye, she raises her voice to a regular conversational level. "That sounds wonderful. Thank you for taking the time to speak with me. That will be all."

The cook also spots the intruder, and she bows. "Your Highness," she says and shuffles off as quickly as her legs will carry her.

"Getting comfortable, I see." The intruder saunters over, a smug look in her eye. "Ordering the servants around, strutting down the halls of the palace like a queen. Predictable."

What is predictable, the Enchantress would argue, is this damned woman and how she's always following her around.

"I'm just trying to make an unfamiliar place more comfortable for my husband," she says with more civility than she feels. "That's all."

"Save the act for my brother," the woman says. "I see you for what you are."

"And what's that, dear sister?"

"I'm not your sister," the woman hisses, stepping closer. "My brother has taken fancy to many strumpets like you over the years. Pretty things who think they can change and control him. They never last. Sooner or later he finds some other pretty thing to toy with and casts the old ones aside. You will be no different."

"Then I shall take comfort in the knowledge that *you* will remain to watch over him. It's quite remarkable how devoted you are to your brother. Is that why you never married?"

The woman bares her teeth like a kerit bear. "A harlot may cover herself in expensive silks and gemstones, but a heap of dung with glitter is still just a heap of dung."

"Fascinating insight. You clearly know more about animal excrement and prostitution than I do, so I'll defer to your superior wisdom."

The woman and the Enchantress watch each other like two poisonous serpents who know that should they lunge for each other, neither will survive.

The spell is broken when a throat clears next to them.

"Your Highness. A word." A masked Jasiri in crimson and gilded aerosteel has joined them, radiating deadly power. His voice is a strange metallic echo.

"If you'll excuse me, sister," the Enchantress says. "Perhaps we can continue this conversation another time."

"Oh, I'm sure we will."

The Enchantress leads the Jasiri away, remaining silent until they've reached a safe distance. She feels a pair of eyes watching her, but they don't dare to follow.

"Report."

"The one you asked us to watch sought out the sanctuary yesterday," the Jasiri says. "He fled the scene shortly after arriving; we suspect he may have sensed he was being followed."

"So it *is* him." *But what is he doing in the city?*

The Enchantress brings a hand to her crimson jewel, a discomfiting sensation settling into the pit of her stomach. She thought she'd wiped the enemy's agents from the game board by purging the apostate sanctuary, only for *him* to arrive. There is also the troubling matter of *whom* he arrived with.

None of it can be a coincidence.

There are too many variables in this plan of yours, too many moving parts that may break.

Words the Enchantress brushed away when Prophet said them, but now she's beginning to appreciate their significance. Who knew that orchestrating a world war would be so complicated?

"What are your orders?" the Jasiri asks. "Shall we eliminate him?"

The idea moves the Enchantress near to sickness. "No," she says. "Leave him be. Keep eyes on him, however. Watch the one he follows as well."

The Jasiri nods, then leaves her to her troubled thoughts.

13: Isa

Isa first experienced the beauty of the botanical gardens almost a decade ago—*the feeling of the whole world in the palms of her hands, her mother chasing after her, telling her to slow down, but she wasn't listening because the sunlight felt like a warm bath on her skin, her single golden necklace chiming a melody with each step.*

She ran around the beds of roses whose petals shifted color when sung to. Past the clumps of artistic vines that formed moving reflections of her, like magical mirrors made of foliage. Past the tulips whose scent made her laugh uncontrollably. All the wonders of the garden seemed to have been made for her enjoyment; she was a princess, and she knew it made her special.

It wasn't until she was years older that she understood that the people who'd made the garden's wonders were even more special than her.

That they were gods, and she a mere mortal.

Isa arrives fifteen minutes before high noon and settles down on a bench looking out onto a secluded water lily pond, in the shade of a tree with downy leaves. The cup-shaped flowers floating in the pond shimmer like glitter dust. A pair of large, translucent insects zips around the water lilies almost too fast for her eye to track, dazzling her with their golden sheen, their fluttering wings catching the sunlight like stained glass. Minutes go by.

The glazed dome rising next to the garden entrance can be seen toward her right, over the branches of other downy-leaved trees. Obe and Ijiro will be lurking somewhere close by, though hopefully not too close. The last thing she wants is to give her guest a reason not to trust her.

Not that he should, says a voice in her head. *He should not trust you at all. He should stay as far from you as possible.*

At exactly a minute to high noon a tall, slender youth walks down the stone path to the pond, approaching her bench. He is obviously foreign, given the unusual white garment wrapped in folds around his hips and thighs, as well as those spectacles of his, which conceal his eyes, and the lack of clan markings on his neck.

He's also quite obviously a mystic. The ornate staff is a dead give-away. So's the cloak draped over his bare chest, one of those magical cloths popular with the wealthy of this city these days, an emerald green with stars that actually twinkle even in bright sunlight. And only a mystic would wear so much jewelry.

Somehow, he still manages to look benign.

"Our only advantage is that he isn't aware of what he holds," the Arc said to Isa. "If he were, we would all be in grave danger."

She remembers the warning in the high mystic's voice. He wasn't afraid, exactly—Isa doubts the man fears anything—but he was worried. He truly believed that the danger he spoke of was real.

"A beautiful day to enjoy the gardens," the young mystic says when he's close enough, planting his staff onto the stone underfoot. "Do you mind if I join you?"

"Please, honored. Be my guest." She moves to make more room on the bench and gestures at the empty space.

"Much obliged."

He settles down next to her, holding his staff upright with one hand. She notices how he keeps a somewhat cautious distance between them. *This is him, the one whom the Arc spoke of, the one who holds the key to my people's salvation.* She didn't think he would be so young. She envisioned something akin to a Jasiri, a hulking warrior with a stern countenance and fire in his eyes, or a proud prince with a haughty sneer. He is neither. His KiYonte is accented but cultured, polite. He is approachably handsome.

"So far I've seen sunflowers with petals that retract when observed," he says. "I've seen an orchid larger than a grown man. This garden is filled with many wonders. What is it about this pond that drew your attention?"

His reflective spectacles make it difficult to tell where he's looking. He might be staring out into the pond, or he might be studying her out of the corner of his eye. "Focus your eyes on that lily over there," she says, pointing toward the water. "See those insects? They are venomous skimmers, supposedly the fastest insects in the world. I'm told they were engineered by the botanists here to keep the insect population under control."

He leans forward, appearing to investigate. "Ah. I see them. They really are beautiful." He watches them in silence for a moment. "Like living rays of light, are they not?"

"A fitting description."

Sitting back, he says, "You KiYonte are fortunate. Such a garden would never exist where I come from. My people have an appreciation for art, but they would never consider using magic for purely aesthetic purposes. It would be condemned as a misuse of Ama's benevolence. But I have seen much proof in this city that they are mistaken. Art and beauty are clearly worthy ends unto themselves."

"Every culture has its own vices and virtues," she says. "You might envy the beauty of our art, but I have always envied the cohesiveness of your tribe. You stand united as one people despite your many clans. Would that my people could be the same."

"We're not as united as you would think," the mystic says. "But I see your point." He faces her. "I also see that I'm at a bit of a disadvantage here; you seem to know who I am, yet I know nothing of you."

"My apologies, honored." She offers a hand. "I am Andaiye Saire, handmaiden of Her Majesty King Isa. You are Emissary Musalodi Siningwe of the Yerezi Plains, are you not? Please feel free to call me Andaiye."

They shake hands. His skin is warm to the touch. "Well met, Andaiye. But did you really just say you're the king's handmaiden?"

A pang of guilt visits Isa's chest. He seems sincere, and here she is, lying to him already. *But I have no choice.*

"Does that alarm you?"

"It surprises me," he admits. "It's not what I expected."

"What were you expecting, if I may ask?"

"Someone older, for one thing. A mystic, for another, given the message I received. Definitely not a representative of the king."

The equivocations come freely to Isa's lips. "The king is young, and I am her most trusted servant, so she sent me to speak to you in her stead. As for the message, it was transcribed by a mystic in the Red Temple."

"I see." He studies her for a beat, an unreadable smile exposing the large gap between his upper incisors. "I have to ask, Andaiye—what could have possibly drawn the king's attention to me?"

"We know you met the supreme justice on our clan's behalf," Isa says. "We also know you promised to shelter our people in the event of our violent persecution. Not many foreign dignitaries have been willing to even acknowledge the perils facing us; the fact that you have shows you're a man of principle."

Of course, she doesn't mention how it was she, through the merchant Mwenemzuzi, who manipulated him into doing these things to give her the pretext for approaching him, although she had not planned for him to meet the Shirika. An unforeseen slice of good fortune.

The young sorcerer isn't smiling anymore. "Let's not get ahead of ourselves," he says. "I will do what I can, should the worst come to the worst, but I would rather refrain from needlessly involving myself in matters of politics."

Isa expected resistance. She meets the mystic's gaze. "A perfectly reasonable position. But if I may ask, honored emissary, what was the result of your meeting with the supreme justice?"

He grimaces, turning his face away.

"The worst is coming," Isa presses. "If we do nothing, it will sweep my people off the face of the earth. Her Majesty would rather prevent such a fate than wait for it, but she needs allies. She needs help. You showed that you might be someone we could trust; were we wrong?"

He looks out into the pond, and for a second Isa fears she has lost him, that he'll get up and walk away.

"The message said you could help me find a way into the Red Temple," he says.

Illogically, some part of Isa despairs at his decision to stay. "We can."

"I assume you'd want something in return."

"A favor of sorts," she says. From the shoulder bag sitting by her legs, she takes out a folded piece of paper and hands it over. "Her Majesty needs someone to enter the Pattern Archives and acquire the spells on this list."

He frowns, unfolding the paper. His frown deepens as he browses through the list. There are at least a hundred spells written there, in all six disciplines. Lifting his gaze, he says, "I'm not sure I understand. Why me? If the king has a mystic to transcribe messages for her, why can't she ask that same mystic to enter the Archives and get these spells for her?"

"Allow me to be frank with you, honored emissary," Isa says. "Her Majesty needs these spells so she can win the support of a group of independent mystics. Ordinarily, yes, we might have employed the king's mystic for this task, but he's a member of the orthodoxy, and they all take binding vows that forbid them to share magical knowledge with outsiders. He couldn't help us even if he wanted to, and for the record, he does. Independents on the other hand are barred from the Archives, hence their need for spells in the first place. Our only recourse is to seek the help of a trusted foreign mystic who can pay his way into the Archives and get us the spells we need."

The Yerezi sorcerer takes his time to absorb the information she's delivered. He twists his serpentine staff back and forth between the thumb and forefinger of one hand, staring once again at the list.

Isa finds herself wondering what agenda has kept him seated this long. Surely getting into the Red Temple can't be all there is to it. If he's wise, and she thinks that he might be, he could simply wait for her to be forced out of the Red Temple, which, barring miraculous intervention, will happen sooner rather than later.

His reflective spectacles unnerve her when they turn back to her. "So you're asking me to steal these spells from the orthodoxy, thereby gaining the king independent support."

Isa waits for him to finish his line of thought.

"But what would such support even accomplish?" he asks. "Would it really make a difference? Or is this just a stalling tactic, delaying the inevitable?"

"You now know that the Shirika are indifferent to our plight," Isa reminds him. "Independent support would bring magic back on our side, a victory that would go a long way toward deterring those who would slaughter us. It would also buy us more time to find a permanent solution, which has to be enough for the time being."

"Perhaps you're right, but I'm not sure what you're asking me to do is possible. How would I sneak all these spells out the door? If their security is even halfway decent, they would catch me as soon as I tried."

"We don't need you to steal the actual spells, honored emissary, only make copies."

The mystic shakes his head. "Writing out a copy of a single spell can take hours, and there are many spells on this list. I suppose I could use my talisman to save time, but why do I sense that would only land me in trouble?"

Another question she anticipated. "Because the system in use at the Archives doesn't allow devices that can capture and store information. If your talisman is such a device, it would be detected at the entrance, and you'd be forced to relinquish it. Writing out copies is also forbidden; visiting mystics are expected to memorize spells on the premises. No copies, no loans."

"I'm sorry, Andaiye, but I simply don't have the time to memorize all these spells. One, maybe two at best, but not the whole list."

"We don't expect you to," Isa says, and at the mystic's puzzled expression, she makes her final move of the conversation, reaching into the shoulder bag yet again.

This time she extracts an ornamented rosewood case with a gilded latch. He hesitates for a moment when she presents it to him, but eventually he reaches forward and accepts. She watches him carefully as he opens it and stares at what's inside.

He breathes out a curse in a foreign tongue. "But where did you get this?"

Isa looked inside the case just once, right after the Arc handed it to her. What she was looking at, she couldn't say, but she could tell that it was powerful given the reverence she saw in the old mystic's eyes. "Where I got it isn't important. All you need to know is that it will be invisible to whatever security charms are in place at the Archives. I was also informed you would recognize what it is and what it can do for you."

"This is a talisman," the mystic says, awe palpable in his voice. "But there's something strange about it." He moves to lift the item out of the box, but she places a hand on his arm to stop him.

"Please. Let us be discreet."

He has a dazed look about him, which tells Isa the high mystic was right. Whatever this thing is, it isn't something he can resist. "Of course," he says, closing the box. "Of course."

"Consider this gift a show of good faith. When you're done, transcode the spells onto the memory cube you received yesterday. I assume you still have it?"

"The one that told me to come here? Yes. An ingenious artifact."

"Do this for us, and we will help you complete your pilgrimage. That's a promise." Deciding that she has played her part for now, Isa picks up her shoulder bag and rises from the bench. "I wish I could stay awhile longer, but I'm afraid I must leave you here. It was a genuine pleasure to meet you, honored emissary, though I wish we had met under better circumstances."

"Wait," he says. "How will I reach you? Afterward, I mean."

They will be watching him and will know when he's been successful. For a second Isa considers coming clean and telling him everything. Then that second passes. "We'll be in touch," she says and walks away.

It would be prudent for her to retreat behind the safety of the temple's lightning wards now that she has completed her mission for the day, but an hour after leaving the botanical gardens, Isa's carriage draws to a stop in front of an old Northtown residence with a red door.

The residence is one of many three-story homes crammed along a narrow street in what is probably the most agreeable neighborhood in the district. Leafy vines creep up the trellised walls, hiding the cracks and peeling paint, but the streets are clean, and lovely gardens flourish on the balconies and terraces.

Obe and Ijiro watch from the carriage as she walks up to the red door and knocks. A bucket draws her eye when it squeaks where it hangs beneath a nearby gutter, waiting to collect rainwater. There's a window with its shutters open next to it, and she thinks she sees the curtains flutter like someone drew them closed quickly.

She looks away as the red door swings open, bringing the aroma of roasting fish to her nose. The morose-looking man on the other side is barefoot, wearing a simple blue tunic over gray trousers. His gaunt face is partly hidden behind a thick beard, and his widow's peak heightens the effect of his slight glower. The black markings on his neck are those of the Rhino.

"Your Majesty." His voice is almost a growl. "We were expecting you."

"Bwana Amidi. Thank you for agreeing to see me."

He grunts. "One can hardly refuse a king's demand for an audience."

She sent Amidi a written message requesting to see him in private, expecting a snub given his cold reception the first time they met, but he surprised her by responding positively.

So why the death glare?

"My message was explicit that this was a request," Isa says. "You needn't have received me if you didn't wish to."

"A polite request from a king is as good as a demand, Your Majesty." Breaking eye contact, Amidi steps aside, gesturing into the house. "Please come in. There are many eyes that watch this door."

Propriety might have demanded that she apologize and leave the man alone, but Isa knows she will never win if she lets herself give up at the slightest inconvenience.

She steps inside, and Amidi closes the door behind her, leaving her standing in a hallway whose floor is so thoroughly polished she can almost see her reflection when she looks down. Taking the hint, she begins to unlace her sandals, but Amidi quickly puts a stop to it.

"That won't be necessary, Your Majesty. I will not dishonor my ancestors by having a king walk barefoot in my house. Please, follow me." He's halfway down the hall before she can protest.

She follows him past a curtained archway into a living room of grass mats and brightly colored cushions. Eight people of varying age and height are waiting for her inside, standing with their heads bowed respectfully, their hair and skin shiny with ointments. Likely they bathed and wore their best garments just for the occasion, which Isa finds at once touching and embarrassing.

Standing proudly to one side of the room, Amidi says, "Your Majesty, may I present to you my family," and goes on to introduce all eight by name.

The first thing Isa notices is that some don't have marks on their necks. Stranger still is those who do have different marks and look so dissimilar from each other it is unlikely they're related. Yet Amidi calls them his daughters and sons and brothers and aunts.

Other peculiar details catch Isa's attention. One of the younger boys has a scar sealing his right eye shut. The eldest woman has a hunted look about her. A man Amidi's age might be muttering to himself and won't lift his gaze off the floor.

"It is lovely to meet you all," Isa says once the introductions are over. "Thank you for receiving me into your home."

"You honor this house with your presence, Your Majesty," says the stout young woman in an orange caftan, introduced as Tuliza, Amidi's eldest daughter. She has a pleasant face and a mass of tight curls crowning her head so luxuriantly Isa feels a twinge of envy toward her. She must be adopted if she is indeed Bwana Amidi's daughter, since she bears the Lion's mark on her neck.

Isa finds that her interest in this family has been piqued. "The honor is mine, Bibi Tuliza," she says.

The young woman brightens like Isa has granted her a palace filled with gold and gemstones. "Oh, just Tuliza, please. I'm too young for titles."

"As you wish, Tuliza."

"You may go now," Amidi says to his family. "Do not disturb us until we are finished."

Seven of them file out of the living room obediently, leaving Isa alone with Amidi and his eldest daughter.

He gestures at a mat littered with pillows. "Please make yourself comfortable, Your Majesty. We may not have much, but this room is warded against prying ears. We may speak here without worry of being overheard."

As she complies, sitting down in Amidi's living room, it strikes Isa that this is her first glimpse into the livelihoods of the city's common folk. While she is used to lounging in rooms adorned with the finest silks, here the fabric on the cushions, clean though it is, looks faded. Her living rooms and bedchambers are always coordinated works of high-end interior design, but here the furnishings and sculptures of stone and wood were put together with no regard for color, contrast, or theme, an eclectic mix, like the family who inhabits the space.

And yet it manages to look more like a home than the impersonal and palatial rooms of the Summit. Lived in. A place where meals, laughter, and conversations are regularly shared.

Or maybe, says the cynic in her, *you're just another spoiled princess glorifying the simplicity of common life from the safety of your gilded dome. Would you enjoy living here if you had no choice?*

"Would you like something to drink, Your Majesty?" Tuliza offers, and Isa politely declines.

Tuliza goes on to settle down next to her father, who says, "My daughter is privy to all that happens within these walls. She will be joining us."

"Of course." Isa had hoped to speak with the man alone, but she won't dictate the terms of their meeting in his own house. "Your home is lovely," she says. "Thank you again for receiving me."

Unsurprisingly, the compliment fails to thaw Amidi's expression. "You probably have questions about my family. Let us get them out of the way so we may arrive at the purpose of your visit."

Tuliza gently slaps his arm, clucking her tongue in disapproval. "But you embarrass us with such discourtesy. Forgive him, Your Majesty. He may seem brusque, but there is a good man buried beneath all that brooding. Ours is a home for victims of violence against nonconformists," she explains. "He opened it in honor of his wife and young son, who were murdered during a sanctuary purge over twenty-three years ago. I myself came here as a young girl after my parents were stoned to death near our home. He pays for most of our keep with his wages from the city guard, though we receive regular donations from our sanctuary."

I'm a princess in a gilded dome, Isa thinks, suffering a surge of disgust for her own privilege and the ignorance it nurtured. *While I bathed in scented water and wore emeralds in my hair, people were being stoned to death in the same city for the crime of believing something different.*

"I have no words," Isa says. "I'm sorry for your losses. You really are a good man, Bwana Amidi."

"I neither want nor need your validation. Same goes for your pity."

"Father!" Tuliza cries.

"What? Should I be punished for speaking the truth?"

"No, but you shouldn't be rude to our royal guest!"

"It's fine," Isa cuts in. It's beginning to look like Amidi wasn't the one who accepted her request to meet. "This is your home, and I have clearly intruded."

"You're welcome here, Your Majesty," Tuliza says. "And I, too, am sorry for your recent loss. You are no less a victim of mindless cruelty than we are." She scowls at Amidi. "My father ought to remember that."

At this he turns his face away from her, dropping his gaze to the floor. He remains surly, but his voice becomes much less confrontational. "I thought I made my position clear when we last spoke, Your Majesty. Until Healer Majii agrees to support your cause, I'm not sure there's anything for us to discuss."

"I'm not here to discuss nonconformist support," Isa says. "I'm here for an unrelated matter. A personal matter."

Amidi looks up from the floor.

"Go on, Your Majesty," Tuliza says, her eyes beaming with the satisfaction of being proved right. "My father is intrigued."

They probably betted on what Isa was coming here to discuss. She doubts they guessed right.

Figuring that Amidi is the type of man who appreciates bluntness, Isa comes straight to the point. "To be perfectly frank," she says, "I seek to perform the rite of the Dazzling Tree, and I believe you're the man who can make that happen."

Two sets of eyes blink at Isa, betraying nothing of the thoughts transpiring behind them. "I'm afraid I don't know what you're talking about, Your Majesty," Amidi says, and this time Tuliza remains quiet.

Isa knew this meeting was never going to be easy, so she plows on. "There is not much to occupy the wandering mind of a princess growing up in the palace, so I kept the boredom away with books. From my studies I understand that partaking in this rite is not only a show of deep respect for the undercity and its people but also a chance to receive a boon from the Dazzling Light himself. Am I wrong?"

For the first time since she met him, Amidi smiles, but it isn't friendly. "Knowing the world through books is not the same as knowing it in fact. Books can lie or stretch the truth until it is unrecognizable."

"I'm well aware of that, Bwana Amidi. But in this instance, I believe what I read. I believe Engai is real, and I believe that you, as an elder of his sanctuary, could lead me to him if you were so inclined."

Amidi shakes his head, so clearly affronted Isa thinks he's about to kick her out of his house. "You presume to know whom my sanctuary venerates because you read a few books? And even if you were right, do you think I would acquiesce in giving you my blessing to traipse around the warrens? You, who only recently deigned to step into the undercity, and only then because your enemies left you no choice?"

"Father—" Tuliza begins.

"Be quiet!"

"I am not here to make demands, Bwana Amidi," Isa says. "I am not here to intimidate you. I am here to beg for a chance to earn your respect and maybe, just maybe, receive a blessing in my hour of need. You're free to refuse. I will leave you be, and you will not see me here again."

The words seem to allay his anger. Still, he keeps glowering. "Why should I help you? What has your kind ever done for me and mine?"

"Perhaps nothing. The same system that hurt you so many times showered me and my family with privilege, and we never complained. So you're right; you don't have to help me. And maybe we finally got what we deserved, as the orators preach in the streets. Maybe I deserved to weep over the corpses of my family and to be thrust into a war between the high mystics, my future in service to designs I cannot escape. Maybe. I don't know. All I know is that I'm here to *beg* for your help, Bwana Amidi, and not as a king or a princess but as a desperate woman."

She had meant to stand resolute against the sway of her emotions, but she has to wipe her eyes before tears can form.

Then she becomes annoyed at the amazement she sees growing on Tuliza's face, as though it shocks her to see a king display human emotion, but she realizes she might be misinterpreting the reaction when Tuliza speaks next.

"And a woman with a mask of thorns shall beseech you beneath the shadow of silence."

Isa shudders. "I beg your pardon?"

"Words from a dead sibyl, told to my father many moons ago," Tuliza explains, her voice full of awe. "We wondered what they meant at the time, but now, here is a king whose mask-crown is a painful burden, beseeching my father's help in a room warded against spies." She turns her wide-eyed gaze to Amidi. "This has to be it!"

Amidi is visibly troubled but makes a dismissive gesture. "You're reading too much into vague and unreliable divinations."

"You know I'm right," Tuliza insists. "This can't be a coincidence."

"Even if it isn't, it'd be foolish to grant her request. No one has returned safely from the rite in years."

Though Isa has no way of knowing she was the one the sibyl spoke of, she seizes upon the prophetic words. "All the more reason to let me do it. What would happen if the power sustaining the undercity were to run out?"

"That's actually becoming a real concern," Tuliza admits. "The power crystals haven't been replenished for some time."

"I am determined, Bwana Amidi," Isa presses. "I may be a king, but every step I take has been planned for me, designed to advance the machinations of the orthodoxy. Coming here is the first time I've acted solely in my own interest. Even if I fail to find the grace of Engai in the undercity, the chance to earn your respect is worth everything to me."

"I don't think you understand," Amidi says. "The journey down to Engai will almost certainly kill you. No one who's gone down there in the last several years has returned. And you won't be allowed to carry weapons or take guards. You'll have to rely solely on Engai's grace to protect you."

Isa's spirits fall as she suffers a debilitating tingle of dread at the idea of descending into the warrens of the undercity on her own. *You just said there's little you won't do for this chance,* she reminds herself. *Don't prove yourself a liar and a coward.* "Those are odds I am willing to take," she says, keeping her voice from wavering.

A heavy expression settles on Amidi's face. There is little trace of hostility in his voice now. "You realize this would be an act of apostasy, don't you? It may very well be the single most egregious act of apostasy in the kingdom's history."

"The suns bring warmth and growth to all creatures of the earth," Isa says. "The stars and comets mark the passage of time. I am a king and a child of the Mother, but even I must recognize that she is not the only force of good in the world. My father, devoted to the Mother though he was, also recognized this truth. It was why he was as tolerant of the undercity sanctuaries as the Shirika would allow him to be."

"Curbing the Shirika's bloodlust couldn't have been easy," Tuliza agrees. "I wonder if that's why they turned against him in the end."

Amidi curls his lip in a sneer. "They turned against him because they have empire in their sights and they needed a puppet who would gladly do their bidding. That's how you know they aren't gods, as they claim. They're just as flawed and greedy as the rest of us."

Tuliza gives a long-suffering sigh. "Here we go again."

"Do you know why we all bear these unsightly marks, Your Majesty?" He tugs his tunic down and lifts his chin to better expose the tattoos on his neck.

"I know the stories," Isa says, careful not to elaborate.

"Everyone blames the first headmen for disfiguring us like this, while the Shirika are seen as neutral or even reluctant participants. But it was the Shirika who orchestrated the scheme. They used the marks to strip magic away from most of the population; then they divided us against each other so we wouldn't band together against them. Why do you think they set things up so the rest of the kingdom would despise you and your people, Your Majesty? And why do you think they made sure you had no power of your own but the fact of their support?"

Isa's father wholly believed that the Shirika were divine and that their will was the will of the Mother. Isa believed this, too, once, but now she's not so sure. If they can disagree and scheme against each other, then their will cannot emanate from a common source.

"I have learned a lot about my true place in the order of things over the last few weeks," she says. "That's one of the reasons I'm here."

For the longest time Amidi considers her like he's trying to see through her skin to the substance beneath. Isa endures the stare without flinching from it.

At last he sighs. "Your Majesty, I must remain steadfast in my earlier position. I cannot offer you the support of the nonconformist community until you have won the trust of the independents. That said, when the Sibyl Underground spoke to me of this moment, though she did not tell me what decision to make, she implied that I would be better served by letting go of my grievances. So even against my better judgment, I will help you in the matter you have come for today."

Tuliza pats Amidi gently on the arm. "A wise decision, Father."

Pressure releases from some cavity in Isa's chest, and she feels the urge to hug the man. "I cannot express my gratitude enough, Bwana Amidi. I have not known the taste of hope in a long while."

"Do not thank me just yet," he cautions. "The rite will be ten days from now. If you're still determined, then you will descend to meet whatever fate awaits you in the undercity. But it's more than likely you won't return from your journey, so I suggest you put your affairs in order."

"We will pray to the Dazzling Light for your success," Tuliza says, and despite her warmth and encouragement, Isa feels a shiver climbing down her spine.

I will walk the depths of the undercity on my own. I could die there, and it would be all over for me and my people.

"I thank you, Tuliza. I have known you for a short while, but I already consider you a friend." To Bwana Amidi, she says, "A week from now, I will be ready."

14: Musalodi

Skytown

In the afterglow of yet another sumptuous dinner in the garden, Salo decides it's time to tell his friends just how much trouble he's about to invite into their lives.

"I have a few things I need to discuss with you," he says. "You all know I met with someone mysterious in the city earlier today, and yesterday I spoke to the queen. You've probably been curious about what was discussed, and I'm sorry for keeping it from you until now, but I wanted to make sense of it first."

Sitting across the dinner table, Tuk sticks a toothpick into his mouth and leans back into his chair. "No harm done," he says. "Just spit it out already."

Where to even begin? "I'll start with my conversation with the queen. Long story short, she's concerned about the regent's expansionist intentions, and . . . well, to put it bluntly, she wants me to do something about it. Stop him before he gets started, so to speak."

Both Tuk and Ilapara gawk at him. "You're joking," Ilapara says.

"I wish I was. Alinata can probably confirm it for you. I'm sure she already knows."

The Asazi runs a finger over the rim of her empty wineglass. Ilapara looks at her, then back at Salo, her mouth agape. "How the devil are you supposed to do that?"

Salo takes a second to think about how to best phrase the queen's command. "Basically? Find out what his enemies are planning and see if I can't help them along."

"That's an awfully, *awfully* vague plan, Salo," Tuk says. "Not to mention treacherously dangerous. As in you-could-lose-your-head-for-this dangerous."

"It's not a plan, more like the sketch of one. And I admit, I wasn't sure how I'd begin to fill it out until this afternoon."

"The mysterious meeting," Ilapara says, and Salo nods.

He tells them about his meeting with the king's handmaiden. He can still remember the frisson he felt when he first glimpsed her sitting alone by the pond. A handmaiden, she said, a mere servant, and yet she spoke with an irresistible authority, her voice holding him in place even when he wanted to get up and flee as fast as possible from her dangerous plans.

"You aren't actually considering this, are you?" Tuk says. "The Archives are well guarded, Salo. Breaking their rules would only get you into trouble."

"I agree," Ilapara says. "I think you should stay out of this. The Red Temple isn't going anywhere, and neither are you. It's better to just wait out the power struggle, then finish your pilgrimage after the dust settles."

Salo gives a tired sigh. "Don't you see? This isn't just about the Red Temple anymore. I have to at least try to give the queen what she wants, or she'll never let me go back home."

"You're still talking about stealing from a heavily warded stronghold," Tuk says. "How are you going to pull that off?"

Salo extracts a golden chain from the leather pouch on his hip and tosses it onto the table. It jangles as it settles, catching everyone's attention with its polished sheen. The chain holds a conspicuous pendant set with a large crimson gemstone that glitters in the twilight. "With this," he says.

While Alinata eyes the necklace with unconcealed curiosity and Ilapara squints at it with a dubious expression, Tuk's skin grows pale. He leans forward to snatch the pendant from the table.

Speechlessly he studies it, his expression blank, and then his eyes flick up to Salo. They have darkened to the color of tar. *"Where did you get this?"* he asks, subvocalizing his question and sending it along their newly forged mental bond.

His alarm confirms Salo's suspicions about it. "A gift from the king's handmaiden, as it happens," Salo says out loud, choosing not to leave the others out of the discussion.

"But *where* did she get it?" Tuk asks, aloud this time, his strident voice implying that the answer is a matter of life and death.

"I have no idea."

Bemused, Ilapara leans toward Tuk to get a closer look at the necklace. "All I see is a chain with a large ruby. What am I missing?"

"It's Higher technology, isn't it?" Salo says, watching Tuk.

The young man turns the gemstone over in his hands, visibly perturbed. "I can't believe my eyes, but this is a metaformic crystal."

Salo has never heard of that term. When he first saw the pendant cradled in its box, he thought it was some kind of talisman, like his red steel serpent, but he's since recognized that it's so much more.

"Will someone please start making sense?" Ilapara says.

"It's a ciphermetric device, Ilapara," Tuk says sharply.

She blinks at him, unamused.

"It's a device like Salo's talisman," he elaborates, "except it hosts a metaform within its lattices, an arcane mind born of Red magic."

"Oh, it's a lot more powerful than a talisman," Salo interjects. "I haven't figured out its secrets yet, but I can tell you that much."

"How interesting," Alinata remarks.

"This shouldn't be here," Tuk says. "You don't just find these things lying around. Not in the Enclave, and certainly not here in the Redlands. First, everyone starts walking around with charmed fabrics, then this? It's beginning to look like someone here is messing with Higher technology, which, if true, would be bad news for everyone."

"Why, though?" Alinata asks. "Why does this upset you so much?"

"Because if someone is doing this, Alinata, then they have an agenda, and whatever it is can't be good. Higher technology appearing in Yonte Saire right when there's talk of a resurgent Ascendancy? Can't be a coincidence."

Ilapara regards Tuk through slit eyes. "You gave your moonfire gauntlet to the Tuanu," she points out. "Are you sure *you* didn't drop this metaform or whatever when you passed through the city last time?"

Tuk makes a frustrated noise. "Come now, Ilapara. The gauntlet was a considered choice. I knew the Tuanu would only use it to defend themselves. They won't be sharing it with anyone else." He wags the golden chain in his hand like it's sinned against nature. "And I certainly didn't come with one of these. Like I said, you don't just find them lying around. The Enclave keeps a registry of every metaform in existence and has strict rules about who can own one and who can't. If you're unauthorized and you have *this* in your possession, you'll be hunted down with extreme prejudice. I couldn't have arrived with one even if I wanted to."

Alinata's eyes fall onto the pendant again, shining with deeper interest. "Is it really that powerful?"

"Let me put it this way," Tuk says. "If it ever came to light that *this* ended up here of all places, to say the Enclave would be horrified would be putting things quite mildly."

Pensive silence descends on the table, spooling around the gemstone. Still, Salo decides that he has more pressing problems right now.

"If the Enclave wants their artifact back, they're welcome to come and get it," he says. "In the meantime, I'm going to use it to help the king and hopefully put a stop to Kola Saai so I can maybe get away from this nightmare while we're all still alive."

Ilapara hums in agreement. "I won't argue with that last part, but I still don't see how the amulet is supposed to help you."

"The king's handmaiden implied that it can conceal its power and slip past the security wards in place at the Archives," Salo says. "I just have to figure out how to get it to do that, as well as how to surreptitiously copy dozens of spells. I guess I'll have to spend a couple of days playing around with it; then I'll go to the Archives. Thoughts?"

He looks pointedly at Alinata, the queen's eyes and ears. He's sure every word they've spoken will be relayed back to Her Majesty by sunrise tomorrow.

Put on the spot, the Asazi presses her lips together in displeasure. "It's in our interest to stop Kola Saai and his ambitions, and helping the king is a step in that direction, so I say go ahead. I do advise you to be cautious, however. The magic of that crystal might be powerful, but it's unfamiliar to you. Know what you're doing."

"What she said, I guess," Ilapara says.

Tuk, on the other hand, shakes his head yet again. He lets out a long sigh, giving the chain back. "I won't tell you what to do. Just know your limits, all right? You're obviously a talented mystic, but there are things even you can't do. Don't let yourself forget that."

He doesn't attempt to experiment on the gemstone until much later that night, when he is alone in his study, at his desk. The air is pleasantly cool, so he's left the doors leading out into the gardens open. Only a single lamp is active in the room, releasing its enchanted Mirror light from within a yellow crystal mounted on the wall behind him.

He feels a stirring of excitement as he rubs his thumb over the facets on the crimson jewel. He can sense it brimming with enchantments and reserves of raw essence. To his cosmic shards he might as well be holding a piece of the moon itself.

This sense of unrestrained power is all he's gotten from the gemstone, though. He can feel it trying to communicate with him, but it's as if he's gazing into a pond of cloudy water, knowing something lurks beneath the surface and yet lacking the faculties to see it.

"Like we're speaking different languages," he mutters, and as soon as the words come out of his mouth, he senses that yes, this is exactly the problem. "So how do I get you to understand me?"

He decides to test the waters with his talisman. He brings it closer to the chain, and at his command the red steel serpent uncoils from his left wrist, lifting its head so that it faces the gemstone. Its crystalline eyes flash with lights that pierce the stone, and Salo waits while it conducts its analysis, sensing that the results won't make things any clearer, but at least it'll be a start.

Except the talisman starts to writhe uncontrollably on his wrist. At first, he watches, dumbfounded; then he feels his mental connection to the talisman growing weaker, and he starts to panic. He drops the gem and bolts away from the table to put some distance between the two artifacts, but the serpent continues to thrash about as though it has been cut in two. Its coils loosen completely, and it falls off his wrist to the carpeted floor, stilled.

He makes a strangled sound in his throat. His talisman once belonged to his mother. It holds a record of every project he's ever worked on, including the prose of his Axiom. It's his only link to home.

He crouches down to pick it up, praying to the moon to be merciful, but the talisman remains limp in his hands, eyes inactive. "No, no, *no*! Please . . ."

He prods it with his mind but comes up empty. Its core has been erased of every enchantment that makes it a talisman. It might as well be a lump of rock.

Salo almost bites his tongue off. *How could I be so stupid? How am I supposed to talk to the queen now? How will she tell me when it's time to go back home?* He almost shrieks at the top of his voice.

No, he tells himself, keeping his temper under control. *Don't panic. Surely whatever happened can be undone. You just have to figure out how.*

The amulet is still where he left it on the table. He strides over and picks it up, giving it the evil eye. Outside, gentle rains begin to pitter-patter on the roof, pouring down the glass windows in rivulets.

He settles back behind his desk and activates his shards, trying hard to get a sense of what might be going on within the crystal, but he gets nothing. Where a moment ago, the gemstone felt as though it would burst with essence at the slightest touch, now even that sensation has evaporated, leaving only a faint, rhythmic hum. If the gemstone were a pond of cloudy water before, now it has become an ocean.

This is pointless.

Eventually Salo gives up and retires to his chamber, thinking he might figure out a solution after getting some sleep. He lies on his bed, clutching the dead talisman in one hand and the gemstone in the other, fuming silently at his foolishness. Then his eyes gradually grow heavy, and he gives in to the peace of sleep.

When next he opens his eyes, the world has become an infinite white expanse where the ground and sky appear one and the same. The whiteness is all-pervasive, and there are no shadows, though Salo can't see any obvious light source.

Blocks of electrified glass populate the environment, zipping through the air. A colorful nebula of glowing dust can be seen rising toward one horizon.

His gaze is drawn to the nebula and the presence lurking inside, slithering within the luminous interior. He thinks he glimpses a giant pair of eyes watching him when a bolt of lightning arcs out of the gaseous cloud and spreads across the white sky in a fractal pattern. Thunder rumbles across the expanse like a rolling drum.

He stands speechless, blinking at the nebula, then around himself, trying to figure out where he is and how he got there. Then a figure emerges from the whiteness, and his heart thuds when it resolves into a wickedly handsome young man wearing nothing but a bloodred loincloth.

"Niko?" Salo says, his voice a disbelieving whisper.

As always, Aneniko is the picture of strength and confidence, the quintessential vision of a Yerezi man. At first, he seems surprised, and then he beams as he closes the distance between them. "Salo? Is that you?"

How? Salo wonders. *How are you here, wherever "here" is?*

Before he knows what's happening, Niko has swept him into a crushing embrace. His skin feels hot, their bare chests pressed so close together Salo thinks he can feel the other man's heartbeat trying to drown out his own.

"By Ama. It really is you." Niko pulls back just enough to look Salo in the face, his eyes shining with awe and wonder and relief and something Salo desperately hopes he isn't imagining. "I've missed you so much."

Caught in Niko's strong arms, Salo can barely breathe. "You have?"

"Terribly." Niko's smile is beatific. He lifts a hand to gently caress Salo's cheek. "I should have never let you go alone. I should have taken your blessing and come with you."

Salo shivers at the touch, the sweet words making him light headed. Blood rushes to his every extremity until he feels like he could float. *Is this really happening?* He looks into Niko's eyes. "I don't understand."

"I was a coward, Salo," Niko says. "Watching you ride away was the hardest thing I've ever done. I wanted to come after you, but I was afraid of what people would say. It was stupid of me, and I'm sorry."

This. If this moment lingered for the rest of eternity, if Niko held him like this forever, if he leaned a little closer and—

Wait. Stop. Something doesn't make sense.

"How can you be here?" Salo wonders out loud.

Niko had begun to lean in, but now he stops, a puzzled frown creasing his forehead. "I don't know. Does it matter?"

"You're not real, are you," Salo realizes, the heat and euphoria that had swept him away turning to cold sludge in his gut. "You're a dream, telling me what I want to hear."

Salo has dreamed about Niko before. He has dreamed about Niko *a lot*. It hasn't ever felt this real, though. And yet it can't be real.

Once again, he looks up into the distant nebula dominating the white sky, where lightning continues to shoot out in mysterious patterns. When the slithering presence within is briefly illuminated and he sees the vague shape of a massive serpentine head, he begins to understand what's happening.

"This is a construct," he says. "The metaform cannibalized my talisman and has figured out how to communicate with me." He looks back at Niko. "But how are you here? You don't have a talisman, and even if you did, you can't use it to communicate because you're not a mystic."

"I don't know what any of that means," Niko says, so earnest and sincere Salo almost believes him. "I'm just happy we're together."

How easy it would be to stay here and indulge in this beautiful dream. How perfectly tantalizing.

"But that's the thing, isn't it?" Salo says, looking into Niko's lovely brown eyes. "We're not together, because the real you never wanted me."

Even though it feels like ripping open an old wound, he steps out of Niko's arms, a wave of sorrow sweeping over his being and surprising him with its force. He turns away from the hurt on Niko's face.

"Salo, have I upset you?"

"Goodbye, Niko. You can't be here anymore." And because Salo has uttered the words, they become true. Niko disappears in a white haze, still looking at Salo with longing and confusion in his eyes.

Dear Ama, I'm pathetic. Salo faces the colorful cloud in the sky, his sorrow heating up into anger. "My talisman was important to me," he shouts. "You stripped its memory apart and destroyed it."

The presence within makes the nebula ripple with its movement, its crystalline snake eyes shining briefly in the glow of a lightning flash. Salo also catches the glint of red scales. *"Deconstructing the inferior cipher core was necessary to acquire the vocabulary to communicate with the master."*

The words fill the air around him, seeping through his skin and directly into his mind, almost like telepathic communication with his talisman.

"You didn't have my permission," he says.

Once again, the metaform's response isn't spoken but understood. *"The master's desire to communicate with this metaform was interpreted as permission."*

"There was a lot of important information stored inside my talisman. Things I needed. What am I supposed to do now?"

"This metaform copied and stored all data from the inferior cipher core. This metaform is also capable of replicating all the functionalities of the inferior cipher core."

The presence might convey information telepathically like his talisman, but it feels lucid and purposeful, and that makes Salo uncomfortable.

He looks around at the networks of electric blocks moving through the air all around him and understands what the metaform has said. Each of these blocks is a memory, some copied over from the talisman, others native to the construct.

That still doesn't explain why Niko's ghost made an appearance. "Why did you poke through my memories and use them against me? You had no right."

"The master controls all manifestations within the construct."

"Are you saying I *wanted* you to conjure a fake Niko to fawn over me?"

"This metaform cannot speculate on the master's intentions."

Salo seethes with fury and shame, though he's not sure what upsets him more—that the Niko who was affectionate with him wasn't real or that this artifact could read him so well as to know his deepest desires.

"Are you conscious?" he asks.

"This metaform is neither sentient nor self-aware."

That's a relief. No reason to be ashamed if it can't judge him. "What are you capable of?" he asks, and immediately regrets it.

Every electrified block in the sky, thousands of them perhaps, comes to a complete stop. Then a tidal wave of information floods into his mind with enough force to bring him crashing to the ground. He curls into himself with his palms pressed against his ears, groaning in pain. "Stop!" he shouts.

At once the deluge eases, and his mind, which had become so crowded he couldn't hear his own thoughts, clears up again.

"What the devil just happened?"

"Apologies. This metaform performed an instantaneous data insertion into the master's short-term memory, but it seems the new vocabulary is ill suited for high-speed transference to a human mind."

Salo grits his teeth. "How about from now on, you give me your answers in packages I can tolerate."

"This metaform will henceforth avoid performing data insertions unless instructed otherwise."

Perhaps it isn't so intelligent after all. Still feeling a little off balance, Salo picks himself up off the white floor and into a seated position, stretching his legs out in front of him and leaning back onto his palms. The nebula is still sparkling with lightning, briefly illuminating the shape of a large snake moving within, while the blocks in the sky are in motion again.

He's still upset about the loss of his talisman, but a part of him appreciates that the metaform adopted its serpentine appearance. *Maybe I shouldn't think of it as completely gone,* he muses. *Maybe it's simply part of a greater whole now.*

"Explain why I'd ever want you 'inserting' anything into my short-term memory."

"Instantaneous data insertions would allow the master to quickly analyze large sets of information and choose which portions to retain in his long-term memory before his short-term memory is purged."

"That actually sounds useful," Salo admits. "But not if it'll knock me off my feet every time, so let's avoid it for now."

"Understood."

"How about security?" he says. "How do I make sure no one else but me can make use of you and access your memory?"

"This metaform paired with the master upon activation. No other entity can access its memory or functionality without his permission."

"Just so we're clear, am *I* your master?"

"Affirmative."

"How do I know you're not lying to me? How do I know you aren't already loaded with prose designed to spy on me and what I do here?"

"This metaform is incapable of deceiving its master. This metaform is also designed to protect itself from malicious prose."

"But of course, you'd say that."

The metaform remains silent. Perhaps it was not designed to respond to sarcasm.

Salo looks around the barren expanse. "Can I change the environment to look however I want it to?"

In answer, some of the electric blocks in the sky change course and approach, arranging themselves in front of him. Visually, there's nothing to tell them apart from each other, but in this construct, sight is merely superficial. Beneath it, everything is prose and ciphers. Salo understands just by looking at the selection of blocks that they represent the tool set with which he can shape the construct, a more intricate tool set than his talisman could have provided him.

He whistles, impressed. He could transform this expanse into a replica of his old workshop or a meadow as stunning as the queen's golden plain. He could envision something else entirely. So many possibilities. Sadly, they will have to wait.

What's important right now is to find something that will help him in the Pattern Archives. "How do I go about masking your nature from those who might detect you?"

"A simple command will suffice."

That will make life easier. "How about capturing visual information from the real world and storing it here?"

In response, the blocks hovering in front of him disperse, and a different set of blocks takes their place, each one offering a unique way to collect and store visual information.

"I'll need to know exactly how they each work."

Thorns of lightning radiate away from the nebula, the air around Salo becoming charged with knowledge that could explode into his mind like a flooded river bursting its banks. But this time the metaform keeps the tide at bay. *"The functions will take some time to explain."*

It might be useful to investigate these data insertions and see if he can't lessen the negative effects. The utility of quickly absorbing large amounts of information would be endless. But that will have to be a problem for another time. "Before we get started, what are you called?"

"This metaform has no name but that which the master gives it."

Salo takes a moment to think of an appropriate name. He never felt the need to name his talisman, since he saw it as little more than a tool. But this new entity, even though it claims to be nonsentient, has a voice, and it answers his questions like it can reason. A name seems inescapable, if only to make it seem less alien. "Then I shall call you Ziyo, short for Owaziyo, for you are wise and know many things."

The boom of thunder reverberates across the environment before the metaform replies. *"This metaform will now respond to the name Ziyo."*

"All right, Ziyo. Let's see what you can do."

◆　◆　◆

Two days later, early in the morning, Salo bathes and gets a haircut in preparation for his visit to the Pattern Archives in Midtown.

He dresses appropriately, wearing new linens and coppers and a deep-blue blanket cloak with silvery cogs that spin. A thin copper band sits on his head, and a golden chain rests around his neck, set with a crimson jewel most people will mistake for a large, expensive ruby. He looks at himself in the mirror and is satisfied with his appearance.

There's a hint of approval in Ruma's eyes when they bid each other farewell in the foyer. Tuk and Ilapara are already waiting for him by their rented carriage; they smile teasingly as he approaches.

"You're starting to take longer than I do when you dress," Ilapara remarks.

"Leave him alone," Tuk says. "Good looks are hard to maintain."

Salo rolls his eyes, entering the carriage. He's paid both of them more than enough money to take care of any clothing-related issues, but for some reason they both insist on sticking to what they know whenever they head out.

As the carriage rolls down Skytown, Ilapara, sitting across from Salo and Tuk, acquires a mischievous expression. "I'm surprised you found the time to leave the residence, Tuksaad," she says. "What with you and Alinata being so . . . busy of late."

Tuk's eyes turn brilliant green. "Do I detect a note of disapproval in your voice, Ilapara? Or is that jealousy?"

"Oh, please. You're not my type. You're too short, too pretty."

"Nonsense," Tuk says. "I'm everyone's type if I want to be, and I'm just the right amount of pretty."

Salo looks between them. "What are you two talking about?"

"Only what's been right in front of your eyes this whole time," Ilapara says casually, and Salo has to think for a second before it finally hits him.

He gapes. "You mean, they've been . . ."

Amusement sparkles in Ilapara's eyes. "Yes."

"Since when?"

"Probably since the day we got here."

Salo gawks at Tuk, who shrugs. "I'm young, handsome, and virile, and I won't be shamed for enjoying it."

"But Alinata is an Asazi," Salo says.

"What the devil is that supposed to mean?" Ilapara says.

"I'm only saying that . . . aren't Asazi supposed to be . . ." He stops. Words. Why are they suddenly so difficult to speak? "Are you planning on marrying her?" he asks Tuk, who blanches almost comically.

"My goodness, no."

"And . . . she knows this?"

"Of course! We're just having fun. There's nothing more to it."

Salo moves his lips but finds himself speechless, which makes Ilapara snort with laughter.

"By Ama, you're such a traditionalist."

"No, I'm not!" Salo protests. "I'm quite untraditional, as a matter of fact."

"Look at your face, Salo. You're scandalized."

"I've just . . . you know what? Never mind. Your bodies are your own, and you're both old enough to know what you're doing."

Salo is grateful when they speak no more of it, but he can't help the vague feelings of discontentment that well up inside him. He doesn't identify the cause until the carriage stops at a crossroads and he sees, out the window, two men holding hands as they walk down the street. They stop by a vendor selling trinkets on the sidewalk and appear to have a lighthearted debate about what to buy. Maybe they tease each other, then they laugh, and one leans forward to kiss the other on the lips.

To Salo's surprise, the world keeps spinning. No one stops to gawk.

And that's the thing about this city, isn't it? Here a woman can have a wife, men can practice magic and hold hands in the streets, and it's nothing to whisper about.

Why was I denied that? Why couldn't I be with Niko in that way and have it mean nothing to everyone else? Or . . . maybe even be celebrated?

The carriage arrives at their destination just minutes later. From outside, the Pattern Archives are a three-story building with a glass-paneled atrium and a courtyard entrance. Only as they walk through the doors do they realize that there's more to the structure than meets the eye.

Sunlight floods in through the glass roof and scatters on the tiled floors, which literally glitter with precious metals. Actual moongold was glazed into the tiles in elaborate designs.

"This is so wrong," Ilapara says, glowering at the floor like it has personally offended her. "I should not have to work hard for something others use to pave floors."

The entrance hall flows naturally toward an ebony desk of the finest craftsmanship. Behind it sits a mystic in immaculate white robes; he's in the middle of writing when Salo spots him, but he looks up and smiles brightly when they approach.

"Mother's grace, visitors. Welcome to the Pattern Archives. How may I help you?"

Given his experience with Mosi and Ewa Akili, Salo is rather taken aback by this mystic's bubbly attitude.

"Ama's grace, Red-kin," he says, looking around the opulent surroundings before resettling his gaze onto the Akili. Or could this be a Msani—a member of the artisan class? But the Msani wear orange and bronze, so this mystic is probably a scholar. Akili it is. "I'm here to purchase access to your spell archives, honored Akili."

"Wonderful! Do you have a bank vault in this city by any chance?"

"I do."

"Then this will be straightforward." The Akili, Salo presumes, gestures behind him, where a complex arrangement of patterns stands out in relief on the wall. "Please cast your Seal over here. The moment you do, this amount will be charged to your vault." He pushes a piece of paper across the table, tapping it with a finger. "Your Seal will then be active on those doors over there for exactly ten days." He points to the two heavy-looking doors down a passage to the right of the desk. "The good news: You may come and go as you please during those ten days, even at night. You may also study any of our spell prototypes for as long as you wish, for as many times as you wish."

"All right," Salo says, wondering what a spell prototype is. "And the bad news?"

"Here we call it the not-so-good news," the Akili corrects him. "Unfortunately, no prototype can leave the Archives. In addition, you may not produce copies of our prototypes in any way, shape, or form, at any time. Attempts to violate these rules will result in immediate and permanent expulsion from the Archives and prosecution by the House of Law. There will also be no refunds of any fees paid. Questions?"

The amulet around Salo's neck begins to feel heavy. He narrowly avoids gulping. "That's clear enough, I suppose." He picks up the piece of paper the Akili pushed over to him and blinks, then shows it to Tuk and Ilapara. "I can't make sense of this amount," he says, speaking to them in Sirezi.

Ilapara's eyes bulge at the figure. Tuk whistles, shaking his head. "My goodness. Let's just say it's a fortune and leave it at that."

"Can I even afford it?"

"Oh, sure," Tuk says confidently. "It's a lot, but it'll hardly make a dent in your vault."

"Exactly how much is in there?" Ilapara wonders out loud.

"Too much," Tuk tells her.

Salo studies the paper again. "So I just cast my Seal over there, and that's it?" he asks the Akili.

"Once the transaction completes, yes. That'll be it."

Salo goes ahead and activates his shards, flicking his staff toward the patterns carved on the wall. A vision of shifting geometric shapes appears in the air in front of the patterns, subtly morphing into a crystalline cube spinning rapidly beneath a strobing red star. The Seal's hypnotic magic will tell anyone who looks at it of its owner: a mystic born to a great house of leopards.

The Seal interfaces with whatever sorcery is hidden in the carved patterns, and Salo feels the sensation of being watched, evaluated. Beyond this, he can't tell exactly what's going on.

While the Akili waits silently for the process to complete itself, Ilapara considers the mirage with a troubled expression. "This looks familiar," she says and doesn't have to explain why. She saw something similar in the Pavilion of Discovery, when the Forms rearranged themselves to look like Salo's Seal.

"These things are awesome," Tuk says, not picking up on her mood. "We don't get them where I come from. Did you design it, or did it just happen?"

"It sort of just happens," Salo replies. "But it's somewhat determined by your Axiom and the way you see yourself, I think."

"The Dark Sun has a literal black sun as his Seal," Ilapara says, her voice haunted. "Horrific."

Salo shivers with half-repressed memories. "If I had that kind of Seal, I don't think I'd ever cast it."

The patterns on the wall finally glow with a reddish light, and the Akili smiles. "Thank you, honored patron. All funds have been paid, and I will have proof of payment by the time you leave."

Salo banishes his Seal, skeptical that his entrance could be so simple. "Thank you, Red-kin."

"I can't believe you just paid that much money for something," Ilapara mumbles behind him, earning a glance from the Akili, almost as though he understands her.

"I'm afraid your companions will have to wait here," the Akili says. "Only patrons are allowed inside."

"Of course." Salo glances hesitantly at his friends.

"I'm sure we'll find a way to entertain ourselves," Tuk says.

"I might be a while."

"It's a big city," Ilapara says.

He'd hoped he wouldn't have to commit a crime on his own. "I guess I'll see you later then."

They bid each other goodbye, and Salo sucks at the gap between his teeth as he watches them go.

"Do you have any magical artifacts in your possession?" the Akili asks, drawing his attention.

"My staff," Salo says and lifts it.

The Akili inspects the staff, then flicks his gaze over Salo, a hint of surprise in his expression. "Is that all?"

"Yes. Will that be a problem?"

"Not at all, honored patron." The Akili directs Salo down the hallway toward the forbidding doors. "Cast your Seal on the doors to open them. The wards will detect any artifacts with prohibited enchantments; if the doors don't open, it means you're carrying something that can't go inside. Should that happen, you can leave whatever it is here with me and collect it when you leave."

"Understood." His heart thumping rapidly inside his chest, Salo walks toward the doors, where he casts his Seal yet again. He senses currents of magic rippling all around the doors, promising a nasty reward for anyone foolish enough to try breaking in or stealing something from inside.

For a while, the red star winks at him from above its spinning cube, and he begins to wonder if the promise of the metaform was a lie. Then the Seal disappears, and a loud clanking sound reverberates across the hall as the doors unlock and then swing open on silent hinges.

Breathing out in relief, he walks through the doors.

More ostentatious displays of wealth await in the hall beyond—winged statues hovering above their plinths, a shallow ornamental pool with water lilies from the botanical gardens, murals encrusted with gemstones.

And it turns out, as he suspected, that there really is much more to the Pattern Archives than meets the eye. Most of the structure is belowground.

He quickly learns that the Archives are housed in seven cavernous subterranean chambers: one for each discipline of Red magic and another much larger chamber for multidisciplinary spells. Patterned carpets, expensive furniture, and plush upholstery give each chamber a unique flair. Floating crystals provide lighting between the shelves. He should be used to the wonders of this city by now, but Salo is still astounded by what he sees as he tours the library, that such vastness and grandness could exist belowground.

And the number of shelves! There are so many shelves each chamber has multiple balconies just to accommodate them all. And instead of books, they hold thin rectangular plates of aerosteel stacked horizontally in grooves for easy retrieval. From a placard mounted on a wall, he deduces that these plates are the so-called prototypes the Akili spoke of.

In each chamber he visits, Salo notices a few people ambling along the aisles, perusing the seemingly endless selection of spell prototypes. Others are lounging in strategically placed alcoves or at tables, deep in the process of memorizing the patterns engraved on the plates they've chosen. Among them are a number of students from the House of Forms in their white or orange robes, but some of the patrons are clearly foreign.

He decides to begin with the Void craft archive. First, he takes a stroll around the chamber to familiarize himself with how the spells have been shelved. He spots only one other person in the chamber, ensconced in an alcove on the main floor, too busy studying the patterns of a prototype to notice him.

It seems the spells have been sorted into multiple categories, as one would expect of Void craft, including kinetics, metamorphosis, and time magic, with each prototype tagged and color coded to indicate casting difficulty. A spell for a simple static barrier has been marked with a white tag, while a sound-dampening field is marked yellow. There is a spell for small-scale telekinesis designed to manipulate fluids, marked orange, and a spell for conjuring complex shapes of pliable force, marked red.

The black tags are the fewest. One of them is attached to a spell that can shape the Void into pockets of space in which time moves at a different speed than the rest of the world. Another is attached to a spell for storing items in the metadimension. Yet another to a spell for entangling one's mind and body with those of a beast for shape-shifting.

So. Many. Spells.

On the highest balcony with a wide view of the chamber, Salo looks out at the endless shelves and sighs, daunted by the sheer number of spells. The vaulted ceiling and lofty walls seem to taunt him with all the knowledge they contain. Ten days? It would take him a lifetime to learn even a fraction of what's in this chamber alone. Ten days is barely enough to learn even one spell.

You're not here for yourself, a voice inside his head reminds him. *You came here to do a job.*

"Might as well get it over with," he mutters and heads back down to the main floor.

The list Andaiye gave him includes several spells housed in this archive. After only a minute of searching, he finds the first one marked by an orange tag, a spell of thin force fields supposedly ideal for performing surgical incisions and keeping them pried open while the healer works on the patient. He pulls the plate out of its groove and takes his time marveling at the maze of ciphers engraved across its face.

Such lovely prose. He knows little about the art of healing, but he can tell that a lesser spell architect might have filled more than several plates with ciphers just to achieve a spell with the same effects. These people managed to fit everything onto one plate. And being so lean, it will be energy efficient. Used together with a good Axiom, this advantage would only be amplified.

Time to get to work.

Salo awakens his crimson jewel with a thought, sending part of his awareness into the construct so that he's at once standing in a chamber of the Pattern Archives as well as sitting cross-legged in a white expanse while a great crimson serpent watches him from within a glowing cloud.

During his experiments in the construct, he played around with the metaform's ability to capture and store visual information, adjusting its parameters until he found a method subtle enough for his purposes in the Archives.

While the version of himself in the real world continues to study the plate like it has engrossed him, the version in the construct utters a command.

"Ziyo, capture an image of this plate using the low-power settings I gave you. Tag it with a bar of orange light."

"Acknowledged," Ziyo replies. A silent heartbeat elapses; then it says, *"Scan complete."*

And there, hovering in the construct in front of Salo, is a perfect copy of the prototype, and as per his instructions, a bar of orange light glows along one edge of the plate.

The version of him seated there reaches for it, and even though he knows what to expect, he's still shocked at just how real the copy feels in his hands. The metaform captured every detail about it—weight, texture, color—so that holding it in the construct is nearly indistinguishable from holding it out in the real world.

No wonder Tuk was so disturbed when he saw the amulet. Such power could be dangerous in the wrong hands.

Salo looks around, partly expecting an Akili to leap out of the shadows and accuse him of theft. The dim crystal light illuminating the aisle flickers, but he remains alone.

It really shouldn't be this easy. He came expecting to find spell books similar to those his people use, where he would have to copy each spell one tedious page at a time while trying not to look suspicious. He even practiced on books back at his Skytown residence. He expected to spend at least five minutes per spell.

It took him less than a second to capture this prototype.

His blood runs cold as an insane idea slithers out of some shadowy corner of his mind.

You are too curious for your own good, he can almost hear his father say.

But it might not even be possible, he says to the voice. *I only want to conduct a little test. That's all.*

He replaces the spell prototype he just copied and picks up the one beneath it, pretending to be interested. In the construct, he says, *"Highest balcony. First shelf to the left. Prototype in the upper left corner. Can you see it from here?"*

"Affirmative," Ziyo replies.

That particular shelf is behind him and on a different floor, with at least a dozen other shelves standing between them. Yet the metaform can see it.

Salo's heart skips a beat. *"Go ahead and scan the prototype for me like you did the other one."*

Less than a second later, another aerosteel plate pops into existence in the construct, floating in the air in front of his seated form. A white bar of light glows along its edge. It's the spell for static barriers he saw earlier.

"Scan complete," says the metaform.

Keeping a lid on his excitement for now, Salo says, *"Now do the one beneath it."*

Another plate appears, also marked with a white bar. *"Scan complete."*

"Do the next three."

In the space of a breath, three more plates appear. *"Scan complete."*

"The next ten," Salo says, and this time the metaform takes several seconds to respond, but the result is the same: ten more plates appear in the construct, hovering in the air in front of Salo with their faces turned toward him, one edge glowing with a bar of colored light.

Out in the real world, he covers his mouth to smother a giddy laugh. Could he really do this? And even if he can, should he really?

It's theft, says the rational part of him.

But I paid to be here, says the rest of him.

You're only supposed to copy the spells on the list.

Ignoring his better judgment, Salo forges ahead. *"Can you arrange these copies exactly how they are arranged in the world?"*

"Affirmative," Ziyo responds, and Salo watches as the plates reorient themselves and fly away, one moving to hover just in front of him while the other fifteen stack themselves on top of each other some distance away.

He was wondering what shape he would give to his construct. Now he thinks he knows.

"How fast can you make a copy of every prototype in this chamber?"

"Calculating." Ziyo's glowing nebula sputters out lightning, and thunder rumbles across the construct. *"With full resource allocation to the task, approximately fifty-three minutes."*

A gamble with a massive penalty for failure, but Salo reminds himself he's no stranger to such risk. *"Go ahead and begin,"* he says, and the metaform complies.

15: The Enchantress

Skytown

The Enchantress stands quietly by her husband's right side in a grand hall of the Summit, where eleven thrones are arranged in a circle in mimicry of the sacred Meeting Places. Only four headmen are present in the hall, seated on their thrones. The other six, who returned home to their provinces, are represented by proxies. Everyone has been listening for the past several minutes as the newly crowned Kestrel bickers with the frustrated herald over who's culpable for the assassination at the New Year's Feast.

"Blood for blood!" shouts the new Kestrel, his avian eyes glowing with the scarlet fire of a redhawk. He is young—it has not been two comets since he left the Sentinels—and the mask hasn't quite settled onto his face, but he speaks before the headmen without faltering or mincing his words. "I don't care that the arrow wasn't meant for my father. The Saires killed him, and there will be retribution."

The herald, seated on one of the thrones on behalf of the king in hiding, looks at the verge of pulling out his own hair. "He was our ally, for the Mother's sake! What would we gain from his death? This is obviously a setup!"

"How is it a setup?" the young headman demands. "Did a Saire not fire the arrow that killed my father?"

"Even if he did, you cannot condemn us all for the actions of one madman. The Royal Guard was bewitched into killing their own king. Can you say the same didn't happen here?"

"I don't care," the Kestrel says mulishly. "All I know is that a Saire murdered my father, and I want retribution."

They argue in circles, their tempers growing hotter. The regent remains silent throughout, and so does his younger brother, who stands on the left-hand side of the regent's throne, grinning like a feral dog.

"I say execute the assassin and be done with it," the brother says. He would not have dared open his mouth were this gathering a Mkutano, where only the king and headmen may speak while the fire burns in the hollow at the center of the circle of thrones. But this hall is no Meeting Place.

"That will not be enough," declares the Kestrel.

"A payment from the Crown, then," the brother suggests. "And an official apology."

The Kestrel remains implacable. "There will be blood, or there will be war."

This makes the regent's brother grin wider, clearly pleased by the rage he has stoked.

Fool, the Enchantress thinks, wondering how no one can see what should be so obvious to them. She hasn't told her husband, but she knows through her network of spies that it was actually his hot-tempered idiot of a brother who orchestrated the Kestrel's shoddy assassination.

He hired a cutthroat from a Halusha immigrant death cult, whose members live in the undercity, then employed the services of an underground tattoo artist to brand the assassin with a fake Saire mark—a crime so offensive in the kingdom it's always punished by death.

Idiot that he is, the Enchantress's brother-in-law left footprints all over the place, forcing her to secretly clean up after him. She had to order the deaths of nearly a dozen people just to tie up his loose ends, and while she didn't hesitate to do so, she certainly didn't enjoy it. If his discovery wouldn't compromise what she's trying to achieve, she would have fed him to the Shirika by now.

"Assassins are often tools, Your Highness," the herald says. "He hardly acted alone. Surely you want to know whose hand wielded him against your father."

"Of course I do," the Kestrel growls. "But it doesn't change the fact that a Saire shot the arrow."

"So you agree there needs to be a thorough investigation into the matter."

"That goes without saying."

The Enchantress smiles behind her veil of golden strands, sensing a scheme in the air.

"Then I propose we let the inquisitors of the city guard take over," the herald says to the gathered princes and representatives. "And I propose we move the Mkutano by the Summit to the Requiem Moon. There can be no formal gathering of the princes until this matter is resolved. What if the same thing happens again?"

After a thoughtful silence, the Buffalo speaks. "I concur," he says. "Until the culprits behind the assassination are exposed, we cannot risk the princes gathering in one place at the same time. I second the motion to postpone the first Mkutano of the year to the Requiem Moon."

As the headmen and proxies nod in agreement, the Enchantress gains a heightened respect for the herald. He correctly assessed the mood of the hall and used it to his advantage. *A wonderfully executed move.*

"Now, hang on a minute," says the regent's brother. His infuriating grin has disappeared. "What does the Mkutano have to do with this?"

Clearly, the fool is too dense to recognize that this battle is already lost. Speaking out against a popular motion will only invite suspicion.

The Enchantress has to do damage control. "I fear the herald is onto something," she says, and her husband stiffens in his throne while his brother casts her a venomous look. She continues. "Perhaps the assumption that the wrong headman died is erroneous. Perhaps it was only meant to *look* like a failed attempt on the regent, when in fact, the dark deed proceeded exactly as planned."

Silence grows in the hall as the implications of her words sink in. The herald's face pinches together like he's tasted something he's not quite sure he likes. He obviously hates the regent and sees him as his mortal enemy, and yet here is the regent's wife, voicing support for his argument.

He seizes on the moment. "That's exactly what I was saying! Someone took advantage of our desperate position to commit murder and lay it at our feet. We're being framed."

"Pathetic excuses," says the regent's brother, but the young Kestrel, who was demanding blood not a moment ago, now appears less sure of himself, adjusting the ill-fitting mask on his face.

"Whatever the truth," the Enchantress says, "it needs to come out so we can know that our headmen are safe." She glances at her brother-in-law just so he knows the spear she's about to conjure is aimed straight for his heart. "I suggest, my princes, that instead of the inquisitors of the city guard, you submit this matter straight to the Shirika through the House of Law. Should you convince them to involve themselves, the truth will be sure to come out; then the true culprit will be punished."

The Jackal, the only other headman present, nods in agreement. "I think that's a fine idea. If I didn't have business in the city, I wouldn't be here myself. We need to know how a headman was killed right in front of us before we meet again. The Shirika will not fail to uncover the truth. I put forward a motion to submit this case to them."

"I second that motion," the herald is quick to say.

Finally recognizing the peril he has wandered into, the Enchantress's troublesome brother-in-law keeps silent, pressing his lips tightly together. The regent himself has been quiet throughout the discussion. It does not sit well with him that his peers might now think him a vicious thug. He wants their fear, but mostly he wants their respect, which he believes is the bedrock of his legitimacy.

He was convinced the Enchantress was responsible, despite her denials. She can tell he's no longer so certain. Clearing his throat, he shifts forward in his throne, one elbow leaning on his thigh, and speaks with a confident voice. "A motion has been put forward and seconded to postpone the Mkutano at the Meeting Place by the Summit to the afternoon of the Requiem Moon. All those in favor?"

Wisely, he raises his hand first. The herald has an almost manic look on his face as he lifts his hand, like he can't believe his luck. Everyone else seated on a throne does the same, including the new Kestrel.

"The motion passes with unanimous support," the regent says. "A motion has been put forward and seconded to petition the Shirika to investigate the Kestrel's assassination at the New Year's Feast. All those in favor?"

Once again, every hand goes up. The Enchantress almost laughs at the look on her brother-in-law's face. Who knows; maybe she'll allow the Shirika to gobble him up for the fun of it.

"The motion passes with unanimous support."

When the meeting adjourns, while the regent rushes off with his guard captain to some other meeting, the Enchantress lingers in the marble-columned gallery outside the hall, making small talk with some of the representatives. She nods at the herald as he hobbles past her, earning a curious stare before he continues on his way. She feels her prey watching her, perhaps debating whether he should approach her even though she already knows what he will do.

Just as she expects, he follows her when she begins to leave the gallery. "Sister, a word."

She stops, feigning mild surprise. "Of course, brother. How may I help you?"

"What do you want?" he says after making sure there are no ears to hear them. "To make this go away."

Though he resembles her husband, he doesn't possess nearly as much charm or authority. He's also quite a bit taller, so she has to look up into his eyes. "You'll have to be more specific. To make *what* go away?"

"I don't want this going to the Shirika. I want the assassin executed and this charade to be over. No harm was done to you."

"Wasn't it, though? My husband—your brother—almost died. I'd like to know who was responsible."

"He was never in danger, and we both know it. Tell me what the devil you want and stop toying with me, woman."

"What I want, brother," she says, "is your complete, unconditional loyalty."

"You have it," he says without hesitating.

"I want you to behave yourself. You don't make any moves without asking me first. And whatever you were plotting against your brother—and I know you were plotting—I want it to end right this second, or the Shirika will be the least of your worries."

"It's ended. Are we done?"

"For now."

He regards her momentarily, hatred flashing in his eyes. "You know, I always thought you were a vapid little creature my brother used to warm his bed. I see that I was wrong."

"I am fiercely protective of what's mine," the Enchantress says.

"I will not underestimate you again." He inclines his head and begins to walk away. "A good day to you, sister."

Later that night, the Enchantress and her husband collapse onto the sheets of her bed, their skin slicked with sweat from indulging in each other's sensual talents. As they descend from the high of their climax, their loud breaths fill the chamber, mingled with laughter.

The Enchantress rolls onto her side to face her husband, seeing that his thoughts are already drifting.

He's been distracted all night.

"What is it?" she says.

His chest rises and falls, his eyes glistening in the light spilling into her dim bedchamber from an open patio door. He's staring at the ceiling like he can see past it to whatever secrets are in the night sky. "I had a chance to kill the king today," he says.

The Enchantress stills as a pang of alarm cuts through her postcoital haze. "You did?"

"One of my spies spotted her somewhere in Northtown. Looks like she's been sneaking out of the temple dressed like a common girl." His eyes remain distant. "She's either brave or profoundly stupid."

"Is that why you left the meeting in such a hurry?"

"One word from me, and it would have been over. I would have won." His voice is subdued and tinged with regret, which is a relief to the Enchantress. A dead king would have complicated the plans of her accomplice.

"I gather you didn't go ahead with it," she says.

He shakes his head. "I have the blood of one king on my hands already. I don't wish to test the spirits by staining myself with the blood of another. Besides, maybe the wedding isn't a ruse and I'll get what I want anyway."

A ripple of displeasure makes the Enchantress frown. The wedding. She really shouldn't care, but it annoys her how easily her husband would relegate her to the position of second wife. But this is a trifling matter in the grand order of things. "A wise decision. Better for her to give you her crown than for you to be seen taking it by force."

"That's what I figured," he says and turns onto his side to face her. They watch each other in the dim lighting. "You didn't do it, did you."

"Do what?"

"Hire the assassin."

"I told you I didn't."

"But you know who did," he says. "How?"

She traces a line up from his navel to his chest. "I have my ways, husband."

"Right." He regards her, amused, frustrated. "Ways you can't tell me about."

She draws lazy circles around one of his nipples. "I'm glad you understand."

"I assume the culprit is at your mercy now."

"I made sure he understands his position."

"Why did you let it happen? If you knew. Why didn't you stop it?"

Drawing back her finger, she turns onto her back so she's looking at the ceiling. "The head of an enemy handed to us on a platter? Frankly I was annoyed I hadn't thought of it myself." When the prince remains silent for a time, she tilts her head to look. He's still watching her, mysterious thoughts shining in the depths of his eyes. "What is it?" she says.

"It's nothing," he replies, then seems to reconsider, his gaze going far away again. "It's just, sometimes I wonder if we're not making a mistake. All this change, the bloodshed. Will I still recognize myself when it's over?"

She turns back to him, this time cupping his face with a gentle hand so that she has all his attention. His doubtful eyes look into hers, seeking comfort.

"You have been anointed to bring these lands into a new age," she says. "It won't be easy, but that is why the high mystics chose you. A lesser man could not have done it."

She knows the words have hit their mark when the prince smiles. "How about *you* remind me why you chose me again?"

She laughs, kissing him, and they ravish each other for the second time that night.

◆ ◆ ◆

A year after seeking the help of a dark priest in the cover of night, the duke and duchess of the Two Suns Eclipsing welcome twins into the world, a girl and boy so perfect their hair and skin appear to glow with the light of the suns.

The children are a delight, and the duke and duchess are utterly enamored with them, for each day they seem to grow even more beautiful. Even more lovely. Even more perfect.

Perhaps too perfect, but the duke and duchess do not worry about this. Not at first.

As the children grow further into their many talents, however, it becomes clear that these are no ordinary children. They rarely cry or misbehave. People listen when they talk. Rain clouds part when they step outside to play. Broken things they touch somehow become fixed. The world itself seems to shift around them to accommodate their whims.

Troubling, to be sure, but the duke and duchess write these abnormal talents off as mere idiosyncrasies. After all, the children are innocent, wonderful, full of joy.

But other people start to notice them. Friends of the duke and duchess. Rivals. Enemies. The imperial court itself. They watch with awe and envy as the girl becomes a brilliant academic and public speaker, an icon of style and glamour who gathers a court of fawning young aristocrats. They hold their breaths as the boy matures into a preternaturally gifted swordsman, defeating battle-scarred champions in contests across the land. Aristocrats and commoners alike are enthralled, and people begin to whisper that the house of the Two Suns Eclipsing is on the rise, that a new empress will soon sit on the throne.

That in fact, a new empress must *sit on the throne, for who better to rule the heavens than she whose smile can make the suns rise? And who better to sit by her side than he whose beauty is like starlight?*

Too proud of their children, too filled with love for them, the duke and duchess fail to realize the threat they have become to the powers that be. They fail to notice the venomous stares from the highest echelons of the

Court of Light, the invitations to the empress's palace growing fewer and further between.

They fail to realize that their days are numbered, that what they hold most dear has carved a path to their own destruction.

Their enemies descend like shadows one night, and in one fell swoop, the house of the Two Suns Eclipsing is struck from the face of the earth.

◆　◆　◆

In the early hours of the morning, just as the first sunrays lance across the skies from the east, the Enchantress's metaformic jewel reaches out to her from her bedside table, piercing through her dreams to announce that a distant associate wishes to speak to her.

Without opening her eyes, she allows the metaform to lift her consciousness from her bedchamber and into a plane that transcends distance. Here she takes shape on the main deck of a vessel of sky and wind, a palace of polished wood sailing across a canopy of golden clouds on the currents of a magically generated jet stream.

Matrices of metal struts wrapped in crimson membranes extend from either side of the vessel's hull like the wings of a damselfly. They seethe with eddies of Storm and Void craft, reddish vapors coming off the membranes like steam. Having sailed such a vessel several times before, the Enchantress recognizes that she is on the main deck of a moon-powered windcraft.

Morning is slowly unveiling itself in the city outside her bedchamber, but here the suns rose hours ago, infusing the blanket of clouds beneath the windcraft with a warm glow. To her side a man is seated by a table on the deck, pouring tea from a kettle into a porcelain cup. When she sees him, she draws her violet nightgown tighter around herself, wishing she had taken the time to make herself more presentable.

"Prophet."

The man sets the kettle down and stirs his tea with a silver spoon. "Enchantress. I would offer you tea, but . . . well. You shall have to enjoy it vicariously."

Surprised, the Enchantress takes another look at her surroundings. It seems Prophet has projected her into his real environment rather than a metaformic construct, the first time he's done such a thing in all the times they've communicated remotely. He is usually secretive, hiding behind faceless figures in constructs of grand architecture or impressive natural phenomena. Today he has appeared as he is.

Solemn and gracefully thin, Prophet bears the face of a benevolent emperor. His grizzled beard and dreadlocks give him a leonine aspect; his silver eyes are a startling contrast to his dark skin. Those who do not know him might mistake those eyes for wells of kindness and generosity, but the Enchantress has seen how they can perform the calculus of death without ever losing their shine.

Even so far above the world, Prophet is dressed as a genteel lord of the Enclave. A bloodrose blooms out of the chest pocket of his charcoal-gray waistcoat, worn over a perfectly pressed lily-white shirt with silver cuff links. His metaformic jewel is the centerpiece of his silver-and-diamond necklace. He is the picture of a cultured mystic of Higher Red magic.

All a ruse, of course. An effective one at that.

Silently, the Enchantress ventures to the port gunwales. If she squints, she can make out the slight shimmer of the vessel's microclimate force field, which keeps rains and powerful gusts of wind at bay. Far beneath the layer of golden clouds, she glimpses a glittering tract of turquoise waters. Given the relative position of the suns, she figures they belong to the eastern Inoetera—or the Ioethean, as it is known beyond the Redlands.

Turning away from the view beneath the windcraft, the Enchantress folds her arms and leans against the gunwales. "I take it you're on your way east. Must be earthshaking if you're going there in person."

Prophet takes a sip of his tea, crossing his legs at the knee. There might be other people on the deck, but the Enchantress would never know—his metaform has given them complete privacy. "I would have sent my favorite operative in my stead," he says. "Alas, she ran off to start wars in the hinterlands."

"I'm sure you'll manage," the Enchantress says. "Is it the Vigilants?"

"Ostensibly, they appear to be an unrelated sect. Secretive, always kept to themselves, but something about the New Year excited them enough to start selling off their homes and possessions, buying old ships, tents, dried foods, and the like. It's making a lot of noise. I intend to find out what they think they know."

The Enchantress considers his words. "Sounds like they're preparing for a journey," she remarks.

"More like a pilgrimage."

"To where?"

Prophet's eyes flash, pearly teeth showing in a grin. "Where else but to meet the new Hegemon?"

Disbelieving her ears, the Enchantress looks askance at him.

"Oh yes, you heard me right." Prophet smiles from above the rim of his cup as he sips. "Of course, they claim not to know *where* said Hegemon is at the moment, but that seems neither here nor there, as far as I can tell."

"They're raving mad," the Enchantress says. "I assume they've all been arrested by now."

"Quite the opposite, actually," Prophet casually states. "The eastern polities have been itching for a chance to defy the West and display their combined strength. So they've banded together in support of the sect's freedom of religion. Naturally, neither Empire nor Enclave is pleased. I've even heard talk of joint military action against the entire eastern hemisphere as punishment."

She can hardly believe it. The Empire and the Enclave, the suns and the moon—adversarial powers since time immemorial—*uniting* against the East? Throw in a new Ascendancy rising in the South, and the drums of war will beat so loudly as to be deafening.

But why is there worry in Prophet's eyes? Is war not the outcome they both seek?

"It must be the weakening Veil," the Enchantress says, struggling to keep her zeal contained. "The whole world can feel it, even if they don't recognize it for what it is. They sense that something is stirring in the air."

She is mildly disappointed that Prophet fails to display the same level of enthusiasm. "Perhaps," he says, looking into his teacup. Then his silver eyes flick back up, and she sees that a new and somewhat unsettling light has taken up residence within them. "Normally, I wouldn't involve myself directly in such a high-profile affair, but the timing of this sect's activity is suspicious, to say the least, especially considering what you're doing over there."

This is why you wanted to see me, she realizes. "There can't be any connection to my work," she says. "I'm an ocean away in the most isolated region on the planet. It'll be months before the outside world gets wind of what's happening here."

"Even so, talk of a new Hegemon while you're orchestrating a sham Ascendancy could hardly be a coincidence. Something you did must have made unanticipated ripples."

She wonders if she should tell him about the high mystic and their plan. That the Ascendancy they are working to resurrect will be much closer to the real thing than she's led him to believe. That the key to its power is within her grasp.

A thought strikes her. *What if Prophet is right and this sect is reacting to events in this city? What if they sensed the key's existence? What if they aren't crazy?*

"Possible, but doubtful," she says, in part to herself. "I've been careful."

Prophet smiles in that way he does whenever his students over-estimate their talents. Of all his smiles, this is the Enchantress's least favorite. "Don't forget that the world is chaotic, Enchantress. Even with all the information at your fingertips, there will always be limits to your ability to control which way the wind blows. Be careful you don't find yourself an unwitting instrument in someone else's designs."

She smothers a prickle of annoyance, remembering how much she respects and admires her old mentor. "You taught me well, Prophet. I will be careful."

He nods. "One last thing before you go. I recently received intelligence that a Vigilant operative from the Empire might have snuck across the desert several months back. It's possible she's in your city as we speak."

The windcraft seems to spin around the Enchantress, the false sense of gravity breaking beneath the force of her shock. But then her mind hooks onto one of the last words he spoke. "Did you say *she?*"

"Find and neutralize her," Prophet says. "The last thing we need is Vigilants planting roots in the Red Wilds."

Her relief is immense. *It's someone else. He doesn't know about him.* At the heels of that thought are curiosity and a much less intense, though still pronounced, sense of alarm at this "she," this other Imperial interloper. *Who could she be, and what is she doing here?* "I will look into it."

"Let me know when it's done. You are dismissed."

When she awakens from her bed, the first thing she does is call for the pair of Jasiri warriors she trusts the most. If a Vigilant operative from the Empire is in this city, they will find her.

And then she will interrogate her herself.

16: Isa

Undercity

Just outside the sanctuary of the Dazzling Light, Isa is forced to lie to her two guards so they don't follow her past the sanctuary's entrance.

"I'll be in there the whole time," she says to Obe and Ijiro. "When the vigil is over, I'll come straight out."

The two Sentinels, both dressed as civilians, regard her unhappily. "I don't understand why we can't come with you," says Obe. "We're not supposed to let you out of our sight, yet you keep asking to go off on your own. You're making our jobs difficult."

She could not attract suspicion when she left the temple, so she wore a simple sleeveless dress of white cotton and a head wrap of cheap printed brocade. "I'll be fine," she assures Obe. "And it's a private ceremony. Invitation only. I'm sorry, but you can't come."

A man in an ivory boubou appears by the sanctuary's open door, his face set in a permanent frown. "We are ready to begin," he announces.

"I'll be right there, Bwana Amidi," Isa says to him.

Obe watches him distrustfully as he disappears back into the sanctuary, then gives Isa the same look. "So you're praying with apostates now?" he says in a low voice. "What will the high priest say if he finds out?"

"The term is *nonconformists*. And he won't find out because you won't tell him. Promise me, Obe. Under no circumstances will he know what I'm doing here." She hardens her voice when he blinks at her in silence. "Obe?"

"Fine. I promise. But I still think it's crazy you're associating with . . . these people."

"I need them, Obe, and I need them to trust me. That won't happen with guards following me around."

"We can stand in the background and be real quiet," Ijiro suggests, breaking his silence. "You won't even notice we're there."

"What he said," Obe agrees, jerking a thumb in Ijiro's direction.

Isa feels her patience begin to wear thin. She may well be dead by morning, and the longer she waits out here, the more tempted she is to let these Sentinels whisk her back to safety and end this mad scheme. "I need them to see me as one of them," she says, somehow holding herself together. "You'll just be a reminder of my otherness, and I can't have that. I'm sorry, but this is my final word."

She turns to enter the sanctuary before she can change her mind.

"Isa . . ."

The helplessness in Obe's voice stops her.

He cares for me, and I encouraged it, because I care for him too.

By impulse she turns around and rushes back to kiss him on the lips. She imprints the sensation firmly onto her mind, a keepsake for both of them should the worst come to pass.

His face cycles through conflicting emotions when she steps back, and this time, as she turns to leave, neither Sentinel has anything to say.

The rite begins as soon as the doors close. Isa, Bwana Amidi, Tuliza, and two dozen other congregants stand in the sanctuary's candlelit main chamber, facing a wall upon which a mural is carved. The mural depicts a fig tree crowned by a starburst pattern whose rays appear to spin in the weak lighting. Its roots disappear into a shallow pool extending away from the wall in a half circle. Isa isn't sure, but the water in that pool seems to shimmer with its own glow.

Amidi is the most senior member of the sanctuary as far as she knows, so she's surprised when an elderly lady steps forward to speak while he remains among the gathered people. The woman is dressed in a white caftan and head wrap and speaks to the congregants with the graciousness of a loving grandmother.

"The rite of the Dazzling Light is one of the undercity's oldest and most sacred traditions," she begins. "All are welcome to participate, be you a member of this sanctuary or a visitor. With this in mind, I ask tonight's participants to please step forward."

Amidi and Tuliza are the only people here who know Isa's true identity. They betray nothing with their faces as she steps forward and presents herself to the elderly priestess. No one else joins her.

The priestess waits in silence, heightening Isa's sense of isolation with every passing second. She presses a hand to the secret pocket by her side and takes comfort from the hard edges that meet the tips of her fingers.

"There are two types of people who seek the Dazzling Light," the priestess eventually says, addressing the sanctuary but staring into Isa's eyes. "The first seek it to prove a point, either to themselves or to someone else. The second are drawn to it because they feel certain inexplicable truths in their hearts, whose presence is undefinable yet real, like the suns hiding beneath the horizon just before dawn. If you belong to the first group, I beg you right now to reconsider your choice and step aside. I don't care what you've heard before; this rite is not a game. It is not a gamble. Finding the Light is its own reward. If it isn't what is driving you forward tonight, then you are here for the wrong reasons."

Isa keeps her feet still.

"This is your last chance, young woman," says the priestess. "If the Light is not why you are here, then you should step aside and spare yourself."

In the sanctuary's silence, no one moves.

"So be it." Turning away from the congregants, the priestess approaches the carved tree, and while everyone watches, she bends over to pick up one of several empty gourds sitting on the pool's rim and fills it with water. "We call him Engai," she says as she returns with the gourd in hand, cradling it like a precious object. "The spirit of the Dazzling Light who shines in the darkest places to give hope, warmth, and knowledge to those who seek it. But we recognize his other incarnations, too, which are understood and venerated in different ways. Some honor him as Nyami Nyami, the spirit of life-giving waters. In other places they know him as Adroa, he who straddles the line between good and evil. But he is one and the same, each incarnation embodying a single aspect of his greatness. Tonight, we commit a willing soul into Engai's care—"

"Two willing souls. I, too, will seek the Dazzling Light."

Everyone is speechless as Tuliza steps forward to join Isa at the front of the gathering. Her hands are trembling—Isa can *see* them trembling—but she stands with her chin lifted high, as if expecting resistance.

Behind her, Amidi watches in horror, mouth agape. "Tuliza! What are you doing?"

She speaks without looking back, her voice so racked with fear Isa wonders what has possessed her to step forward. "I'm sorry, Father. I've made my decision."

"I will not allow it."

"It is my choice," she says.

"Tuliza, you cannot."

"Bwana Amidi," the priestess says in a kind but resolute voice. "With all due respect, you cannot forbid the rite to an adult who has chosen it freely."

"But she is my daughter!"

"Even so." The priestess studies Tuliza, worry aging her face. "Are you certain this is what you want, Tuliza? It has been years since the last successful rite. In all likelihood, you will not return from your journey alive."

In her yellow ankle-length dress, belted at the waist, and a simple headband holding her curly hair back, Tuliza might look even less prepared for the undercity's depths than Isa. Insanely, she remains unmoved. "I seek the Light just as my father did before me."

Having failed to order her into submission, her father resorts to pleading. "I barely survived the rite, Tuliza. I know what's down there. Please, for my sake, don't do this."

"I'm ready," Tuliza says to the priestess, who nods even as Amidi continues to plead.

Isa tries to catch the other young woman's eye, but Tuliza's gaze has fixed on the carved tree ahead.

"To the Dazzling Light we commit these two willing souls," the priestess says, resuming the rite. "Guide their footsteps as they seek your radiance." She approaches Isa with her gourd, raising it to her lips. "Drink."

Isa obeys, swallowing down two gulps of the water before the priestess withdraws the gourd. Her mouth is left with a metallic tang.

She stares intently at the floor as the priestess offers the water to Tuliza. Amidi's faint sobs are the only sound in the sanctuary by the time she is done. Isa spares him a glance and feels her heart break at the choked despair she sees on his face. The congregants around him try to comfort him with kind, gentle words, wrapping their arms around his shoulders, but he remains inconsolable.

The priestess speaks. "Now is the time to say your goodbyes, and then I shall take you to where your journey begins."

Only now does Tuliza rush to Amidi and surround him in a tearful embrace. "I'm sorry, Father. Please forgive me."

The man envelops her with his arms like he thinks he'll never see her again, and they cry onto each other's shoulders. "My daughter," he says.

Tuliza, trying to console her father, kisses him once on each tearstained cheek. "I love you. Now and forever."

"Participants of the rite," the priestess says, "the time has come. Please follow me."

An archway to the right of the carved mural and the pool leads out of the sanctuary's main hall. While Tuliza extracts herself from her father's embrace to follow the priestess, Isa approaches Amidi to make promises she's not sure she can keep. Maybe it's the pity. Or maybe it's the guilt she now feels for bringing this sorrow to Amidi and his family. "I will watch over her," she tells him.

Amidi's tearful gaze is almost accusatory. "She is my daughter."

"And she will come back to you," Isa says. "I promise."

He probably knows that her promises aren't worth the grains of dirt beneath his sandals, but he nods nonetheless. Isa almost feels the weight of his hope settling onto her shoulders like a yoke.

Without another word, she follows Tuliza and the priestess through the archway and out of the main hall.

The priestess brings them to a smaller chamber in which the focal point is a bronze fig tree sculpture nestled within a niche on the back wall. The chamber is otherwise barren, save for the many elongated crystals sticking out slantwise from sconce-like contraptions all along the walls.

Together the crystals paint the corners and edges of the chamber in varicolored light.

"The crystals here are the center of a network that feeds the homes and shops of the undercity with warmth and clean air," the priestess says. "Without them the undercity would not be habitable. There would be no lights, no circulation of air, no clean water. They are, in essence, our most valuable resource. But our supply of fully charged crystals is dwindling, and if it is not replenished, we will run out of power in less than three years.

"As pilgrims of the rite, each of you must select a crystal from the wall; even when empty, they burn with a light no darkness can extinguish and will burn even brighter upon drinking from Engai's tree." She motions to the walls with her hands. "Go ahead. Select one. It doesn't matter which one you choose, since they're all nearly depleted and will need to be replaced soon anyway."

They both comply. Tuliza extracts a golden crystal from its sconce while Isa chooses a milky stone with a white radiance. Even though it's supposed to hold a reserve of magical power, its surface is so cold it's almost frosty.

"There are many ways down to the warrens of the undercity," the priestess says after they've made their choices. "But those who walk the rite always begin here. It behooves me to tell you to be honest in your search. If you act dishonorably, the path will not reveal itself to you, and you will not succeed. Understood?"

Isa joins Tuliza in nodding in agreement, resisting the urge to touch her secret pocket again. The priestess searches their faces and must be satisfied with what she sees because she reaches for the bronze tree behind her and tugs at a branch as though pulling down on a lever. Immediately, a deep rumbling rises from the floors, shaking the chamber like an earthquake.

The niche and the tree it holds begin to descend until they disappear, sinking into a depression on the floor and leaving behind a gaping portal of blackness where the sculpture once stood.

The entrance to a hidden staircase.

Staring down into that unknowable breach, Isa doesn't think she imagines the musty wind rushing out of it, nor the distant echo of her name pitter-pattering over and over again from its depths like the sound of a pebble tumbling down a steep rock face and into an abyss.

Whatever brain malfunction made her brave enough to come this far almost rectifies itself right then, but somehow she finds the courage to remain still.

"Mother's grace upon you both," the priestess says, stepping aside. "And may Engai illuminate your paths."

Next to Isa, Tuliza's crystal torch is trembling in her hand as she blinks at the portal, breathing like she's about to take a dive into deep waters. The priestess looks on with sympathy but remains silent.

"You don't have to do this, you know," Isa says, and Tuliza nods more times than is necessary.

"I know." She releases a long and shaky breath. "I just felt compelled to. I guess I didn't want you to go alone."

She holds her torch aloft and sounds calmer when she speaks next. "Shall I go first?"

The voice Isa thought she heard earlier floats out of the portal again, beckoning to her. Her better judgment begs her to turn around. Instead, she says, "Allow me," and steps forward into the unknown. Despite the brightness of her crystal, the gloom seems to slip over and around her like a shroud as she descends the staircase.

And then it swallows her whole.

Water drips just out of sight, but she never sees it. Dampness fills her nostrils, condensing on her skin, the smell of wet things and sewage. Beneath it all, that faint echo at the back of her mind, calling her name over and over again.

For thirty minutes, Isa walks with Tuliza through the dank tunnels in silence. She becomes curious about the faded markings she keeps seeing on the walls wherever the layers of grime aren't thick enough to obscure them. She stops at one point to investigate, thinking she can see shapes vaguely familiar to her, like the ghosts of effaced words on a palimpsest, but they don't resolve into anything she recognizes, so she moves on.

The tunnels curve, slope down, and split in places. They lead to dead ends and staircases that wind down to deeper floors. Isa once read that the undercity is much older than the city itself; at the time it seemed far fetched, but now that she's here, she can almost feel the age and silent history pressing against her, forcing her to breathe it in. When they come to their first four-way juncture, they wordlessly choose to go straight ahead, neither of them willing to take the risk of a wrong turn.

"When is the path supposed to show itself to us?" Isa whispers.

Even in the cool and damp air, Tuliza has sweat on her forehead. She wipes it off with the back of one hand while the other holds on to her torch with a death grip. "We just have to keep going. Eventually we'll see it."

It is only gradually that Isa comes to realize she's been drugged.

She once smoked a red herb with her brother Ayo in the woods near the Summit's sacred committal grounds and spent the whole day laughing at the silliest things: the way a caterpillar crawled up a tree, the way a leaf spiraled in the wind, the way Ayo began to resemble a monkey. She remembers the feeling of something sitting on her brain, throwing her thoughts off their regular straight lines and into the absurd.

That's not quite what she feels now. There's no light-headedness, no euphoria, no desire to skip or sing at the top of her voice. She's still afraid, but her skin begins to tingle, and her eyes begin to see farther than the reach of her torchlight, convincing her that her mind is being interfered with.

A hallucination flashes before her eyes: These same tunnels, but filled with light. The walls are pristine and pearlescent. Panels of moving images are mounted onto them like windows into other dimensions. Someone calls her name from somewhere far away. She turns to look behind her, but the vision flees from her eyes like a visor coming off her face, leaving her in darkness once more. A chill grips her spine as the echoes of her name continue to ring in her ears.

"Did you see that?" she asks Tuliza, failing to suppress her alarm.

Tuliza tenses visibly as she searches the way ahead. "What did it look like?"

Like nothing I can describe. "I'm . . . not sure," Isa says, still reeling from the images. "I think there was something in the water they gave us. I feel a little odd."

"I feel the same," Tuliza says after a pause. "Perhaps the path is revealing itself to us."

Or perhaps we were drugged.

More flashes appear ahead, ribbons of light that race along the edges of the tunnels until she blinks, and then they're gone. She tries to shake the hallucinations off, but they keep tormenting her, almost like she's seeing through two pairs of eyes. Tuliza seems immune to the effects for the most part, at least until they come upon a string of neon-green pebbles floating in the air just ahead.

And then she freezes in perfect terror.

Stopping next to her, Isa warily regards the strange lights, unsure if she wants them to be real or another figment of her imagination. "You see that, too, don't you?"

"I see it."

Tuliza's stiffness forces Isa to take a second look at the string of glowing pebbles. It is only as she sees the lights throb along the pebbles from one end of the string to the other that she realizes they aren't pebbles at all but scales.

In a terrific display, the beast the scales belong to lifts and spreads its membranous tail, which glows along its ridges with enough strength to cast shadows. Isa is almost hypnotized by the swaying motion of the appendage; in the light of its own bioluminescence, the ninki nanka is a heavily built silhouette standing low to the ground on four stocky legs. Rows of barbed teeth come into view as it uncouples its monstrous jaws, and a luminous forked tongue slithers out to taste the air.

Isa has seen enough drawings of this creature to know exactly what it is. She and Tuliza stand motionless, their breath turning to ice in their lungs.

The beast roars.

"Your Majesty," Tuliza squeals as the walls around them shudder.

"Stand very still."

Slowly, carefully, Isa reaches for the object in her pocket, a plum-size cube of bronze with openwork patterns that expose a maze of ivory gears and crystals within. She slides a little knob along one edge of the cube to bring it to life.

"Your Majesty!" Tuliza cries when the giant reptile begins to charge.

With a shaking hand Isa holds the cube out in front of her, standing her ground, but the beast keeps coming. She closes her eyes, muttering a prayer to the Mother. An earsplitting roar forces her eyes wide open, and she almost loses her nerve at the sight of the beast so close to her, close enough that she can smell its breath, but it has stopped and is now tossing its head back and forth as though in agony.

Possessed by courage she has never known, she steps forward with the cube held out before her. The ninki nanka roars as it shrinks back like it has been burned. She steps forward again, and it retreats, snapping its jaws in threat. With her thumb she pushes the knob on the cube as far as it will go, and this time the beast roars once before turning around and scurrying off into the gloom.

A moment of astonished silence. "We're still alive," Tuliza remarks. She brings her halo of torchlight as she moves to catch up with Isa. "Why did it run away?" Amazed, she stares at the cube, which Isa is still holding out in front of her. "What's that?"

Isa keeps still until she's certain the beast has left them. Only once she's rediscovered her breath does she lower her cube and start walking again. Tuliza follows, still confused.

"It's a sonic repellent," Isa explains. "I had one of my Sentinels commission it for me from the House of Axles. It was enchanted to emit sounds irritating to beasts with acute senses of hearing. And since there's no light with which to see down here, the beasts of the undercity are extremely sensitive to sound."

Tuliza tilts her head to one side. "I don't hear anything."

"The sounds are too high pitched for human ears, but to the beasts they are unbearably loud."

"I see," Tuliza says after a long pause.

Isa glances at her, noting the sharp transformation that has occurred on her face. Where she was petrified not a moment ago, now she looks betrayed. "You don't approve."

"I wouldn't presume to criticize you, Your Majesty."

"Speak your mind, Tuliza. I'm not so petty I'd hold your opinions against you when we're both risking our lives."

"We're not supposed to carry such things on the path to Engai," she says. "We are meant to rely solely on his grace to protect us. That box is cheating."

Isa lets out a sigh. "I wasn't going to leave my survival down here up to chance, Tuliza. My people need me alive. And I certainly wasn't going to stand back and watch you get mauled to death."

Tuliza shakes her head, the picture of disappointment. "The tree might not show itself to us after this. Engai does not take kindly to those who cheat."

"Maybe, but at least we're still alive." Isa studies the other young woman in the torchlight and is struck with shame and guilt by the sadness she sees there. She looks away, fixing her gaze ahead. "You think less of me now."

"I thought you were honorable," Tuliza says. "Yet here you are, buying your way ahead with expensive artifacts. It is an insult to everyone who's walked this path, many of whom lost their lives."

"So you would have rather I let us die just now?"

"If you had begun this path with an honest heart, perhaps we might not have encountered that beast in the first place. Perhaps it could sense that you were cheating."

"Somehow, I doubt that. No one has returned safely from the rite in years, and I'm sure many of those who died were honest. And even if you're right, I don't have the luxury to play fair right now. I'm sorry if that disappoints you."

"Fairness is never more important than when it is the hardest choice. I thought you understood that."

Isa clamps down on her jaw to stop herself from saying something abrupt. The air between them becomes tense like a string pulled to the point of snapping.

"We must continue," she says.

They walk on.

The hallucinations grow more insistent. Flashes of the tunnels like images stolen from someone else's memories. Echoes of her name ricocheting off the walls, interposed by roars that make the floors shake.

As they descend a staircase, Isa thinks she sees the ghost of a young boy standing at the landing below, one hand braced against a window of colorful images mounted onto the wall. She blinks, and the image vaporizes, the effect of seeing it almost throwing her off balance.

"Are you all right?" Tuliza says, eyeing her with worry.

She takes a breath, finds her center, and presses on. "I'm fine."

◆ ◆ ◆

Perhaps due to the deepening influence of the adulterated water, they navigate the labyrinths by instinct. Down staircases. Past intersections. Through chambers pockmarked with corridors like the inside of a beehive. Some tunnels just *feel* right; others exude a repellent aura. Others invite Isa by giving her flashes of themselves from a different time. She turns right when she catches sight of a phantom woman doing the same, even though the woman disappears in the next half breath.

Despite the eeriness of it all, Isa finds that she cannot distract herself from the sting of Tuliza's disappointment. She can't say why, but it matters to her what the other young woman thinks.

"I wish I could be as idealistic as you, Tuliza," she says, her voice sounding strange after their long silence. "Or as faithful in the gods. But not long ago I came face-to-face with the true extent of the world's contempt for me. My brother Ayo and I irritated each other constantly, but I loved him, Tuliza. I loved him so much I cannot put in words what I felt when I stood over his disemboweled corpse. That image is the last thing I see every night just before I fall asleep and the first thing I see when I wake up in the morning. I also see my cousin floating in a bath full of her own blood. I see my mother with a gash so deep into her skull her brains were seeping out. And I see the same fate waiting for my people if my enemies succeed. How can you expect me not to use whatever advantage I can get?"

Compassion softens Tuliza's expression. "The world is merciless, Your Majesty, and its darkness must ultimately prevail over our bodies. That is the way of things. I learned this truth as a child when a group of angry men decided to take their frustrations with the world out on my family. But we must not let the darkness triumph over our souls! Do not let it distort who you are and turn you away from the path you know to be right."

Bitterness wells up in Isa's heart. "Then maybe I've always been a cheater and a liar. Maybe the darkness peeled away the layers of falseness that surrounded me and revealed me to be rotten."

"I don't believe that."

"You hardly know me, Tuliza."

"I know the young woman who knocked on my father's door a week ago, the king who spoke from the heart and with conviction, who humbled herself before a common man when others in her position would have spoken with pride. She's the woman I followed into the undercity."

"And now you're stuck with me," Isa murmurs beneath her breath, lifting her torch as they come to a wall cutting off further passage down the tunnel.

"A dead end," Tuliza says. "We should turn back."

"Wait." Another ghost superimposes itself onto Isa's reality, producing a visual distortion as it walks by, like underwater ripples. While Isa watches, it waves a wrist over a panel on the wall, causing an aperture to appear in front of it. The ghost walks through, and the aperture closes behind it. Darkness returns to Isa's eyes as the vision dissolves.

"What is it?" Tuliza asks, perhaps noticing the sweat beading on her face.

Ignoring the question, Isa steps up to the wall, gulping as she lifts her wrist in imitation of what she saw in the vision. There is no panel she can see—everything is covered in centuries of grime—but sure enough, there is a hiss as a section of the wall ahead slides away to reveal a portal that wasn't there before. More gloom awaits beyond.

Tuliza blinks at the portal, mystified. "How did you know that would happen?"

"I . . . had a hunch," Isa says, and she trembles as a wind rushes out of the opening to meet them, carrying a distinct voice on its wings.

Come forth, says the voice, and motionlessly, they both stare at the portal, Isa questioning her sanity.

"Did you hear that?" she says.

"I heard a whisper," Tuliza says, confirming Isa's worst fears.

"I think this is the way," Isa says.

"I sincerely hope so."

Side by side they walk through the portal and into the shadows that have beckoned them forward. Isa is grimly unsurprised when the portal closes behind them.

Sounds begin to permeate the visions that keep flashing before her eyes. Voices. People talking in a tongue she can't parse. They walk through a large, circular chamber, and for a split second she sees hundreds of people seated on tiered rows that ascend in longer and longer semicircles. When the vision dissipates, she lifts her torch to better illuminate her surroundings only to find that she is standing on the base of a ruined amphitheater.

"This was once a place of gathering," she says, amazed by her own words. "People actually lived here once upon a time."

Tuliza casts her gaze about skeptically; then something catches her attention up ahead. "I hear movement."

"Tread carefully."

A bloodcurdling screech greets them as they exit the amphitheater and enter a ruined hall with a high ceiling. A staircase climbs up to a series of colonnaded floors that overlooks the hall; to Isa's horror, a trio of frightful creatures with glowing ridges and fanned tails is converging upon a smaller, rodent-like beast they've successfully cornered on a landing of the staircase.

Isa seizes Tuliza's arm, intending to pull her away slowly. But the young woman digs her feet into the ground. "Your cube!" she whispers, wiggling the fingers of an open palm with maddened urgency. "Give it to me!"

"Tuliza, we need to get out of here," Isa whispers through gritted teeth.

Tuliza looks her in the eye, strangely lucid despite the clear and present danger. "Trust me."

Against her wiser instincts, Isa goes ahead and gives away her only form of protection and is helpless as she watches Tuliza dash for the staircase, *toward* the hunting monsters.

"Tuliza!" she screams.

But the young woman is already climbing up the ancient staircase, holding her torch high with one hand while the other clutches the enchanted cube.

Almost as one the ninki nankas stop stalking toward their cornered prey and roar at the intruder, gaping their maws so wide Isa thinks they could swallow her down in one gulp.

The one nearest to Tuliza charges down the stairs on its clawed legs but stops just a few yards shy of her, repelled by the artifact. She brandishes the cube in front of her like a weapon, screaming like a madwoman. "Back off! Away!"

The beast roars in defiance but is forced back by the torrent of noise from the cube.

"Run, vile beasts! Go find something else to eat!"

After only a few seconds in the cube's vicinity, the creatures reach their limits and turn to flee, roaring in indignation.

"That's right, you hell-spawned lizards!" Tuliza shouts after them. "And don't think of coming back!"

Also terrorized by the cube, the giant rodent hisses at her, its muscles tensing like it's about to pounce, but it stays put. Tuliza retreats from it slowly, showing she means it no harm. Isa is incredulous as she watches her climb down the stairs, never turning her back to the creature she just saved.

Only when Tuliza is back within arm's reach does Isa remember she has a tongue. "What the devil were you thinking?"

Tuliza has a crazed look in her eye, like she herself doesn't quite believe what she's done. "The giant rats of the undercity are gentle, sacred beasts," she says. "I couldn't just stand by and watch one die."

Isa tries not to scowl. "I think I'll take that now."

Almost reluctantly, Tuliza hands over the cube, and Isa says nothing as she returns to the business of walking. She seethes for a full minute before she can't hold it in any longer. "So you're fine with using the cube to save a rat but not our own lives. Is that right?"

"You shouldn't have come with the cube," Tuliza insists. "But perhaps Engai will be appeased now that it's been used for a good deed."

Isa shakes her head, amazed by the sheer lunacy. "So what happens when the ninki nankas come back for that creature? Will you camp down here and guard it for the rest of your life?"

"We gave it a chance to return to its burrow. It might live for another decade."

Unbelievable, Isa thinks, her blood still charged from the encounter. Lacking the energy to knock some wits into the other young woman, she decides to let the matter go. "I sense we're getting close. No more heroics until we're back home safely."

Tuliza has the wisdom not to argue.

A ruined metallic structure dominates the next vault they enter. It is cracked in many places, pieces of it scattered across the dusty floor, but the parts of it that remain intact vaguely suggest that it might have once been a sphere of sizable proportions.

A sphere that fell from a great height and shattered as it hit the ground.

Following this thought, Isa lifts her torch and looks up, wondering where the sphere might have come from. Above her the ceiling gapes into a cavernous opening, the mouth of a vertical shaft that goes on until it disappears into the shadows.

She gasps as she glimpses the ghost of a different reality: a shaft reaching so high above her she cannot see where it ends, illuminated by a massive sphere spinning at its center, which shines with a radiance that makes her eyes water.

By the way Tuliza braces a hand against her chest as she looks up, Isa knows that this time she isn't alone in her hallucinations.

"So you see what I see?" she asks, still staring up at the lingering vision.

"It was a sun," Tuliza says, breathless. "Its light powered everything in this ancient city."

"Not a city," Isa says, though she cannot say how she knows this. "Something far stranger."

The gloom reasserts itself as the vision fades.

They continue past the ruined sphere and see that the symbols carved onto the walls are still visible despite the centuries of dust and decay. There are *countless* symbols, a vast cache of unknown history preserved here in the dark, where few eyes will ever behold it.

Never having seen such symbols before, Isa can't possibly understand what they mean, and yet some seem to fix themselves in her mind, giving her intuitions. Ideas. *Knowledge*, even if in the loosest sense of the word.

Coronations of monarchs. Earthshaking battles. The rise and fall of great houses and empires. They come to a set of surviving symbols depicting a naked man and woman standing side by side, the man lifting his right hand in greeting. Behind them is a series of arcs and lines, and a star shines on the man's far right. Isa gets the *feeling* from looking at them that the symbols were once a celebration of . . . something.

Tuliza is drawn to them, too, and moves close enough to trace the path of a ray shooting away from the star with her finger. "These markings. They mean something."

In the torchlight, a fragment of knowledge seeps from the symbol and into Isa's mind, almost like something she once knew. "The star is a map," she says with a surprised shiver. "To somewhere very old and far from here." Somewhere incomprehensibly far and old, so much so the proportions of it make her dizzy.

What is this place? Where am I?

A breeze unexpectedly rustles through her skirts, bringing a chill to her skin.

"I see you, daughter of kings. Come forth so I may know you."

Scared witless, Isa moves her torch about, scouring the chamber. She sees nothing but ruins and dust. "Who said that?"

The look on Tuliza's face is enchanted. Crazily, she says, "I think we must follow the voice."

"Are you actually insane?"

"I heard my name," she says and starts walking.

"Tuliza, wait!"

But Tuliza is already halfway toward a portal that has opened in the chamber, where the breeze emanated from. Isa catches up to her just as she vanishes beyond the portal.

"Tuliza!"

The portal is open, but Isa cannot see anything past the threshold, not even Tuliza's torchlight, as though she fell into a pit.

Isa stands paralyzed, regretting her decision to come down here, thinking that maybe she should turn back, but the thought of leaving

Tuliza gives her a sick feeling in her stomach, so she braces herself and walks through the portal . . .

◆ ◆ ◆

"Tuliza?"

Isa's torch scatters its white glow across a dusty floor that spreads away from her feet. She blinks several times, wondering if she hasn't developed selective blindness, but then she sees a streak of light flitting in the air above her, accompanied by the melodious trill of a songbird.

"Come forth, daughter of princes. I have been waiting."

She swallows and takes a few tentative steps forward, following the echo of her name, which she heard as clearly as she can hear the crunch of her footsteps and the rapid hiss of her breathing.

"Tuliza!" she whispers, but Tuliza doesn't answer.

The streak she saw earlier arcs toward her, and only now does she see that it is a small bird whose radiant wing tips leave behind threads of pure light that linger where it has flown. It flits over her shoulder and alights on an invisible perch some distance away.

The perch turns out to be a branch that comes alive with dazzling bioluminescence. It awakens the branches next to it, then the ones next to those, setting off a chain reaction that ripples outward from the bird like a pulse, gradually illuminating the shape of a thick trunk and the many roots that spread across the floor from its base.

The next thing Isa knows, she's standing before the largest fig tree she has ever seen, whose pliant boughs hold an inner brightness she can't look directly into. Many other luminous birds swarm around its branches, trilling their endless melodies.

The Dazzling Light, and it is more beautiful than I imagined.

Isa's legs weaken and fold, bringing her down to her knees in reverence. The exhaustion of the long journey catches up to her, leaving her almost out of breath.

"Great Engai," she says in a trembling voice. "I am unworthy."

A wind blows across her face, filling the air around her with a presence that prickles her skin.

"Yet you sought me out, daughter of kings. Why?"

Isa wanted to ask for a way to save her life. But now that she's here, she can't get what Tuliza said to her out of her head. "I am beset by evil, yet to escape it I must partake in more evil, and I see no other way out for me. But there must be another way. A more righteous way. I'm here to beg that you show it to me so I may walk it. Shine your Light on me, Great Engai. It is all I ask."

"Alas," says the wind, *"some evils were preordained and cannot be escaped. With your aid a tyrant shall rise from the ashes of your kingdom and strike fear into the hearts of many. From a throne of blood shall he rule over multitudes. This, you cannot stop."*

"Is there no hope for me, then?" Isa asks, dreading that this was all for nothing.

The breeze stirs again, its answer a cold hiss. *"Not in this life, daughter of princes, not for you."*

Isa's eyes fill with tears.

"There is, however, a gift, if you shall have it."

She wipes her eyes, fighting the desire to give up and yield her life unto the undercity. What is the point of anything if there's no hope? "I'll take whatever I can get," she says.

And the branches of the trees whisper in the wind, the birds taking off in a great cloud of radiance that spreads into the seemingly infinite darkness. *"Then gaze into my Light, daughter of kings, and receive the last gift I shall ever give, for I have waited for this day long enough, and now that it is here, I shall fade into the night like the rest of my kind."*

When Isa looks into the Dazzling Light and accepts the gift, she's suddenly suffused with a hope more intoxicating than any she's ever known.

Her eyes are opened to a forgotten past that moves before her like an arrow shot from a bow; she sees it arc over eons of history during which Engai reigned from the highest peak of a mountain range, his roots so widespread they covered a whole continent, his light so pervasive it shone on all who sought it, guiding his people to greater heights of prosperity. She sees the descent of fiery destruction onto his domain and his desperate but ultimately futile attempt to save his flock. She sees an exodus to save the gates to eternity, then cities descending from the skies and gods making their homes in the suns and moon.

None of it makes sense, but the visions resonate with some distant part of her and fill her with grief, as well as a small insight into the nature of Engai's gift: *There's no hope for me. Not in this life. But there can be hope for everyone else.*

As the visions end, she glimpses a winged figure within the tree's blinding glow. Still kneeling, Isa dares to ask. "What are you?"

"I was once a spirit of heaven; then a queen flung me down to the earth to lie in wait for this moment." A mighty sense of relief fills the air as the leaves of the fig tree begin to dislodge from their branches and float upward. *"And now my vigil is at an end."*

"I don't understand," Isa says. "Why are you leaving? If you're not here, how will your people continue to know your light?" *Who will power the undercity?*

"I have held on to the last fires that once fueled my domain for long enough. They are yours now. Your torch shall not be depleted, not even for a thousand years." As the fig tree sheds its leaves, its branches waste away and disintegrate, their inner glow evanescing into nothing. *"A final warning, daughter of kings. My branches wove across a breach in the Veil. When I dissolve, the breach shall be opened."*

And then a last gust of wind whooshes past Isa, pelting her with so much dust she has to shield her eyes with an arm. When it's over, an almost unnatural silence descends all around her.

She blinks her eyes open, getting back up to her feet. Her torch has acquired a much stronger glow, but something else grabs her attention: a golden crystal beaming at her some distance away.

"Tuliza?" Hopeful, she starts to run toward the light and almost cries in relief when she sees the young woman kneeling next to her discarded torch, seeming lost. "Tuliza, we need to go. I think something is coming."

Tuliza looks up, her expression hypnotized. "I know the truth now," she says. "I finally know the truth!"

The floors begin to shake.

"We have to go now!" Isa grabs Tuliza by the arm and forces her up. She collects the discarded torch, shoving it into Tuliza's chest, but the other woman remains blissfully oblivious to the impending threat.

"Don't you see?" Tuliza says. "Engai is a malaika, and Yonte Saire was built upon the ruins of his vessel, which once sailed across the stars. All this, the undercity, it was a vessel of the stars."

A chasm rips open in the floors, unleashing from its hellish depths a one-eyed fiend straight out of folklore. It rises on enormous bat-like wings, its bony, humanoid form shrouded in a most unusual medium—a misty blackness that conceals even as it illuminates. A black light. An antilight.

Tuliza snaps out of her trance, pointing at the fiend with a trembling finger. "Is that . . . but it can't be."

But it is, Isa knows, for a breach to the underworld has torn open right beneath Yonte Saire, and that creature is only the first of their problems. It flexes its great wings as it hovers above the fissure, blinking its massive eye and searching the air like it can't see their torches.

An advantage they can't afford to waste.

"Run," Isa says quietly, and Tuliza obeys.

17: Musalodi

Lying on his bed in his chamber, he blinks up at the ceiling, giving up all hope of falling asleep. A low, indistinct drone has been harassing him since morning. He can't tell where it's coming from, but he felt it turn on like a beacon earlier in the day, and it hasn't let up. Every time he closes his eyes to concentrate on the sensation, a migraine begins to throb beneath his temples, forcing him to stop. It's slowly eating away at his sanity.

Deciding he might as well make use of his wakefulness, he gets up from his bed, puts on his slippers, and heads downstairs to his study. With his metaformic amulet hooked around his neck, he reclines on the chaise by the window and sends his consciousness into the gemstone, materializing a second later inside a construct of white space and floating blocks of electrified glass. A colorful nebula billows slowly in the featureless sky as a sinuous figure moves within it; as soon as he appears, the figure lowers its head to look down and partially reveals itself to be a massive red serpent.

"Hello, Ziyo," he says to the metaform.

"Ziyo greets the master," comes its reply, lightning arcing away from the nebula.

He stretches his neck from side to side and yawns. "I want to resume the combat scenario from last time. But first, can you show me all the spells for conjuring illusions with tactile surfaces? I'd like to start playing around with your enchanting functionalities tomorrow."

Thunder rumbles across the sky as the metaform searches its memory; then a cluster of spell prototypes appears floating in the air in front of Salo, flat faces turned toward him, tags of red or orange bars glowing along their bottom edges.

Through a limited form of data insertion into his short-term memory, Salo understands exactly what the spells can do just by looking at them. They are each a marriage of Mirror and Void craft—light and force—extracted from the multidisciplinary archive, though designed with different outcomes in mind. Some, for example, are better suited for producing static illusions with rigid surfaces, while others can mimic the texture of fluids. Salo points when his eyes fall on a spell designed specifically to create dynamic phantoms of human beings. The tag attached to it is a red bar of light, marking it as a rather challenging spell to cast.

"That one." The aerosteel plate floats toward him, and he catches it, scanning its cipher prose with his hungry gaze. "Yes. This will do." He looks up at the nebula with a crooked smile. "Begin insertion at the lowest speed."

"Acknowledged."

It's been three days since he completed his stealthy pillaging of the Pattern Archives—almost a week since his first visit. His metaformic amulet, small as it is, now hosts thousands of spells in all six disciplines and thousands more that employ multiple crafts. He had to temporarily dispense with visual forms for the prototypes when the construct started to look cluttered; he has a more permanent solution for them in mind, but for now he's been preoccupied with exploring Ziyo's many other abilities.

Like the data insertions to his short-term memory. Through hours of headache-inducing trial and error, they both figured out that the solution to making the insertions tolerable was for Ziyo to slow them down significantly from instantaneous to a steady trickle, giving Salo a gradual awareness of the delivered data set, which he could then choose to purge or retain in his long-term memory once the insertion was complete.

The first spell he learned back in Khaya-Siningwe took him days of intensive study and memorization to master. With Ziyo's data insertions, he mastered the prose of a telekinetic spell of Void craft in less than three hours and has since managed to learn four other new spells, bringing his spell repertoire up to seven.

That alone would have made the amulet worth killing for, but Salo was even more impressed when he found out how the metaform could simulate spell casting within the construct. Not only that but also combat scenarios, allowing him to practice his spells safely.

He's done nothing else since the discovery. And not because he desires to use his shards for war, but his visit to the House of Forms showed him that there are mystics out there who can slaughter roomfuls of armed men in the time it takes to blink. What if he had to defend himself or his friends against such a monster? What if, Ama forbid, an army of them set upon his clan and attacked his kraal? He would be completely outclassed.

The only choice for him is to improve. After what he went through when Monti died, he knows he can't afford to be complacent.

While the prose of a new spell begins to trickle into his memory, Salo banishes the floating prototypes and summons the combat scenario he used during his last visit.

Grass begins to sprout from the featureless white floors until the construct becomes a verdant plain broken on the horizon by granite mountains. He drew deeply on his memories of home when he built this environment, and any of his clanspeople would immediately recognize the distant plateau with the drystone village or the lake of sparkling water sprawling in the east.

But he allowed himself a liberal measure of artistic license, transforming the sky into a celestial dream where giant bloodroses bloom next to ringed planets and burning comets in a violet star field. A red moon hangs so low and swollen it almost seems a ladder of practicable height might actually give access to it, while Ziyo's nebula, the only thing remaining from the original construct, inhabits a large swath of the new sky.

This is probably as far as he could have gone with his talisman. With the metaform, however, it is simply the foundation of the real construct he intends to build.

"Staff," he says, and an exact copy of his witchwood staff flies toward him from out of thin air. He catches it and holds it with both hands in a fighting stance, leaning into the training he received when everyone still expected him to join the rangers.

He learned the hard way just how well the metaform can simulate the consequences of battle—sometimes the pain and fatigue linger even after he's left the construct—so he bolsters himself with a breath, knowing he won't be able to cheat his way to victory.

"Begin," he says.

A life-size, spear-wielding stone mannequin appears in the plain right then, its face covered behind a mask with the elongated and blocky features that typify Yerezi sculpture. It immediately rushes Salo with its spear, seeking to impale him in the chest.

Experience has taught him not to take too long besting this first mannequin, since it only grows faster and more skilled the longer it stays alive. With his staff, Salo turns the mannequin's thrust aside and retaliates with a kinetic spell in the form of an invisible clenched fist. It hits the mannequin in the chest with enough force to shatter it into pieces.

One down.

A heartbeat later, two identical stone mannequins replace the first and move to flank him, approaching with single-minded purpose and no sense of self-preservation. Once again Salo acts quickly, swinging his staff in a wide arc as he unleashes another spell of Void craft. His shards glow with essence as he conjures an invisible wave of force in the wake of the staff; it augments the reach and power of the swing so that when it slams into both mannequins from yards away, one loses its head while the other is cut in half crosswise from shoulder to hip.

Three down.

Four stone figures appear next, surrounding him. He tries the same thing with another kinetically reinforced swing of his staff, but this time they anticipate him, each one leaping dexterously out of harm's way and then rushing him with machinelike doggedness.

That didn't happen last time. The simulation must be getting tougher.

Before they can surround him, he springs off the ground, calling upon a rather arduous joint spell of wind and force to give himself lift. The mannequins stop and look up as he soars above them, turning head over heels in the air before his feet touch the ground a good twenty paces away.

He didn't want to get here so quickly, but the evasion spell pushed him beyond the limits of his single ring of power, forcing his Axiom to start borrowing processed magic from the future. Every spell he casts now will be increasingly difficult as his debt to time grows larger.

The stone warriors halve the distance in seconds, their spearpoints gleaming menacingly. With a release of Storm craft, Salo envelops all four of them in a depression of electric potential while conjuring an opposing influence around the tip of his staff. They're still more than twenty feet away when a fractal of lightning bolts away from the staff and blasts them to pieces.

Eight mannequins replace them, instantly surrounding him. His shards are now smoldering furiously; he knows that at this point he could either leap away again or cast his most offensive spell. Either way, he won't be able to perform any magic for at least a minute while he pays back his debt to the future.

He makes his decision as the mannequins converge upon him. Lifting his free hand, he clenches it into a fist, then pulls it down with a shout, expending his remaining power in a razor-thin disk of force that explodes away from him faster than the speed of sound. The spell flattens the grasses as it hurtles outward, and the eight stone figures are each cut in half at the waist.

Sixteen more replace them. Salo gulps, holding his staff in a defensive stance. He swivels from one side to the other, not knowing how to start defending himself against so many attackers without using magic.

He lasts three seconds. He bats one thrust away and ducks from another, but a sharp pain explodes into his back when a mannequin impales him from behind. Unable to speak, he looks down at his chest and, to his horror, sees the head of a bloody spear sticking out of him.

"Stop!"

The mannequins immediately disappear, and his body is restored to its original state, though the pain of being run through with a spear takes a while to abate. He falls down to his hands and knees, panting with exhaustion. His Axiom lets him cast spells well beyond the norm for someone at his level, but one ring of power really isn't much at the end of the day. A sustained battle is out of the question.

"Impressive, but you rely too much on magic to do your fighting."

Startled, Salo looks up, only to be met with Niko smiling down at him, resplendent in full regalia, his greaves and vambraces of red steel polished to an almost mirrorlike finish. Salo lets out a groan. "Seriously?"

Impervious, Niko takes an admiring look around the plain. "Did you dream up this place? It's nice."

Salo pushes off his hands and knees and gets up, brushing the dust off his palms as he stares at the ranger. He shakes his head. *What the devil is wrong with me? Why do I keep conjuring him?* "Niko, what are you doing here?"

Niko grins, folding his arms. "I saw you sparring with those demon things. Your magic is incredible, but maybe you're using it too much. You need to mix it up a little. Turn that staff into a spear or get a sword."

"They're not demons," Salo corrects him with a half-hearted scowl. "They're mannequins controlled by the metaform. And why am I explaining this to you? You shouldn't even be here."

"I guess I hated how we left things last time," Niko says. "At the least I'd like us to be on good terms. Hey, how about we spar while we talk? I promise I won't be too hard on you." His grin becomes devilish. "Not unless you want me to be, of course."

Heat creeps up Salo's neck and face. "I've completely lost it. I have. I mean, listen to you."

"Yes, listen to me," Niko says. "You're here to train, right? So let's train."

It's a bad idea but not one Salo hates entirely. Niko was right, after all; he's too reliant on his magic.

He shakes his head and conjures two spears, one in either hand. "I don't know why I'm entertaining you right now. You're not real."

Niko tilts his head to one side as he accepts his spear. "But how do you know I'm not real?"

Perhaps to convince himself of the truth, Salo humors him. "Easy. Can you tell me where you are? I know I'm actually in my study in Yonte Saire, for example. What about you?"

After a thoughtful pause, Niko replies, "I can't say."

"And what about what you were doing just before now? Do you know?"

Niko frowns, a contemplative look in his eyes. "Huh. I can't remember. That's odd, isn't it?"

"Not even a little," Salo says. "Because you're not real. I conjured you subconsciously just like I conjured these spears. As far as you're concerned, there's no before because you didn't exist until now."

Absently, Niko chews on his lower lip, staring into the middle distance. "Maybe you're right," he says. "But I'm here right now, so let's make the most of it." He steps back, lowering the point of his spear. "Try to get me in the chest. It's not like you can hurt me in here, is it?"

He would be wise to banish Niko's likeness and forget he ever existed. Instead, Salo attacks him with his spear, thrusting for his chest.

Stepping into the Ajaha training glade back in Khaya-Siningwe never failed to make him feel inadequate and like a fraud, like he was pretending to be someone he wasn't. Those feelings don't rear their heads today, however, even as Niko evades his every thrust with barely any effort. He thinks it might have something to do with the fact that he's training for his own reasons now, not to prove a point to someone else.

At a break in their rhythm, Niko stands his spear upright and eyes Salo curiously. "If I'm not real, as you say, how come I feel real to myself?"

Salo digs the butt of his spear into the ground. "All right. Tell me something only Niko would know. Something I can't possibly guess."

Niko looks pensively at the ground, then peers up at Salo as his lips twist into a smirk. "I liked chasing after you whenever you ran from the kraal. I pretended I didn't have a choice, but I always volunteered."

Salo shakes his head, feeling even more pathetic. "That sounds like something I would make up and have you say to me."

"Fine. How about this: Remember when I asked you to go hunting with me last year?"

"How can I forget? Three days and nights with you and my brothers mocking me for everything I did wrong. I can't remember why I ever agreed to that."

"I never mocked you," Niko says, a tad defensively. "And I tried to get your brothers to back off."

"Not that it helped."

For the first time since he got here, Niko hesitates, seeming unsure of himself. "It was supposed to be just you and me, but . . . I panicked at the last minute and asked them to join us. I guess I wasn't ready to admit what I was feeling. I was . . . confused."

This isn't what Salo was expecting. In fact, this Niko sounds so real it's making him feverish and divesting him of his self-control. He shifts on his feet. "You've said that before, that I confuse you. You also said you wished I was normal."

Niko lets out a dry snort. "Well, to the pits with normal. I don't want it and I don't need it. Not if it means I have to deny what I feel or at best become like your uncles, hiding in plain sight."

Salo knows what Niko means, though he wouldn't say that Aba D and Aba Akuri hide their love for each other, exactly. Their wedding ceremony was quite public, for one thing.

It's just that, in order to silence those who would question their masculinity, both men chipped away at themselves until they were made of hard and uncompromising edges that cut like jagged glass.

"They never smile, you know," Niko says. "Not even at each other, at least not in public. It's like they think if people see them being affectionate, they'll seem weak. Unmanly. I don't want to be like that." Niko frowns at the ground, looking uncharacteristically vulnerable. "Don't get me wrong, all right? I like being an Ajaha. I like training with my kinsmen and observing our traditions. It's what's expected of me, and I have no problem being that person because it happens to be in line with who I am. But I also really like you, Salo, and I don't want to have to hide it or turn myself into a machine so that my feelings are socially acceptable. If that makes people perceive me as less of a man, so be it. So long as I never have to watch you ride away again."

Salo reminds himself that this isn't the real Niko, that it *can't* be him, and this makes him irrationally angry, so angry he lifts his spear and moves to attack. "You have an army of admirers." He thrusts at Niko's neck, but the ranger dodges to the side too quickly. He follows, intent on drawing blood. "I'm sure you could have your pick. So what the devil's so special about me?"

Niko's eyes flash with surprise, only to harden and narrow to slits. He tosses his own weapon aside, and upon Salo's next thrust, he moves so quickly that the next thing Salo knows, he's disarmed, tackled, and pinned to the ground by Niko's weight, his arms held down by the sides of his head. Niko says nothing until Salo stops resisting. Then time seems to stop as they stare into each other's eyes.

They've never been this physical with each other. Salo isn't certain what to make of it. The one thing he knows for sure is that he doesn't want it to stop.

"Niko, what do you think you're doing?"

"You have no idea, do you?" Niko says in a strange whisper. "You have no idea what I see when I look at you."

A shudder runs through Salo's entire being. He tries to be rational, but his thoughts are almost too electrified for speech. "It doesn't matter what you see. The real Aneniko never saw me that way."

"The real Aneniko doesn't know how to let himself be himself. He's trying to learn, though."

"So you admit that you're *not* him."

Niko stares with his keen gaze; then his eyes glint with wicked purpose. "If I say I'm not, will you let me kiss you? After all, what would it matter what we do here if it's not real?"

Breath. Salo tries to remember how to get it into his lungs. *He's not real. He can't be.* "You've assumed I'll return your affections. What if I don't? Maybe I don't even like men."

Niko lifts an eyebrow and makes a show of looking down at their pelvises, then smirks, satisfied with himself. "Somehow I doubt that.

I can feel your . . . affections pressing up against me. And in any case, I'm not real, remember? You imagined me, which means my desires are reflections of *your* desires: if I want you, it's because you want me to want you, which you would want if you want me."

Outside the construct, in the real world, someone knocks on the door to the study and calls Salo's name. He is immensely relieved and a little irritated.

"I have to go," he says to Niko. "Don't be here when I come back."

Niko responds by bringing his fingers to caress Salo's chin. Just once, but Salo doesn't think he'll ever forget the sensation.

"See you around," Niko says, and his smile stays with Salo as he withdraws his mind from the construct and opens his eyes.

It's like waking from a dream. There's a crystal lamp burning just outside the window next to his chaise. Little insects flutter around it, giving its light a varying brightness. He blinks, turning his gaze away, and the rest of the dim study takes a while to come into focus around him.

Tuk is standing by the open door, his shirtless form backlit by a lamp in the hallway. By the way his arms are folded, Salo can tell he's not pleased, even with his face cast in shadow.

Salo sits up, planting his feet onto the rug beneath him. "Hello, Tuk. Did you need something?"

"It's past midnight," Tuk says in an accusing tone. "You don't come for dinner anymore, you don't leave your study, you barely sleep. You're obsessed with that thing. I'm concerned."

"That thing" being the amulet dangling around Salo's neck. He brushes a finger over his chin, where Niko touched him just seconds ago. "Is that what you came here to tell me?"

"Did you even feel the earthquake?"

"What earthquake?"

Tuk makes a disapproving sound. "There's a Sentinel begging to see you outside. He seems distraught, but he won't tell us what he wants. Says he'll only speak to you."

An earthquake? Wait, a Sentinel? He must be here for the king's spells, which Salo transcoded onto the memory cube as he was requested to do. But why now, and why come here when they were so discreet the last time?

"How curious," Salo utters.

"I think you mean troubling."

"That, too, I guess." With a sense of foreboding, he gets up, crosses the room to his desk, and picks up the memory cube. "I suppose we should find out what he wants."

Tuk continues to watch him with gloomy eyes, blocking the way out the door. "It's not my place to tell you what to do—"

"I value your advice, Tuksaad. You can tell me anything."

"What I'm trying to say is, your queen's expectations aside, getting more involved in local politics is a bad idea. Keep that in mind when you talk to this guy."

Salo looks down at the floor. "I know, and I don't intend to go any farther than I've gone already." He looks up at Tuk, and their gazes cling. "I promise."

Tuk's worry seems to lessen, his eyes lightening a shade. Finally, he steps aside. "After you."

The Sentinel out on the drive is the same young man who slipped Salo the message box over a week ago. Ilapara and Alinata are already there, watching him suspiciously from the porch as he paces back and forth, rubbing his hands together.

His eyes widen as soon as Salo emerges from the residence. "Honored sorcerer! I need your help! The king is in trouble!"

Standing somewhere behind Salo, Tuk lets out an audible groan. Salo ignores it, moving past Ilapara and Alinata and approaching the distressed Sentinel. "Calm down, Red-kin. Where is she right now?"

"In the undercity!" the Sentinel says, his eyes wild with panic. "She told us she was attending a prayer service; then there was an earthquake and the mystics started evacuating everyone, but I couldn't find her, and they wouldn't let me look for her. But I know she's still down there! You have to help me."

By her hardened expression, Ilapara is unconvinced. "This is absurd," she says in Sirezi. "Of all the mystics crawling in this city, the guards, the Sentinels, he comes here? Something doesn't smell right."

The same thought has crossed Salo's mind. "Why have you not sounded the alarm?" he asks the Sentinel. "Why have you come here?"

Fighting back tears, the Sentinel, who says his name is Obe Saai, babbles through an explanation: the king was doing something she didn't want her Faro protector to know about, so she made her guards promise not to tell him under any circumstances, and since she has enemies who would seek to kill her the instant they knew she was out of the Red Temple, the Sentinel didn't know where else to go but here.

"I shouldn't have let her go alone," he says when he's done, looking haunted. "If she's dead, it'll be my fault, Mother above."

The sheer force of his distress is surprising to Salo considering the Sentinel is supposed to be an indentured guard. Also surprising is Alinata's reaction.

"We have to help, Salo," she says, the urgent edge to her voice betraying how much this matters to her. "The king is in trouble, and the high mystic protecting her doesn't know. Her death would be the end of everything."

"That's overstating things a little, don't you think?" Tuk mutters, though his protest lacks enthusiasm, like he partly agrees with her.

"I thought the king was sequestered in the Red Temple," Salo says to the Sentinel, who sniffs as he wipes his rheumy eyes.

"She's been coming out disguised as a servant."

Salo stills as a realization strikes him. "By Ama. That young woman I met in the botanical gardens . . ."

"Yes." A flicker of hope sparks in the warrior's eyes. "That was the king, and she needs your help, honored sorcerer."

Tuk utters a curse while Ilapara shakes her head again. "I really hate this city," she mumbles.

A sentiment Salo shares, but he could hardly refuse to help now, not when he remembers the king's face so clearly. Not when she was desperate enough to meet him in person.

He considers the memory cube in his hand; it looks like he won't be needing it tonight. Swallowing down his nerves, he makes his decision. "Tuk, Ilapara, Alinata. Get your weapons and ready your mounts. We're going to the undercity."

◆ ◆ ◆

Obe Saai's muscled zebroid sets an almost frantic pace as he rides it into the night, leading them down a path that rounds the Skytown hill and cuts through a wooded park into Northtown without crossing the river.

An unpleasant essence pervades the air tonight, like stench from a peat bog or a field of manure, and it grows stronger as they enter the city's most populous neighborhood. Salo wrinkles his nose, wondering if something has gone wrong with the sewage system somewhere.

The stores along the streets are barred and shuttered. The market stands are empty and covered in sackcloth. But there are more people up and about than he would have expected for such a late hour.

On one particular street, a number of people have gathered around a three-story building enveloped in flames. As they approach the building, Salo considers stopping to help, but then he sees the crowds parting for a woman in bronze-colored robes mounted on a sable antelope. Everyone watches as she lifts a staff of aerosteel with one hand, filling her cosmic shards with magic, and then Salo's ears pop as she conjures a high-powered construct of wind that begins to suck out all the air from the building in a visible vortex. Starved of air, the fires immediately subside, and the gathered crowds cheer.

At another building they see a similarly dressed mystic using Void craft to levitate rubble from a collapsed section. Wounded people on stretchers are being carried out of the building and into carriages marked with the twinned helixes of the House of Life.

Was the earthquake really that bad? Salo wonders, completely amazed that he didn't feel it.

As they arrive at a crowded square, the rancid aura in the air gets so obnoxious he almost gags. The people milling about the square seem unconcerned by it, though. Some are gathered around fires crackling inside drums. Mothers are breastfeeding their babies, and elderly people are sleeping on mats laid out on the ground. They all look dispossessed.

Must be evacuees of the undercity.

Ahead of Salo, the Sentinel stops and points toward the mouth of an alley on the west end of the square. "The entrance we used to the undercity is down that alley. The sanctuary is a short walk from there." He seems to spot someone he recognizes. "Ijiro!"

A husky young man seated on a crate by a storefront gets up and jogs over, looking relieved. "Brother Obe. You're back."

"Have any other Sentinels shown up?" Obe asks.

Ijiro shakes his head. "Not yet, but the herald will know something has gone wrong by now. He might send a squad to come investigate."

"Then we'll have to find the king and return her to the temple before that happens." To Salo, Obe says, "Honored sorcerer, this is Sentinel Ijiro Katumbili. He was on duty with me when the king disappeared."

Ijiro bows his head respectfully. "I had begun to despair, honored sorcerer. But now that you're here, I have hope."

"I'll do what I can, Red-kin. But we need to get moving."

"Agreed." Swiftly, Obe dismounts his zebroid and hands the reins over to the other Sentinel. "Ijiro will watch your beasts." He gives Mukuni a questioning glance. "They aren't dangerous, are they?"

"Oh, they're quite dangerous, but they're under my command," Salo says. He dismounts, staff in hand. "You have nothing to fear."

They leave Mukuni, Ingacha, and Wakii with Ijiro and walk across the square in a group. The crowds get thicker as they enter the alley.

Ilapara's expression is skeptical as she looks at something straight ahead, flexing the grip around her spear. "Anyone else notice we're headed straight for a cordon of Jasiri?"

She's right. Three Jasiri warrior mystics armed with spears are blocking access to a descending staircase at the end of the alley, instantly recognizable in their eyeless horned masks, gold-and-aerosteel armor, and crimson robes. The trio alone seems to be enough to keep the restless crowds several yards back.

"Suddenly I feel itchy," Tuk says with a grimace, his eyes shining in the light of the streetlamps. "Which means we're headed toward something likely dangerous. I *knew* there was something off about that earthquake."

Tuk's comment makes something connect in Salo's mind, and only now does he recognize the unpleasant fetor in the air for what it is: not a smell at all but something worse, something he can feel oozing around his cosmic shards like slime.

"Black magic."

"I feel it too," Alinata says, troubled.

"Wonderful," Tuk says.

Is this the funny feeling that's been troubling me all day? Salo wonders. He tries to concentrate on it now but is forced to stop when his temples throb with sharp pain. He comes away with the certainty that whatever is happening here is separate from this other sensation. One is a rancid wrongness coming from somewhere deep below. The other is a beacon calling to him from an unknown place, like a melody he can't quite hear.

He feels like he's losing his mind.

A man in a white boubou has dared to come close to the Jasiri and is shouting at them at the top of his voice. "My daughter is still down there! Let me pass!"

The trio of Jasiri remains unmoved. "Step back, Bwana," says the one in the middle. "The undercity is on lockdown until the threat's been neutralized."

"Gah!" The man throws his hands up as he stomps off. "It's like talking to machines!"

"Looks like they aren't letting anyone pass," Tuk mutters to Salo.

"We'll just have to ask nicely."

Obe lets Salo take the lead as they emerge from the crowd and approach the cordon. He's thinking about what to say when the central Jasiri addresses him by name, sounding surprised. "Emissary Siningwe?"

Stifling his own surprise, Salo dons a facade of confidence he doesn't feel. "You know who I am?"

"I was there when you were presented to the prince regent," the Jasiri explains, and Salo has to consciously avoid a sigh of relief.

"I see."

"A strange time to be about, honored emissary. Do you not feel the corruption stirring in the air?"

"I feel it, but a friend of mine has been trapped in the undercity. I need to go down and search for her."

"I would not recommend it. The warrens will soon be overrun by fell creatures."

"What happened?"

"We suspect a breach into the underworld has torn open deep below the surface. There have been similar incidents before, but never on this scale. Anyone still down there by the hour's end will be a lost cause. We've been ordered to close all undercity entrances until the breach has sealed itself."

"I'm not ready to give up yet, honored Jasiri. Please, let me search for my friend."

"How would you even find your way?" the Jasiri responds. "You're new to this city, and it's a maze down there."

"I'm determined," Salo says.

The Jasiri looks to his comrades, who both remain silent. "I hope, for your sake, that you know what you're doing," he says, then steps aside.

Salo thanks him and leads his party down the staircase, leaving the three Jasiri to face shouts of protest from the crowd.

Walking alongside him, Tuk has a grin on his face even as his eyes remain pitch black. "A breach into the underworld tearing open right beneath our feet. Just what this night was missing."

No one answers him. Salo tries not to even think about what they're walking into. "We need to hurry," he says and hopes they're not already too late.

◆　◆　◆

The city beneath the world's beating heart swallows them up like the tangled bowels of some massive, long-dead beast. It's a honeycomb of tunnels, galleries, and vaulted chambers so alien to Salo he cannot conceive how a sane human being could have possessed the mind or the will to construct such a place.

What's eerier is the stillness haunting the halls despite clear signs that a vibrant community inhabits them. Smoldering grates left unattended. An eatery where people left their plates on the tables. Dwellings with doors left open. The people down here must have abandoned whatever they were doing at a moment's notice.

Just as well, Salo thinks. He can almost taste the vileness of the underworld on his tongue, and beneath the tapping of their footsteps he can hear the echo of roaring things.

Things he can feel getting closer.

Obe Saai seems to know his way and leads the party through the maze at a brisk pace. They come to an open door near the end of a long corridor of flickering lamps. Beyond is a candlelit chamber with the carving of a tree set onto the back wall.

"This is the sanctuary," Obe says, searching the chamber as though he might spot his king hiding in the shadows. "She came in through this door and never returned. I searched inside during the evacuation, but she wasn't there." He looks at Salo with red-rimmed eyes. "I think she might have left through a secret exit."

While Tuk, Ilapara, and Alinata spread deeper into the chamber to investigate, drinking in the scene with obvious curiosity, Salo wanders toward the carving and the pool of water at its base. Something about that water tickles his senses and draws him in. He crouches down to get a closer look at the pinkish glow he can see rippling across the surface. Definitely enchanted.

He finds himself wishing he had his talisman before he remembers he has something even more powerful now. Seamlessly, he partitions his consciousness, and a likeness of him appears in his metaformic construct, settling down on a conjured couch in the original white environment. "Ziyo, can you tell me what's special about this water?"

The metaform responds barely a second later. *"The water contains trace elements of essence-infused moongold underpinning a rudimentary memory charm."*

"Hypnotic Blood craft?"

"Yes."

"Can you tell me what the memories are? Avoid any risk of infecting yourself with malicious prose."

"Analyzing," Ziyo says and speaks again a second later. *"It appears the memories are fragments relating to a certain path to a deeper level of the city's substructure."*

In the real world, Salo gets back up, trying to make sense of this.

"But why would she use a secret exit?" Alinata asks, returning from somewhere deeper in the sanctuary. "Unless she was evacuating like everyone else. Maybe she's safe and you just don't know it."

"I'd know it," Obe says. "I was at the door. I watched everyone come out and waited until the mystics had to force me to leave." He hangs his head. "There's a rite she told us about, but I didn't take her seriously at the time. People go down to the lowest level of the undercity to find some ancient spirit, and if they survive the trip, they gain the respect of the people down here or something. I think she might have decided to do it."

"If I had to guess," Salo says, pointing at the pool, "she probably drank some of this water as part of the rite. It contains a charm with memories for a path deeper into the undercity."

Everyone takes a moment to digest this.

"So to recap," Tuk says, "a breach to the underworld tore open while the king was performing a rite that had her going down to the deepest level of the undercity. Does anyone else think this is *not* a coincidence?"

The candles in the chamber seem to create autonomous shadows that lurk in the corners. "Probably not," Ilapara says, the only one among them to continue using Sirezi. "But the Jasiri was right. How are we supposed to find her down here? She could be anywhere. Not to mention we can't find a secret exit."

"I have an idea," Salo says. "Hold on." While in the real world his eyes go unfocused, in the construct, his likeness addresses Ziyo's nebula. *"My talisman could detect mind stones and life signs even from a mile away. You can do the same, right?"*

"Affirmative."

"Excellent. Scan for all human life signs in as much of the undercity as you can."

What Ziyo gives him is even better than he hopes. A mirage of red light appears in front of his likeness, showing a translucent maze of burrows and tunnels like the inside of an anthill. It's a three-dimensional map of the entire undercity, and within that map are a number of blinking white lights and many more black points clustered together, seething through the tunnels like a plague.

Ziyo doesn't have to tell him what those black objects are. "Dear Ama. This place is crawling. And there are other people still down here."

"Then she could be alive," Obe says.

Looking at the mirage in the construct gives Salo another idea. *"Ziyo, can you tell if there are any secret exits nearby?"*

"A hidden staircase north of your position leads down to a distinct sector of the undercity."

"Show it to me."

The mirage blows up so that he sees the staircase illuminated brighter than the rest of the maze, and indeed, it looks like the entrance to it is a few rooms to the north. "Follow me," he says to the others and leads the way out of the main chamber.

A shriek from somewhere below makes the walls tremble, reminding them of what they will face should they linger here. While Tuk, Ilapara, and Alinata start mumbling to each other, Salo grips his staff tighter to focus his mind on the task ahead. "What do you mean, 'a distinct sector'?"

"Pardon me?" Obe says behind him.

"Sorry. I was conferring with my invisible familiar."

"Oh. Carry on, then."

"Ziyo?" Salo says, this time subvocalizing his communication.

"The network of tunnels beneath you is markedly different from the rest of the undercity in composition and structure," Ziyo explains. *"It also gives access to the labyrinth's deepest cavity."*

"Show me the life signs within this sector specifically."

The metaform obeys, and all blinking lights on the three-dimensional map disappear except for two located somewhere near the bottom.

They aren't moving. A closer inspection tells Salo that they're trapped in a small pocket of space just outside a seething mass of black dots.

Not trapped, he realizes. *Hiding.*

The secret staircase is in a chamber lit by an assortment of colorful crystals. Ziyo shows Salo the mechanism for accessing the staircase, which involves pulling down on a lever disguised as a branch on a bronze tree. As soon as the lever moves to its lowered position, the bronze tree and its niche descend into a hollow in the floor, leaving an open doorway to a staircase.

Tuk takes one look at the doorway and walks to dislodge a crystal lamp from a wall. "I think we're supposed to grab one of these." The others quietly follow his example.

Staring at the open portal, Salo suffers a powerful spasm of fear. "I sense two people hiding at the bottom of this path," he tells the others. "If the king is alive, and if she used this exit, she'll probably be one of them."

"Then we have no time to waste." Obe makes to enter the portal, but Salo puts a hand out to stop him.

"Wait. It'll take us too long to get there if we just walk. Let me think of something." In the construct, he says, *"Ziyo, what's the absolute fastest way down to the bottom of this sector?"*

On the map, Ziyo highlights a vertical duct running throughout the entire depth of the undercity. *"A three-thousand-foot drop down a shaft from one level below. However, under free fall, the descent would be lethal to a human."*

Not ideal, but it surprises Salo how the shaft seems to be sitting almost directly on top of the two life signs. That makes the decision for him. *"Show me the way to this shaft."* To the others, he says, "Keep close." And then he descends the staircase.

◆ ◆ ◆

"Even with the torches I can't see a damned thing down here," Tuk complains minutes later. "Did I ever tell you how much I hate dark and confined spaces? There could be a horde of tikoloshe waiting twenty feet ahead of us, and we wouldn't know."

Salo responds by lifting his right hand in a fist and filling the witchwood ring on his middle finger with essence. Yellow Mirror craft explodes out of the ring's citrine stone, its rays bringing daylight to the tunnels. "Better?"

"Much better," Tuk exclaims. "At least now we'll see what's coming to eat us and have enough time to say our last prayers."

Either the earthquake or eons of neglect left parts of the tunnels in this sector in severe disrepair. They have to leap over a section of collapsed floor and then crawl through a grimy duct before they come to a chamber housing the mouth of the shaft. It yawns before them like a massive gullet, devouring their torchlight so that they cannot tell how far down it goes. Not even Salo's enchanted ring can penetrate its depths.

Silence enfolds them as they stare down into the gloom.

"So," Ilapara says, "I'm assuming there's a reason you brought us here, Salo. Hopefully one that doesn't involve this gaping chasm of death."

Salo wipes sweat off his brow. "Actually, this shaft will take us down to the bottom. Practically within several feet of whomever we're rescuing."

Obe leans down so he can take a closer look. "Are we supposed to jump?" He sounds dubious, though his expression suggests he's actually considering it.

"It's a three-thousand-foot drop, Sentinel Obe. You'd die."

"Lovely," Ilapara remarks.

"I don't know." Tuk examines the chasm with a pondering look. "I feel like I might survive. It'd hurt something fierce, though. And someone might have to pick my splattered guts off the floor and stuff them back inside me."

Alinata gives him a hooded stare, unamused. "Thank you, Tuk, for that wonderful image."

Tuk replies with a wink.

"I don't see how this helps, honored sorcerer," Obe says.

"Well. I was hoping . . ." Salo lets his sentence trail off while raising his eyebrows at Alinata in invitation.

She exhales loudly. "I suppose you're going to ask me to fly us down."

"Walking would take a while," he says. "And whoever's down there might not have that much time left."

She considers it. "I can only carry one person at a time, though."

"That will have to be good enough."

Obe appears surprised by this development. "You're a mystic?" he says to Alinata, who gives him an imperious glare.

"No, but I'm close enough to one to get the job done."

He glances down the shaft again, his fists clenching by his sides. "I'll go first."

"That might not be wise," Salo cautions. "We'll face significant opposition down there."

"Perhaps I should check what we're walking into first," Alinata suggests. "Then I'll let you know."

"Good idea."

The Void's touch chills the air as the Asazi wraps it around herself like a blanket, blurring from view while black-feathered birds take her place. A second later the birds surge upward before tucking in their wings and plunging into the abyss.

"Dear Mother," Obe exclaims.

While the others wait with bated breath, Salo keeps track of Alinata's rapid descent through the map in the construct, seeing her birds displayed as little white dots plummeting down the shaft. He watches them reach the cavity at the other end of the shaft, sweep the cavity in a circle, and then hurtle back up.

"She's coming!"

Her ravens soon emerge from the chasm and gather at the edge into a young woman in pale kitenges and red steel.

"There's one devil of a welcoming party at the bottom of this shaft," she says, looking grim. "Quite literally."

A burst of moonlight briefly blinds them as Tuk summons a flash-brand from one of his rings, a Void weapon in the form of a long and curved sword with a golden radiance. Sparks of red lightning ripple along its engravings. "Take me down first," he says.

"Agreed," Salo says, which makes Obe frown again.

"Why?" the Sentinel demands.

"Because I have the best chance of surviving until the rest of you arrive," Tuk replies, then looks at Alinata. "Bring Ilapara down next, then Salo." Speaking again to Obe, he says, "Do you have any experience with underworld creatures?"

Obe stands straighter, looking mildly affronted. "No, but I can hold my own against any enemy."

"What's down there won't be like any enemy you've ever faced, friend. You might want to hang back."

"He's right," Salo says. "There's no need to put more lives at risk than is necessary. Perhaps you should wait here."

Obe unsheathes the blade by his side without breaking eye contact. "I'm coming with you. Even if I have to jump."

A little intimidated by the look in his eye, Salo nods. "As you wish. Tuksaad, are you ready?"

"Always."

"Then we're all in your hands now, Alinata."

Once again Alinata brings the Void's cold bite into the air, this time wrapping it around Tuk as well, and they dematerialize into a flock of ravens that swoops down into the shaft. The chamber grows dimmer with their torches gone.

Salo knows exactly when they've reached the bottom because he feels Tuk immediately drawing strength from his blessing as he begins to fight for his life.

"I'm in hell down here!" he sends along their mental bond, the force of his fear and excitement swelling along the tether like a tide. It almost brings Salo down to his knees.

"Hold on!" he sends. *"Ilapara will be there soon."*

While Tuk battles against unknown horrors, Alinata races back up the shaft, and several long seconds pass before her ravens issue forth from the darkness. Ilapara is already waiting expectantly with her torch and spear, and she doesn't hesitate when the ravens surround her and take her into the Void.

Biting his lips nervously, Salo watches as the ravens disappear to deliver yet another friend of his unto the jaws of death. Obe seems calm, considering, and Salo hopes for the young man's sake that his confidence isn't just a pretense.

The ravens return and don't even give Salo a moment to steel himself before they swoop down on him and transpose him into a realm of absence. He has drawn the Void into his cosmic shards and has become familiar with its unsympathetic character, but being *in* it is an entirely different experience, like drowning in an infinite ocean of loneliness and sensory deprivation, where his existence is simultaneously meaningless and without end.

He's aware of his rapid plunge down the ribbed shaft, the thickening stench of rot and manure, the earsplitting roars, the desperate battle waiting for him, and then suddenly he is there at the bottom, standing next to the ruin of a giant structure that might have once been a sphere. Tuk has dropped his torch and summoned a second flashbrand. Ilapara has dropped hers, too, so she can hold her weapon with both hands. The tikoloshe are almost clambering over each other to get to them, white fire beaming out of their eye sockets.

And there are so many burning eyes the torches are almost unnecessary, and more keep crowding in through a wide entrance on the other side of the broken sphere. As the ravens flutter back up the shaft, Salo glimpses Ilapara spinning with her bladed spear amid a group of malformed skeletons that tower over her. One is sundered in half by the maneuver, but they have surrounded her on all sides, and it's only a matter of time before she's inundated.

When he first encountered tikoloshe, Salo's weakness cost him Monti's life. The second time he became paralyzed with fear long enough to put the lives of his friends at risk, and Tuk was injured as a result. Today he doesn't allow himself to hesitate.

The citrine stone on his ring dims as he diverts essence into his shards and calls upon a spell of telekinetic Void craft to reinforce his staff. He swings with all his might, and the wave of magic that follows the swing flattens down a trio of demons pressing toward Ilapara. As one they fall apart into dust, but Salo doesn't give in to the temptation of being amazed at what he's done.

"Duck down, Ilapara!"

She's surrounded, thrusting her spear to keep the encroaching wraiths away. "What?"

"Duck down!" Salo shouts again.

Ilapara drops low, and Salo quickly swings his staff in another Void-powered attack, launching a horizontal wave that slices into the necks, skulls, and shoulders of the tikoloshe surrounding her. They disintegrate, and she has a baffled look on her face as she straightens back up. Then her eyes widen.

"Watch out! Behind you!"

He looks up just in time to see danger leap toward him from atop the ruined sphere. But then Tuk is there, meeting the leaping tikoloshe with the swing of a flashbrand. A cloud of dust billows around him as he cleaves it in half, and he slides toward his next target, swinging his other weapon in an attack that slices cleanly down a rib cage, then executing a powerful kick that sends the demon flying off into a crowd of its fellows, where it disintegrates upon impact.

Even in the heat of the moment, Salo is astounded by what he sees. Tuk was already an extraordinary swordsman. Now he's just ridiculous.

The floors shudder when something emits an earsplitting screech from outside the confines of the chamber. Salo senses in this screech a much greater evil than the tikoloshe and immediately understands that should it catch them here, none of them will leave this place alive.

The birds descend from the shaft one last time, depositing Obe Saai into the battle. Alinata takes shape next to him with a knife of shadows in either hand, throwing one across the chamber, where it impales a tikoloshe in the skull. She discorporates again and surges forward, ripping through the body of another tikoloshe, leaving a trail of dust in her wake.

"The king is hiding behind a door in this chamber!" Salo shouts, hoping his voice carries over the din. "I'm going to seal off the entrances. Watch my back!"

Ilapara teams up with the Sentinel to keep Salo's immediate surroundings free of demons. Obe proves to be rather competent with his sword, though Alinata takes it upon herself to make sure he's never overburdened.

In the construct, Salo consults the map for the exact dimensions of the cavity so he can begin weaving a defensive barrier, using his staff to keep his mind focused. The others continue to fight around him while he employs his spell of Storm and Void craft barriers, erecting the ward from the base up. Tessellated hexagons of force and lightning rise flush against the walls, sealing off the entrances and stemming the ceaseless flood from the underworld.

With only one ring on his cosmic shards, he has to borrow Storm and Void craft from the future, using now what his shards will have to process later. But the technique is unsustainable and taxing on the mind, and unlike in the simulation, it will leave him with a real migraine and a temporary inability to cast spells.

Nevertheless, the ward grows around them and manifests as a warped dome given the cavity's irregular shape, though Salo has the presence of mind to leave an opening at the top so that the shaft remains accessible and another where he detected the two life signs. He completes the ward just before the evil presence he sensed arrives.

While the battle rages around him, Salo's eyes are glued to the entity that hovers into view beyond an entrance he sealed off. Its form is slightly distorted by his semivisible ward, but he can clearly see its single gigantic eye and its leathery wings, as well as a mouthful of razor-sharp teeth. More alarming is how the tikoloshe trapped outside the ward step out of its way and gather behind it, like it's their leader.

With a clawed talon the creature reaches forward to test the ward, tilting its head curiously. Sparks of red lightning radiate from its finger, but the lightning is apparently too weak to harm it.

Only when Tuk shouts something at him does Salo pry his gaze from the horrific creature and see that the cavity has been cleared.

He points. "Over there! They're behind that door." Without Ziyo he wouldn't have known it was a door, given how it's almost indistinguishable from the rest of the walls, which are carved with strange symbols.

Obe runs for the door and bangs repeatedly against it while he shouts, "Isa! Isa, are you there?"

A muffled voice responds. "Obe?"

"Isa! Isa, it's me."

There's a hiss as the door slides open, revealing two young women huddled together in a space hardly large enough for one person. Both are covered in dust, holding their unusually bright torches like weapons, but at the sight of Obe one of them drops her guard and rushes to embrace him. "Dear Mother, I've never been so happy to see you."

By the way they hold each other, Salo finally divines why the Sentinel was so determined to rescue her.

"You actually came," she says, her voice laden with emotion.

"I had help," Obe says and looks over his shoulder at Salo, gratitude shining in his teary eyes.

The young king finally takes stock of her surroundings, her gaze traveling across Ilapara, Alinata, and Tuksaad and then finally landing on Salo, whose shards are still glowing. Her eyes widen as she recognizes him. "Honored emissary."

"Your Majesty," Salo says, inclining his head respectfully.

"I suppose I have you to thank for my rescue."

By her hesitation, Salo figures she probably feels embarrassed for lying about her identity when they first met. That hardly matters right now. "You can thank me later, Your Majesty. Let us get you to safety first."

". . . Yes. All right."

"I have to ask, though," Tuk says, his eyes shining almost neon blue in the torchlight. "How the devil did you survive what we just fought through? Erm . . . Your Majesty."

"It seems I have a knack for hiding from danger," she says. "You're the second mystic to rescue me from a closet, Emissary Siningwe."

"She saw a vision that led her to the door," says the full-figured young woman behind the king, stepping forward. "Then we barricaded ourselves behind it." She waves shyly at everyone. "I'm Tuliza, by the way."

"Questions and introductions later, everyone," Salo says, straining to maintain his ward. "In case you haven't noticed, we have an audience."

Everyone looks at the creature outside the ward, and the woman named Tuliza gasps. "That's the popobawa we saw earlier. I can't believe it's real!"

"It's quite real, unfortunately," Salo says. "Alinata, are you ready?"

The Asazi gives her weapons up to the Void and partially blurs from view as ravens begin to swirl around her. "Say the word."

"This time Ilapara goes in the vanguard, then the Sentinel, then Her Majesty and her companion. I'll bring up the rear since I have to maintain this ward. Tuk, you'll go second to last in case I need you."

Tuk nods, twisting the flashbrands in his hands. "Got it."

"Alinata."

She wraps Ilapara in the Void, and they ascend the shaft. The rest of the evacuation proceeds as planned while Salo maintains the ward, the creature outside watching the whole time, waiting.

When he's left alone with Tuk, his nerves start to get the better of him. "I'm afraid of what will happen when I drop this ward."

Tuk stares at the hellish creature. "You could go up first."

"There's no way I'm letting you fight that thing alone. I'll be fine."

"Are you sure?"

Salo gulps. "Yes."

And so it is Tuk who goes first when Alinata returns, leaving Salo alone in the deepest cavity of Yonte Saire's undercity with a demon staring at him from across a dying ward. The terror that grips him almost breaks the courage he cobbled together at the joints. The popobawa, as Tuliza called it, can probably smell his fear, which is likely why it grins, showing him its frightful mass of serrated teeth.

Salo looks away. The seconds tick down; then Alinata appears at his side, and it's his turn to go up. He tries to maintain the ward even as his body enters the Void, but eventually the distance between the ward and his cosmic shards grows too wide, and he is forced to relinquish the spell.

A large winged shape enters the cavity and climbs the shaft after them, and there's nothing he can do but watch.

18: The Enchantress

The night is well underway when the Enchantress walks into an interrogation chamber at the end of a narrow hallway, two masked Jasiri trailing behind her. Located in an abandoned section of the undercity several levels removed from the residential and commercial sectors, it has held many political dissidents and enemies of the Shirika, many of whom have never again seen the light of day.

Dull, wall-mounted crystals cast a jaundiced light across the interior, where a wiry bronze-skinned woman sits with her head bowed, her hands shackled to the top of a sturdy table. A third Jasiri is standing guard behind her, silent as a mountain.

The Enchantress takes a moment to study the prisoner. "How did you find her?" she asks the Jasiri.

"It was as you said, Your Highness," he replies. "We posted the symbol you showed us in taverns and shebeens around the city, and someone heard her asking questions. Then we followed her to an apartment in Northtown to interrogate her. She was wearing this." The Jasiri dangles something hanging on a silver chain. A Fireblue pendant wrought into the symbol of an eye.

The Enchantress frowns behind her scarlet veil. That pendant erases any doubt that this woman is her Vigilant spy. Put a black circle inscribed within a square inscribed within an octagon, and no Vigilant will be able to resist the chance to hunt down a nest of supposed devil worshippers.

Lifting her veil to reveal her face, the Enchantress approaches the table cautiously. She knows that the shackles on the prisoner aren't there merely to keep her in place; they are there to mute whatever sorcery she might possess. She knows this because she instructed the Jasiri to use them. Without her guidance they would have used a regular muting collar instead, which, though effective at nullifying Red magic, would not have worked on this particular prisoner. Standing close to her now, the Enchantress knows she made the right call.

"Did she put up a fight?"

"Initially," answers the Jasiri. "But she calmed down when she realized she couldn't defeat us."

"Thank you, gentlemen. If you could give us a moment alone. I'd like to have a little chat with her."

The Jasiri look at each other. The one behind the prisoner shakes his head. "Your Highness, I'm not sure that's a good idea."

"You've shackled her, haven't you?"

"Yes, but—"

"I'll be fine. Come on. I don't have all night." The Enchantress lowers herself onto the seat across the table from the prisoner. She enraptured her Jasiri well, so they file out of the chamber without further protest.

"We'll be right outside, Your Highness," the last one says at the threshold; then the door shuts, leaving the Enchantress alone with the prisoner.

The prisoner doesn't raise her head. Her straight hair was clipped short for practicality rather than for beauty's sake. The dirty brown tunic she's wearing is a little too large for her frame, but the Enchantress sees military training in those lean shoulders of hers.

"A lord of the suns and a Vigilant, here in the heart of the Red Wilds." The Enchantress chooses to speak in the ancient tongue of Syliaric, the adopted tongue of the Enclave beyond the Jalama, knowing that the prisoner will understand it. "What has brought you so far from home, my dear? I can only imagine the risks you must have taken."

The prisoner remains silent.

"You won't tell me? Then I suppose I shall have to guess." Without moving a muscle, the Enchantress extends a subtle spell across the room, so quiet it fails to engage her cosmic shards. It takes shape as a psychic membrane of hypnotic Blood craft designed to detect fluctuations in brain physiology: useless to the uninitiated, a boon to those who know the workings of the mind.

She begins with a statement she knows to be false in order to establish a baseline. "Let's start with the fact that you obviously don't bow to Valor, since you were smart enough to surrender. A true Valorite would have sooner died. You draw your power from Verity, the white sun."

That rouses a derisive chuckle from the prisoner.

"Not impressed? Then let me try harder." With the baseline set, the real interrogation can now commence. "I know you're from the Empire," the Enchantress says, "and if you were able to resist the Jasiri even for a few seconds, you must know how to handle yourself in a fight."

A tremor in the psychic membrane tells the Enchantress she's onto something.

She keeps pushing. "A mystic of Valor from the Empire who has obvious military training." A sharp spike in the membrane betrays the prisoner's surprise, making the Enchantress smile. "Did I say you were *not* a Valorite? I must have misspoken. You reek of self-righteousness. What else could you be?"

The prisoner remains still, but sweat begins to collect on her forehead. She must have realized what's happening and is now—rather predictably—struggling to maintain a protective barrier around her mind. That might have worked to ward off an intrusive mind-reading attempt, but it does little to mask her physical responses to the questions, which are all the Enchantress needs.

She gets up and paces for a time, thinking through the facts. She knew many lords of the sun quite intimately during her old life in the Empire, sometimes against her will, but it gave her a deep understanding of the way they think, even the few who apostatize into the Cult of Vigilance.

"If I had to guess, I'd say you're former imperial intelligence. It's almost impossible to prove, but no other organization in the Empire has been infiltrated by the Vigilants more successfully. You were likely identified as impressionable and proselytized by a superior officer. But are you still working for them, or have you gone rogue?" The Enchantress stops pacing to eye the prisoner. "What were you doing in this city?"

The prisoner is almost shaking from the effort of shielding her mind.

"You were recruiting more Vigilants," the Enchantress says, closely monitoring the psychic membrane. It's unperturbed. "No? So you were spying on the royal court." The membrane remains flat. That isn't it either. "You were here to bring something."

Though the prisoner feigns calm, her internal response to the statement produces an obvious spike in the membrane. The Enchantress steps closer to the table, moving in like a shark after tasting blood.

"You were here to bring an object." A tremor, but not enough of one. "Some kind of artifact." Not that. "Knowledge." A spike, and the prisoner frowns in concentration. "Technology?" The spike doesn't move. "Magic."

The prisoner finally looks up, her brown eyes bloodshot and full of rage. "Get out of my head, you evil bitch!"

Stunned, the Enchantress presses a hand against her chest. "You were here to bring solar magic to the Red Wilds?"

A powerful spike. The prisoner continues to glare. She must have put up a good fight, because her face is swollen and bruised.

"Is that even possible?" the Enchantress asks, and her jaw almost falls at the membrane's positive reaction. "How many have you taught? Where are they?"

The prisoner's face twists with hatred, her imperial accent giving her words a distinctive lilt. "I know who and what you are, Luksatra of the Seven Mountains. I see the stain you harbor inside your heart. You are a mistress of the devil. An enemy of humankind. But you and your ilk shall not succeed."

It costs the Enchantress a tremendous feat of effort to keep herself from reacting to that name. She blinks, opening her mouth to speak, but the floors suddenly move beneath her, dust falling from the ceiling as the room shakes on its foundations. When she hears a loud rumbling like the sound of a rockfall, she begins to think the roof is about to collapse on top of them.

Then the tremors stop, and the door bursts wide open.

"Your Highness, we have to leave," says one of her Jasiri. "An earthquake down here is never good news."

She takes a moment to recover her composure. For a moment she thought she was about to die. "You're right. I've gotten what I came for anyway."

"What do we do with her?" the Jasiri says, nodding at the prisoner.

The Enchantress glances at the woman, thinking. "Kill her."

"As you wish." The Jasiri draws his blade and approaches, but the Enchantress stops him with a raised hand.

"Not while I'm here, obviously. Wait until I'm gone."

"Yes, Your Highness."

To the prisoner, she says, "I will find your students, and I will destroy them."

"You will never win!" the prisoner shouts, but the Enchantress is already out the door.

The other two Jasiri fall in behind her while the third remains in the interrogation chamber. She walks briskly down the corridor, intent on returning to the Summit so she can inform Prophet of what she has discovered.

But a pile of rubble brings her to a standstill.

A cave-in has completely blocked the way forward.

Stifling a nervous shiver, she turns around, facing her guardians. "Please clear a path. I don't fancy dying down here."

They trade looks. "We're Mirror mystics, Your Highness," one of them says. "We have no magic that can move these rocks."

The Enchantress rubs her eyes. "Use your hands, then. And be quick about it. Something wasn't right about that earthquake."

She makes space for the Jasiri, and they both get to work. The third one joins them not long after, offering no details about what he's just done. The Enchantress doesn't ask, though she finally lets herself shiver.

In a different time, in a land far away, the priest who aided the duke and duchess of the Two Suns Eclipsing is greatly saddened when he hears news of their demise.

It is a story that shocks the Empire: a house whose star was on the rise, cast down without warning, their futures stolen away in the night. No one claims responsibility. No one is arrested. There are too many people who wished the duke and duchess evil because of their two brilliant children, and some even whisper that the kill order might have come from the Court of Light itself.

As for the priest, he cannot help but mourn the family as though they were of his own blood, for the children he gifted the duke and duchess were his crowning achievement, the culmination of decades of experimentation and arcane research.

Indeed, he had meant for them to be his legacy, their ascent to the highest seats in the Court of Light proving once and for all that the moon's power is not inherently evil. If children born of Red magic could be so perfect even in the eyes of the suns, how then could the moon be a sister to the Adversary? How then could those who call upon her power be corrupt at heart and worthy of hate and persecution?

In his grief, the priest succumbs to a foolish plot to salvage his work. Before the brother and sister can be given over to the consuming sunlight of a funeral temple, their souls sent along with their parents' into the Infinite Path, he orchestrates a most unholy crime, stealing away their corpses and bringing them to his home, where he casts spells to preserve their flesh.

Being old and wise, the priest knows there's no magic on earth that can return a soul to its dead vessel, but he spends many days capturing the structures of their minds in minute detail, the information in their flesh, the stories in their blood, the marks on their skin.

But the project is more demanding than he anticipated, and the days turn to weeks, the weeks to moons, the moons to comets, until at last the old priest becomes weary and decides he can go no further. Before his encroaching senility can confine him to his deathbed, he shelves all the materials he has gathered over the years and finally commits the siblings to the heavens with a spell of moonlight.

As their bodies dissolve away on twin altars, the priest reflects on how appropriate it is that the moon be the one to guide them into infinity, as she was the one who breathed life into them in the first place.

Little does he know that decades later, his successor several times over will discover his notes and see within them not a misguided attempt to revive the dead but a breakthrough in the science of creating synthetic humans, promising to finally meet the Empire's demand for pliant bed slaves.

Little does he know that decades after his death, his beloved children will return, except they won't quite be his children. At least not as he envisioned them, and certainly not as he intended them to live.

Little does he know, and it's just as well, for if he did know what would become of his creations, he would weep.

It takes two hours for the Jasiri to move enough rubble to allow escape from the collapsed corridor. During that time the Enchantress becomes aware of a tainted influence thickening all around her, seeping up from the floors and permeating the air.

Keeping her power concealed beneath a field generated by her metaform means that her own faculties of sensing the magical world are often compromised, but this influence is so dense she can almost feel it coating her skin. The shadow she keeps hidden in some corner of her soul rears its head and attempts to rise to the surface, finding affinity with the influence, but she beats it back down with sheer force of will. Still, her gums begin to itch, and she has to battle against the urge to growl like an animal.

"We should be able to pass through now, Your Highness," says one of her guardians. He tilts his head as he notices the look on her face, and the Enchantress isn't even sure what he sees. "Are you all right?"

She inhales, coming off the edge as she takes back control. "Yes." *Just what exactly is happening here?* "We need to get back to the surface. Now."

One Jasiri leads the way forward while the other two follow behind the Enchantress. Her veiled senses are further irritated when she senses a sustained burst of magic released elsewhere in the undercity. The shadow inside her roars with fury, filling her with the desire to find the source of the magic and destroy it. She wrestles the shadow into submission.

Another passage the group used on their way in collapsed on itself, so they have to turn around and find a different way. It is as they turn into a new corridor that they come face-to-face with a creature of nightmares feasting on the bowels of a dead man.

The thing might have been human once, but now it runs on all fours, its spine bent awkwardly, its flesh long since rotted off its bones. Dust and the deathly energies of the underworld seethe all around it, and for a second they all freeze as they stare back into its unblinking torch eyes.

It roars, bits of human flesh clinging to its bloodied teeth, only for its lower jaw to be cleanly sliced off as the Jasiri in front of the Enchantress unleashes a concentrated beam of monochromatic red light from a glowing palm. The beam slices through the monster's torso and legs as well, bringing it crashing onto its meal in a pile of bones and dust.

"There will be more," he says, lowering his palm. "We must keep moving."

He takes a step forward and is swallowed up as the floor gives way beneath his feet. Watching him disappear, the Enchantress slaps a hand over her mouth to smother a scream. Strong hands grab hold of her and pull her back from the chasm.

"Come on, Your Highness. We must find another way."

The Enchantress stares up into the faceless mask of her rescuer, then back at the hole in the floor. "What about him?"

"He'll live if he's of any worth."

They continue on.

There are more demonic creatures roaming the halls, alone or in pairs, clearly forerunners of an incoming wave. Her remaining Jasiri silently cut through them with spells of destructive light, prodding her onward with martial efficiency. She feels her self-control unraveling as she battles the dual impulses assailing her: the fear of suffocating down here or falling to mindless underworld beasts, and the urge to let free the shadow inside her and join the beasts in their rampage.

Soon she climbs a staircase and emerges into an undercity residential neighborhood with clean walls and floors, wider galleries, and doors leading to apartment dwellings.

"The exit to the surface won't be far from here," says one of the Jasiri. He points at a street sign indicating directions to a commercial hub with egress to the surface. "This way."

They hurry into the curving tunnel beneath the sign, one Jasiri in front and the other behind the Enchantress. She becomes less sure footed when she hears shouts and the sound of crashing things.

"I sense a battle ahead," says the Jasiri in the lead, his shards brightening as he readies himself for the worst.

The Enchantress braces herself, too, but is still unprepared for what greets them at the other end of the tunnel. They come to a dead stop.

"Conceal us," she commands.

Quickly, the lead Jasiri casts an illusion spell that surrounds them in a light-distorting field, making them invisible.

In the large cavity of the commercial hub, a group of young people has been cornered by a one-eyed creature with a pair of perforated leathery wings spread wide enough to close its prey in. Two of them are carrying crystals shining with a glaring brilliance, yet their light fails to completely illuminate the beast's features, as though it is surrounded by a light-resistant medium.

The Enchantress and her Jasiri watch from behind their distortion field as one of the youths rushes the creature with his sword raised high.

"Obe, no!"

There is a bespectacled mystic in the group, his shards alight with magic, but his magic must be temporarily depleted, because he's unable to stop the beast from slapping his friend away with a vicious swipe of a clawed hand. The young man flies, hitting a wall hard before slumping to the ground, one arm bent at an unnatural angle.

At first the Enchantress can only watch in silent horror as the beast advances on the others. And then her eyes fall on the figure who puts himself in front of the group, his twin swords flashing with magic that shouldn't exist on this side of the Jalama.

Her heart drops inside her chest. The floors threaten to tear open and devour her. She already knew he was in the city, but to actually see him is a painful jolt to her spine.

It should be easy to let him die here. He once promised that he would never leave her, but when the chance for a better life came to him, he didn't hesitate to take it, abandoning her to suffer alone at the hands of their cruel mistress.

She should hate him, and a part of her does. Indeed, a part of her will never forgive his betrayal. But she still remembers the day when they both came to life on the cold steel altar of an ambitious necromancer and immediately recognized each other from a different time, when the suns smiled down on them and their futures were full of light. That life was never hers, nor was it his—they are not their progenitors. Yet the echo of love she felt for him was strong and unwavering.

Without thinking, the Enchantress unleashes the shadow she welcomed into her soul when she became Prophet's student and was inducted into his inner circle. It surges to the surface of her skin and tries to take over, but she wrestles to keep it under her control.

Time stops. The world stills as the Veil that blankets reality becomes visible, everyone around her blurring into ghostly outlines. The only thing not affected is the one-eyed creature, which, noticing the change, stops advancing on its prey and turns its angered gaze toward the Enchantress.

"Leave them be," she says to it, the shadow supplanting her voice so that it's deeper and more resonant. "Go back from where you came. All of you."

The creature snarls, its thicket of teeth dripping with poisonous drool. "You do not command me."

"Look again." Just for a second, the Enchantress allows the shadow to show itself in its entirety. Teeth break out of her gums like thorns, her fingers lengthening to claws. "Go back. Your time has not yet come."

The creature steps forward with a growl, and she hears herself growling back. It takes a mighty force of will to keep the shadow on a leash, until at last the creature screams in frustration and scurries out of the hub and back to the breach whence it came.

The passage of time resumes as the Veil lifts. Fighting the shadow back into its cage takes so much of her strength her knees give out, forcing one of her Jasiri to catch her.

"Your Highness, let me carry you."

Spent and utterly drained, the Enchantress allows herself to fall into the arms of her guardian and be whisked away. The last thing she sees before her eyes close is her long-lost brother and his friends rushing to collect their fallen comrade as they flee to the surface, none of them the wiser as to what has just transpired.

Interlude: The Sister

A shield of rage protects the Adversary as she faces a spirit of misery and desolation at the shores of a subterranean lake.

"Show me," she says, the opening note of an all-too-familiar song.

"It is futile," the spirit tells her. *"For even if you tasted all the sorrows of this lake, you would not have done any of its victims any good. Your grief is wasted, your rage impotent. There can be no recompense for the souls entombed here, only the silence of nothingness. Give in, and you shall know peace."*

The spirit attempts to break through her shield, drilling into it with its twisted, tentacled limbs, but the shield holds, and the Adversary remains resolute. "Show me," she says again.

At length, the spirit complies, releasing another memory from the lake, yet more evidence of the inequity of those who would preserve heaven at the cost of justice.

She is young in the memory, but her brother is younger, and the medicines he needs for his sickness are more expensive than her meager wages can cover. So she paints her eyes and lips after sunset, brushes her hair back, slips into something flimsy, and roams the shadowy streets of her city, those loveless places where people go for quick, loveless transactions that leave them feeling a little more dead inside, a little more numb.

There are other girls who wander these parts, and many of them stare out at the world through grim, empty eyes, bodies carrying deadened souls, living ghosts going through the motions. She is not yet quite like them—she still knows the taste of joy; she feels it every time she hears her little brother laugh—but she can feel herself slipping. Girls like her were never meant for the shadows.

A wagon machine rolls by. It is a cloudless night, and the rings of the world are faint bands of color in the sky against the pale moonlight. She simulates a smile, slides one hand down her jutted hips—this is something she has practiced in front of a mirror, her fishhook, and tonight it works on her first try.

The wagon machine stops next to her, the door opens, and she slips inside. The man within drinks her in with his eyes, and she bats her eyelashes, pushing out her chest. She's done this a few times before, so she can do it again. At least that's what she keeps telling herself.

What she doesn't know is that the lawmen of her city don't much care for girls who do what she does.

She doesn't know that when she disappears tonight, no one will look too closely.

She doesn't know, in fact, that she will never see her beloved brother again.

A day later, her bruised, battered, and lifeless body lies in an unmarked grave, somewhere beneath a lonely tree, never to be found.

Another forgotten victim of an indifferent universe, but she doesn't have to remain so. There are gods who wield the power to give her the justice she deserves, yet they choose not to lest they lose their thrones in heaven.

In her rage, the Adversary renews her solemn vow of enmity with these gods. There will be justice, even if heaven must fall.

PART 3

KAMALI
*
JOMO
*
ILAPARA
*
MUSALODI

Tronic ivory:

Like tronic bone, tronic ivory is the result of alchemical meta-plasia induced by the presence of raw essence within a live animal's limbic system. As essence infestation deepens, the dentins are transfigured into a material harder than ordinary ivory, valued across the Redlands for its beauty and unparalleled ability to store reserves of raw essence.

With respect to enchantments, there is no functional difference between tronic bone and tronic ivory. Tronic ivory, however, is significantly more expensive, as it is stronger and makes for more attractive ornaments and jewelry.

From On Arcane Materials, *an encyclopedia published by the House of Forms*

19: Kamali

Undercity Prison

"Today your worthless lives belong to me," says the mshamba. "I don't care who or what you were before. Jasiri. A prince. You could have been a motherdamned Faro, and I still wouldn't give a shit. You. Are. Mine."

The mshamba is a bald giant of a man in a black loincloth and an aerosteel breastplate as scarred as his face, no doubt left that way to show off his many triumphs over death in the arena. He holds a whip coiled in one hand as he paces in front of thirty unlucky prisoners in manacles and garments of brown sackcloth, all of them lined up against a wall in the undercity prison.

It's been a week since the earthquake that shook Yonte Saire, and these prisoners have been selected to provide a distraction for the thousands who will show up to the Northtown arena a little later today. A man who was once Kamali Jasiri of the Fractal, now simply Kamali, stands among the prisoners, though he differs from the others in his calm expression and the metal collar around his neck. The mshamba means to frighten them, but even with the collar muting his cosmic shards, the prospect of death doesn't frighten Kamali. Death simply means returning to the Mother.

I am not a bad man, he tells himself. *The Mother will welcome me, and I will walk the Infinite Path.*

"As my runners, your job is simple," the mshamba says in a booming voice. "You will double my winnings by staying alive long enough for my team to kill the enemy runners first. After that? You can get eaten by undead for all I care. I won't lose sleep if I never see your ugly faces again. There's more human refuse where you came from."

I am not a bad man. I shall walk the Infinite Path.

A part of Kamali regrets not knowing *why* he must die, why he was driven to murder eight men and steal memories from two other mystics as well as several Faraswa servants, then from his own mind, too, ensuring that none of them would ever remember *it*, whatever *it* was. A part of him wishes he knew why he must now suffer humiliation in front of thousands. But he knows he must have felt he had no other choice than to do what he did, for in his heart he knows he is not evil.

I am not a bad man. I can't be.

One of the prisoners starts sniveling. "I'm not supposed to be here!" he cries. "Not today. There's been a mistake."

Kamali shakes his head. Nothing good can come from attracting the mshamba's attention. Sure enough, the man bares his yellowed teeth like a feral beast and marches over to the weeping prisoner, a scrawny runt of a man with matted dreadlocks and the mark of the Buffalo upon his neck.

With a voice made for carrying across an arena, the mshamba can make any wall shudder when he shouts. "What's your name, boy?"

The prisoner snivels something inaudible.

"Speak up!"

"Fanaka, my lord."

"A weak name for a weak boy." The mshamba hawks and spits. "You carry the stink of an easy life about you, like a chicken fattened for the slaughterhouse. Well, you're in it now, boy. You're in shit so deep you'll be wearing it for lipstick by the time the chikara sinks its claws into you this afternoon."

"Please, my lord! I'm not meant to go today!"

The mshamba takes a step closer. "Maybe I wasn't loud enough when I said it the first time, so let me say it again: You belong to me. I *own* you. Contradict me again, and a chikara will be the least of your worries."

The prisoner shrinks before the much larger man, holding his manacled hands up in a gesture of appeasement, but he must really believe what he's saying because he keeps with it. "Please, check the papers. My sentence doesn't begin today. There must be some mistake. I swear it."

Kamali expects to witness a gruesome beating, but the mshamba levels a frown at the three prison guards standing behind him. "What's he on about?"

The prison guards exchange glances; then one of them starts scanning through the sheet of paper in his hands with the aid of a finger. "Fanaka, was it?" he says and licks his lips nervously as the finger comes to a stop. "Fanaka Wanyati?"

The prisoner gives an eager nod.

"Uh . . . it looks like he's right, mshamba." The guard winces and scratches his head. "Fanaka Wanyati isn't scheduled to enter the arena until two weeks from now."

"Then what the devil is he doing here?" bellows the mshamba, causing all three guards to flinch back.

"A clerical error, mshamba. We'll fix that right away."

"Bah! I'm not waiting around while you half wits fix your mess. You'll have to bring my prisoner to the arena yourselves." The mshamba turns his fierce gaze on the evidently relieved Fanaka and points at him. "Shit for lipstick, boy. I'll be back for you. Be sure of it."

Fanaka weeps as the guards lead him back to his cell. Some of the other prisoners look on with envy. Kamali doesn't envy him, though. In fact, he pities him, for he has only prolonged his suffering to delay the inevitable. The coming weeks will bring him only dread and nightmares, yet the outcome will be the same.

"All right, you worthless scum!" A number of prisoners cower at the mshamba's loud voice. "I want good behavior in the tunnels. You walk in single file with your head forward. No talking. Try anything funny, and I'll make you rue the day your slut mother spread her legs to spawn you. Now hop to it!"

◆ ◆ ◆

One of the prisoners is a woman. A Faraswa woman, wiry, with short hair and tensors that twist from her temples and behind her head in a rather arresting pattern. She walks a few places up the line in front of Kamali as they follow the mshamba through the labyrinth of the undercity, herded by the mshamba's riders, who keep shouting nasty words at them.

It is not the fact that she's the only woman among the prisoners that catches Kamali's attention, nor is it the fact that she is Faraswa. Rather, it's that she differs from the others in the same way he does.

She isn't afraid. The other prisoners keep shuddering and looking over their shoulders whenever a distant creak or jangle reaches their ears; they probably haven't forgotten that these same tunnels were crawling with mapopobawa and other beasts of the underworld only a week ago. But there's no fear in the taut lines of the woman's shoulders, only alertness.

Kamali finds himself wondering what she did to end up here, what wrong turn she made in her life, but he's always been an introspective creature, so those questions inexorably turn inward: *What if I made the wrong turn? What if I killed those eight men for no good reason at all and then tried to hide the evidence? What would that make me?*

As a mystic, he was tried and judged by the seven members of the Shirika, including Mistress Talara, his coven master. She did her best to convince her colleagues to be lenient, but with eight dead guards and two Akili lying unconscious in the House of Life, an example had to be made. Six of the seven Faros found his crimes worthy of death, much to the satisfaction of Mosi's and Ewa's families.

Kamali can remember the grief on his mistress's face as she stripped her Axiom from his shards, expelling him from her coven. She wanted an explanation, anything that could help save his life, but knowing nothing of his crimes himself, he could give her nothing, save to say that he believed he wouldn't have shed so much blood if he didn't believe he was acting in the coven's best interest.

I am a good man, he tells himself. *I would not have shed blood unless my coven came under threat. I am not evil. I can't be.*

A whip cracks behind him, scourging the poor fool at the back of the line. The man howls in pain, which incites the muscled rider who whipped him to have another go at him. "Scared of mapopobawa, are you, boy? That's funny, because what you're about to face is ten times worse! Now keep your eyes forward, or I'll gouge them out!"

The stinking labyrinths are a city unto themselves, but the mshamba clearly knows his way around. Soon they surface into the tunnels beneath the arena, and by the muffled roars of the crowds above, there must be a fight already underway, perhaps one gang squaring off against another in demonstrations of strength. Whatever it is, Kamali knows it's only the appetizer; what comes next will be the main course.

As he and the other prisoners get herded into a heavily guarded armory, growls from beasts caged somewhere out of sight ripple across the stone floors and vibrate straight up their legs. Two prisoners let out feeble whimpers and get whipped for it. Meanwhile one of the mshamba's riders yells out instructions as he struts up and down with a dangling whip.

"If the chikara comes out and you're still in the arena, say your last prayers. Otherwise, you see a rider who isn't us, you run. That's why they call you runners. You see a column of light somewhere, that means there's a flag there. If you're brave enough, go for it. I'll personally pat you on the back if you make it to the enemy gate with a flag, because that's more prize money for us. It also means you get to live another day. But be warned: one of the enemy riders will be guarding the gate. If we're in the vicinity, we'll help you out with that; if not, you're on your own. And if I see *any* of you fighting each other for a flag, I swear to the Mother I'll cut your worthless balls off before I kill you myself."

Kamali has never been fond of the savagery that passes for entertainment in this arena, but he knows how a battle-pit match is supposed to unfold. It's always two teams of five riders and thirty runners each. Convicts versus destitute fools—the runners, that is. The gangs toss a special moongold coin long before the match to determine which gang gets which.

Convicts run for the privilege of living until the next time they get chosen, and the destitute and debt ridden get to run for a chance to win money. Carrying a flag past the enemy gate is the key to success, but with sixty runners competing for a maximum of fifteen flags while facing an army of undead, a team of enemy riders on wild beasts, and the chikara when it's released, the odds of even a single runner leaving the arena intact are often slim.

Once the rider is done shouting at them, the prisoners all get their shackles unlocked, though Kamali's collar remains secured around his neck—knowing what he is, no one dares to remove the artifact cutting him off from his shards. It's entirely unnecessary, of course, what with his expulsion from his mistress's coven; after all, without her Axiom he cannot harness the spirits tattooed onto his skin. But keeping the collar there makes them feel safer around him.

Not that he blames them.

The prisoners each get steel weapons and cheaply made armor if they want it and if it fits. Kamali refuses the armor but chooses a long, single-edged blade with a slight curve and a simple round shield for improved survivability. The blade is nothing like the aerosteel-and-moongold weapon he carried as a Jasiri, which could cut through stone if the hand moving it was strong enough, but it'll have to do. At the least it means he'll die fighting, which is the best death any Jasiri could wish for.

He also takes off his threadbare sandals so he can feel the ground beneath his bare feet. A trained Jasiri can sense motion through vibrations underfoot and can walk on lit coals without suffering a single burn simply by denying the heat its power over him. He has no need for shoes.

"No armor, Jasiri?" The mshamba gives him a cocky grin from a good distance away. "What, you think you'll have spells to save you?"

The man is a giant, wearing a breastplate as strong as any breastplate can be, yet he's afraid of a prisoner with a pitiful excuse for a sword and a collar muting his sorcery. It makes Kamali smile a little.

"I don't need armor," he says. "It'll slow me down. Besides, the options you have here aren't worth their weight in salt. I'd be better off going in naked."

The mshamba's smirk skews into a sneer. "You Jasiri call yourselves warriors because you have magic on your side, but there'll be no magic for you today. I look forward to seeing you get chewed up like the brat you really are; then we'll see how tough you talk."

"I hope not to disappoint," Kamali deadpans.

The mshamba spears him with a long glare before stalking off.

Kamali glances at the Faraswa woman and notices her watching him from across the armory, but she looks away as soon as he catches her at it, turning her attention to the two short blades she has chosen for herself. Like Kamali she has refused to wear armor, and she's ripped her sackcloth tunic up so that it's a close-fitting garment wrapped around her chest, exposing the lean strength of her arms. From the tattered remnants of the tunic she fashioned a belt to cinch her trousers tightly around her slim waist. His curiosity tempts him to approach, but they said no talking, and it's not like it matters anyway, since they'll likely both be dead soon.

"All right, runners. I hope you said your prayers, because the malaika of death is about to start collecting. To your gate!"

◆ ◆ ◆

A slight wind blows into the mouth of the tunnel through the closed iron gate, bringing with it the stench of death and rotting things. Combined with the stink of unwashed bodies, it swirls around Kamali like a hateful shroud.

His long dreadlocks might have swayed in the foul breeze, but his jailers shaved them off after his conviction. His beard too. He'd grown them out for years, and when the razer slid across his skin, he felt like he was losing some unquantifiable part of his manhood. It took every ounce of his sanity to remain still, to not reach for the hand emasculating him and snap it in two. To accept his punishment.

I am not evil, he kept telling himself. *But I butchered eight men.*

Drums begin to clatter beyond the gate, followed by thunderous roars from the spectators. When he became one of the Jasiri, the physicians at the House of Forms carved his back while he was awake, removing a vertebra from the lumbar region of his spinal column and replacing it with a facsimile of charmed moongold. The Jasiri's second heart, they call it. His was sapped nearly dry of essence when he was convicted, but he has since replenished a portion of its reserves through battle meditation.

He reaches for it now with his mind, letting the essence flow up his spine and to the rest of his body. His heart begins to pump rapidly but steadily, packing his muscles densely with unreleased energy. The colors around him become more vivid, the sounds become sharper, and his lungs draw more strength from each breath.

He might be without a coven, and the collar sitting uncomfortably around his neck might be muting his cosmic shards, but he is still a Jasiri, and his body has not forgotten it.

The spirits infused into the colorful tattoos on his body wait patiently at the edges of his mind: the dingonek, the chameleon, the great spearfish, the peregrine. He won't be able to call upon them today, but he finds their presence comforting.

A horn blares somewhere in the arena. Kamali tightens the grip on his blade and slants his gaze to the side. The woman prisoner is watching him. This time she doesn't avert her gaze.

Her eyes are like the double sunrise, a dance of luminous yellows and reds that he could bask in for hours. In another life, he might have liked to know her, ask her out for a drink, and hear her story. But it's not another life, so all he does is nod, and she nods back, and it's a fleeting moment of solidarity during which they imagine what roads they could have walked together, what secrets they might have whispered to each other.

The gates open and the moment ends.

Light. The glaring suns. An immense oval structure rising around him. A roaring multitude. Corpses discarded across the arena floor like the toys of a particularly savage child.

They are the first to rise against them.

Under the sway of a necromantic spell of Blood craft, cast from the private box reserved for the mystics on duty, the corpses lift themselves off the dusty earth like oversize puppets, standing on putrid limbs, and all at once they declare in a hoarse, rasping cry: "You shall soon be among us."

And then they attack.

Each wields the weapon he died with, if not with the same skill, then with twice the tenacity. They plague the air with their stench, some with wounds boiling with worms. When Kamali runs out of the tunnel, he has no direction in mind, only a simple goal: survive for as long as he can.

He ducks as a walking corpse attempts to cleave off the top of his head. With a burst of energy from his second heart, he slams the rim of his shield into the corpse's rib cage, feeling bones give way under the blow. He bashes the corpse again with the flat of his shield, and there's a loud metallic report as a skull breaks and crushes upon steel. A filthy blade comes in toward his right; by reflex he swivels on his feet to dodge and lashes out with his blade. A rotten head flies off its shoulders a fraction of a heartbeat later.

Movement to his left. Kamali lowers his body, bracing his feet on the sands and tucking his shield into his left shoulder in time to tackle the incoming corpse. Another one emerges from the fray on his right even as the first one topples over his shoulders; he summons a burst of speed to block a strike to his face and reply with a swift decapitating blow, pivoting in time to hack the first corpse in the skull as it struggles to rise. Putrid brains and blood spew forth.

With the dingonek he could have leveled the arena in minutes. With the peregrine he might have simply flown off. As it is, he tears his way through the undead one swing at a time, feeling no sympathy for his enemies, for their fates have already been sealed.

I am returning to the Mother, he tells himself. He and the other prisoners begin to spread away from the mouth of the tunnel, whose gate is now shut, and into the daunting landscape of limestone walls and staircases sprawled out before them.

The theme is a moving multilevel maze today, where the structures change alignment on a whim. Capricious walkways and platforms float in the air, moving up and down and sideways in no apparent order. Kamali bats away a thrust aimed for his chest and leaps onto a staircase just as it swings right. His heightened reflexes allow him to maintain balance when his feet land on the moving staircase, but then it lifts off the ground and begins to rise.

When he briefly looks up as the staircase takes him higher into the air, he sees himself in one of the mirages floating above the arena like giant windows. It seems he has caught the attention of the illusionists on duty today and possibly whoever is maintaining the maze.

Kamali probably knows who they are, as the arena's entertainments are always manned by students of the House of Forms. He shouldn't be surprised that they'd pay special attention to him. Likely, they have a point to prove.

Keep away from the platforms, then. He grits his teeth and leaps off the staircase before it takes him any higher, landing in a crouch and rolling forward to take the force off his knees. He cuts down corpses as soon as he finds his feet.

A brilliant bar of white light appears toward the center of the arena, shooting up into the sky with the promise of life to whoever reaches it first. The crowds roar in excitement; then roars of a different kind terrorize the arena as the rider teams are released. Kamali can't see them directly from his vantage point in the maze, but the hovering windows of Mirror craft give him a clear picture; it seems the enemy riders are on juvenile dread rhinos, while Kamali's team rides mutated wild boars. Both creatures are terrible creations of Blood craft and were chosen for the teams by the spin of a wheel.

As they emerge from their gates, the riders crack their burning whips, which were rubbed thickly with an oily resin and set aflame so that they would give off a pale-yellow steam. It used to be that riders prioritized protecting their runners, but that changed when they realized that the crowds roared louder when they focused on whittling down enemy runners instead.

Kamali ignores the bar of light. That's always where the riders first clash before they start mauling down each other's runners one by one. Better to be as far from it as possible, at least for now.

But the undead are relentless. They don't give him a moment's rest, forcing him up a staircase and onto a long floating platform despite his vow to stay off them. Predictably, the platform begins to rise almost as soon as he steps onto it, taking him and five undead high above the arena floor. One corpse isn't quick enough to leap and ends up clinging to the platform with a rotted hand. Kamali severs the grasping fingers with the rim of his shield before turning his attention to his fellow passengers.

As the platform begins a slow lateral spin, the undead warriors hack and slash at his body, keeping him in motion, forcing him to push himself to the limits of his strength. His shield rattles as he blocks multiple slashes from the front. He retaliates with an impaling thrust into the head of a corpse. Somewhere the bar of light turns yellow, which means a runner on the opposing team has picked it up. Kamali subconsciously keeps track of it as it moves through the maze; at some point he hears a scream, and then the bar turns red and starts moving in the opposite direction.

He has no sooner cleared his platform than he sees a second one rising to meet him, bringing an even larger contingent of undead with it. His face is on at least two of the floating windows of Mirror craft, and he's almost certain he's the cause of the rising tide of cheers that engulfs the arena. These people are eager to see him die.

Sudden anger floods his veins, joining the thrill of battle to charge his blood with even more strength. They want entertainment? So be it. His death will be the greatest spectacle they've ever witnessed. He throws his shield to the side, and with a roar he leaps off his platform to meet the incoming horde, landing in their midst. Then he carves them.

His sword becomes so laden with filth it no longer reflects the sunlight. His face must be a ghastly sight as well, but he doesn't care anymore. The madness he has been keeping at bay has finally taken over, the bloodlust of a Jasiri in battle, when he knows he is becoming his own apex, the best of what he is and also the worst.

Beneath him the battle continues. One of his fellow prisoners gets transfixed upon the horn of a dread rhino. An enemy runner falls screaming when a rider licks his back with a burning whip. It is death and it is glorious and it is returning to the Mother.

When his platform is a gory mess and he's the only one left standing, Kamali raises his sword and roars in defiance. To his surprise, the crowds reciprocate with a ferocity that sobers him a little.

And then he sees her. She's a lithe figure somewhere below, hopping from one floating platform to another with grace as she escapes the attentions of a rider on a dread rhino, and when the maze conspires to bring her into the path of a phalanx of undead, her twin blades lash out quick as the fangs of a viper. Kamali is so taken by her he almost tips over when his platform begins to tilt.

They will never kill him this way. A few hops and leaps later, and he hits the ground. Then a loud peal assaults his ears as a column of light appears in a clearing not far away. He looks and sees a little white flag standing at the base of the column, waiting for someone to pick it up.

He stares at it for what feels like minutes. Is someone trying to save him? He could make it to the other gate if he really wanted to. But to what end? He'd only be back here sooner or later.

He is still undecided when the woman arrives and stops on the other side of the bar of light. But as their eyes meet through the brilliance, the question becomes settled for him. He will die here today.

"Go on," he says. "Take it."

Her sun-touched eyes gleam back defiantly. "I don't need any favors from you."

He doesn't know what to say and doesn't even get the chance to think up a reply, because a terrified man in a gray dashiki runs out of a passage and into the clearing, freezing when he spots Kamali and the woman eyeing each other next to the flag.

The man is an enemy runner, perhaps in his thirties, with no markings on his neck, which means he's a foreigner, as many runners from the other team often are. Must be truly desperate if he's willing to risk his life in this arena for the slim chance of winning coin.

Kamali makes a decision. "You don't want it?" he says to the woman, who shakes her head.

So he walks to the flag and picks it up. The bar of light follows the flag, turning red as soon as he touches it. He knows this will attract any enemy rider in the vicinity.

He'll just have to be fast, then.

"You," he says to the enemy runner. "Follow me. I will take you to our gate." When the man sputters in shock, Kamali points with his sword. "Move, or I leave you here to die."

He turns around and leads the way through the maze toward his own gate. The other man follows him, and curiously, so does the woman. She runs up a staircase and starts hopping across the floating platforms, keeping up with them. Kamali stays on the ground, unwilling to risk the platforms while he's carrying the flag. Better to keep his location somewhat of a mystery.

"A rider has caught your scent," the woman warns.

Kamali parries a slash from a corpse and cuts off its head in one move, then looks over his shoulder to make sure the foreigner is still following. He is.

"What's the quickest way to the gate?" Kamali asks the woman, since she enjoys a better view up there.

"The maze keeps moving, so I don't know," she says. "Follow me."

So he does, and it's not long before they emerge from the maze and return to the mouth of their own gate.

There's a rider guarding the gate, sitting astride a monstrous wild boar. He tilts his head in confusion upon seeing Kamali and the woman, but his eyes fly wide open when Kamali passes the flag over to the foreigner and the bar of light turns yellow.

Kamali doesn't think. His legs move, and in a heartbeat he closes the distance and launches himself into the air, the muscles of his sword arm rippling with strength. Next thing he knows, he's split the shocked rider's face in half, and they're both tumbling off his mutant beast.

Freed of its rider, the wild boar charges at the foreigner with a deafening squeal, but the woman veers into its path in time to sink one of her blades into the base of its throat, bringing it down almost on top of her.

"Run!" she says to the foreigner.

And the man runs, his flag clutched tightly in one hand. The gate opens as soon as he reaches it and closes when he steps beyond the threshold. He pauses briefly for a tearful thank-you before he vanishes into the tunnel to claim his prize. Loud boos and cheers erupt all around the arena.

As Kamali gets up to his feet, his grinning face is on half the floating windows of Mirror craft. The other half show the woman as she finishes off the boar.

Kamali laughs deliriously as a realization dawns on him, making the woman frown as she rises from the dead beast.

"We just killed our own rider, and the match hasn't stopped," he says. "Do you know what that means?"

The woman shakes her head, looking both curious and amused.

"It means killing riders is not against the rules." Kamali's manic grin widens. "There are nine left. I bet I can get more than you."

She smiles, and it is right then that he falls in love with her.

"We'll see about that," she says, and together they go hunting.

20: Jomo

Sitting in a private box on the north end of the arena, Jomo underscores a passage of handwritten text in his little green journal.

The text describes a scandalous affair wherein a headman is infertile but never finds out because his mother, a staunch traditionalist, arranges for his younger brother to secretly impregnate his wife, thereby preventing the spread of unpleasant rumors about his virility—or lack thereof. The prince goes on to raise all four of his sons to adulthood, never the wiser that they are in fact his nephews. According to the journal, he remains oblivious to this day.

With his pen Jomo circles key details in the titillating account, even though he probably won't be using the information since the headman in question is already an ally. A real pity, Jomo would say. This could have been excellent blackmail material.

But there are other secrets in the journal about other powerful people. Affairs. Bastard children. Family feuds. Devil worshipping. Elea Saai was right when she told him the secrets in his mother's little green book could start wars. His challenge now is to leverage those secrets into an advantage, a task that is proving more difficult than he would have expected.

A bead of sweat rolls down his temple despite the presence of little hexahedral contraptions mounted on the ceiling to siphon heat and humidity from the private box. He wipes the sweat away with his golden shirtsleeve and lifts his gaze off the journal, peering over the parapet.

Down on the arena floor, the former Jasiri and his Faraswa accomplice are still hunting down riders on both battle-pit teams, rousing the crowds to fever pitch with each kill. Their exploits are displayed in vivid detail on the giant mirage windows floating in the air so that the only way to escape them is to close one's eyes.

Jomo grimaces as one of the mirages briefly focuses on an undead corpse with half its face missing. He's never liked the arena and its ghastly amusements. He came here once before with his family and found the spectacle grotesque, a low form of entertainment for the uneducated. But even he must admit that today's match is hard to look away from.

Also in the private box, smoking a pipe while leaning over the parapet, is Odari, the snake-eyed Sentinel. He chuckles and shakes his head as the Jasiri is shown leaping off a floating platform onto an unsuspecting rider and his rhino. The rider is subsequently dismounted while the Jasiri takes charge of the beast.

"What were they thinking, putting an armed Jasiri in there?" Odari says, puffs of smoke escaping his nostrils. He proceeds to answer his own question. "Actually, maybe it was a stroke of genius because these matches were getting too predictable. Look! The woman's about to get another one."

On the window floating directly across from the private box, above the arena's south end, the Faraswa woman hurls sand into the eyes of the rider whom the Jasiri dismounted. In a rage he cracks his burning whip, which he managed to hang on to as he fell off his beast, but she evades and slides toward him, and in the next split second there's a blade lodged in his groin.

Odari cheers, thoroughly amused. "Oof, right in the balls! I'm never pissing off a Faraswa woman, that's for sure."

Wincing in sympathy for the unsexed rider, Jomo subconsciously covers his privates with his journal. "This is repugnant," he mutters. "How can you watch such a thing and laugh about it?"

The Sentinel looks over his shoulder, his chapped lips curling upward. "Is this your first time here, boss?"

"I've been here once before," Jomo says, slightly irritated by Odari's flippant tone. "Hated it the first time, hate it even more now. Barbaric."

The violence seemed distant to him that first time, something that only happened to other people and therefore nothing to give him nightmares when he slept. Today it feels real enough that it could reach out from the arena floor and from the delirious crowds to tear him apart limb from limb, the same way it did his family.

Maybe it's because of the anti-Saire placards he's seen flying above the heads of many spectators. He also hasn't run into a single clansperson today. The last time he was here, wealthy Saires populated most of the private boxes.

Kito has been standing guard just outside Jomo's private box. He steps inside now with an announcement. "Boss. You have a visitor."

"It's about time," Jomo says, relieved that he didn't come here for nothing. He closes his journal and tucks it into a pocket, along with his pen. "Please let him in."

"I'll give you your privacy," Odari says as he follows the other Sentinel out of the box.

On the night of the earthquake, Isa told Jomo she was going down to the undercity to partake in a night vigil in an apostate sanctuary. Obviously, Jomo objected, but his cousin has a way of getting people to do as she wills, so he let her go.

When she returned to the temple with a badly injured and unconscious Obe Saai, and he learned from Ijiro what she'd *really* gone there to do and that the only reason she'd survived her insane plan was the intervention of some foreign mystic, he was so furious he couldn't stand the sight of her for two days.

At least she's no longer insisting on any more excursions to the city. The downside is that he now has to meet the mysterious ally who supposedly saved her life.

Jomo gets up with the aid of his cane to greet his guest and is entirely unprepared for the young woman who walks in. She pauses as well when she sees his face, and for a moment they watch each other, speechless.

When he first saw her, on the eve of the New Year, she was standing outside the Summit's state room looking like she wanted to be far from there. In that look he recognized a kindred soul: Here was a woman who had an eye for bullshit. A woman who saw the lights and glittering marble floors of the palace for the snake pit they actually were.

Today she's wearing a red sundress and a coal-black head wrap piled above her head with a leather shoulder bag hooked beneath one arm. Her lips are painted black and her eyes ringed with kohl.

"You," she says, clearly surprised to see him.

A grin takes over Jomo's expression. "You're not stalking me, are you? Not that I'd complain if you were."

Amusement makes her eyes crinkle. "No. I'm here to speak to the herald on behalf of a friend. You *are* the herald, are you not? Or did I walk into the wrong box?"

"You're exactly where you need to be." He offers a hand for a handshake. "Jomo Saire at your service. And you are . . . ?"

She shakes his hand, the hint of a smile on her lips. "You may call me Ilapara."

The calluses he feels in Ilapara's grip tell him she's not the pampered type. This is someone used to working with her hands, perhaps even holding a weapon.

"A delight to finally put a name to the face," he says. "I'd have brought wine if I knew I'd be in such pleasant company; as it is, all I can offer you is a seat."

"That's all right. I won't be staying long anyway." As they settle down next to each other, her worldly eyes flash like she might be teasing him. "Besides, you haven't known me long enough to judge me pleasant."

"Oh, I can often tell right away that I'm going to like someone, and I doubt I'll change my mind about you."

"Anything is possible."

"And some things are less possible than others. Tell me, Ilapara, what do you make of our city's pastime?"

She seemed in good spirits, but her expression takes a turn for the somber as she gazes down at the arena. "I regret knowing it exists."

Another reason to like her, and yet Jomo is suddenly filled with shame. "The night we first met, you witnessed the public assassination of a headman. I imagine between that and this and all the other stuff in between, you probably think my people evil."

Ilapara shakes her head, surprising him yet again. "Who am I to judge? I know how easy it is to become inured to evil simply because you feel powerless to stop it." She gestures at the spectacle unfolding before them. "Take these games. I'm sure there are many who recognize the cruelty of them, but look at all these people cheering! How do you get them to stop? How do you even summon the will to try? Easier to keep your head down."

The faraway look in her eyes tells him this is a subject she has pondered extensively. "Perhaps we can take heart in the fact that the Jasiri and his friend have decided not to play by the rules. I don't think what we're witnessing has ever happened before. The sad irony is that his survival would only make the sport more popular. People will be talking about this match for years."

"He doesn't deserve this," Ilapara says in a quiet voice, again with a haunted look. "No one does. I sincerely hope he survives."

Regret makes Jomo silently chastise himself. He should have known better. "I'm sorry I suggested meeting here. I thought a crowd would make it harder for spies to watch me."

"I understand."

Jomo regards Ilapara unabashedly, trying to make sense of her relationship to the person he thought he was coming here to meet. "So. Your master is the Yerezi mystic who saved my cousin. How did he end up with an Umadi retainer?"

"I'm Yerezi, actually. I only dress and speak like an Umadi woman because I've been living there for the last three comets. And I am *not* his retainer. I am his friend."

"Well. That teaches me to make assumptions." Jomo looks her over again. "Is your friend here?"

"He's in another private box," Ilapara says. "He came as a guest of the Valau ambassador, so he couldn't speak with you in person."

"A pity," Jomo says. "I would have liked to meet him."

"Perhaps you'll get your wish." Something pleasantly mysterious shines in Ilapara's eyes; then it dims. "How is Sentinel Obe Saai? Last I saw him, he was . . . not in a good state."

"He's recuperating," Jomo hedges. "He couldn't go to the House of Life, so they treated him at the temple. His right arm had to be amputated due to the corruption in his wounds."

Ilapara grimaces, shaking her head slowly. "I'm so sorry to hear that."

"He's actually taking it better than you'd think," Jomo says. "Didn't even shed a tear when they told him he'd lost his arm. He's a stubborn bastard. He'll pull through."

"I pray that he does." After a commiserative silence, Ilapara bends forward to extract a smaller leather pouch from her shoulder bag, then places it on the floor between their chairs. "Listen. The memory cube is in the bag; everything requested was successfully transcoded onto it. The other item is a communication device my friend enchanted. Void craft, or something. My friend would like to speak to you and the king; he'll be waiting for you at the Paragon's seventh flash. Use the device then, and only in trusted company."

Jomo has to actively prevent himself from immediately reaching down and unearthing whatever is in the leather pouch. What memory cube? *Damn Isa and her endless secrets.* "How does this communication device work?"

"Pull down the brass lever when the time comes," Ilapara says. "Then you'll just have to let it in. I was told it's intuitive."

"How do I know it's not harmful? Nothing against your friend, but I don't know him. I barely know you either."

"And here I thought you already liked me," she says with a sly grin.

"That's beyond a doubt. But you're still a beautiful and mysterious woman doing the bidding of a foreign mystic I've never met. I definitely like you; I'm just not sure I can trust you."

"Then I suppose you'll just have to trust your instincts," she says. "All I can give you is my word that we mean you no harm."

Jomo finds himself drawn in by her sharp gaze. *I'm not thinking with my head, am I?* he realizes. "Ah well. What's life without a little risk anyway?"

She smiles again, at least until a terrific roar shakes the walls, followed by a crazed bout of cheers from the watching crowds. "What's happening?"

On the arena floor, only a few figures can still be seen moving in the chaos of the kinetic maze—two mounted on beasts, the other three on foot. The Jasiri and his friend are in the latter group, and no more undead are shambling about.

Jomo explains, "As the match draws to a close, the chikara is released, and whoever is still alive has a few minutes to run for the gates."

A large trapdoor gives way on the floor in the center of the arena, much to the satisfaction of the crowds. They roar even louder as a living nightmare rears its head and slithers out of the darkness, the walls of the maze flying off to make way for its bulk.

Jomo shudders, profoundly horrified by the sight. Though the creature possesses the tusks and great flapping ears of his clan's totem animal, its jaws and body are those of a monstrous serpent.

Ilapara curses in a foreign language. "Is that . . . is that a grootslang?"

"Looks like it," Jomo says, though he's never seen one with his eyes before, only drawings that, in retrospect, clearly failed to capture the sheer horror and wrongness of the real thing. "The last time I was here, the chikara was some kind of giant monitor lizard from the Jalama. I thought that was bad, but this . . ."

The maze starts to move faster, walls actively blocking off routes of escape for the runners and riders alike. On one of the floating windows, the grootslang is seen springing forward to intercept an unlucky runner, trapping him with its coils. He disappears between its jaws when it lunges.

"How are they supposed to survive this?" Ilapara says, horrified.

"Normally the riders work together to wound or even kill off the chikara, give the crowds a show, but there aren't enough of them today."

And yet, even with the grootslang unleashed, the Jasiri and his friend make a point of hunting down the last rider from the opposing team, who falls off his rhino from a dagger picked up from the ground and thrown expertly into his neck. The duo then flees for their gate and makes it through just before it slams shut. The resulting cheers are such that Jomo can feel them in his bones.

"Well. There you have it." A disbelieving laugh escapes his lips, his heart racing faster than the celebratory drumbeats from the musicians a few levels down. "I can tell you this much; their mshamba won't be pleased. He's lost a lot of riders today. At least they had the sense to leave one of them alive to give him the win."

"Will they kill him?" Ilapara asks quietly. "The Jasiri."

"Probably not. It'd look bad if they did. I suspect the next time they choose him, though, they'll make it impossible for him to survive. Might even send him in with his hands still bound. He's a dead man walking."

"Wasn't he already?"

The cynicism in her reply makes Jomo wonder why she's concerned about the Jasiri's fate. "I suppose he was."

He's still thinking about it when she bids him goodbye and quietly exits his private box. He stays long enough to watch a sorcerer cast a spell on the monstrosity in the arena and lull it into returning to its lair.

When Jomo leaves minutes later, he vows never to return.

As soon as he arrives back at his commandeered office in the temple, Jomo arranges with Isa, through a patient votary who conveys their messages back and forth, to meet just before the seventh hour after high noon outside a chamber of prayer and meditation located in the citadel's residential wing.

At dusk he picks up the pouch Ilapara gave to him and makes his way down the temple's cloistered walkways of stone and bamboo, grumbling silently about Isa's choice to meet in a prayer room of all places. She's been especially devout since her return from the undercity, spending hours at a time in meditation or reading religious tomes in the temple's library, a change Jomo has found troubling.

Devout people make him nervous. And it's not just how they remind him of his own lax spirituality—he can't remember the last time he prayed in a sanctuary—but he also often finds them unreasonably inflexible. Dour. No sense of humor whatsoever, and he would know, having been surrounded by votaries and grim Jasiri for the last several weeks. And now Isa.

As he's rounding a corner and entering the mouth of a cloister open on one side to a lawn-covered quadrangle, he sees the flash of a red robe ahead. Immediately, he backtracks, cursing the squeaking protest of his leg brace, but it doesn't look like he's been spotted. Carefully, he takes a peek around the corner.

Isa, wearing a simple white dress with a train, is walking with the terrifying high mystic, their backs toward Jomo. They stop at the entrance to the prayer chamber, facing each other, and for a heart-stopping moment Jomo thinks she's invited him to their meeting. But then the old man bows and walks on, leaving Isa alone.

Jomo waits until the high mystic has moved out of sight before entering the cloister and revealing himself to his cousin. She brightens as he approaches, although she seems somewhat guarded, like something is weighing down on her but she's trying to pretend that it isn't.

Oh, Isa. Why won't you trust me and let me in so I can help you? Why do you feel you need to keep secrets from me?

"Does he know?" he whispers when he's close enough for her to hear him, jerking his head down the cloister, where the Faro disappeared.

"Know what?" Isa says, genuinely puzzled.

"What happened last week. Have you told him yet? Because if you haven't, I feel like he'll take one look at me and just know. Honestly, Isa, sometimes I feel like he can read my mind."

Isa frowns, checking that the high mystic is out of earshot, then grabs Jomo by the arm and pulls him toward the prayer room. "He knows I was in the undercity," she says in a low voice. "He doesn't know the rest, and I'd like to keep it that way, so no more talking about it where we could be overheard. There are mystics everywhere, remember?"

"Fine," Jomo says and lets himself be dragged into the mostly empty chamber.

There is a clicking sound as Isa locks the door behind them; then she takes his arm again. "Come."

The sweet scent of wax explains why the floors are so shiny. A stained glass mural depicting a twilight moonrise dominates the front of the chamber, lit from behind by many candles so that it fills the room with a palette of warm colors. Rolled-up mats and cushions have been stacked on one side for worshippers to use, but Isa picks up two chairs and places them in the center of the room, facing each other.

Jomo blinks at her as she settles down on one of them. "Why are we here, Isa?"

She smiles at him. "I recently found out that the temple's prayer rooms are all warded to be soundproof. We'll have more privacy here than in my chambers."

"Wait, really? That's . . . actually quite useful."

"I know, right? Now sit down already and show me what you've brought. Your message mentioned a communication device?"

Jomo moves to lower himself onto the other chair, sighing as he stretches out his bad leg, then hands over the leather pouch. Her eyes sparkle with interest when she extracts the first item, a patterned cube of aerosteel, which Jomo assumes is the memory cube. The second item is an oval ornament with a golden luster and a set of concentric rings freely swinging about the same axis inside a circular hollow. A brass lever juts out of a vertical slit along the ornament's side. It might be a clock or a useless trinket. Jomo wouldn't know either way.

"So what did you think of him?" Isa says as she studies this second ornament.

"Of who?"

She makes an annoyed sound. "Who else, Jomo?"

"I didn't meet him," Jomo says. "He couldn't come, so he sent a friend." He proceeds to tell Isa about his meeting with Ilapara, even disclosing their first encounter at the Summit on the eve of the New Year.

"I see she made an impression on you," Isa says, teasing him.

"I suppose she did."

"There were two young women in the group that saved me and Tuliza. Both impressive fighters. She might have been one of them."

"I figured she was, since she asked after Obe," Jomo says, to which Isa tenses. Watching her, he says, "How is he, anyway? I should probably pay him a visit later on."

"He's . . . coping," she says, not looking Jomo in the eye.

"And you? I know you blame yourself for what happened to him. Are you coping?"

"I don't regret going down to the undercity," she says without hesitating. "I just wish he didn't have to pay for my choices."

Deciding to change the subject, Jomo points at the little box sitting on her lap. "So are you going to tell me about the memory box? Or should I keep pretending I don't know it exists?"

She sighs, ending her scrutiny of the oval communication ornament. "How much time do we have until seven?"

Jomo fishes out his golden timepiece to check. "We have a few minutes."

It proves to be enough time for Isa to fill him in on the utterly insane plot she hatched with the high priest to win over the independent mystics of the undercity, which is itself part of a plot to rope the Yerezi mystic into alliance with them, and this is where Jomo's mind starts to jam like the gears of a rusty machine.

"But why?" he asks. "What could you possibly want from him?"

By the look on Isa's face, she knows just how crazy she sounds right now. "You know what Bloodway pilgrims come here to do, right?"

Jomo thinks about it. "Don't they come to get treasure from the inner sanctum or something?"

"Or something," Isa agrees. "Well, the way His Worship explained it to me, most mystics can't choose what treasure they retrieve from the sanctum, if they manage to retrieve anything at all. It's a game of chance. But the Yerezi mystic allegedly possesses a key that will give him full control over what he gets."

"Okay . . . so he has some kind of magic key. Why is this important?"

"Because we want to influence his choice so that he retrieves a specific item that will help us put a stop to interclan hostilities, perhaps for good."

Jomo squints at her, unbelieving. "There's an item that could do that?"

"So says the high mystic, and I believe him."

Dear Mother, she's serious. "What's the nature of this item, and why haven't I heard of it before?"

"I don't know what it is," Isa says, looking away. "Not many people do, and the high mystic has yet to tell me. I suspect it's a topic rarely discussed outside the orthodoxy."

So we only have the high priest's word that this fantastic object exists. Great. "What if the Yerezi refuses to help? What if he decides he's better off choosing something to help his own tribe instead?"

"That's why it's essential we make him not only sympathetic to our cause but also absolutely convinced that helping us is acting in his own self-interest."

"How the devil will you do that?"

Her eyes glitter with purpose. "Very carefully."

Jomo stares at her. "Don't tell me you risked your life in the undercity just so he could come save you."

"No." Isa looks down at the artifacts in her lap, flicking one of the rings on the ovoid so that it spins. "That was . . . fortunate."

"I think we fundamentally disagree on the definition of the word."

Her eyes flick back up. "We live in a world of endless perils, cousin," she says in a weirdly self-assured voice. "Every new day we see is a blessing we shouldn't take for granted."

It's times like these that Jomo sorely wishes he wielded the power of telepathy. "What happened to you in the undercity?"

Her expression is at once fragile and sincere. "I found hope."

He can't help but sigh. He checks his timepiece and nods at Isa. "It's time. I was told you should push down the lever on the side."

She goes ahead and does just that, moving the lever down the vertical slit. They both stare at the ornament as its rings begin to spin of their own accord. Jomo feels something cold brushing against his mind, or a ghost knocking on the door to his soul, and somehow he can tell that, whatever it is, it's reaching out to him from the ornament. The sensation is as interesting as it is disturbing.

"Do you feel that?" Isa says, breathless.

"I feel it."

"What happens now?"

"I was told it would be intuitive," Jomo says, trying to remember what Ilapara told him. "Strangely, it's like something wants to come into my mind, and I could let it in if I wanted to."

"I feel the same." Isa looks up at him, excitement bright in her eyes. "On the count of three?"

"All right." They count together. "One. Two. Three—"

Oblivion. Nothingness. An eternity of being aware of his insignificance. Of wanting to scream and yet not having the mouth to do so. And it is so cold, and so lonely, and so endless—

A new world explodes into existence around him in a flash of color, and it's like he's stepped into a drunken hallucination.

Where he and Isa were seated in a prayer room of the Red Temple not three seconds ago, now they stand on a marble porch connected to a grand palace floating in the middle of a lake. A sealed double door bars one side of the porch, while the steps on the opposite side descend onto a columned walkway. There's a burning statue of a warrior woman glowering at them from the center of the porch, though a closer look tells Jomo it's not a burning statue but moonfire *in the shape* of a statue, which is even stranger. And the sky . . .

"What in the damned pits?" Jomo walks to the edge of the porch, his mouth agape. "Are those roses in the sky?" There are indeed roses, with comets and gaseous clouds and ringed moons.

"None of this is real," Isa says, mesmerized. "It's a construct like the Meeting Place by the Sea. Coming here even felt the same, but this . . . I've never seen anything like this."

"It's amazing."

"It is," Isa agrees, then looks toward the rotunda of pearly marble rising on the other side of the walkway. "I hear voices over there. Come."

The walkway's roof is a latticed framework enwrapped with glowing vines. As he walks with Isa beneath its length, Jomo keeps to the center since either edge of the walkway is a sheer drop into the lake. This place might not be real, and maybe he knows instinctively that he could simply withdraw from it if he wanted to, but he'd rather not test his luck. Still, he doesn't remember the last time walking was so easy. He almost doesn't need his cane.

The rotunda turns out to be a richly furnished pavilion sitting at the center of the whole structure. Six other walkways radiate away from it, bridging over the water to other porches with closed double doors. The floors feature murals of spike-maned leopards rendered in paint that twinkles with precious metals. In lieu of a domed ceiling, rafters covered in vines sit above the pavilion so that the crazy sky can be seen through the gaps.

Four people are in the middle of a hushed argument when Jomo and Isa arrive through an arched entrance. The youth in black-and-silver finery is the only one seated, an ankle hitched over his other knee; he gets up as soon as he spots them and alerts the others to their arrival.

Ilapara is there, too, still in her lovely sundress. She gives Jomo the tiniest smile when their eyes meet, which of course makes him want to grin like a fool, but he's here in his capacity as herald, so he keeps a lid on it. There's also another pretty young woman he might have noticed in passing at the New Year's Feast, dressed in an agreeable pearly garment with a plunging neckline.

The fourth member of the group is a young man wearing spectacles and some kind of white cloth wrapped around his groin. He greets them first, giving them a friendly, gap-toothed grin, and Jomo silently wonders if the guy didn't bite too hard into a piece of flatbread and lose a whole tooth. That gap is huge.

"Your Majesty," he says, bowing to Isa. "Welcome to my construct."

Isa accepts his welcome with a gracious nod, sliding neatly into a polite, diplomatic mask Jomo has learned successfully belies her cunning mind. "Thank you for having us, honored emissary. Your construct is beyond lovely."

"You honor me, Your Majesty." The Yerezi mystic gives Jomo a respectful bow of the head. "Herald. It is good to finally meet you face-to-face. I'm sorry I couldn't come see you in person earlier today."

"No harm done," Jomo says, looking him over. *This* is the mystic who saved Isa's life? The one with the magic key to the temple's inner sanctum? He looks rather tame.

"I see all my saviors are present," Isa says, smiling at the other three people in the room.

"Allow me to formally introduce them to you, Your Majesty," the mystic says and goes on to do just that. Jomo already knew Ilapara. The bald, insanely attractive girl with the shrewd gaze is apparently Alinata and is an apprentice of her queen, whatever that means. Then there's the short one named Tuksaad, who might be from a northern tribe given the lightness of his skin. Jomo takes an instant dislike to the young man, though he can't quite put his finger on why. Maybe it has something to do with the unusually bright hue of his blue eyes.

"I didn't get the chance to thank you in person for risking your lives for me," Isa says to them. "Truly, each of you has my undying gratitude."

"And mine as well," Jomo puts in. "Saving my cousin has made you all my friends as far as I'm concerned."

"We were glad to help," says the one named Alinata.

"It was quite exhilarating, actually," declares Tuksaad, stroking his chin. "But only after it was over, of course. Definitely wouldn't want to do that again."

Not blue eyes but green, and Jomo adds his accent to the list of things he doesn't like about the guy. *Have I met him before?*

Isa speaks over his thoughts. "I was thoroughly impressed with the way you all handled yourselves despite your youth, and maybe a little envious. Are all Yerezi women as capable warriors as the two of you?"

The Yerezi women exchange significant glances, and Alinata is the one who replies. "We are both . . . atypical, Your Majesty, though in our own ways. In our culture, the art of warfare is largely a man's domain."

"Whoever decided that clearly hadn't met either of you," Isa says, shaking her head. "I wish I could fight like that!"

"They fight better than most men too," the mystic offers with a slanted grin. "So they aren't just atypical women but atypical in general."

"Then I was lucky indeed," Isa says. "Again, thank you. All of you."

To stop Isa from emphasizing her gratitude too much—lest they start asking for favors—Jomo steers the conversation elsewhere. "Speaking of atypical," he says to the mystic. "Forgive me, honored emissary, but you don't look like a woman to me."

While Isa's smile becomes fixed, the sorcerer's lips twitch with amusement. "That may be because I'm not a woman."

"Because as far as I know, your people don't allow male sorcerers to exist."

"I am the first."

"Huh. An awful lot of firsts going around these days."

"Jomo," Isa says in warning, which makes him feign embarrassment. "My apologies. I meant no offense, of course."

"No offense was taken," the mystic says magnanimously. "Your curiosity is justified." He gestures at the couches in the room. "Please, let us sit down. We may speak freely here without worry of being overheard."

Once they're seated on couches and armchairs around a low table, Isa scans their surroundings and says, "What *is* this place? Our royal masks carry a similar enchantment, but I thought it couldn't be replicated."

"Actually, any artifact with sufficiently advanced telepathic and processing ability can host a mental construct," the mystic explains. "Right now, we are in a construct hosted in the amulet you gifted me. Through a spell of Void craft, I entangled the amulet to the device you're using so we could interface with it simultaneously even across distances. So in a sense, I have you to thank for our presence here."

That explanation makes little sense to Jomo, but it annoys him that Isa failed to mention that she "gifted" this mystic with an amulet. He files this fact away to use as leverage if necessary.

"You did me the greater favor by getting me the spells I requested," Isa says. "Because of you, the clinics and sanctuaries of the undercity will now be better equipped and my people better supported. Thank you."

"It was a pleasure, Your Majesty."

"It is a little curious, though, isn't it?" Jomo says. "Specifically, why you were willing to help my cousin as you did. I know she offered you entry into the Red Temple, but that doesn't seem to me a strong enough motivation considering the risk you took."

The mystic smirks, though it doesn't crease the corners of his eyes. "I was also offered an incredibly powerful magical artifact as part of the deal." He gestures at their surroundings to prove his point. "And I am very motivated to complete my pilgrimage, Herald. As a matter of fact, that was one of the things I hoped we could discuss tonight."

Isa steps in to smooth things over. "Rest assured, I will honor my promise. The high priest has agreed to let you into the temple two weeks from today, after the Requiem Moon."

Why wait that long? Jomo wonders.

The mystic scratches his chin, thoughtful. "I would have liked to go in sooner, but I understand this might not be in your hands. Thank you, Your Majesty. And you are right, Herald. I had . . . other motives for helping your cause, which is actually the main reason I arranged this meeting." He glances at his three friends, echoes of their unfinished argument manifesting as subtle frowns and pursed lips.

Whatever the disagreement, he forges on, delivering his words with tact and a little too much caution. "Given . . . recent events, my queen now understands that the best way to avoid a future war with your tribe is for you, Your Majesty, to retain your throne. As such, she directed me to do what I could to assist toward this end. And after I informed her of the undercity incident, she was even more convinced that strengthening our cooperation would be ultimately beneficial to both our tribes."

Jomo gapes, then quickly closes his mouth. Did he hear the mystic right? The pieces of Isa's game seem to be falling in place all on their own. He and Isa exchange silent glances. "Forgive me if I'm being blunt," he says to the mystic, "but I want to avoid misunderstanding you. Are you offering to help us keep my cousin on the throne?"

"It is what my queen has commanded," the mystic says, but he looks uncomfortable now, which tells Jomo that this wasn't his idea. Ilapara and this Tuksaad fellow don't appear overly excited about it either.

"And just so we're clear," Jomo says, "how far would you be willing to go to help us?"

Again, the mystic trades meaningful looks with his companions. "Obviously, neither I nor my companions can act violently against any of your tribespeople, nor can we do anything indiscreet. Carelessly jeopardizing our welcome here would be counterproductive, so we must be seen to maintain as much neutrality as possible."

Courteous, diplomatic, a strong conscience. That could be useful.

"You've helped us twice now without giving yourselves away," Isa says, also diplomatically. "We must continue in that vein."

But Jomo has never been known to be diplomatic. "If I needed you to secretly watch someone, say, one of the headmen, could you do it?"

The mystic leans forward in his seat, his expression anxious. "Now, wait a minute . . . ," he begins, but then Alinata clears her throat and whispers something Jomo doesn't quite catch. Reluctantly, the mystic revises his answer to, "I'd have to look into it, but it's within the realm of possibility."

Interesting. "What about several headmen at once, scattered across the kingdom?"

"Again, not a definite yes," the mystic says, looking beleaguered. "But it's possible."

"I can work with possible," Jomo says, ignoring the inquisitive stare Isa is giving him and the glower coming from Ilapara. He addresses the other Yerezi woman, as she seems more amenable to his plans. "And you're the one who can turn into bats or something."

She smiles thinly. "Ravens, Herald."

"Even better. How fast could you fly to another province and back if you had to?"

"Less than a day."

"Where are you going with this, Jomo?" Isa intervenes.

"Think about it," he says to her. "The biggest threat facing the throne right now is the next Mkutano. Should nothing change between now and then, the headmen will vote to disband the Sentinels, unleashing the militias. But with the help of a mystic"—Jomo points at said mystic for emphasis—"we could stop that from happening. We could get the votes we need." He looks at the guy, almost feeling sorry for cornering him. "That is, if your offer of help was sincere."

The mystic is silent for a time. "We're listening," he says, so Jomo lays out his plan.

"As it stands, I can count on three votes going our way: my own, which I'll cast on my cousin's behalf; the Lion's vote, seeing as he's a sworn enemy of the Crocodile; and the Impala's vote, which we'll be buying at great financial cost. We need three more votes to win, and I think I know how you can help me get them."

He told Isa in passing about the little green journal he received from Elea Saai at the New Year's Feast. But she doesn't know how obsessively he's been poring over its pages, wishing he had the power to weaponize the secrets contained therein. Now it seems the Mother has answered his prayers.

"The first headman you'll help me acquire is the Caracal," he says. "Two comets ago, he got one of his servants pregnant; nothing remarkable in and of itself, but when the woman gave birth, they claimed the child was stillborn. Then the mother disappeared, never to be seen again. I happen to know, in fact, that the child is alive but was hidden because of a rare condition that gave her both the mark of her father's princedom *and* the white mark of the mystic caste. I also happen to know their general whereabouts. What I would like you to do is secretly find them and bring me evidence of their existence."

Silence grips the construct, and a few puzzled looks get exchanged. "Forgive my ignorance," the mystic says, "but why would that help you?"

This is a delicate subject and necessitates someone more tactful to explain, so Jomo looks to Isa for help. Fortunately, she's quick on the uptake and steps in to answer. "Our clan marks prevent us from awakening, honored emissary. Only members of the mystic caste, who are free from clan biases, may know the Mother's embrace. But a child with both marks is immune to this inhibiting effect and could therefore awaken if schooled in the ways of magic."

"Which would threaten the neutrality of the mystics," says Tuksaad in that accent of his, understanding making his skin go pale. His eyes aren't really green, either, but a murkier color—must be the construct messing with Jomo's vision.

"That's the belief, yes," Isa answers him.

"So what happens to children who have both marks?" he says.

Isa struggles with the next part. "Such infants are . . . euthanized at birth. Hiding them is considered a serious crime."

"You mean they're murdered," the mystic says, predictably repulsed, and when no one disputes this, he correctly deduces the tenor of Jomo's plan. "So you intend to use this child's existence to blackmail the headman into supporting you."

"I'll use whatever leverage I can get," Jomo says. This doesn't win him any sympathetic looks, so he lifts his palms placatingly. "I don't actually intend to expose the child, all right? The threat of doing so should be enough. I'm not a monster."

The mystic shakes his head, clearly troubled. "I'm not sure about this."

"I don't like it, either, but we're literally fighting for our lives here. Thousands of my people could die if I fail them. I can't afford not to make use of any advantage I have."

That little reminder of what's at stake brings another silence to the pavilion.

"Where's this child right now?" the mystic asks.

"In the Caracal province," Jomo says. "We can discuss the specifics later."

"All right."

"Next, I need you to put eyes on the Buffalo. It's another case of a secret bastard, but this one is a grown man and a condemned criminal sentenced to die in the arena on the Requiem Moon. The Buffalo tried to cut secret deals to get him off but was unsuccessful. I strongly suspect he hasn't given up, though. He's planning something, and I'd like to catch him in the act."

"He's in the city, I presume."

"Yes, and so's the Jackal, whom I'd also like you to watch. I believe he's having an affair he wouldn't want exposed. If you can find evidence of this and bring it to me, I might be able to use it."

"Great. More blackmail," Tuksaad says, and Jomo's hackles rise.

"Do you have a better idea to get the votes I need?"

The little man's fickle eyes shine defiantly. "Not really."

"Then keep your judgment to yourself."

"Jomo . . . ," Isa says.

Clearing his throat, Jomo retracts his glare and continues. "One more headman to keep an eye on is the Hare. It's possible he's a worshipper of Arante and is harboring a Black mystic of the Inoi tribe in his hometown. If true, the Shirika would strip him of his crown, so he definitely wouldn't want anyone finding out his dirty little secret. He's in his province right now, so it's the ideal time to spy on him. And feel free to watch the other headmen if you can. The new Kestrel, the Buffalo, and the Jackal are in the city. The rest are in their provinces. Let me know as soon as you find something I can use."

The uncertainty on the mystic's face makes Jomo wonder if he hasn't been too forward. Almost as if she can read his mind, Isa makes a tactical retreat to soften his hard sell. "If this is too much for you, honored emissary, and I'm sure it is, please don't hesitate to say so. I'd hate for you to needlessly compromise your safety or the safety of your friends."

Good, Jomo thinks, silently applauding his cousin. *Give him the chance to take a step back, and his conscience will force him to step forward. It always works with the moral types.*

Jomo taps his fingers together while he waits for the mystic to make his decision, and it strikes him right then just how young they all are, playing dangerous games they have no business playing. But neither he nor Isa asked to be here, and the same is likely true for this mystic and his friends. This is simply the lot they were given in life, and they can either succumb or fight with everything they've got.

"Doing nothing means definite war," the mystic says eventually, "so our safety will be compromised either way." He releases a heavy breath. "Your Majesty, Herald, let us think through how we can help you acquire these three votes and get back to you tomorrow. Same time?"

Jomo looks to Isa, who nods. "Very well," she says, and in his heart, Jomo prays that they haven't all just signed their death warrants.

21: Ilapara

Skytown

Focus. Breathe. Tuksaad has clearly done this before; Ilapara can see it in his sparkling green eyes and the way he holds his sticks as they circle each other. To think he asked her to go easy on him. The lying shit.

Following a rash impulse, she lowers her sticks and levels a daring look at him. "Stop holding back. You clearly know your way around stick fighting, and you're blessed now. Give me your best."

He, too, lowers his sticks, a dangerous shadow dimming the brightness of his eyes. "You can't handle my best."

She lifts her sticks and falls back into a fighting stance. "Try me."

Tuk seems to think about it, then shrugs. "If you insist."

And then she's fending off what feels like three fighters banding together against her. Attacks come from her flanks, her back, her front, delivered by an enemy who seems to have turned to mist. Even when she reaches deep within herself, her sticks swipe through nothing; she sees him in front of her and strikes, but by the time her stick should connect, he's already whacking her from the side. The assault continues for a full minute before a low kick catches her from behind; then the garden spins as she tips over and lands hard on her back.

A completely illegal move, but Ilapara asked for it. She lies still for a time, her chest heaving as she pants. Her skin burns so much she feels like she's been flayed alive.

Tuk's face appears above her, looking absolutely smug. "Are you all right there, Ilapara?"

"I'm disappointed, Tuk," she says between breaths. "Is that all you've got? I barely broke a sweat."

His green eyes twinkle down at her. "You look pretty drenched to me."

"What, this?" She wipes her forehead, and her hand comes away damp. "That's just the humid air."

"I'm sure." He offers a hand to help her up. "Come, let's go have a drink."

"Good idea."

The servants left lemon-infused water with actual blocks of ice on the table in the garden, a slice of the legendary winters of the far south right here in the jungles. Ilapara and Tuk quench their thirst while they relax by the table, staring at the city sprawled out beneath Skytown. So calm on the surface, she thinks, yet in truth it balances on the edge of a deadly knife.

The skies have been a bit moody today. Perhaps it'll rain sometime later. Ilapara sinks deeper into her chair and enjoys the cold wave that steals across her body from the pit of her stomach. Tuk does the same, putting his feet up on another chair. He wears black whenever he leaves the residence, but when he's here, he wraps his hips in khangas with cheerful pastel shades. The one he's wearing right now is peach with white spirals. Her haltered dress is . . . well. It's mostly red.

"So, Tuksaad," Ilapara says after a long, companionable silence. "How come you got so good at fighting? It can't just be talent. No one gets that good unless they're motivated."

His eyes were clouded over with his own thoughts; now a touch of something sad enters his gaze. "Answer your question first, and I'll tell you. What drove you to be the warrior you are?"

She breaks eye contact, discomfited by having the question thrown back at her. She should have known better; avoiding personal histories has been an unspoken rule since they all met each other. "Don't we all just stumble through an endless succession of choices, mistakes, good fortune, bad fortune, and then we suddenly find ourselves where we are? Did I plan to be a warrior? Did I plan to be here? I don't know."

"You're avoiding the question," Tuk says, eyeing her intently.

She gazes into her glass. Her past is a knot of bitterness in her heart, and she would rather leave it undisturbed. "I guess it started out as a way to prove my worth to my father. I'd disappointed him by getting kicked out of the kraal's grammar school, so I—"

"Hang on. Stop right there." Tuk sits up, his eyes bright with fascination. "Did you say you were kicked out of school?"

It shouldn't be funny, but Tuk's amazed expression makes Ilapara bite her lips to stop herself from laughing. "Yes."

"Why? You didn't argue and pick fights with your instructors, did you?"

"Close, but not quite. One of my classmates wouldn't stop spreading nasty rumors about my uncle. I guess she and I had words, and the instructors took her side over mine."

"I see," Tuk says. "And by 'had words,' you mean . . ."

"Maybe there was a broken nose involved."

"Ha! I knew it! So what happened next?"

"Around the same time, I discovered my uncle was secretly a talented fighter—"

"The same uncle that horrid girl was spreading rumors about?"

Ilapara nods, remembering how ecstatic she was to see with her own eyes just how wrong everyone was about him. "He fought off a gang of Umadi hunters on his own, but he made me and the others who saw it promise not to tell anyone. He agreed to teach me his secrets, though." The levity Ilapara had begun to feel recedes, and in its place comes the sting of old grievances. "Except my father was even more disappointed in me when he found out, and our chief wouldn't let me earn my steel at the Queen's Kraal when I asked." She swallows the hard lump in her throat. "So I left, and here we are."

Tuk continues to watch her with a lopsided grin. "Kicked out of school, huh?" He chuckles as he leans back into his chair. "I'm never forgetting that one."

"You still owe me an answer," Ilapara says pointedly, and she almost regrets her words when the humor in his eyes dims a little.

"I guess I do." He stares down at the city for a time, idly twisting the ring on his right middle finger. His gaze is distant and shadowed, like he's sifting through a thousand heavy memories.

"So an aging lord of the empire visits a high-class pleasure bath to enjoy the company of pretty atmechs," he begins. "It's not his first time there, and it's not unusual for a powerful man to indulge his desires in such a place. But today one of the toys on offer catches his eye, and he can't look away. So what does he do?"

Tuk smiles as he answers his own question. "Why, he decides to buy the toy for a fortune and take it home, and the owner of the bath is all too happy to let him. Except it's not lust that moves the old man but something else, a light he sees in the atmech's eyes, something most of his kind refuse to believe exists in the toys that adorn their beds and sate their lusts." Tuk's gaze seeks Ilapara, glistening with emotion. "Do you know what he saw?"

She shakes her head, too enraptured to speak.

"A soul," Tuk says. "He saw me, Ilapara. A person. I was confused, at first, because no one had ever been interested in me outside what I could offer them in bed. Sex is what I was made for. My first memory is sex. But he wouldn't even touch me, and when I tried to seduce him, as I thought I was meant to, he became sickened and upset." Tuk's bewildered expression mirrors what he must have felt back then. "I didn't understand what he wanted from me. Why had he purchased me if not to use me as I'd been used my whole life? Why did he want to teach me how to read and write? Why did he care if I was happy, when I didn't even know that happiness was an option for me?"

Ilapara remains silent and attentive as Tuk recounts his tale.

"He was more of a father to me than anything else. His wife had passed on, and his adult children had distanced themselves from him, so he was lonely and in need of company, and I suppose I filled that gap. I was the son who worshipped and idolized him and he the father I never knew I wanted."

For a moment, Tuk seems wistful, but then his mood clouds over.

"Our affection for each other is what destroyed us both in the end," he says. "One day he decided to cut his children out of their inheritances and bequeath all his wealth to me. *All* of it. I didn't know what this meant at the time—we never discussed his wealth, I didn't care for it, I didn't *want* it. But he did it anyway, and when his sons found out, they blamed me for his decision, and then they butchered the old man right in front of me. They tore him apart, Ilapara, and all I could do was watch. I couldn't even move. There was so much blood."

Tuk doesn't wipe his cheeks when they glitter with tears. "Afterward they framed a servant for the crime and sold me off. I was too afraid to tell anyone what I'd seen; they knew I'd never talk, and for the first time in years I was back inside a pleasure house. Except this was nothing like the first one. This one served a clientele with more . . . violent tastes.

"I prayed for death every second I wasn't battered unconscious. To be utterly helpless, Ilapara, to be dirt beneath the boots of people who hate you simply for existing . . ." When he looks at her, his irises are as scarlet as embers of moonfire. "I won't ever be weak again."

Tuk's story stays with Ilapara when she goes inside to bathe, and it haunts her still as she applies her face paints in front of her dresser. She pauses as she lifts a brush daubed in black lip paint, looking at herself in the mirror.

You're not in Umadiland anymore, she thinks. *There's no need for you to keep painting your face like this.* She could return to the lighter colors of her people and stop wearing veils. But she doesn't because dressing like an Umadi girl long ago became a symbol of her rebellion against her people, whom she hasn't forgiven for shunning her.

But hasn't the outside world consistently proved to her just how lucky she was to have been born Yerezi? What are her grievances against her people compared to the hell Tuk suffered? What is her indignation compared to the plight of the Faraswa people, or to that of the Saires, who now fear stepping out of their homes? After everything she's seen, do her people, despite their flaws, deserve her continued scorn?

A knock on her door breaks her out of her thoughts, and the servant outside announces that Salo would like to see her in his study. In the end, she goes ahead and brings the brush to her lips, deciding not to think too much about it right now. After sprinkling herself with fragrance—which she can afford with her wages these days—she heads downstairs to answer Salo's summons, only to hear his voice as she descends the stairs to the foyer.

". . . None of them are to enter the study without my permission, understood?"

Ilapara's eyebrows shoot up at the hardened edge she hears in his voice. The steward Ruma Sato gives her a nervous glance as she stops nearby with her arms folded.

"Absolutely, honored emissary."

"Good. Oh, and one more thing, Bwana Ruma." Salo is bouncing up and down on the balls of his feet like he's full of pent-up energy. "Could I please have more of that wonderful beverage the ambassador sent me? And if you could prepare the sponge cakes you served for breakfast, that would be wonderful. Leave it all in the drawing room when it's ready."

"Right away, honored."

Salo flashes the steward a grin. "Excellent." And then he turns around and strides away without acknowledging Ilapara's presence.

Glowering, she jogs to catch up. "Someone's excited today."

"Yes. Quite." At the door to his study, he pauses with his hand on the doorknob. "I figured out a brilliant solution to my surveillance problems." A thought seems to strike him. "Speaking of which, I have a request to make of you."

"I'm listening. You did summon me, after all." She has half a mind to chew him out for that, but he doesn't seem to catch on to her displeasure.

"Not here," he says, opening the door. "Somewhere more private."

They enter his study, where he has spent most of his waking hours since the first meeting with the herald a few days back. Sometimes she worries about him, shut inside these walls, his mind off in that construct of his. It can't be healthy.

As she closes the door behind her, he settles down at his desk, where he starts rummaging through a pile of sheets scrawled all over with magical script.

"So?" she says. "What's the request?"

There's a white mug holding a sweet-smelling beverage on his desk. He lifts it up and takes a sip without looking away from his papers. He points across the room. "Take a seat. Tuk says he'll be here in a minute."

Salo is aloof today, but Ilapara tries not to lose her patience. She moves to sit down like he asked and notices that the cipher shell they used to enter his construct the other day is still sitting on the low table in front of the couch. Another golden orb with spinning rings sits next to it, which she assumes is responsible for the swarm of metal skimmers zipping around the dormant ceiling lamp in regular patterns.

She frowns. Those insects weren't supposed to be for sale, but Salo bribed the store clerk into breaking the rules during his last visit to Midtown. Ilapara could only watch as he parted with an eye-popping amount of money for them.

Her frown deepens when she notices how the mechanical insects seem to keep popping in and out of sight, like needles threading through pockets of light and shadow. "I don't remember your toy insects doing that," she says. "The disappearing thing."

"They aren't toys," he says irritably. "They are artifacts of complex magic, and I'm going to make them even more brilliant, because *I* am brilliant. With my amazing Axiom and my workhorse of a metaform, I can cram as many enchantments as I want into their tiny cores without spell overwrite. I'm so brilliant sometimes I astound myself."

I am not my emotions. "Have you found a use for them?"

"Yes, but I'd rather not explain now."

"Well, forgive me for asking."

"I forgive you."

Ilapara grits her teeth. "Have you slept at all lately, Salo?"

"Who needs sleep when you have this?" He taps his white mug, oblivious to her mounting anger.

"Yeah? And what's that?"

"A stimulating Valau beverage the ambassador sent me. I haven't needed sleep in three days! And best of all, it silenced that infernal beacon that wouldn't stop. It was driving me up the wall, I tell you. But now I can't hear it, and I'm awake, and I could work forever."

"What beacon, Salo? What are you talking about?"

"The beacon, Ilapara. It was like a worm in my head, but now it's gone, and good riddance." Salo knits his brow at the paper in his hand, then crumples it into a ball and tosses it aside. "That won't work." He continues to fuss over his papers until the door opens and Tuk steps inside, his hair dripping wet. Salo scowls at him. "Took you long enough, Tuksaad."

Tuk brushes his hair back. Despite her anger, Ilapara gives him a soft smile when their eyes meet. "I needed a good soak," he says, "but I'm here now. What's the emergency?"

"We'll talk about it in my construct," Salo says, to which Tuk sighs. "Do we really have to?"

"Yes, Tuk." Impatiently, Salo shoos him toward the cipher shell on the table. "Come on. Chop-chop. I don't have all day."

It's almost comical how high Tuk's eyebrows go. When his face swivels toward Ilapara, seeking explanation, she mimes that she is just as confused.

He comes over to sit down next to her, leaning over as he speaks beneath his breath. "Is that an obnoxious impostor, or has this room finally broken his mind?"

The subject in question has leaned against his chair and gone still, probably already waiting for them in his construct. "He hasn't slept in days," she whispers back. "And he's been drinking some kind of stimulant the Valau ambassador sent him."

"Ah." Tuk makes a face. "Let's pray this is a phase and not the new normal." His grimace deepens as his eyes fall on the cipher shell. "I suppose we should join him."

Ilapara shivers with the memory of using the device the last time. "Unfortunately."

She watches as Tuk pushes down the lever on the artifact, and then together they let their minds fall into the shell, passing through the cold nothingness of the Void and appearing in the construct seconds later. Lightning flashes from the nebula in the otherworldly skies as if in welcome. The last time they came here, they materialized on the porch with a cloud of swirling blackness. Today they appear next to a large musuku tree with glowing round yellow crystals for fruit. As with the other porch, the heavy double doors here are sealed shut, presumably leading nowhere if Salo was honest when he told them there was nothing behind the doors.

"Dear Ama, I hate the Void," Ilapara says, shuddering.

Tuk hugs himself like he's cold. "Agreed."

After they shake off the chill of their transit, they cross the walkway and join Salo in the fancy rotunda. He's already seated, tapping his foot on the floor as he waits. Even in the construct, he doesn't seem quite himself today.

"Why are we here again?" Tuk says as they sit down. "Are we meeting the herald?"

Salo grins mirthlessly. "Well, Tuksaad. I figured since we're trying to commit subversion, espionage, and extortion in a foreign tribeland, we'd better do it somewhere no one can overhear us."

Tuk blinks at him, unimpressed. "For future reference, I still disagree with this course of action. Vehemently."

"So do I," Ilapara says, reviving the argument they've been having ever since Salo fell into the king's orbit.

"Yes, that much is clear, but I've given you chances to opt out, which you can still do if you want." Salo pushes his spectacles up his nose. "My chances would be a lot worse without you, but I won't hold it against you if you don't want to risk it. It's your choice."

This is emotional blackmail, and he knows it. Ilapara almost growls. "Just tell us how to help."

"It's not going to be easy to surveil a whole bunch of powerful people without getting caught. If we're going to pull it off, I'm going to need to spend as much time as I can immersed in spells and enchantments. Which means I don't have time to leave this study. So. I need the two of you to pick up a few things for me in the city."

"You're having us run your errands?" Tuk clicks his tongue. "It's a good thing you pay us well, Salo."

On an ordinary day, Salo might have chuckled, but today the humor is lost on him. "I need someone to go down to Midtown and get me more cipher shells. The smaller kinds. Bracelets, necklaces. I think I saw rings. About a dozen of them should do, and don't ask me why. I simply don't have time to explain. The next thing I need is—"

A resonant metallic clang comes from across one of the seven walkways. Ilapara is stupefied when she looks and sees the double doors on that porch swinging open and a young man in a red loincloth walking out. Salo doesn't seem to notice, since he keeps talking.

"Uh . . . Salo?" she says, interrupting him. "Who the devil is that?"

"Who's who?"

"The Ajaha I just saw coming out of those doors over there, by the ice-and-lightning statue. I thought you said there was nothing behind the doors."

Salo stiffens, his expression going taut. "I don't see anyone."

A blatant lie.

"I see him," Tuk says, leaning forward with curious blue eyes. "Tall, muscular fellow holding a cat. Oh! He's waving." Tuk beams as he waves back. "Well, hello!"

The Ajaha is indeed waving and holding a cat. As they watch, he sits down on the steps of the porch and continues to stroke and nuzzle his feline friend like it's the most normal thing to do in the world. Bewildered, Ilapara swivels her head back to the parlor.

"Salo?"

"Don't worry about him," Salo says with a glower, though despite his words, his hands have curled into fists. "He's . . . a memory. He's not real. Focus on what's important, like the books I need from the library at the House of Forms. I have borrowing privileges there, so if someone could go there for me and get whatever is available on complex multi-disciplinary enchantments, I'd appreciate it. Guys? Are you listening?"

Both Tuk and Ilapara struggle to look away from the curious ranger and his cat. Is that a mini version of Mukuni?

"Yes," Tuk says, distractedly. "Books on enchantments from the House of Forms. Want to handle that, Ilapara?"

She shakes her head. "I'd rather not go back there for obvious reasons. I'll get the shells."

"And Alinata is off hunting after the cursed child," Salo tells them. "So I guess that leaves you, Tuk."

"That's fine," Tuk says, still watching the ranger; then his eyes snap back to Salo. "Wait. Alinata left? When?"

"About an hour ago," Salo replies, and Ilapara shakes her head, not believing Salo is actually going through with Jomo's crazy plan.

"What's she supposed to do when she locates the child?"

"Exactly what the herald said: get evidence of the child's existence."

"Yes, but how?"

Salo tilts his head to the side like this is an unreasonable question. "With a cipher shell, obviously."

"That explains everything," Ilapara says.

Her sarcasm flies over his head. "Good. One last thing before we get to the other matter I want to discuss. Steward Ruma tells me there are many alchemists who sell their wares in the undercity. If you can discreetly find me an alchemical sedative that induces instant unconsciousness when injected into the bloodstream, that would be great. Nothing lethal or permanent, of course. All the better if it's quick to disappear from the body, leaving no trace of itself. But it has to be instant."

"An interesting request," Tuk says, watching Salo like a hawk. "Should we be worried?"

"Not at all." Salo gets up, rubbing his hands together like he's nervous. "Now, to the other reason I brought you here. I know you're skeptical about what I'm doing, but hopefully you'll feel differently after I've shown you the resources I now have at my disposal. Last time, Alinata was here, so I told you there was nothing behind the doors on the other side of the walkways, but . . . well. I lied. You see, this whole structure is actually . . . maybe I should just show you."

He sets off toward the ranger, then stops at the mouth of the walkway to beckon them over. Ilapara and Tuk quietly get up and follow.

She noticed before that each of the seven porches connected to the central rotunda features a unique work of art; the one ahead of them is a leopard of red lightning lounging on a slab of ice.

When they reach the porch, the ranger looks up with a rather handsome grin.

"Hey, Salo," he says. "Hey, Salo's friends."

Salo ignores him. "Keep walking. He's not real."

This doesn't seem to offend the ranger, given how he goes back to nuzzling his cat with a content expression. Ilapara stares at him brazenly, barely noticing that Salo has opened the doors.

"Guys," Salo says, sounding exasperated. "In here."

Ilapara and Tuk pry their eyes from the ranger and follow Salo into a large hall with an arched framework of rafters open to the sky in place of a roof. The rafters are festooned with active Yerezi glowvines that crisscross each other almost thickly enough to form a canopy, and the sight of them inflicts on Ilapara a sharp twinge of homesickness. Even the wicker furniture strewed around is Yerezi, though it somehow manages to look at home alongside the grandness and opulence obviously inspired by KiYonte architecture.

Row after row of shelves fill the hall between carpeted aisles, with more shelves on the balconies overlooking the main floor. At first glance Ilapara thinks she might be in some kind of library; then she notices the distinct lack of books. Instead, the shelves here hold plates of metal slotted into horizontal grooves, each with a colored bar of light glowing along its front-facing edge.

Strange, but it fails to distract Ilapara's mind from the ranger. "So you have an Ajaha just lounging around your construct with a cat," she says to Salo's back as he takes them farther down the widest aisle.

"Yes."

"That's a little curious, Salo."

"I guess it is."

"I don't suppose you could tell us why he's here?"

"No."

"Why not?"

Salo comes to a stop, hanging his head. When he turns around to face them, he appears resigned, the look on his face holding no trace of his recently acquired arrogance. "I don't know why he appears, Ilapara. He comes mostly at night, and it's not deliberate on my part, but I let him stay when he comes because . . . because I miss him and I like the feeling that he's here with me even if he's not." Salo gulps visibly. "Is that a problem?"

In his voice Ilapara recognizes the fear of rejection, that his admission will somehow lessen her opinion of him. She doesn't think it does. She doesn't think it should. She regrets that he thought it would.

She shakes her head. "No, Salo. It's not a problem."

"I can't say I blame you," Tuk says. "He's quite easy on the eyes. And polite. And a lover of cats. All wins in my book."

Relief loosens the tension in Salo's shoulders, and his lips quirk, a hint of his old self coming to the surface. "Yes. I had the same thought."

"So what are these?" Tuk asks as he walks to a nearby shelf and pulls out a metal tablet.

Salo exhales loudly, his hands tapping his thighs in a nervous rhythm. "That's a spell prototype from the Pattern Archives. Or a copy of one. So are all the others."

Tuk jerks his head up. "Salo, there must be thousands in this chamber alone."

"Yes."

"And there are six other chambers." Tuk gasps, color draining from his face. "You didn't."

Ilapara can't even say she's surprised. "I think he did," she says, eyeing the damned fool. "I think he really did."

"You stole the Pattern Archives!" Tuk exclaims. "I don't know whether to be impressed or horrified!"

"You should be horrified, Tuk," Ilapara tells him, and as the scale of Salo's reckless crime hits her, she has to resist reaching for his throat and trying to choke some sense into him. "What the devil were you thinking? Do you have any idea what could happen if the wrong people found out?"

He has the gall to look irritated. "That's why we're all going to make sure that doesn't happen. No telling anyone else. And Alinata can't know, or she'll report it to the queen, and who knows how she'll react."

"The king was here, Salo! And the herald! What if they saw?"

"And you gave them a key to this place," Tuk says grimly. "You do know a high mystic lives in the Red Temple, don't you?"

"Relax, both of you," Salo says. "The doors won't open for anyone I haven't authorized, and no one can enter the construct unless I allow it. We'll be fine."

Ilapara continues to shake her head in disbelief. "I've never met someone so intent on getting himself killed."

Tuk laughs as he looks around the hall with sparkling eyes. "I have to admit, this is pretty amazing."

"Until it gets us all killed," she reiterates.

"But that won't happen, obviously," Salo says, "because I won't let it." He claps his hands together. "Well then. Now that the secret is off my chest—whew—I think we're done here. I have a lot of work to do, and you both have places to go. So. See you out in the real world."

And then he disappears from the construct with a flash, leaving Ilapara glaring at the empty space where he stood. "Sometimes that boy makes me regret ever running into him," she says.

"I think we both know that's not true," Tuk says.

"Right now, it is," she says, but the smile on his face says he doesn't believe her.

"Come," he says. "We can race down Skytown to make ourselves feel better."

Alinata has returned by morning the next day. Ilapara runs into her in the hallway outside the bathing chamber, her skin beaded with drops of water, a towel wrapped around her body.

When she first met the woman, she thought her reserved and watchful behavior symptomatic of a devious and calculating character. A part of her still thinks this—Alinata is an Asazi from the Queen's Kraal, after all, and no one there makes it far up the hierarchy without a cunning mind. But Ilapara has come to understand that Alinata is not in herself a bad person. She is simply fiercely loyal to her queen.

The hall is empty, but Ilapara speaks softly. "I take it since you're back, you found the child."

Alinata nods, not meeting her eyes. "She lives with her mother in the western mountains of the Caracal province, among an isolated community of spirit worshippers. They weren't difficult to find once I knew where to look."

"So what happens next?"

"The herald makes use of the evidence, I suppose. Salo has arranged for me to deliver it to him in an hour's time."

Ilapara watches the Asazi. Had they not spent the past few weeks living in the same house, she might have thought her indifferent to the child's fate, but she has learned to see past the dense veneer Alinata wears all the time. "I can tell you don't like this any more than I do. So why go through with it?"

The veneer cracks just a little, and Alinata's gaze hardens. "I don't have a choice."

"Yes, you do, Alinata. You could tell the queen that you and Salo are in over your heads here. What she expects you to do would be unreasonable for an experienced Asazi and a much older mystic, let alone the two of you. We've been lucky so far, but sooner or later, you'll make a mistake. Then what?"

"War is coming to the Redlands," Alinata says. "Our actions here will determine whether the Yerezi tribe is still intact when it's over. No risk is too high if it means securing the future of our people."

"Is it the future of our people you care about or your own future in the Queen's Kraal?" An unfair question, perhaps, but Ilapara doesn't take it back, even as Alinata's eyes flash with indignation.

"I have served the tribe since the moment I could walk. I was chosen for this mission because I'm not afraid of doing what needs to be done, even if it means sacrificing my own life. Don't you dare question my loyalty."

With that, Alinata turns her back to Ilapara and walks away.

Ilapara follows. "What about sacrificing the life of your tribesman?" she says. "I know you worry about Salo just as much as I do."

At the door to her chamber, Alinata pauses, her shoulders rigid.

"Salo made his own choices," she says. "And so did you."

The Asazi then enters her chamber and shuts the door.

During a break in her daily exercise session with Tuk later that afternoon, Salo comes by clutching a shiny item in either hand, frowning as though in concentration. His mood has only worsened since yesterday, so they've both taken to avoiding him. As he strides nearer, Tuk sinks deeper onto his recliner, turning his head to Ilapara and making an apprehensive face. "What now?" he whispers.

"No idea," she whispers back.

Salo doesn't greet them when he arrives. He simply discards the items onto their laps, one each for Tuk and Ilapara, then folds his arms. "I forgot to hand these over to you this morning, so. Here you go."

Ilapara picks up her item, a thin golden wristlet with bands of tronic ivory and little carnelian crystals. She looks over and sees that

Tuk's item is identical, save that his crystals are black stones of smoky quartz. "What are they?" she asks.

"Cipher shells, obviously," Salo says. "I enchanted them when I was practicing with my metaform. They both hold three charms, two of which are the same, while the third is unique to each shell. Ilapara, to use your first charm, make a fist and twist to the right. Repeat to deactivate. Twist to the left for the second charm. Press on the central crystal for the third charm, but use it sparingly since it'll rapidly deplete your power cell. Tuk, you can control all your charms by thought and use them as often as you please."

Ilapara looks up from her wristband. "Wait. Why is his different?"

"Because he has my blessing, Ilapara, which gives him instinctual control over charms I cast. His blessing will also continually replenish his power cell with essence, so he'll never have to run out. You'd have the same if I blessed you, too, but you've made it clear I'm not worthy of your trust. Anyway, try them out and let me know what you think."

With that, Salo turns around and walks away, leaving Ilapara to glower at his back. "What a manipulative asshole."

"He's not himself," Tuk says, snapping his band around his left wrist. "I think he's under a lot of stress."

"Well, he'd better destress soon, or I might have to strangle him."

Tuk chuckles as he sits up, swinging his feet off the recliner. "Come. Let's see what these things do."

Ilapara's first enchantment turns out to be a film of Mirror light that envelops her entire body, passing over her eyes like the fabric of a sheer veil and reminding her of the time she possessed herself with the spirit of an inkanyamba. But the resultant grimace on Tuk's face almost prompts her to yank off the wristband right there and then.

"What do I look like?" she asks, dreading the answer.

"Like someone I've never met," he says. "Even your clothes have changed color." His eyes turn green, and he tilts his head. "I must say, Ilapara. That nose. Yikes. I feel the urge to reach over and pull it down just a little lower."

"Are you saying I'm now ugly?"

"You've definitely looked better," Tuk says with a laugh.

Ilapara quickly twists her balled hand to the right to deactivate the charm, then again to reactivate it. There are subtle distortions in her field of vision each time. "What about now?"

"It's a different disguise," Tuk says, amazement in his voice. "And a little better looking."

More attempts confirm that the disguise the wristband gives her is different each time. And then she starts twisting her wrist to the left, activating the second charm.

". . . Now I can't see you at all," Tuk remarks.

"What?"

"It's a stealth charm. I can't see you."

She looks down at herself and sees nothing different. "But I can still see myself."

"It's so uncanny how your voice seems to be coming out of nowhere."

Ilapara relinquishes the charm and stares in wonder at the wristband, salivating at what else it might have in store for her. Heart racing, she presses down on the largest carnelian crystal.

The moment she does, a field of light with a reddish tint wraps itself around the contours of her entire body like a suit of spectral armor. With restrained alarm she studies the layers of red light enveloping her arms, chest, and legs. She lifts a hand to touch her face but meets a smooth, hard surface instead.

This time there's no humor in Tuk's expression. "That's Void armor, Ilapara," he says. "Just one step away from my flashbrands. And he's had the metaform for what, less than a month?" Tuk shakes his head. "I'm beginning to see why the law of zero contact was a good idea."

Remembering Salo's warning, Ilapara presses down on the crystal again to deactivate the charm. And then she surprises herself by laughing as she stares down at her wristband. "This is already the most valuable item I've ever owned. Do you know how much I could sell it for? I could probably buy this house and have change left over. I can't believe Salo just gave it to me."

"He has a metaform and a whole library of spells. Combined with his unique Axiom, these wristbands are probably the floor of what's possible now."

"What about yours?" Ilapara says. "Let's see what it does."

"Oh, I already know what mine does," Tuk says, except his lips don't move, and his voice comes from the reclining chairs behind Ilapara. She turns around to look and feels her jaw almost hit the floor when she sees an exact copy of Tuk lounging on one of the chairs, stirring his coconut water with a grass straw.

She turns back to the version in front of her, whose eyes sparkle with laughter as his smile widens.

"Tuk?"

"I'm actually over here," says the Tuksaad on the recliner. "That over there is a phantom I've been controlling this whole time. I never actually got up from my chair."

Ilapara allows herself a moment to be astonished, looking several times between the real Tuk and his phantom. "I'm guessing you have invisibility and . . . a replica you can control?"

"I can disguise myself too." With a ripple of light the phantom's nose lengthens and becomes hooked, his eyes dim and inch closer together, his cheeks sink into themselves, and his mauve khanga shifts to a pale yellow.

Ilapara leans forward to take a closer look. Most Mirror craft illusions she's seen thus far have been easy to identify as such due to their ghostlike character. This one looks solid as rock. "Your phantom is really ugly, Tuk." She pokes it in the stomach and is met with resistance. "Can you feel when I touch it?"

"No," the phantom answers.

"But how can it speak?" Ilapara asks. "How can an illusion have a voice?"

"There are kinetic spells involved," the phantom says. "Vibrations. I don't really know how I'm controlling them; I just am. Hey, stop poking me. It looks weird."

Ilapara retracts her finger and stares at the phantom. "The skin feels odd, but I'd have never known without touching it."

"I doubt the illusion's very strong. If you hit it hard, it'd probably explode."

An idea strikes her, and she turns to address the real Tuk, still on the recliner. "Why don't we find out? Might as well practice how to use these things in a fight."

By the time she remembers that it's a bad idea to give him such an opening, it's already too late.

"I like how you think," he says.

And then, cheat that he is, his ugly phantom attacks before she's prepared herself.

Salo summons them to his study again three days later. Many of the cipher shells she bought him in Midtown are all over the place along with their internal organs, some sitting on his desk, others on the low table across the room. But the mechanical insects, which had become a regular feature of the decor, are no longer present.

"Where are the skimmers?" she asks, craning her neck to stare up at the ceiling.

"I sent them out," Salo replies. "Most of them, anyway."

His hoarse voice forces her to take a good look at him. He's always been lithe, but he's grown even thinner over the last few days, which is no surprise seeing as he rarely joins them for meals. Dark bags have also begun to swell beneath his spectacles.

"What do you mean, you sent them out?"

He looks up from his desk, his brow creased in confusion. "Oh. Didn't I explain what they were?"

"No, you didn't," she says with a pointed look. "You were too busy gloating over your own brilliance."

He winces, looking away. "Sorry about that. I was trying to cram too much information into my short-term memory, keeping myself alert with a stimulant . . ." He sighs. "I've stopped all of that now. The stimulant especially. It improved my productivity, but it gave me indigestion and mood swings."

Ilapara suffers a stirring of pity for him. "You look exhausted, Salo."

"I know, and hopefully I'll get some sleep today once your mission is complete."

"Mission?"

"Yes. Here, watch." He puts out a hand, palm facing up, and there's a flash of gold as a metal skimmer appears out of thin air and flutters onto the hand. "I turned the skimmers into my little spies. They came with spells of kinetic Void craft already transcoded into their cipher cores, which was how they could fly, but I added a few more. Entanglement with my amulet. A stealth charm. A joint Mirror-and-Void charm to give them sight and hearing. I can now have unbroken surveillance on as many targets as I have skimmers."

Ilapara doesn't have to be a mystic to understand the implications. Someone with an army of stealthy, highly mobile little spies would quickly acquire a trove of dangerous information.

"So you control the skimmers with your mind?"

"If I want to, but there're too many for me to control all at once, and I can't do it all the time. My amulet does most of the mental heavy lifting."

The skimmer on his palm flutters its wings and lifts off, then vanishes with a twinkle.

"As impressed as I am," Ilapara says, "this city is crawling with mystics. Won't they detect your spies if they get too close?"

Salo shakes his head. "I used a stealth charm so robust my skimmers can skip through walls. Only a talented Void mystic can detect it, and even then, they have to be actively looking for this exact spell. I *have* noticed a few places warded against all types of stealth magic, though, mostly the Shirika strongholds like the House of Law and parts of the royal palace. But the skimmers can go pretty much everywhere else."

Ilapara is quietly alarmed that he has already tried to infiltrate these places. "Again, Salo, I'm impressed." *And I pray to Ama you know what you're doing.*

"Thank you. But I suspect you'll be even more impressed with this." From his desk he picks up a golden earring and hands it to her. "Put this on."

She reaches for it, uncertain. The jewelry's ornate, with silver and tronic ivory, designed to clip around the ear. She knows for a fact that it cost a prince's ransom, since it was one of the cipher shells she bought for him in Midtown when he sent her there.

"Go on," he prompts her, lifting his crimson amulet and slinging it around his neck.

With a wary sigh, Ilapara clips the earring onto her left ear, leaving a hand nearby in case she needs to take it off quickly. But nothing happens. "Now what?"

"Now you wait here." Salo extricates himself from behind his desk and dashes out of the study, leaving Ilapara to stare at the door, baffled and a little annoyed.

A second later her ear vibrates, startling her. At first, she thinks she imagined the tiny voice she heard, but the earring vibrates again, and Salo's voice is unmistakable.

"Can you hear me?"

She gasps. "Yes. Can *you* hear me?"

Salo's chuckle comes through with a metallic timbre. *"That's the point, Ilapara."* He reappears in the study a moment later, looking extremely pleased with himself. "All right. Looks like it works. Of course, you wouldn't need it if you took my blessing, not to mention how much stronger and faster you'd get, but . . . well. To each her own."

"I'm not having this argument with you again, Salo," she says as she runs a finger over the metal artifact clipped to her ear. "But great job with this thing. And the wristband too. You just might be too good at this. Makes you easy to forgive for being an ass."

Sitting on the edge of his desk with one knee up, he smiles. "Thank you for not strangling me. I know you probably wanted to."

"You have no idea."

The door opens right then as Tuk enters the study, dressed in a black knee-length shirt hemmed with silver embroidery and matching pants. "I'm late again, aren't I," he says, grimacing like he anticipates a scornful reaction. "Sorry."

"It's all right, Tuk," Salo says. "And I'm sorry for the appalling way I've acted toward you both this last week."

Tuk relaxes, his expression turning sunny. "You're under a lot of pressure, so I understand. Besides, I knew you'd be back to your old self."

"Thanks for your faith in me."

"It is not undeserved," Tuk says. "You said you had a mission for us?"

"Yes." Salo straightens and rounds his desk, settling back down on his chair. "I need you and Ilapara to investigate the source of a strange signal in Northtown."

"A strange signal?" Ilapara says, intrigued.

Salo rubs his temples, visibly worn out. "On the night of the earthquake, I felt something . . . turn on. A beacon, maybe, and it hasn't stopped hounding me since. The stimulant helps drown it out a little, but I'm not going down that road again. Anyway, I can't sleep. It's like a vibration or a drone, and I can feel it loosening the teeth from my gums. I didn't know where it was coming from until my skimmers traced it to an abandoned apartment in Northtown, but whatever it is, it's hidden somewhere the skimmers can't get to. I need you guys to go there and find it and possibly turn it off before it drives me to madness."

"My goodness, Salo," Tuk says, his eyes yellow with concern. "Why didn't you say something?"

"I thought I was imagining it. But my metaform confirmed that there's something there. I just don't know what."

"Then I guess we'll find out," Ilapara says. "But how will we know where to go?"

"I'll guide you from here. And my friend will be following you." A skimmer flashes into view as it zips past Ilapara's head only to wink out a second later. "Take a carriage and get off at the Northtown market square. You'll walk the rest of the way. Make sure to keep your Mirror disguises active. Questions?"

Ilapara and Tuk look at each other, then shake their heads. There are always questions, but for now the path ahead seems clear enough. "You'll owe us for this," Ilapara says.

"I know." Salo pulls in a ragged breath and lets it out slowly, wiping his eyes behind his spectacles. "And I appreciate you sticking with me despite your reservations and my rude behavior. You're both the best. Now please get going before I bite off my own fingers."

22: Musalodi

Skytown

Magic is alive in Yonte Saire. It permeates every corner of every street like an invisible mist, anchored in place by a network of ancient relics scattered across the city. These relics, holy shrines to the people of Yonte Saire, make the moon's essence thicker in the air, providing constant power to the many enchantments built into the city's ecosystem.

Pumps that supply homes with potable water. Reclamation centers to process waste. Streetlamps that burn brightly in the night. Even the living fence growing around the city's perimeter draws from the moon shrines, and so do some of the magically reinforced towers of Midtown.

It is a marvel of arcane artifice a scholar of magic might enjoy studying in detail, and had he the time to spare, Salo might have done just that. As it is, the thickness of magic in Yonte Saire has meant that his skimmers can roam the city without much risk of detection.

They swarmed out of his study on a drizzly morning and fluttered into the bleak skies, unseen and unheard, silent dancers swaying to a melody sung through the Void. With Ziyo's help he spread them across Yonte Saire like a plague, casting an invisible net of surveillance that continues to penetrate nearly every shadow in the city.

They watch and they listen, never lingering in one place for long, perching on trees, streetlamps, and windowsills. Skipping through walls and ceilings, sinking beneath roads and easing into sewers and tunnels. They crawl into cracks on walls and crannies in the bark of trees. They lurk in flower beds and in gutters on rooftops. Everything they see and hear they send to their hub for Ziyo to analyze and categorize and for Salo to sift through like the pages of a picture book.

He sends his mind into his construct as soon as Ilapara and Tuk leave for Northtown. Even now the unknown beacon continues to gnaw at his sanity like a fly buzzing endlessly around his ears. At first, he thought he could keep ignoring it, but the headaches and the sleeplessness soon became unbearable.

A constellation of floating mirrors awaits him in the central pavilion of his construct, each displaying the field of view of a single skimmer. He designed the mirrors to let anyone push them around the room and resize them at will, taking inspiration from the visions of Mirror craft he saw in use at the arena. He settles down on a chaise and draws the mirrors closer with the flick of a hand. The tiny simulacrum of Mukuni he conjured yawns at him from its perch on the other side of the room.

"Show me the apartment," he says.

One mirror comes to the fore as the metaform obeys, showing him the view of a multistory Northtown tenement building from an external vantage point. Vines crawl thickly up the trellised walls. Wet clothes were hung to dry on the balconies. The curtains are drawn inside the apartment in question, but Salo's skimmers have already investigated the interior. No one has been in there for at least a week.

"Show me Ilapara and Tuk," he says.

Another mirror comes forward, displaying the faces of his friends as they sit inside a carriage rolling down the Skytown road. He told them he'd be watching, but he feels compelled to announce his presence so they know he's listening.

"Hello," he says, transmitting his voice through his mental bond with Tuk and to Ilapara's earring through the metaform. At the same time, he commands the skimmer riding with them to make itself visible.

"I just wanted to let you know I'm here. I don't want you thinking I'm spying on you."

Both their eyes flick toward the skimmer, and it almost looks like they can see him through the mirror. Ilapara is shown frowning as she adjusts her earring. *"You can see us right now?"*

He chuckles at the incredulity in her voice. "Yes, Ilapara. I can see you."

"Am I the only one who thinks this is creepy?"

"It is creepy," Tuk agrees. *"And now you know why it horrifies me that a metaform ended up here. In just a few weeks, Salo used it to create a surveillance system any despot would kill for."* Tuk's expression is grim as he gazes into the watching skimmer. *"You wield dangerous magic, Salo. Use it honorably."*

Salo knows Tuk is right, of course. With his Axiom, a metaform, and a full library of spells at the tips of his fingers, it would be all too easy to grow intoxicated with his own power, and there are probably a million ways he could abuse the ability to watch anyone he wants to at any time. He'll have to exercise stringent self-control. Surely he can keep a finger on the city's pulse without egregious violations of privacy.

"Good advice, Tuk," he says. "I'll try not to disappoint you."

"I'm sure you'll do fine."

Salo turns his attention to the other floating mirrors. A skimmer clinging to a wall in a Northtown alley lifts off to follow a nervous-looking teenage boy carrying a bundle of posters as he runs down the alley on bare feet. He stops by a corner to make sure no one is watching before sticking one of his posters onto the wall and running off. The poster depicts a woman carrying two swords as she yells at the observer in defiance. FREE AYANA is the caption beneath the image. To Salo's shock, he recognizes the woman as the Faraswa warrior who fought alongside Kamali during the bloody match he witnessed at the arena.

The arena. And the horrible things that happened there. Things he tries his best not to remember, though the images are rarely far from his mind. He thought he'd be witnessing something akin to the fighting games staged by the Ajaha at the completion of their yearly initiation ritual. What he viewed instead was a bloodbath.

Had he not been there for ulterior reasons, he might have excused himself from the ambassador's private box and fled the scene altogether. His lower lip still hurts from how much he bit himself during the match, and it was all he could do not to reach forward with a spell and pull the Jasiri out of danger.

"Ziyo, do you know anything about this Ayana?"

Bolts of lightning sprawl away from the nebula in the sky above the library before Ziyo responds. *Ayana is a prisoner who fought during the arena match staged last weekend. Ziyo has logged numerous discussions of her performance within the Faraswa community; it appears there are many who believe her survival was evidence that she is blessed by the ancients. There is a growing movement among the city's Faraswa population to demand that she be acquitted and set free.*

Salo stares at the image on the poster, intrigued. "Have you seen or heard anything about these so-called ancients?"

From multiple logged conversations, Ziyo has deduced that the word ancients *among the Faraswa people alludes to a former, more exalted state the tribe once enjoyed, to which a return is promised in their legends. It seems the emergence of a powerful warrior from among them is one of the signs that this return is imminent.*

The exalted state could only refer to the period before the Faraswa lost their ability to awaken, during the height of their empire. According to the histories Salo has read, their mystics were so powerful they could call down redhawks to fight for them. It is even said that the two transcontinental roadways of the Redlands were their creations, built to facilitate the spread of their dominion, which left lasting marks on every tribe. And then, so the stories go, they were cursed for allowing sun worshippers into their midst.

"Have you heard anything about why she was sentenced to death?" Salo says.

"It appears she was arrested and convicted for a string of Southtown assassinations. All her victims, male and of moderate wealth, were slain as they slept. Advocates of her release believe she acted in vengeance for the violent rape of young Faraswa girls."

An uneasy feeling slides down Salo's spine. A part of him sympathizes with her anger, especially given the unjust treatment of the Faraswa people in this city, but she still killed several people in their sleep. *She hardly deserves to be mauled in an arena, though, does she? And neither does Kamali.*

"Show me the undercity prison," he says, his heart beginning to thud faster.

Perhaps it was the lingering sense of guilt that moved him, but Kamali was one of the first people he searched for when he released his skimmers, if only to ascertain whether the Jasiri continued to draw breath. He'll never forget what Kamali did to those eight guards, but he did it to keep Salo's secret from getting out, which he wouldn't have needed to do had Salo acted differently.

No matter how he looks at it, Salo knows he must bear at least some of the responsibility for the deaths of those guards and Kamali's present fate.

The lone skimmer that infiltrated the undercity prison flies through a grate and out of the ventilation duct it was hiding in. Its field of view is transmitted through the Void to a mirror in front of Salo's couch in the construct, and he watches as it flies down a vast cylindrical well with a watchtower rising up its center. Hundreds of prisoners are being held in brightly lit alcoves along the circular wall—an arrangement that allows the guards in the dim observation room atop the central watchtower to see all cells at once, while the prisoners themselves, caged in permanent brightness, can never know when they're being watched.

It is a pitiful sight. Dirty, hopeless prisoners disconnected from the passage of time, languishing in their cells as they are continuously bathed in relentless, sleep-depriving light. The bars of their cells contain shock charms of Storm craft to discourage misbehavior. So do the walkways outside the cells. Kinetic charms of Void craft allow the guards to open any number of gates remotely. Salo already knows that all these enchantments are pinned to a central hub in the watchtower.

"Is Ayana here?"

"Affirmative."

"Show me."

The skimmer continues downward, stopping to hover outside a cell one row up from the base of the well. The occupant is indeed a Faraswa woman lying down on her bed with her eyes closed and her head resting on interlaced hands. One look at her striking face is enough to confirm that hers is the face depicted on the posters.

"Keep a close eye on her and monitor any developments regarding Ayana in the city."

"Acknowledged," the metaform replies.

"All right. Check on Kamali."

The skimmer rises and flies across the well, past the watchtower, to a cell many rows up, where it finds the occupant performing a series of stretches completely in the nude save for the metal collar locked around his neck. Brightly colored tattoos strain against his well-muscled arms, chest, and abdomen. His moves are so hypnotizingly graceful Salo feels heat crawling up his cheeks and has to force himself to refrain from intruding any further on the man's privacy, directing his skimmer to avert its gaze.

He clears his throat. "Er, Ziyo, check on the other prisoner, please."

The skimmer flies farther up to a cell near the top of the cylindrical well. The dreadlocked young man within is huddled up in a corner on his bed, hugging his trembling knees to his chest, his cheeks streaked white with dried tears. Exactly as he was when Salo first found him. With a heavy heart, Salo moves the skimmer along.

"Watch them both as well, Ziyo."

"Acknowledged."

"What about the Wavunaji situation? Anything to report?"

Three mirrors move to the front of the array. One shows two city guards in brown tunics patrolling a street in Midtown. Another shows a worker in the city's water-reclamation center taking orders from a mystic in bronze robes. The third mirror shows a man overseeing the offloading of grain sacks from the wagons of a large spirit-powered vehicle near the Northtown wheelhouse terminal. The only thing they all seem to have in common is that none of them belong to the Saire clan.

"Ziyo has identified three figures at the forefront of the Wavunaji. It appears the movement has successfully infiltrated the city guard and various other associations of laborers."

Salo frowns as he focuses on the two city guards in the first mirror. "That's troubling," he says. "Have you witnessed any interclan persecutions thus far?"

"Several members of the Saire clan have been arrested in the past two days for various charges and are being held in the city guard jailhouse. The city guard has also enforced restrictions on the exit of Saires from the city." A new mirror floats forward, showing the field of view of a skimmer near the main northern gate. *"This happened an hour ago."*

In the vision, city guards posted by the gate are shown dragging unwilling Saires off a wheelhouse they boarded in Northtown. As he watches the surreal incident unfold, Salo fears that the violence is about to escalate, but it seems the watchful presence of a contingent of Sentinels stops the guards from taking things too far. There's even a shouting match between a Sentinel and a guard when the latter's rough handling of an elderly Saire woman precipitates her fall. What surprises Salo is that both men are from the same clan. A Jasiri watches indifferently from the gatehouse.

"This is insane," Salo breathes and shudders to think of what would happen without the restraining influence of the Sentinels. "Ziyo, expand surveillance on members of the Wavunaji. Alert me the second anything of significance happens."

"Understood."

Someone enters the room, and Salo doesn't have to look to know who it is. "You're early again," he says. "You didn't used to come pester me until much later."

"Hey, if it was up to me, I'd never leave." Niko settles down on a couch across the room and picks up Mukuni's much-smaller replica, stroking its fur. His eyes are lit with mischief. "I miss you when I'm gone. Even if you won't let me kiss you."

"Quit it, Niko." Still, Salo feels a pleasant tingle spreading down his cheeks as he returns his gaze to the mirrors. "Why *do* you go, anyway? Why not stick around all the time? Not that I want you to. You'd probably annoy me to death. I'm just wondering."

"I can't say." Niko is thoughtfully silent for a heartbeat. "You know, sometimes I wonder if I'm not dreaming when I come here."

"This isn't a dream. I know because I'm awake, unfortunately."

"Maybe you're right." Niko nuzzles the cat in his arms. "What are you up to, anyway? I was hoping we could fight those stone dummies again. We make a good team."

Salo wouldn't admit it out loud, but fighting waves of hostile mannequins alongside Niko has quickly become his favorite pastime since the day they first tried it. "I can't right now," he says. "I'm watching over my friends, so maybe try not to distract me so much." He flicks an array of mirrors across the room. "Here. Be useful and keep an eye on these."

"As you wish," Niko says. "I like being useful."

In Northtown, Ilapara and Tuk have just gotten off their carriage near the market square, both wearing Mirror disguises that conceal their true appearances.

"We're here, Salo," Tuk sends.

"Walk in the direction of the wheelhouse terminal, then take the second left turn after the market. The apartment building is along that road."

Neither Ilapara nor Tuk replies, but they begin threading through the crowded market in a northern direction. Salo directs them so that they approach the apartment building's back door, in a rubbish-filled alley most people would hesitate to enter alone, even in broad daylight.

"The green door to your right is where you need to go," Salo says as they draw nearer.

"We see it," Tuk says. *"Should we be expecting company on the other side?"*

Following Salo's command, the skimmer watching the apartment flies down and skips through the wall to check. "There's no one there right now. When you're inside, take the stairs and climb up to the fourth floor."

"Got it."

Ilapara reaches the door first. She pulls on the handle. It doesn't budge. *"Locked. What now?"*

Tuk steps forward, drawing strength from his blessing and spooling it into his arm. *"Allow me,"* he says and shoves the door open, breaking the lock and cracking the door in places.

"That works, too, I suppose," Salo says.

Ilapara isn't nearly as impressed. *"So we're vandals now?"*

"Do you know how to pick locks, Ilapara?"

"No, Tuk, I don't."

"Then you're welcome." Tuk opens the door and gestures inside. *"After you."*

They enter the building and hurry up the stairs, but as they reach the fourth-floor landing, one of the two skimmers following them spots trouble. "Wait," Salo says. "There's someone in the hallway."

The elderly woman in the hallway takes her time rummaging for her keys in her shoulder bag. She finds them eventually, only to let them slip through her fingers. Salo sighs as he waits for her to pick them up from the floor and use one of them to open her door. Only once she's sealed herself inside does he let Tuk and Ilapara continue.

"Okay, it's safe now. Hurry. The apartment is the third door to your left."

They proceed to the door, where Ilapara turns the knob to no avail. *"Damn. Another locked door."*

Tuk's eyes twinkle at her. *"Do you have another way to open it?"*

"Just do it, Tuk."

"If you insist." As before, the locked door violently gives way to his strength, though this door opens into a living room in disarray. Shards of glass are strewn all over the floor. A table lies with all its legs broken, as though someone was slammed forcefully onto its surface. The grass mat near the table has a conspicuous splotch of brown, like dried blood.

Salo has already seen this with his skimmers, but Tuk and Ilapara take a moment to absorb the scene. *"What the devil happened here?"* Ilapara says.

"I don't know," Salo tells her. "All I know is that the signal is coming from the bedchamber to your left. Look for hidden compartments in the floor. There's something there, but my skimmers can't see it."

"I'll go check it out."

While she goes in search of the mystery behind the signal, Tuk remains in the living room, taking in the destruction with curious blue eyes. *"If I had to guess, I'd say that whoever lived here was abducted."* He crouches by the bloodied grass mat, lifting one corner closer to his face. *"It looks like they put up a fight, though."*

"I guessed the same," Salo says. "No one's been here since I started watching the place. Shit, Tuk, you forgot to close the door. Someone's seen you."

"Who are you?"

Tuk gets up and turns around with a broad smile, probably aiming for winsome, but with his Mirror disguise at work, the expression isn't quite so effective. *"Hello there, friend."*

A girl who's seen maybe thirteen comets folds her arms and frowns suspiciously at him from the hallway. *"You're not my friend."*

"Not yet, but I could be."

The girl is unmoved by his attempt to charm her. *"What are you doing here? This isn't your house."*

"I'm . . . looking for other friends of mine." Tuk takes a step closer to the girl, drawing her attention away from the ransacked living room. *"I was supposed to meet them earlier today, but they didn't show up. Do you know anything about where they might be?"*

The girl sizes him up dubiously, but she must not believe him a threat, since she stays put. *"There was a woman here a few weeks ago. I haven't seen her in a while. Wait, how did you get in?"*

"With a key. Tell me more about this woman." Tuk puts a hand in his pocket and fishes out a silver coin, which he holds up for her to see. *"I'll make it worth your while."*

A shrewd light enters her eyes as she stares at the coin. *"Add another rock, and I'll tell you what you want to know."*

"Done." Tuk puts his hand in his pocket and retrieves two more silver coins. *"I'll even add a third if you forget I was ever here."*

To her credit, the girl barely reacts, though her eyes widen almost imperceptibly, like she can't quite believe her luck. *"She was a foreigner. Bronze skinned. Stayed for maybe three or four days, and then she was gone. I think the last time I saw her was the day of the earthquake."*

Tuk extends the coins to the girl. *"You've been most helpful. Now, remember, you never saw me."*

She nods, taking the coins, and then she flies down the hall like she thinks he'll change his mind. Salo sends a skimmer after her just to make sure she doesn't break her promise.

Deeper within the apartment, Ilapara has found something. *"Tuk!"*

This time he pushes the door closed before he follows the sound of her voice. A skimmer tracks him as he enters the bedchamber, where Ilapara has moved the bed and dresser around in search of a hidden recess in the floor.

"No secret compartments," she says. *"But take a look at this."* She points at the stylized chalk drawing of an eye, previously concealed beneath a rug of leopard skin. It's outlined with thin lines, one end of the eyebrow extended in a looping curve. *"Why does it look so familiar?"*

Salo moves the skimmer to take a closer look at the drawing and realizes that he, too, has seen it before. "Tuk, don't you have a necklace with a pendant like that?"

For some reason Tuk has gone pale. He stares motionlessly at the eye on the floor.

"Tuk?" Ilapara says.

He licks his lips, eyes turning dusky. *"Salo was right,"* he says. *"There's something hidden here."* He digs out the pendant of his necklace from underneath his shirt, showing that it is indeed identical to the drawn eye. *"But you need this to get it out."*

"Why? What is *that?"*

Instead of answering, Tuk takes the pendant off his neck and crouches down, dangling it over the chalk eye. It swings on its chain like a pendulum, once, twice, then thrice. On its fourth swing the eye flares with light, and an ornamented box is revealed to be hovering above it. Salo is enthralled as he watches Tuk reach forward and pluck the box out of the air. Even more astonishing is how the distant drone that has dogged him for over a week suddenly goes quiet.

"Tuk, what the devil did you do?" Ilapara demands.

As the eye's magical light dims, Tuk gets to his feet, lifting the box appraisingly. It is small enough to fit in the palm of his hand. *"Someone hid this in the Void right above the symbol, and only a pendant like mine could have retrieved it. What I don't understand is why Salo could feel its presence."*

"Well, I can't feel it anymore," Salo tells them. "It's stopped. Tuk, you'll have some explaining to do when you get back. Right now, take the box and get out of there."

"Right." Tuk eyes the box silently for a moment longer. Then he slips it into his pocket and walks out of the room. Ilapara is visibly perplexed as she follows him.

"You continue to impress me, Salo," Niko says. "The magics you've employed here are beyond anything I thought possible. I've been asked to join the queen's honor guard, but I'd give it all up to be with you up there."

"You've been asked to join the honor guard?" Salo asks, although on second thought, it shouldn't be surprising at all. Only the most distinguished young Ajaha and Asazi are ever raised to the queen's honor guard, so it's only natural Niko would end up there with the likes of Alinata. Except that this Niko couldn't possibly know if such a thing even happened. "Wait, don't answer that. Sometimes I forget you're not actually real."

Niko usually shrugs this off, but today he frowns. "You keep saying I'm not real, but the more I come here, the more I find that hard to believe." His eyes become hooded. "You know what I think?"

"What?"

"I think you know deep down that I'm real; you're just afraid to admit it."

"Why on Meza would I be afraid?"

"I don't know," Niko says. His gaze is simultaneously probing and uncertain. "Maybe you don't trust me not to abandon you again."

Salo almost protests, then pauses to think about it. He can still remember the day in the training glade when he hoped to ask Niko to come with him but got turned down before he'd finished uttering his request. The rejection stung him, to be sure, but is he still holding a grudge against Niko? He doesn't think so.

The real problem is that he can't be sure this Niko isn't flattering him with lies. There are no consequences in this construct, no one to hear or see what they do. Niko could woo him with sweet nothings all day long, and Salo would still never be certain that, in the real world, with their tribespeople watching, this same Niko wouldn't cast him aside to preserve his reputation just like he did in the glade.

So maybe his guess is a little bit right. "Niko . . ."

"Hold that thought," Niko interjects. "I sense I'm about to leave this place." He wags a finger in Salo's direction. "But this conversation is far from over."

The ranger is subsequently engulfed in a flash of light that takes him with it when it dies out, leaving the cat lounging alone on the couch. Salo tries not to feel disappointed by the sudden departure.

What if he's actually real? he wonders. Despite all that's logical, the evidence seems to imply that he is. He comes mostly at night, when the real Niko would likely be in bed. If he comes during the day, it's for brief spells, when Niko might be taking a nap. He talks like Niko. He knows things about himself that Salo doesn't know.

"But how the devil do I bring him here?" Salo asks, the question weighing heavily on his mind. Ziyo, who at times feels omnipotent, has proved useless where this mystery is concerned.

Eventually, Salo withdraws from the construct to get some much-needed sleep.

◆ ◆ ◆

Dinner with Ilapara, Tuk, and Alinata is quiet later that evening. Shades of dusk play out in the skies above the garden, while the city below comes to life in a light show of twinkling crystal lamps.

Salo keeps stealing glances at Tuk. The young man's appetite is usually voracious, but today he's gazing into his peanut soup as he stirs it without end, his eyebrows bunched together in thought. The blue pendant dangling around his neck seems especially conspicuous today.

At first, Alinata's presence makes Salo reluctant to bring up the subject of the mysterious package from the Northtown apartment, but impatience gets the better of him, and he places a newly enchanted voice-scrambling cipher shell on the table, pulling down on its lever to turn it on. A membrane of invisible force immediately enwraps the table like a bubble, acting to distort their voices and thwart any potential eavesdroppers.

The action draws Tuk out of his thoughts, and he lifts his head. Upon seeing the inquiring look on Salo's face, he places his spoon on the table and crosses his arms over his bare chest. His pendant glints in the twilight as he sighs. "I suppose I owe you an explanation."

"Yes, Tuk," Salo says. "I think you do. But first—Alinata?"

The Asazi looks up from her plate. "Yes?"

After taking a moment to think through his phrasing, Salo says, "I understand your duty to the queen as her apprentice; I really do. But I beg you not to relay whatever's about to be discussed. She doesn't have to know every single detail of our personal lives, does she? And I don't want to have to keep excluding you from conversations. I'd like us to trust each other more going forward, but mutual trust requires us to be able to speak to each other in confidence. Is that possible?"

Alinata's face is impassive as she thinks about it. "I won't repeat any aspect of this conversation to the queen. Happy?"

"For now. Tuk?"

The mysterious box was sitting in his lap. He puts it on the table now, giving Salo his first look at it with his own eyes. The box is an exquisite piece of woodwork, featuring intertwining lines running across its surface and a gilded catch.

After unfastening the catch, Tuk opens the box to reveal a vial with a smoky blue liquid resting within. As Salo leans closer, he sees flashes of light illuminating the cloudy contents, as though a lightning storm has been captured and stoppered inside.

"What is it?" Ilapara asks, also leaning forward.

Tuk caresses one side of the box like it's the most precious thing in the world. The look in his eyes speaks of too many emotions all at once. Loss. Longing. Awe.

"The name translates to Rhapsody of the Stars," he says, his voice subdued. "It's a rare elixir used to reach a state of mind in which communication with the gods is thought to be possible. Or should I say, with one god in particular. You know him as the Star of Vigilance."

Salo and the others digest this silently. He finds he has more questions now than before. "Who put it there, and why was it giving me sleepless nights? And what does it have to do with you and that pendant of yours?"

Tuk places both elbows on the dinner table and rubs his face, releasing a heavy breath. "Maybe I should just start from the beginning."

He goes on to tell them the story of his life in the empire across the Dapiaro, where he was once the adopted son of a wealthy lord and lived like a prince in a palace of gold and sunlight. That was, until the lord's true sons grew jealous and murdered their own father, sending Tuk to a den of slavery.

He doesn't speak of the abuses he suffered in this den, but Salo reads the truth of it in his eyes and the way he flushes with emotion. Ultimately, it was only by the grace of the mystic who brought him to life that he escaped that place and was flown on a vessel of wind to the Enclave north of the Jalama Desert. Driven by a guilty conscience, his creator helped him break the sorcerous shackles she had woven into his mind for the benefit of his masters, and then she set him free to become his own man.

"But I was lost," he confesses. "I didn't know what I was living for, and for a while I fell back into old patterns. I drowned myself in sex and opiates, anything to keep me from feeling the chasm of emptiness inside me."

One fateful day he stole a vial of something he thought looked interesting from a traveler he'd slept with. He was looking for another high, but when he drank the glowing concoction, his mind was transported to a realm of light where a voice told him to seek a sanctuary in the city's underground. There he would find his purpose.

"The sanctuary's location was a secret," Tuk says, "but when I found it and told them why I was there, they took me in despite what I was, despite my past, and gave me a home."

He rediscovered and remade himself among the Vigilants, though it wasn't until years later that he was allowed to imbibe another vial of Rhapsody. The voice came to him again, but this time it had a different direction for him.

"It told me I'd find my best self in the forbidden lands across the desert," Tuk says. "So I followed its advice, and here I am."

Salo always feels like his mind is being pried open from the inside whenever Tuk allows himself to discuss his past. His stories never fail to remind Salo that there's a whole world out there that he knows nothing about. A cruel world that Tuk survived even as it tried to grind him to dust. Affection and respect for the young man bloom in Salo's heart.

"So you're a worshipper of the New Year's Comet?" Alinata asks, sounding skeptical.

Tuk answers without shame. "Yes. I also venerate Ama Vaziishe and the two suns. Vigilants accept all the heavens as they are and dream of a day when the peoples of the world are united regardless of which patron they worship, as they once were in the past."

"That's funny," Alinata says. "Because as far as I know, this whole continent has always belonged to the moon. That's why we're the Red peoples."

"I speak of a history before history, Alinata," Tuk says. "A time that was stolen from humanity by the Great Forgetting."

"The Great Forgetting is a myth."

"I don't believe it is."

They exchange intense looks, and though Salo isn't sure about the nature of their relationship, he senses that this might become a major point of contention.

"Let's not descend into a theological debate," Salo says. "I admit, Tuk, I don't quite understand your religious perspective, but if I've learned anything these last few months, it's that my knowledge of the world is limited. It would be sanctimonious of me—or anyone else here for that matter—to condemn you for what you believe, even if it makes us uncomfortable. That said, I want to know more about that box. Was it left in that apartment by another Vigilant like you?"

Tuk looks away from the Asazi, his eyes moody. "I believe so."

"But why?" Salo says.

"I don't know. There was a Vigilant sanctuary here last time I passed through the city, but they were purged sometime before we arrived. Maybe the woman who left the box was here to find them."

"Wait," Ilapara says. "There were Vigilants *here* in Yonte Saire?"

"We're all over the world, Ilapara," Tuk says. "Even here in the Redlands. In most places, we operate in the shadows to avoid persecution. Where we can, we infiltrate places of power to gather information and influence events."

"Sounds like you're an organization of spies," she says, and Tuk tilts his head in thought as he assesses that label.

"In some ways, that's exactly what we are. But every sanctuary does charitable work for the people in its community and provides a home for lost souls. I was a petty criminal who lived on the streets and traded sex for coin to finance my drug habits, but the Vigilants took me in and transformed me into a valued operative. Some of my missions demanded that I spy on people and even shed blood, but I believe everything I did ultimately advanced the cause of justice and freedom. I believe the same about the organization."

"Is that what you're trying to achieve?" Ilapara says. "Justice and freedom for the world?"

Tuk's eyes shine with zeal. "Only through justice and freedom can there be peace, and through peace, unity." He drops his gaze to the table, seeming embarrassed, but his voice remains charged with conviction. "There's another secretive group at work across the world. Wealthier and more powerful than us, even though we outnumber them. All its members are mystics, and not just Red; there are solar mystics among them. We know them only as the Shadows, though they might call themselves by a different name. Where we seek to unify the world, the Shadows seek to break it and expedite the end of all things, which they believe will bring about the perfection of humanity. Our most important mission is to stop them."

There is silence in the garden as Salo, Ilapara, and Alinata fail to react to Tuk's stunning revelations. Salo's mind reels at the idea of secretive mystics working in the shadows and infiltrating the courts of the world to bring about the end of all things. Yet another reminder of his ignorance.

He nods at the box on the table. "I suppose that belongs to you, Tuksaad."

Tuk shakes his head, staring at it. "Then how come you could sense it?" When Salo stares blankly at him, he tugs at his pendant. "Salo, the box was hidden by an enchantment on a pendant like this one. You'd probably call this metal Blue Fire in your language, and it's the only known material that draws from the Star of Vigilance. This enchantment? It wasn't Red magic. It wasn't even solar magic. In fact, it wasn't any type of magic any mystic alive today should know. And yet you sensed it screaming at you from miles away. Do you see why I'm more than a little confused?"

Alinata's eyes sharpen on Salo, and he shifts uncomfortably. His instinct is to deny whatever Tuk is implying, but the question is inescapable: If the enchantment that hid the box was of a type of magic incompatible with his cosmic shards, why *did* he sense it? Could it have something to do with the visions he saw on the Tuanu waterbird and the apparition from the Carving?

"A blue-skinned spirit haunted the skill nexus I used to teach myself ciphers," he confesses. "He haunted my dreams, too, for a while; then I saw him again at my awakening, when he spoke to me for the first time and told me to seek him beyond the gates of the Red Temple's inner sanctum. I cannot be certain, but I have at times wondered if this spirit wasn't . . ."

Salo stops talking when he notices all three of his companions wincing as they rub their temples. A shiver of dread goes down his backbone as he remembers the same thing happening to Nimara when he tried to tell her about his awakening, and to Tuk and Ilapara on the waterbird when they asked about his communion with the Lightning Bird.

A splitting headache, and then they forgot what he said.

"I haven't been hydrating enough," Alinata says as she reaches for a glass of water. "That's always the case whenever I start to get a headache."

"You too?" Ilapara says, grimacing in pain. "Urgh. I think I'm going to turn in early tonight."

Tuk rubs his eyes and squints at Salo. "I'm sorry. Were you saying something?"

He tries not to show just how disturbed he is. "I was saying I think you should be the one to decide what to do with that box, Tuk. I'm just glad I can't hear it anymore. I finally got some sleep today, and I can't wait to get more tonight."

Tuk seems troubled, like he's trying to remember something he forgot. "Thank you, Salo. I don't think you know how much this means to me."

Salo forces himself to smile, though his heart is far from glad. "Don't mention it."

23: Jomo

Northtown

Jomo curses as his carriage slows down to yet another stop. Impatiently, he moves the curtain aside and presses his head against his window, trying to get the measure of the traffic ahead. A groan escapes him when he glimpses a long procession of carriages and vehicles backed up all along the narrow street.

He should have known better than to come to Northtown. Machete-wielding Wavunaji have decided to flood the streets in protest today, hence the slow-moving traffic. It seems they don't like how long it's taking the regent to dismantle the Saire defenses. It galls them how so many elephants are still living in their Skytown and Southtown homes. No doubt many of them have already made plans for which homes they intend to plunder. *Criminals and louts, the lot of them,* Jomo thinks and is thankful that Odari and Kito are accompanying his carriage on their striped steeds, both armed to the teeth.

He didn't need such a conspicuous protective detail before, but the streets have grown dangerous of late. There have been multiple reports of assault, rape, and violent robbery perpetrated against his clanspeople. He's even heard reports of a young Saire girl who was abducted in Northtown three days ago. She's still missing.

The carriage begins to move again, only to come to a stop a few minutes later. Jomo sighs, feeling powerless.

"Behold! An oppressor in the flesh!"

With dread, he peeks through the curtain and feels his heart sink. "Mother damn me to hell. Not this again."

An orator shouting on a street corner has spotted his marked carriage and is now pointing at it for the benefit of his audience. "See how he rides in comfort and splendor while our sons are forced to play honor guard for him!"

Loud boos rise up around the orator like a hailstorm. Something hard strikes the carriage, and Jomo doesn't realize his hands are shaking until he lifts one to draw the curtain closed. He tries to loosen the collar of his emerald shirt, but it's already loose. Against his wiser impulses, he reaches for the bottle of rum next to him, takes a swig, and shuts his eyes as it burns down his throat.

"Your days are numbered, Saire pig!"

"We'll bleed you dry, you crippled bastard!"

Steel hisses nearby as blades come out of their sheaths. "Stay back, or we'll cut you down!" Odari shouts above the racket.

"You are slaves, my son," declares the orator. "All of you. But soon you shall be free."

"Stay back!"

Angry voices draw near. More things strike the carriage. Odari and Kito shout more warnings. Jomo keeps his eyes shut, reaching for the golden pendant in his pocket and turning its dial.

"Let the pig go, my kin," the orator shouts from his corner. "Our enslaved sons will fight to the death to protect him. They have no choice. Let him go for now. He will not escape his reckoning."

The carriage lurches forward so suddenly Jomo's stomach almost heaves. A little later there's a knock on his window. He takes a tentative look behind the curtain and is met with Odari's concerned expression.

He gives Odari a nod to show that he's all right, but he retreats back behind the curtain, turning the dial on his pendant again.

"Salo?"

He waits for a minute, but no response comes. The pendant was delivered to him in a box yesterday while he was having lunch in a Midtown teahouse, by a woman he'd never seen before. A note in the box told him to turn the little dial on the pendant's circular face, and as he did so, he was shocked to hear the Yerezi mystic's voice coming from within its interior. A remarkable little artifact, Jomo would say, except that right now it's not doing what it's supposed to do, and this is not helping his nerves.

"Salo?" he says again.

A second later, the pendant vibrates. *"Yes, Herald. I'm here."*

Jomo relaxes into his seat, forcing himself to breathe. "I thought we were on a first-name basis now. You can call me Jomo."

"Hello, Jomo. Was there something you needed?"

Jomo still hasn't gotten used to the metallic timbre the pendant adds to the mystic's voice. He wonders what his own voice sounds like on the other end of the enchantment. Hopefully he doesn't sound as rattled as he truly is. "The Caracal came back to the city last night. I'm about to pay him a visit. I thought you should know." *I also needed someone to talk to in case I was about to die,* Jomo thinks.

"Hang on." The mystic falls quiet for a moment. *"Okay, I see you. You're on your way to the bridge by the waterfall."*

An eyebrow shoots up Jomo's forehead. Salo has not explained how his method of surveillance works, but Jomo has gleaned from their conversations that it's rather far reaching. "You can actually see me?"

"I can. There seems to be a lot of commotion in Northtown this morning."

"I know. I had to pay a visit to the Sentinel barracks earlier. Thank them for their good work, that sort of thing. Almost got stoned to death just a short while ago."

"Are you all right?"

"A little spooked," Jomo admits. "But I'll live." He takes another swig from his bottle. His heart's almost beating steadily now. "I'll be in a better mood after my meeting with the Caracal."

"Did you carry the cipher shell Alinata gave you?"

Jomo looks over at the gilded artifact sitting on the seat next to him. "I did. And I have to say, Salo, the enchantment on this thing is quite impressive."

"I can't take credit for it, I'm afraid. I bought it as it is. But I did enchant the pendant you're using to talk to me."

"Still impressive. And speaking of which, who was the woman who brought it to me yesterday? I thought I'd met all your companions."

"But you did, Herald."

Jomo tilts his head, frowning. Is that amusement in the mystic's voice? "Then who was she?"

A bright laugh comes from the pendant. *"It's more fun to keep you guessing."*

"Damn you, Salo. And here I thought you weren't sadistic like other mystics."

"Mm. Maybe I'll tell you when you drop by later today. There's something I think you need to see."

"Good news?"

"You'll have to be the judge of that."

"I'll come after my meeting with the headman."

"Would you like me to listen in? Should things get dangerous, I'd be able to offer assistance."

Jomo stretches his fingers before him and finds that they're still trembling. "If it won't be too much trouble."

"It won't."

"All right then. I'll talk to you afterward."

There's a moment of pensive silence, then: *"Be careful, Jomo. And good luck."*

The Caracal of the southeast and headman of the Kachui clan greets Jomo in the drawing room of his Skytown palace in full regalia. He is thin as a rake, but his orange robes, golden chains, and voluminous caracal-hide cloak have added considerable bulk to his form. He holds the golden cane of his princedom firmly in one hand, and the shit-eating grin on his metallic cat mask almost says: *Whose stick is bigger? Mine or that puny cane of yours?*

Legionnaires of his clan stand guard in every corner of his palace, each armed with spears and hide shields. They're all older and more experienced than Jomo's two Sentinel escorts and have no doubt been arranged to stand as they are for the purposes of this meeting. The drawing room itself feels more like a throne room than a place to receive and entertain guests, but of course, that's the intent.

"Ah, if it isn't our three-legged herald." The Caracal approaches Jomo with arms spread in welcome, and they shake hands. "Welcome to my humble abode."

Used to being mocked for his bad leg, Jomo lets the stale insult slide. "Thank you, Your Highness. I'm glad you agreed to meet me. Finally."

"Yes, well. One must be cautious these days. The last time I was in this city, a peer of mine got himself murdered right in front of me. I wasn't meeting anyone back then."

"I understand," Jomo says.

"Would you like something to drink? I arrived from home last night, and I carried with me a few gourds of home brew. My wives are the best brewers in the Yontai, I tell you. It would be my pleasure to share some of it with you, knowing your fondness for intoxicants."

Jomo pushes his pique down his throat. "I'm afraid I must decline. I'm here on business, after all."

The Caracal flicks his metal whiskers in amusement. He looks to his legionnaires and says, "So professional, our young herald," and the men chuckle with him. Jomo feels his cheeks heating up but says nothing. "Very well," the headman says. "Let us talk business."

He leads them to a pair of armchairs, where they sit facing each other, and casts a passing glance at the Sentinels who stand behind Jomo. His eyes linger on the gilded ornament in Odari's hands.

"All right, Herald. Tell me. What the devil are you doing in my house?"

Jomo makes a show of looking around the heavily guarded drawing room. "I was hoping we could have a more private discussion."

"And I'm hoping you'll stop wasting my time. Your mirrorgram implied you had something important to tell me."

"I'll get to that in a second, Your Highness. First, though, I'd like to present you with a gift." Jomo gestures at Odari, who comes forth with the ornament.

The Caracal doesn't even look at it. "You think you can bribe me?" He snorts. "You're more foolish than I thought."

"But this is a special gift, Your Highness. I'm certain you'll agree when you see it. In fact, it's so special I think even the Shirika will appreciate its beauty."

That draws a snarl from the Caracal, but he keeps silent this time.

Fighting back an answering snarl of his own, Jomo nods at Odari. Anyone else might have been nervous, but the Sentinel is as calm as a still lake when he moves a lever on the ornament, causing a static mirage of Mirror light to bloom out of the ornament's citrine crystal.

The Caracal draws in an audible breath as he absorbs the image.

"Exquisite, don't you think?" Jomo says in the silence. "I'm especially fond of the sheer detail in the mirage. Notice the laugh lines on the mother's face as she cradles her daughter. The two marks in perfect harmony on the little girl's neck. The verdant landscape in the background. The charming little hut behind them. Such a sweet, tender moment captured so perfectly." Sharpening his voice like a knife, Jomo says, "It would be such a pity if they could never be rendered in this much detail ever again, wouldn't you say?"

The Caracal leans forward, resting his elbows on his thighs, rolling his cane between his palms. His eyes acquire a bloodthirsty glow. His voice is low, full of malice. "What makes you think you'll walk out of here alive?"

The sips of rum Jomo indulged in earlier must be taking the edge off his fear, because he finds himself mirroring the man's posture. "You think I'm afraid of death? The Crocodile slaughtered my family and took the throne, but I walk the streets of this city in the light of day. I have nothing to lose and everything to gain. There are no lengths I will not go to save my people. Kill me, and this mirage is the last you will ever see of that sweet little girl."

"Out!" The Caracal shoots up to his feet, glaring at his legionnaires with his cane leveled at the door. "Out with you! Now!"

The room clears in seconds, leaving Jomo, Odari, and Kito alone with the headman. He crosses to a sideboard, where he pours himself a glass of spirits and downs it. Then he turns around with his teeth bared in a show of pure hatred. "What do you want?"

"You sure as the pits know what I want."

"I cannot give that to you."

"Then we are done here." Jomo gets up from his chair. "My condolences in advance." He starts to make for the door with Odari and Kito behind him.

"Wait!"

Jomo stops, turns around.

For a moment the Caracal stands there like he's at war with himself. His chest rises and falls with rapid breaths. "Truly, you are as vile an excuse for a human being as your mother was. You are the scum of the world, you evil bastard."

Jomo's teeth grind together. "I don't care for your insults, Your Highness. I care for one thing and one thing only, and if I don't get it, the Arc himself will be paying you a visit soon."

"Gah!" The Caracal hurls his glass across the room. Despite himself, Jomo flinches as it smashes into pieces that scatter upon the marble floor, leaving a wet stain on the wall. "You have my vote, you mother-forsaken son of a whore. Now get the devil out of my house before I skin you alive!"

Jomo leaves the drawing room with as much composure as he can muster. Feelings of guilt try to sink their claws into him, but he doesn't let them. This bastard was prepared to aid and abet a genocide of his people. He doesn't deserve Jomo's guilt.

Hours later, Jomo takes shape in Salo's construct on a porch with a gurgling fountain of blood as its centerpiece. He grimaces at the maca- bre structure and gives it a wide berth as he descends the steps to the walkway.

Salo is waiting for him in the pavilion on the other side, staring at a hovering mirror of moving images. Upon noticing his arrival, he swivels to face him and smiles.

"Herald. I was expecting you a bit sooner. I was beginning to get worried."

Leaning on his cane, Jomo tilts his head. "Weren't you watching me?"

"I try to be mindful of privacy, Jomo. I stopped watching right after you left Skytown."

"Fair enough." Jomo swaggers to his favorite armchair in the room, sits down, tosses his head back, and sighs. "There's this cheap watering hole in Southtown. Bit on the dingy side, but they serve the best rum in the city. My guys and I needed a drink after . . . you know."

"I thought you handled yourself quite well, truth be told," Salo says.

Jomo opens one eye to look at him. "You don't think I went too far? I know you had . . . ethical concerns."

"I did, and I still do," Salo says. "But I've also seen what your people are facing. There aren't any good choices left."

"I'm glad you understand," Jomo says, relieved. He sweeps his gaze across the room. "Where are the others?"

"Running errands."

"What a shame." Jomo would have liked to see Ilapara again. "You said you had something to show me?"

"I did." Salo does something with his hand to summon a floating mirror that fills almost a quarter of the room. "I sent out one of my little spies to the Hare's province, and it witnessed this two nights ago."

The vision must have been observed by a flying creature, since its perspective is elevated. It's nighttime as the view descends upon a compound of huts in a clearing surrounded by dense jungle. A ring of lit torches encircles the compound, casting long and trembling shadows.

Some kind of ritual is unfolding. There are dancers and drummers involved, but the window focuses on the two figures at the center of the ritual: a burly naked man wearing a moongold mask shaped like the head of a hare, and an older woman in blackened sackcloth.

Her forearms light up with magic as she casts a spell, eyes wild, head tilted upward, and Jomo is stunned to see a pair of skeletal evil spirits crawling out of the earth amid a whirlwind, white torchlight beaming angrily out of their eye sockets. They growl and snap their teeth at the gathered people but remain in place, bound by the mystic's power, their clawed talons dangling low enough to almost touch the ground. To Jomo's horror, the masked man kneels before the hellish beasts and begins to pray to them.

Salo turns his face away, visibly disturbed. "It seems the Hare believes these . . . creatures are the spirits of his dead parents. I don't know if that makes him a worshipper of Arante, but he's definitely consorting with a Black mystic."

Aghast as he is, this vision is better than Jomo could have imagined in his wildest dreams. He laughs. "This is absolutely perfect! Dear Mother, Salo. You've just bagged me one more vote. Ha!"

Salo doesn't look as enthusiastic. "I'll send it over to your cipher shell, but it'll replace the image already there, so be warned."

"That's fine," Jomo says. "I don't think I'll need it again. The Caracal knows what's at stake. But tell me you have more good news for me, Salo. The Requiem Moon is in three days. Even with the Caracal and the Hare, I still need one more vote, and the Kestrel has refused to see reason."

"I'm sorry," Salo says. "No more good news right now."

"Nothing on the Buffalo? I know he's plotting to get his son out of prison. That's why he hasn't left the city."

Salo shakes his head. "He's either the most pious, most boring man alive, or he's already made the necessary arrangements. He's behaving almost like he knows he's being watched."

"And the Jackal?"

Salo becomes bashful. "He's . . . uh. Well. He's having an affair with a married woman *and* her husband."

"That's good," Jomo says. "We can use that."

"No, we can't," Salo says. "It's an open secret. They're not hiding it from anyone. All the people close to him know. I don't think it's actionable. You'd only be exposing the fact that you have eyes on him."

"But what choice do I have? I'd rather take my chances than give up."

"I have another idea."

"I'm listening," Jomo says.

"It's crazy and risky, but I've thought about it, and I think we can pull it off."

Jomo waits for him to explain himself, but he drags the silence forever. "Don't leave me hanging, Salo," Jomo finally says.

Salo continues to hold him in breathless suspense as he appears to struggle with what he wants to say. Then he takes a deep breath and forces it out. "What if, instead of waiting to catch the Buffalo trying to set his son free, we get to him first. We break him out of prison, and then we use him to bargain for his father's vote."

24: Musalodi

Skytown

Knowing nothing about breaking a prisoner out of his cell, especially with only a few days to prepare for it, Salo resorts to gathering as much information as he can about the prison and its surroundings. Information will shape strategy, and a good strategy will be the difference between success and losing his head.

He pauses surveillance on all targets and redirects most of his skimmers down to the undercity, where they disperse themselves like smoke and begin to map out in great detail the network of tunnels and sewers surrounding the prison, turning every nook and cranny into a piece of information he can use.

The task takes so much of his attention he finds himself sitting in the drawing room when he comes out of the construct, not remembering how he got there. A servant enters with a tray of sponge cakes and a mug of tea on a silver tray, which he must have asked for, though he has no recollection of it.

"Thank you," he says to her as she places the tray on the side table next to him. "Would you do me a favor? Please summon Bwana Ruma for me. And tell him to come with a notepad and a pen."

"Yes, honored emissary."

Ruma Sato comes in minutes later with said items and a curious lift of an eyebrow. After they greet each other and inquire about each other's day, Salo gestures at the armchair across from him. "Please take a seat. I have a few requests I'd like to make of you."

The steward presses his lips together nervously as he complies. Salo takes no pleasure in knowing he's about to make the man feel a lot worse.

"If memory serves me well, I was supposed to meet with a group of Dulama silk merchants tomorrow to discuss possible trade routes to the Plains. I would like you to postpone that meeting to next week." *Maybe I'll still be alive to take it.*

"And the meeting with Honored Ambassador Iwe?"

"Was that tomorrow as well?"

"Yes."

"Please reschedule every engagement I have tomorrow with my sincerest apologies."

"Consider it done." Ruma hasn't written anything on his notepad yet, and there is a tightness around his eyes that suggests he isn't pleased Salo would think him incapable of remembering such simple instructions.

Salo takes a sip of his tea, seeking to strengthen his nerves, for he knows he's about to precipitate a rock avalanche he won't be able to stop once it gets started. "A Saire merchant prince came here some time ago. I never caught his name. Do you happen to know who he is?"

"Yes. I believe that was one Mwenemzuzi Saire, an influential man in the transport industry. He lives just down the hill."

"I made a promise to him that day. I agreed that I would take in Saires who sought refuge if the threat against them escalated. I believe it's about to, and I intend to keep my promise. So should any member of the Saire clan arrive at my gates from tomorrow onward, and until further notice, you are to let them in. I'm not sure how many we can conceivably take, but I'm not turning anyone away so long as there's space to hold them. Is that clear?"

Ruma gapes like a fish out of water. "But . . . where are we to put them?"

"I think I'll leave that up to you, so you should probably make the appropriate preparations. And yes, I am well aware that this will put me on the outs with certain people up this mountain. Which is why I have asked you to bring that notepad. You said you were a scribe, once. You can compose formal messages, yes?"

"I . . . yes, honored. I can."

"Please send a message to His Highness the prince regent informing him that I will be taking in a number of Saire guests over the coming days, just until the dust settles. Make sure it's clear I mean no disrespect, and do not use the word *asylum*. I may be an ambassador of my people during my stay here, but I'm a pilgrim first and foremost. Emphasize that my actions are in keeping with establishing good relations between my tribe and the KiYonte, for it would greatly sadden my queen to see any of his tribespeople fall to senseless violence.

"Apologize unreservedly for any inconvenience my actions may cause and assure him that any perceived slights are entirely unintentional. Finally, explain that it is my sincerest wish for this situation to be resolved without bloodshed. Did you get all of that?"

Ruma's hand is trembling by the time he's done jotting down Salo's instructions. With a shaking voice he repeats them for Salo's benefit, and when Salo nods in satisfaction, he says, "When would you like me to send the message?"

"As soon as you finish writing it. Send the same message to Bwana Mwenemzuzi as well. Tell him to bring the family he came with last time. I'd like to make sure that they're safe."

"Yes, honored emissary." Ruma fidgets with his pen, wide eyes blinking at Salo. "Was there anything else?"

"That will be all for now, Bwana Ruma. Thank you."

Ruma stares into space for a time. When his eyes return to the present, he nods and rises to his feet. "I'll get to work immediately."

Left alone, Salo lifts his cup to take a sip but pauses when his metaform calls for his attention. One of his skimmers in the undercity has come across a body lying in the dark. He closes his eyes so he can see through the skimmer, and his heart sinks.

She couldn't have seen more than nine comets. The markings on her neck are those of the elephant, which he suspects were the reason she was attacked, killed, and left down here to rot. Without a word, Salo directs the skimmer to move along.

And for a second, just a second, he hates himself and every human being who has ever lived with a blinding intensity and wishes the gods had been wiser than to give them the gift of existence.

25: Ilapara

Midtown

On the morning of the Requiem Moon, about five hundred Sentinels brave the rains and gather in Midworld Plaza, the heart of the Shirika's power over the Yontai, where they begin to sing songs of defiance. They are joined by a large group of Faraswa workers in their coveralls, undercity residents, and a contingent of independent mystics, recognizable by the thin white lines that run down their necks.

Wearing a Mirror disguise that conceals her breastplate, Ilapara watches this with anxious excitement from the large portico of the KiYonte Treasury, lost in a sea of spectators who've amassed from all parts of town to witness the historic spectacle unfolding.

A frail wind gives the rain a gentle slant. Streams gurgle and gush down the drains, and for a time it seems that the city has been washed free of social strata. Skytown merchants in their shimmering silks mingle with Northtown peasants. Academics whisper with hawkers. Strangers who would have never stopped to greet each other on the street share umbrellas. All so they can watch this unlikely group of people defy the mystics watching on from the surrounding buildings, shadowy silhouettes behind their high windows.

Ilapara's heartbeat kicks up as the Sentinel Obe Saai ascends the stepped pedestal at the center of the plaza, where a winged statue looms like a presiding judge. The singers fall silent and look up to him, waiting to hear him speak. A mechanical prosthesis shimmers where his right forearm was amputated.

"Five nights ago," he shouts at the gathered masses, "in this very city, a little girl was stolen from her home in the dead of night. Her abductors hauled her down to the sewers, tortured her, beat her, and left her for dead. Her only crime? Having the mark of the Elephant on her neck."

The rains seem to shy away as he scans the plaza with his gaze.

"What are we, my brothers and sisters, if not creatures of flesh and bone? I bear the mark of the Crocodile, and you the Hare, the Leopard, the Rhino, but do we not all bleed when we're cut? Do we not all wonder at the moonrise and dream when we sleep? Mourn for our dead? Smile at our friends? Curse our enemies? Are we not, at the heart of us, one and the same?

"Many of you feel resentful of the privilege that was bestowed upon the elephant clan. They were put above the rest of us, and many of them used their advantages to enrich themselves. This is true. But let me remind you all that this was by design. They were *put* above us by those more powerful. If they ruled over us, it was because that is what the powers that be decreed. So if we must be resentful, we must resent not our rulers but those who crowned them, for they knew our grievances and had the means to address them but chose not to."

Ilapara casts a nervous glance at the upper floors of the tall buildings around the plaza, where Faros and Akili are watching from their windows. She half expects a bolt of lightning to shoot down and strike the Sentinel dead, but by the look of things, Obe and his comrades aren't the least concerned.

"And yet there are those among us, these so-called Wavunaji, who would convince us that the target of our hatreds should be our fellow KiYonte, who no more chose their marks than any of us here. There are those who believe that our grievances against the Saires make it acceptable to snatch little girls from their beds and butcher them like swine."

"Not on our watch!" comes a voice from among the warriors.

"Down with the Wavunaji!" comes another.

Obe waits for his comrades to shout out their hearts before holding his good arm outstretched, his voice hard as iron. "But each of us here knows their hateful lies for what they truly are. So we have come here in defiance of the express wishes of our fathers, uncles, headmen, of our masters and mistresses, of the orthodoxy itself, because we know in our heart of hearts that it is wrong to stand by and watch as one man paves his way to the throne with the blood of little girls."

"Down with the Crocodile!"

"Death to the Wavunaji!"

Obe's voice cuts across the rainy square like a keen blade, his face twisting with contempt. "Today my uncle will attempt to disband the Sentinels. And why? Because *we* are the last thing standing in the way of his bloody ambitions. But I for one shall not roll over and let him do as he pleases. I shall not shut my eyes as the Wavunaji pillage and murder. And so, no matter how the vote goes today, I will remain a Sentinel and a guardian of the realm, and all those who feel as I do shall stand beside me. I don't know if we can prevail over him and those who support his cause. But I would rather die than live in a world that will sit back and watch! Who will stand with me? Will I stand alone?"

"We are with you, brother!"

"We will not watch!"

As the skies break with new rain, the crowd around Obe begins to sing once more, and their defiant voices make Ilapara's chest swell with feelings of kinship. She was skeptical about being involved in their fight before, but their courage is impossible not to admire. She can't help wanting to see them succeed.

The vibration of her earring tells her it's time to get moving. She walks down the steps of the crowded portico and turns onto an adjacent street. Only once she's out of the crowds does she notice that the voice coming into her ear from the artifact is unfamiliar.

"Hello? Is this working? Ilapara?"

She frowns, adjusting her earring. "Who is this?"

"There you are! Hello, Ilapara. You helped save me from the undercity two weeks ago. Remember?"

"Your Majesty? How . . . are we even talking right now?"

"I'm in the construct. I'm helping Salo coordinate today's . . . endeavor. He's currently handling a situation with the guests in his residence, but I can alert him in the event of an emergency. Don't worry; he walked me through the plan, and I think I have a good handle on how things work around here. You're supposed to deactivate the security enchantments on the prison's southern hub. Correct?"

How surreal to be talking about a prison break with a foreign monarch through an enchanted artifact. Ilapara could almost believe she's dreaming. "Yes. That's what I was told. Tuksaad should be handling the northern hub."

"He's on his way there as we speak. I assume you have the . . . I believe Salo called it the scrambler?"

Ilapara pats the pocket of her flowing one-piece garment and is satisfied with the hard lump that meets her fingers. "I do."

"Excellent. From the maps and notes in front of me, the hub is on the other side of the river, south of the underground prison complex. Salo decided it's best you approach it from a Midtown tunnel accessible through a manhole two blocks east of your current position."

"I'm on my way," Ilapara says as she breaks into a jog. Minutes later she turns into an alley behind a row of upscale artisan stores, which are all closed today, seeing as it's the Requiem Moon. She slows down as she sees a group of pipe-smoking teenage boys loitering near the manhole.

"There are people literally standing on top of the entrance."

"I see them. I suggest you get rid of them before you attempt to enter the tunnel."

"How?"

The king pauses. *"Tell them the city guards are on the way. Better if you look panicked."*

With no other good options, Ilapara starts running again. "Hey!" she shouts, waving her arms. "The city guards are coming!" The boys watch her like she's a strange creature but stay put. "What are you waiting for? They're almost here!"

They look to each other; then one of them decides he doesn't want to take his chances and runs off. The others soon scurry after him, leaving Ilapara alone in the alley.

"That went better than I expected."

"Good job, but you should hurry. It says here that you and Tuksaad must deactivate the hubs simultaneously, and he's almost reached his."

Ilapara is already lifting the grated cover off the manhole. As she descends the ladder, she brings the covering back over her head, plunging herself in near-perfect gloom. Down in the tunnel, just ahead of her, a golden skimmer begins to give off a soft reddish glow, like that of a weak lamp. She follows it.

◆ ◆ ◆

"You're right under the river, crossing over into Northtown," the king says to her some minutes later, sounding amazed. *"It's quite remarkable just how extensive these tunnels are. There are several more levels beneath you, if you'll believe it."*

Ilapara doesn't find this knowledge comforting at all. It's hard enough to have to walk through these tunnels alone given what happened the last time she was in the undercity. "Honestly, I'd hoped I wouldn't have to come down here again."

"I'm sorry. This is the second time you've had to risk your life down there for my sake, and we barely know each other."

Despite her fear, Ilapara finds that she's not upset with the king. In Umadiland she'd gotten used to sitting back and watching while evil trod on the necks of the innocent. But now she's part of an effort to save thousands of lives. "I've never had a cause to fight for," she says. "But this is a cause I can get behind. No need to apologize, Your Majesty."

"You're a credit to your people, Ilapara. I'm blessed to have met you."

That's debatable. "I appreciate it, Your Majesty."

Darkness sweeps over her as the skimmer branches left into a different tunnel. She follows its halo until it comes back into view straight ahead. Her earring vibrates again.

"In a few seconds you'll be entering a restricted zone patrolled by guards. According to Salo's instructions, there's supposed to be a metal grating ahead, which you'll have to kick down, but it's a bit rusty. He seems confident you'll manage."

"Got it."

The circular grating is meant to allow water to flow from her side of the tunnel to the other, cutting off access for everything else. It goes down with two solid kicks, making a racket as it hits the ground.

"Damn. Two guards heard the noise. They are coming your way. Ziyo, please turn off the glowing skimmer."

Light recedes from Ilapara's eyes as the skimmer relinquishes its red halo. She expected trouble, so she's prepared. In one of her pockets is a cloth Salo soaked in an alchemical sleeping draft whose fumes are soporific. She extracts it and holds it in her right hand.

"How far are they?"

"They'll see you in about ten seconds."

No, they won't. Ilapara balls her left hand into a fist and twists once to the left, activating her charm of invisibility. A shimmer of light sweeps over her eyes like a sheer curtain being drawn down. She stalks forward even as she sees an approaching lantern, its yellow light creeping closer.

Up ahead, one of the men pauses like he can sense something in the air. The other one stops too. "What is it?"

"I don't know," says the first, a hint of fear in his voice. "Do you think maybe one of them lizards came up?"

"There are spells to keep the lizards away," says his friend. "They don't come up here."

The first guard doesn't seem convinced. He opens his mouth to speak, but no sound comes out, because Ilapara has already crept around and behind him and has covered his mouth and nose with her treated cloth. His lantern falls and his limbs give out as sleep takes him.

The other guard yelps and starts to draw his blade, but Ilapara dashes forward before he can stab blindly at the air and covers his face. His eyes go wide with terror before the fumes take him and he becomes limp. Ilapara eases him gently to the ground.

"That was . . . impressive."

"We do what we have to do," she says.

"Right. It's a bit of a maze down there, but the hub is not far from you. Can you see the skimmer? It should lead you there."

The skimmer flicks back on again and starts to lead the way forward.

"I see it," Ilapara says. She twists her fist to the left to banish her invisibility, and then she follows the mechanical insect.

Indeed, there are more turns and intersections here than in the warrens she's traversed thus far, but soon the skimmer stops to hover next to a closed box hanging on the wall, broader than it is thick. The box was painted black so as to make it less conspicuous, but in the skimmer's reddish light Ilapara sees a metallic gleam where the layers of paint have peeled off.

"Is this it?" she says.

"Yes. That is the hub. Tuksaad is waiting at the other one. You have to act synchronously, so activate your scrambler when I give the signal."

Ilapara extracts the other item from her pocket, an oval cipher shell with a milky quartz crystal at its center. She holds her breath as she waits.

"Now."

She has to look away as soon as she tugs on the shell's switch because the crystal begins to strobe brilliantly, emitting blinding pulses like recurring lightning flashes. Salo explained that once active, it releases powerful, rapidly changing fields of light and force, which should eventually disrupt the hub's enchantments. A minute elapses before the king's voice comes through Ilapara's earring.

"I'm told the enchantments in the hub have been disabled. You should now be able to safely move about the tunnels immediately surrounding the prison complex. That's it. The skimmer should now lead you to Tuksaad."

This is really happening, Ilapara thinks. Before now, it was just a plan. But with the disabling of the prison's external protections, it has become a reality that could get her executed if she's caught.

It's too late to worry now, so Ilapara steels herself and follows the skimmer.

26: Musalodi

Skytown

The unintentional consequence of being in Skytown is that most of the Saires who've answered Salo's call to take refuge within his gates are themselves residents of the glittering hill. They've been trickling in since yesterday morning, many with their whole families, taking up the lounges, the foyer, and the hallways and even spilling out into the gardens.

It's a war of heavy perfumes and silk that Bwana Ruma and his team of servants have done their best to accommodate. But some of the guests are demanding, to the point that Salo has been forced to abandon his construct and go around answering questions and being a generally reassuring presence.

He almost regrets ever opening his doors.

"But my house will be looted while I'm here," says the matronly woman who's been keeping his attention hostage for the past twenty minutes. "You must send someone to watch over it. Surely you can spare one of your guards?"

Salo shakes his head, struggling to keep his patience. "Again, Bibi, I'm truly sorry, but that's simply not possible. If I did that for you, I'd have to do it for all my other guests; then who would remain to protect the place you've taken refuge?"

The woman waves a hand clad with ivory bangles, dismissive. "We'll be fine. You're a mystic. The Wavunaji wouldn't dare cross you. Besides, I've been told there'll be Sentinels coming."

"Yes. Her Majesty is sending a team of Sentinels our way, as well as to all the other places your fellow clanspeople have gathered. But they're meant only to bolster our security, not replace it."

Her tone becomes pleading. "I beg you, honored emissary; I can't afford to lose my house. It's all I have left."

Salo is saved from giving a definitive response when Ruma Sato appears to his side, looking anxious. "Excuse me, honored. Might I have a word?"

"Let me consider it," Salo says to his guest, "but I have another matter I must attend to immediately." Before she can stop him, he takes Ruma by the arm and leads him away, speaking in a low voice. "Bwana Ruma. I can't afford to entertain the guests right now, so please do whatever you can to make them comfortable."

"About that," Ruma says with a wince. "The servants . . . some of them are unhappy. The workload has been strenuous of late, and the guests are demanding. I'm not sure what to do."

Salo blinks at him for a second. He can almost feel the storm clouds of a migraine gathering beneath his temples. "Have you tried tripling their pay?"

Ruma gasps and stutters. "B-but that would be unreasonable! They're already being paid more than is customary."

"Just do it, Bwana Ruma. Triple your own pay while you're at it, and hire more servants if it'll help. Stock up the pantries and the cellar. Whatever is necessary, so long as I don't have to handle it myself."

The steward remains tense for a moment, then seems to relax. Perhaps he anticipated a more difficult discussion. "As you wish, honored. And thank you. I shall make sure you won't be interrupted further. Will you be in your study?"

"Yes. And by the way, a group of Sentinels and an independent mystic will be coming later on to add to our security. Let them in when they arrive and tell them I'll be out to welcome them as soon as I can."

"Understood."

Back in the peace and quiet of his study, Salo settles down on the chaise, closes his eyes, and enters his metaformic construct, arriving at the porch to the Earth craft archive, where a musuku tree grows eternally laden with fruits of yellow crystal.

King Isa, dressed majestically in golden chains and a strapless gown of peach-colored chiffon, is in the central pavilion, monitoring an array of floating mirrors as she paces in front of them. Most of the mirrors display views transmitted from different skimmers, while the mirror at the center of the array shows the detailed, step-by-step plan Salo wrote to minimize the risk of mistakes.

He gave her access to some of Ziyo's abilities so she could help him watch over and control the skimmers during the mission; at first, he thought she might become overwhelmed, having no experience with magic, but she has adapted to the interface surprisingly well. Salo can't help but mourn for the mystic she might have become had her mark not muted the latent gift for magic in her blood.

He assumes all has gone well since she didn't summon him while he was dealing with the guests. "How goes?" he says as he settles down on an armchair, squinting up at the mirrors.

She answers without a pause in her pacing, the train of her dress trailing on the floor. "Ilapara and Tuk successfully disabled the security enchantments. They're now on their way to the rendezvous point just outside the outer prison ring."

"You seem rather comfortable with the setup here," Salo remarks. "If I didn't know better, I'd say this wasn't your first encounter with an arcane intelligence."

She gives him a sidelong glance. Threads of gold are woven into her braids and catch the light whenever she moves. Salo finds himself admiring her effortless glamour. "I was a studious princess," she says, "so I happen to have a rudimentary understanding of ciphers. It has always fascinated me how similar they are to most other scripts and yet at the same time so . . . different. I used to think I could hear them whispering things to me." She acquires a faraway look in her eyes. "Of course, I was probably just deluding myself."

"Maybe not," Salo says. "Ciphers touch some fundamental aspect of the human psyche, and though rare, some people are born with an instinctual understanding of them. It could be that you're such a person, despite your mark."

She seems thoughtful; then her gaze becomes piercing, as though she were trying to see through him. "What about you? You're clearly capable. Do you have some special affinity with ciphers?"

"No. I had to learn them the hard way."

"Then you had excellent teachers?"

Salo considers the question. Aago taught him to read and write, but he learned ciphers from the Carving. Does that count? "I taught myself, for the most part."

"I guess I'm trying to understand what makes you so different from every other mystic I've ever met," the king says. "Why are you the one sitting here and not someone else from your tribe? Why are you the one who saved me from the depths of the undercity? Why you, Musalodi?"

My mother, Salo thinks. *Despite her often-ruthless ambitions, she had a brilliant mind, and she laid the foundations I would later build upon in my efforts to understand her. That's why I ended up here.* "I don't know," he says instead. "I guess I've been fortunate."

The answer seems to disappoint the king. She turns back to the mirrors, one of which shows Ilapara's dim outline as she makes her way through the tunnels beneath Northtown. Tuk is on another mirror doing the same.

"My cousin has entered the Summit's reception room."

Grateful for the change of subject, Salo gestures to enlarge the mirror showing one of the royal palace's state rooms. He was surprised to find out that, while the palace's private wings were heavily warded against all manner of stealth magic, most of the other sections were not, giving his skimmers free rein to move about undetected.

The state room is not the one Salo remembers, though it isn't any less ornamented. Patterns swirl within patterns on the tiles. Golden statues of the ten clan totems look down from perches on the walls. Elaborate crystal lights droop from the ceiling with enough gold and silver to dazzle the eyes into blindness.

All the headmen are there, along with their retinues and other influential people who have come to petition the princes before they commence the Mkutano in a few hours. Jomo is shown on the mirror as he searches the crowded room, a folder in one hand, the head of his cane in the other. Today he looks princely in his tailored robes of rich blue silk and golden embroidery and the finest black leather boots money can buy. His hair is closely cropped, his beard neatly trimmed. He's a big man, and he wears it well. No wonder Ilapara has a soft spot for him, even though she won't admit it.

Yesterday Salo watched him pay the Hare a visit to his Skytown residence, where he casually presented the headman with evidence of his apostasy. Unlike the Caracal, who reacted with anger, the Hare trembled with fear, all but begging Jomo not to expose his secret. A victory, but Salo felt sick by the end of the encounter, sick that he had helped make it possible. Hopefully today marks the end of these unscrupulous games.

On the mirror in front of him, the man wearing the mask of the Impala turns his head sideways toward Jomo, and their gazes clash. Jomo inclines his head to the wine tables by the side and starts walking there without looking to see if the headman is following.

At the table he tucks the folder under one arm, picks up a glass of wine, and downs it quickly. Watching him, Isa lets out a sigh.

As the headman approaches the herald, a dejected-looking young man at his heels, Salo silently commands the metaform to filter out all the other sounds from the state room and magnify the conversation. He notices a gloomy shadow passing over Isa as she watches the mirror.

"Herald," the headman says to Jomo. *"It is good to see you."* He is a plump figure in blue robes and golden chains. The young man next to him is also in blue—Salo suspects he is the prince's heir—and won't stop staring at the floor.

Jomo sneers at him before addressing his father in a low voice. *"Take it. All the mines in your province, signed over to you by Her Majesty and sealed by an Akili of the House of Law."*

The Impala watches closely as his son accepts the folder and tucks it under one armpit. *"We will have to review those documents, of course,"* the headman says.

"You can review them all you like, Your Highness. But if you go back on your word today, I swear by the Mother I'll trigger the cancellation clause so fast it'll make you dizzy."

The Impala's bovine face settles into an amused expression. *"It is not wise to threaten me, young Herald."*

"That was no threat, Your Highness. It was an oath. I will not take kindly to betrayal."

The headman's son frowns like he wants his father to wreak vengeance for this slight, but the man laughs, reaching forward to tap Jomo on the shoulder. *"Your mother would be proud of the man you've become. Don't worry; I always keep my word."*

Jomo appears at a loss for words, even if for just a moment. He clears his throat, inclining his head respectfully. *"I appreciate it. Now, if you'll excuse me."*

As Jomo picks up another glass of wine and begins to move away from the headman, Salo indulges his curiosity. "I take it there's some bad blood between the herald and the headman's son."

The king clutches at her golden necklaces, looking haunted. "He's a Sentinel, and he was my friend. We . . . had a falling-out."

"I see," Salo says and decides to pry no further.

On the mirror, Jomo has left the state room to get some air. He brings his enchanted pendant closer to his lips, and his voice comes through the construct. *"Salo? The Buffalo is here. Should I approach him?"*

"And say what?" Salo says. "Follow the plan. I'll tell you when it's time."

"Mother above, I hate this. I hate not knowing. How far?"

"Everything is moving according to schedule. If it helps, Her Majesty and I can see you. Maybe take it easy on the wine."

"To the pits with you, Salo."

Both Salo and the king shake their heads but say nothing. They go on to cycle through the mirrors, checking on the sanctuaries across the city where Saires have taken refuge in the thousands. The hope is that, should the vote later today go against them, the Wavunaji will be deterred from courting Ama's wrath by murdering those who've sought her protection. The king placed loyal Sentinels and at least one independent mystic at each of these locations as a safeguard in the event that the deterrent fails to work, but Salo isn't sure this will be enough.

While the king continues to check on the sanctuaries, he brings up the view from Alinata's skimmer. She's in a carriage along the Midworld Confluence, sitting with her legs crossed, staring out the window.

"Alinata. How come you're still on the Confluence?"

She fiddles with the enchanted earring he had to beg her to wear. *"Traffic is brutal this morning. Sometimes I wonder how anyone can stand living in such a crowded place. I've been here less than two months, and I'm already going out of my mind."*

"Hopefully you'll reach the extraction point on time. You might have to ask your driver to go a little faster."

"You know, I just realized you gave me the most boring job, Salo. Why is that?"

"Why did you come to that realization, or why is it erroneous?"

"Don't be witty with me. You know what I mean."

"Your job's important, Alinata. You're the last piece of the puzzle."

"I could have gone down the tunnels with Tuk. I'm blessed; Ilapara is not."

"Yes, but ravens down in the sewers would be a little too memorable, no? Also, Ilapara can turn invisible. You can't."

"Nice try, but I'm not convinced. I think you don't want me down there for some reason."

"What reason would that be?"

"Of course. Why didn't I see this before? There's something you didn't tell me, isn't there? Something the others know that I don't."

Salo curses under his breath. "You are too smart for your own good, Alinata."

She gives a bitter smile. *"What happened to trusting each other?"*

"Baby steps. And there are some things I don't want Her Majesty to know just yet, so I hope you can forgive me."

Alinata makes a moue out the window. *"You're lucky I'm interested in seeing where this goes."*

"Thanks, Alinata."

A knock on the door to his study draws him out of the construct.

"It's me again, honored emissary."

Salo glares at the door. "Seriously, Bwana Ruma? Can't you handle whatever it is yourself?"

"I believe this requires your attention."

"Is the world ending?"

"It might be."

"Dear Ama." Salo sits up, putting his feet on the floor. "Fine. Come in. What's the matter now?"

Salo thought his tone might intimidate Ruma away, but the man already looks like he's seen the devil herself. "There's an Akili at the gates, honored. She has come with a group of city guards. She demands that you let her in immediately."

Salo's heart misses a beat. He closes his eyes, commandeering the view of a nearby skimmer, and sees a woman in black robes standing outside the gates. She's surrounded by a contingent of armed men in brown tunics. An independent mystic and ten Sentinels in green are staring at them from the other side of the gates. "An Akili," Salo says, fear thickening in his veins.

"Yes. From the city guard."

"But why?"

Ruma's eyes are wide. "I have no idea, honored."

Salo takes in a breath as his mind races. *I can't let her intimidate me.* "Allow her to enter with two guards. Unarmed. Two, no more. Let them wait outside."

"Yes, honored."

"And send someone to my chamber to help me dress. I will not be humbled in my own home."

The Akili waiting for him on the wet drive is a walking statue of a woman in a grand black robe and necklaces of moongold that shimmer with cold flames in the daylight. Her brown skin bears a golden shimmer, and her eyes are painted to accentuate their narrow, almond curve, giving her face a somewhat aggressive aspect, the kind that can part crowds with a single frown.

Right now her frown tells Salo she's not happy he's kept her waiting.

Two men in the city guard's brown tunics stand behind her. They're both unarmed, as Salo requested, which seems to have annoyed them, judging by the surly looks on their faces.

Salo's natural instincts are begging him to be conciliatory, to capitulate to their demands, but he knows he needs to be less like himself right now and more like his father, who can be intimidating when he wields his authority. In his shoes he would be proud and defiant, so that's what Salo must be.

He has worn his most ornate circlet. Not copper but the arcane gold this city worships so much. More of it coils down his forearms and up his shins in the form of bands shaped like serpents. The cloth swathed around his hips is a pristine silky white. His blanket cloak is large enough to give him bulkier shoulders and is a deep red with an inner sparkle, as though rays of moonlight were spun into thread and woven into cloth. With his staff in hand, Salo reckons he's never looked more like a sorcerer than he does now.

The ten Sentinels and the undercity mystic part for him as he makes his way toward the Akili, whom they have kept from advancing any farther than the driveway, a cordon of youthful insubordination.

A lone Sentinel is the only other person out on the drive who is taller than he is, so he stands straight to amplify his height advantage. "Welcome to my home, honored Akili. I do wonder about your intentions, however, seeing as you brought an army of guards to my gates."

The guests inside are crammed by the windows, no doubt straining their ears to listen in. Salo can almost smell their fear. He hopes they can't smell his.

The Akili steps forward and presents a folded piece of blue paper. Her golden nails twinkle like the night sky. "Emissary Siningwe, I am Inquisitor Anika Akili of the Prism, arcane investigator of the city guard. We have a warrant to apprehend a list of suspects in your care. We demand that you release them to us at once."

Salo accepts the paper with a frown, which deepens as he skims it. It bears the seal of the House of Law, and there are about fifty names on it—almost a third of the people hiding inside the residence. "Grand larceny," he reads. "Fraud. Embezzlement. Tax evasion. Blasphemy." He looks up at the Akili. "This is quite the list."

"I'm sure you can see that the warrant carries the blessing of the House of Law. You're to release the suspects immediately."

Salo grips his staff to still his shaking hand, and in the background of his mind he calls upon the spell of Mirror craft he prepared for such an eventuality. "The thing I like about you KiYonte is how organized you are. Your laws are so codified and straightforward they are rarely open to interpretation. It is quite ingenious, really. I shall have to suggest to my queen that we do the same for our laws."

With a wave of his hand, he unleashes the spell. So solid is the illusion it floats next to him like an actual page lifted from a giant book, clear for all to see. Salo quietly relishes the awe he elicits from those around him.

"Take this clause, for example. The legal language is a little too technical for me, rather labyrinthine to be honest, but the gist of it is, as I understand it, that I have rights in this city. This residence might be in KiYonte territory, but I am a pilgrim of the Bloodway, and so it is privileged soil. No one can enter without my express permission. Moreover, no one can take anything or anyone from here without my permission. You are here only because I have permitted it. So you do not get to make demands of me in my own yard, understand? It's a grave insult to me personally and to my queen. I am a mystic of Ama Vaziishe, a master of my own Axiom, and the son of a great chief. I will not tolerate disrespect from a subordinate such as yourself. You will apologize to me this instant."

Fury blazes in the Akili's eyes, and every fiber of Salo's body becomes taut with fear, but he hides it under an unrelenting cloak of prideful anger.

His heart leaps as the mystic gives a subtle bow of the head. "You have my apologies, honored emissary."

"Your apologies are accepted. As for this warrant, I respect it, and I respect the law, as I should, but I'm afraid I cannot comply with your request."

She folds her arms, smiling like a hunter who's led her prey into a trap. "You would stand in the way of justice, honored emissary? Have you come here to spit in the face of our ways?"

"On the contrary, my refusal is perfectly reasonable, as well as legal."

"How so?"

Salo points at the illusion. "According to this, I have the right to prevent the arrest and interrogation of any employee of mine so long as I remain a resident of the city, lest they disclose sensitive information pertaining to my household. As it happens, all the people on your list are my employees and have all been privy to information I consider sensitive. Therefore, I have the right to hold them here until such a time as I decide to return to my homeland."

"You cannot possibly expect me to believe this. They're not your employees."

There is a crackle in the air as Salo draws essence into his cosmic shards. "Are you accusing me of lying, honored Akili? You come to my home and insult me, and now you call me a liar? For your sake, I hope you can prove your accusations, else you and I will have a problem."

The Akili all but snarls. "You're playing a dangerous game, honored emissary."

Salo opens his mouth to respond, but then his metaform relays the king's voice straight into his mind. *"Salo, we have a problem."*

He subvocalizes his answer. *"Give me a minute. I'm in the middle of a life-and-death situation here."*

"So are we. Be quick."

Salo gives his unwelcome guest a cold, hard stare. "This is no game from where I'm standing, honored Akili. Gentlemen," he says to the

Sentinels. "Please escort this woman and her guards off the premises. I've had enough of them."

And then he turns his back on the furious mystic and strides back into the palace.

◆ ◆ ◆

Somewhere along the way back to his study, a woman wraps him in a tight embrace. "Mother's grace upon you, honored."

People mouth their gratitude at him wherever he looks, some with tears in their eyes, and it hits him just how much responsibility he's placed on his shoulders. His throat begins to constrict, and he escapes to his study, locking the door and leaning against it to catch his breath.

There is no time to panic. He heads for his chaise and returns to the construct, his vision shifting seamlessly from the study to a library floating in the middle of a lake.

The king is biting her varnished nails in the pavilion, her shoulders tense as she speaks to her cousin through a floating mirror. "Where did you go?" she asks as soon as she sees him.

"Another situation in the residence, Your Majesty." He stops next to her, scouring the mirrors for what might have gone wrong. In one of them, Jomo has secluded himself inside a lavatory and appears at the end of his wits. "What's the matter?" Salo says.

The king takes in his new state of dress with a worried once-over before she answers. "Jomo says the Mkutano has been pushed up by an hour."

He jerks his head toward her so fast he almost sprains his neck. "What?"

"She means, Salo, that we have less than an hour to get the Buffalo's vote!" Jomo explains, his forehead shining in the mirage with sweat.

Salo's balance almost falters. He had a plan. Things were supposed to go according to the plan. "Shit."

"Exactly! This has all gone to shit! I swear the Crocodile must have sensed something. He's getting jittery."

"We can still make it," Salo says. "Ilapara and Tuk made good time down in the tunnels."

Hope and doubt vie for power in the king's glance. "You think so?" *What choice do we have?* he almost says. He faces the mirages. "Jomo, return to the state room. We'll get back to you." Before he can argue, Salo ends the transmission of his voice to the herald's pendant while bringing Ilapara, Tuk, and Alinata into the fold. He addresses them in KiYonte for the king's benefit. "Everyone. Change of plans. We have an hour less than we thought, so we're going to have to hurry things along. I'm dropping all the guards with the stingers. That will give Tuk and Ilapara about twenty minutes to be in and out of the prison before the sedatives start to wear off."

On one mirror, Tuk shares a canteen of water with Ilapara. Their skimmers have led them close to the subterranean entrance to the prison, and they've had to rely on their powers of stealth to deal with the patrols. Both are wearing Mirror disguises that conceal their true appearances.

"Pits. Did you hear that, Tuk?"

Tuk takes the canteen back from Ilapara and packs it into his knapsack. He nods in reply.

"Why the sudden rush?" Ilapara asks.

"The Mkutano has been moved up, so we need the prisoner sooner than we thought. Alinata, you'll have to be at the extraction point in twenty minutes."

On another mirror, the Asazi's carriage is turning off the Artery and into a Northtown neighborhood, its zebras running at a fast trot.

"I'll make it," she says.

"Ilapara, Tuk. You know what to do, right?"

Tuk pats his knapsack with one hand. *"I have the rope, the scrambler, and your detailed instructions."*

"Ilapara?"

She nods, facing the glowing skimmer hovering in front of her. *"Ready."*

"Good luck. A lot is riding on your success."

"Yeah. No pressure or anything."

"We believe in you," the king says, her voice charged with conviction. "You can do this."

He desperately hopes that she's right.

27: Kamali

Undercity Prison

In one particular cell on the fourth-highest row of the undercity prison, Kamali is pulling at the frayed threads of his pillowcase when a shout draws him out of his troubled thoughts.

He swings his feet off his bed and onto the floor, finding his slippers. Slowly, he rises from his bed and walks to the bars of his cell, careful not to come too close lest the charm on his manacle shock him for misbehaving.

He lifts his chin, peering down beyond the catwalk outside his cell. There's a guard lying unconscious near the base of the watchtower. He sees another guard on a lower catwalk yelping and slapping at his neck as though he's been stung by a wasp, only to stagger and fall unconscious just seconds later. Three more guards cry out in pain before succumbing to the same fate.

Kamali feels no pity for them. Most of the guards here are cruel and sadistic, the sort who get off on torturing weak and battered prisoners. But something nefarious is clearly at work.

Other prisoners approach the bars of their cells to investigate. A murmur spreads among them when a rope is flung from above and dangled down the prison's cylindrical well to the bottom. Kamali watches curiously as a figure clothed in black slides down the rope with gloved hands, narrowly avoiding the catwalks, until he reaches the end of his rope, then lets go and lands on the ground with catlike grace.

Like a shadow he slinks over the fallen guard and disappears into the watchtower. Seconds later, Kamali thinks he sees flashes of light strobing out of the windows at the top of the tower; then a sudden jangling sound echoes all over the hollow of the prison, accompanied by a change in his prisoner's manacle.

He stares at it, bewildered. Even with the collar muting his cosmic shards, he could feel the lightning charm thrumming in the manacle's witchwood core, a permanent warning against defying his jailers. But now the charm has gone silent.

What the devil is going on?

28: Ilapara

Undercity Prison

"Listen to me, all right? You have to follow us. There's no time to waste."

The youth inside the brightly lit cell shakes his head forcefully. Like all the other prisoners in this dungeon, he's in a dirty brown tunic, equally threadbare pants, and a steel manacle bound to his right wrist. Unkempt dreadlocks spill over his face. He's hunched up in one corner, as far from the gates as he can go, shrinking away from Ilapara as though she were the malaika of death come to collect his soul.

"His name is Fanaka," comes a voice from her earring. *"You need to get him to trust you."*

Ilapara grits her teeth. "Fanaka, right? Your father sent us to rescue you."

Fanaka shakes his head again, huddling into his corner. "No. You lie. You're here to trick me. I won't fall for it. I won't let you shock me again."

"Do I look like a guard to you? Your father sent us, Fanaka, and if you don't come with us, you'll be monster fodder when you get called to the arena later this afternoon."

A clanking sound ripples across the catwalk and up the chamber; then her left ear vibrates. *"The gates are open, Ilapara. Get him out of there."*

She pushes the cell gate open and strides inside, looming over the prisoner. "If you don't follow me right now, I swear I will leave you here. Every second we waste is more time for us to get caught."

Now Fanaka lifts his head and regards Ilapara like she's a strange breed of creature he's never seen before. "You're not a guard, are you?"

"That's what I've been telling you."

He lets himself relax, eyes wide with hope. "You're really here to rescue me?"

"Yes, now come on!"

"But . . . but the shock!" Fanaka points frantically at the manacle still clutching his wrist. "I can't go out there. It hurts."

"We've taken care of it. Now come and live, or stay and die. It's your choice."

Ilapara turns around and starts making good on her threat. She's relieved when she hears Fanaka's slippered feet pattering on the catwalk behind her.

All around the cylindrical well of the dungeon, prisoners are drifting to the bars of their cells. A few are testing their gates and finding that they're now unlocked. None have yet dared to venture out onto the catwalks, though.

"They'll find us," Fanaka says, jogging behind Ilapara as they descend a staircase to a catwalk on a lower level. "We can't escape this prison."

"They'll be too busy trying to catch all the others."

"What?"

A glowing skimmer leads them farther down the well. Fanaka must see that this isn't the way to freedom because he says, "Where the devil are we going?"

Ilapara accelerates after the skimmer, not looking back. "We have another stop to make."

29: Kamali

Heavy footsteps thud on the catwalks somewhere above him, growing louder by the second. Finally they reach his level and approach his cell. He waits, ready for anything.

"Kamali Jasiri?"

A strange girl has appeared outside the bars of his cell. The guards wear bracelets that protect them from the electrified walkways, but she's not wearing one. He watches her, wondering if he should know her. "Have we met?"

She twists her wrists, and a ripple of light transforms her, shortening her limbs, changing her face and the hue of her clothing. Where she wore a green robe before, now it is crimson, with an aerosteel breastplate protecting her chest.

A spell, and now that it is banished, a tingle of familiarity brings Kamali closer to the iron bars of his cell. "I *do* know you."

She seems relieved to hear that. "Yes. We met at the House of Forms. I was with the Yerezi pilgrim."

"The Yerezi pilgrim . . ."

He roared as he unleashed his dingonek, the spirit tattooed in moongold ink onto his back, and in less than a second its power had flooded his veins, drawing from the second heart at the base of his spine. He knew he had to act quickly before it was too late . . .

The transient flash of memory recedes, its contours too vague for Kamali to make out anything concrete. He grips the bars separating him from the girl like a man begging for his life. "You know what happened, don't you? Why I did what I did? Why I made myself forget?"

Her expression is guarded, but she nods. "I do."

"You must tell me. I don't want to die without knowing." A fact Kamali hasn't admitted until he spoke it. He has sustained his sanity by assuring himself that he is a good man. That he did what he did and made himself forget for a good reason. That he doesn't need to know. But a kernel of doubt has always made him wonder. *I want to know. Dear Mother, I want to know more than anything.*

"We're here to rescue you, Kamali." The girl pushes the gate open and isn't shocked to death. "You must come with me immediately."

Elsewhere in the dungeon, a voice begins to yell: "We're free! The guards are down! The gates are open! Everyone, we're free! Run for the exits now!"

Kamali frowns. "You're breaking me free? But why?"

"There's no time to explain," the girl says. "We have to leave. Now." She makes a twisting motion with her wrist again and is enveloped by a cloak of light that gives her a longer nose, smaller eyes, and much lighter skin, disguising her breastplate while changing the color of her garments to pale blue.

And only now does Kamali notice the other prisoner standing nearby, looking at the girl with a mixture of fear and reverence. Kamali recognizes him as the poor wretch who narrowly escaped the arena two weeks ago.

Another face he saw that day comes to mind, and he steps outside of his cell. The steel underfoot remains dead, just like his manacle. "I will follow you," he says to the girl. "But there's someone I must find first." He walks off without giving her a chance to protest.

Desperate prisoners are now pouring out of their cells and seething along the catwalks and up the stairs in every direction. It'll be difficult to find her in this mayhem, so he resorts to cupping his hands around his mouth and shouting over the railings of the catwalks. "Ayana! Ayana!" A prisoner bumps into him as he runs for the nearby staircase. Kamali ignores him. "Ayana!"

"We need to go!" the girl shouts over the clamor. "There's no time for this!"

Kamali doesn't listen. "Ayana!"

"Look, we're going down to the watchtower. If you're not there in three minutes, you're on your own." Then the girl with the Mirror disguise leads the other prisoner deeper down the prison well, against the flow of escaping prisoners.

Kamali keeps shouting as loudly as his lungs will allow. "Ayana!"

"I'm here!"

His gaze snaps to the source of that voice, and his spirits lift when he sees her running toward him. Without thinking he runs up to meet her, taking her hands in his when he gets close enough.

They didn't have much time to talk after their victory at the arena. All they could do was exchange names before the furious mshamba appeared to promise them death and torture. Kamali can't remember a word of what the mshamba said, but Ayana's name has been on his mind quite a lot since that day.

"Ayana, someone has come to break me free. You must follow me."

He starts to tug her toward the stairs, but Ayana resists him. "Jasiri, Kamali. Wait."

He stops, staring down at her. *She has eyes like the dawn,* he thinks, mesmerized. Today they seem to glow brighter than he remembers.

"I can't come with you," she says.

"I'm not leaving you here."

She smiles, though her eyes fill with regret and longing. He shivers when she reaches up to caress his stubbled jaw. It has been a while since a woman touched him so, and the fact that it is *this* woman touching him fills him with heat. "My path lies elsewhere, Jasiri. But it may yet cross yours again."

"Ayana . . ."

"Listen, I need you to do something for me, all right?"

He barely knows her, but he thinks he would jump to the moon if she simply asked him to. "What is it?"

Rings of white light pulse along her tensor appendages. At first, he thinks his eyes have deceived him, but then another two rings pulse from the base of her temples to the tips of her tensors. The pulses become more rapid, the glow stronger, until it seems she has horns of pure sunlight jutting out of her temples. He watches in awe as white patterns much like cosmic shards appear on her forehead. She lifts a hand in front of her, palm up, and with a blinding flash of white light, she pulls a silver ring out of thin air.

Magic, of this Kamali has no doubt, but not any magic he has ever seen. The ring's silver is strange as well, its luster unnatural, like it was alloyed with molten sunlight.

"Keep this safe for me," she says. "Maybe one day we'll meet again and you can give it back."

Kamali slowly reaches for the ring. It isn't moongold, but there's power inside, a warmth he knows doesn't belong to the Mother. He raises his eyes to Ayana's intense gaze. "What's going on, Ayana? Who are you?"

"Just a woman in the right place at the right time, who wishes she had more time to do this."

She rises on the tips of her toes to bring their lips together, and for Kamali, time slows to a standstill. The feel of her kiss is a study in contradictions, scorching him like the heat of a desert sun even as it makes him shiver as if blasted by a wintry gale. Every nerve in his body awakens, and he feels the spirits on his body stirring with interest.

When the kiss ends, she keeps her eyes closed, a finger grazing her lips. The markings on her forehead flare again, even brighter than before, and Kamali watches her, entranced.

"If Vigilance shines on us both," she says, "I shall see you again. Goodbye, Kamali." And then she blinks out of the fabric of space in a blaze of white light.

30: Musalodi

Skytown

How does one conceal the identity of the prisoners one seeks to break free? When Salo asked himself this question, the answer seemed simple: one breaks *all* of them free.

While Ilapara and the Buffalo's son slither down to the base of the prison's watchtower, Tuk, in a Mirror disguise, leads the other prisoners out through the main entrance above the prison well, shouting at the top of his voice.

"Come on, the guards are down! To the exits before they wake up!"

"Did you see that?" the king says, pointing at one of the mirrors.

Salo doesn't take his eyes off Tuk. "See what?"

"The woman with the Jasiri. She was there one second, and then the next she just . . . hmm. Never mind."

"Where is Kamali anyway?"

On a different mirror, the Jasiri has only just started running down the stairs against the tide of prisoners surging up the prison well. None of them pause to wonder why he might be running down instead of up, because none of them know about the emergency access hatch beneath the watchtower. It leads to a tunnel running beneath the prison for half a mile before rising up a vertical shaft that empties out into a section of the undercity west of the Northtown market.

Kamali eventually catches up to Ilapara and Fanaka, and Salo cracks his knuckles anxiously as he and the king monitor their progress down the access hatch and along the escape tunnel. In another mirror, the reception in the Summit's state room is still in full swing, but it will be winding down any minute now; then the headmen will leave to begin the Mkutano. Meanwhile Alinata has just reached the extraction point.

"I was wondering about the guards," the king says. "How exactly did you take them down like that?"

"The skimmers are near-perfect replicas of the real thing, complete with metal stings," Salo replies. "I coated the stings with an alchemical sedative that causes instant unconsciousness when introduced to the bloodstream."

The king gives him a look somewhere between impressed and disturbed. Then she stiffens as something on one of the mirrors catches her attention. "Salo, we have a problem."

He immediately moves to stand closer to her. The view on the mirror is from a skimmer racing down a tunnel after an indistinct, fast-moving shape.

"What's going on?"

She doesn't have to tell him because in the next breath, the thing stops, craning its neck to look back as though it suspects it's being observed. Its jaws unhinge, and it lights itself up with startling bioluminescence, spreading its tail and lifting it like a sting. There's something so wrong about this vaguely lizard-like creature Salo shudders at the sight of it.

"Dear Ama. What's that?"

"It's a ninki nanka," the king replies in despair. "They normally stay away from the upper regions of the undercity, but the prison is deeper than most settled places. I also think the security hubs we disabled might have been keeping them away. Looks like the noise has attracted them." She points at another mirror, where a second ninki nanka can be seen sniffing the air as it follows the ruckus.

Salo curses. "We can't let them reach the prisoners." He reaches for his bond with Tuksaad, who's currently leading a group of prisoners to an exit near the Sentinel barracks. "You've awoken at least two under-city beasts. If they catch up to you, some of the prisoners will die. You need to hurry."

Tuk slows down but tells the other prisoners to keep running. *"Lead me to them."*

"What? Why?"

"Why do you think? This will all be pointless if no one else makes it out of here alive."

With a muttered curse Salo commands one of the skimmers to make itself visible and lead Tuk toward the approaching monsters.

"Is there a way you can speak through your insects, Salo?" the king asks.

"I wish I had thought of that," Salo says. "Why?"

"Two prisoners are headed straight for one of the ninki nankas," she says, pointing at another flashing mirror. Beneath it, Ziyo has created a three-dimensional map to illustrate what's happening. "If we could warn them . . ."

The skimmer watching these two prisoners flies in front of them and rapidly flashes its halo of light in warning.

"Why have you stopped?" says one of them.

"What the devil is this?" says the other. The skimmer keeps flashing, bathing their dirty and confused faces in a wavering glow.

"Turn back, you fools," the king whispers. "Turn back, or you'll die."

"Come on, it's just a firefly," says the first prisoner. He tries to move ahead, but the skimmer flies to block his path.

"It don't look like a firefly to me," says his skeptical friend.

"We don't have time for this! It's probably just one of the prison's tricks to make us go back. I'm not falling for it!"

He runs ahead, and his friend is forced to follow, both ignoring the skimmer even as it flashes with a stronger intensity.

The king pinches her eyes closed. "Dear Mother. I can't watch."

Neither can I. It's probably cowardly, but Salo doesn't let the skimmer follow. The prisoners disappear into the darkness. Seconds later a roar tears through the tunnels, then spine-chilling shrieks.

Salo stares blankly at the mirror with the king, neither knowing what to say. Then the loud, piercing wail of a clarion shakes them out of their stupor. It's so loud Tuk has to stop running and press his palms against his ears.

"What was that?" he asks.

"I believe the alarm has been raised," the king answers. "The guards are waking up."

Salo's eyes bulge as another mirror begins to flash in warning. "Ah shit. One of the ninki nankas is closing in on you, Tuk."

"From where?"

"Straight ahead."

The creature emerges with its jaws unclenched. Tuk sends a phantom to run ahead of him while he stops to take off his knapsack. The shadow tries to be acrobatic by pushing off one wall with a foot and flipping over the lizard, but the damned creature is too fast. It rears up on stocky hind legs and snatches the shadow from the air, sinking its teeth into his kinetic field. But the shadow bursts into nothing from the force of the bite, leaving the lizard surprised.

The real Tuk pulls out something oval and silvery from his bag, which Salo recognizes as one of the scramblers he enchanted to destroy the prison's security network. Salo's heart almost gives out as the lizard recovers from its surprise and realizes that there's prey close by. Real prey.

It roars as it charges. Tuk stands his ground, one hand carrying the scrambler, the other on the scrambler's little lever. Salo wants to look away but doesn't. "By Ama, Tuk. What are you doing?"

Just before the lizard reaches striking distance, Tuk activates the scrambler, and light blooms from the palms of his hands in rapid flashes. To Salo's surprise, the monster roars as it thrashes about, recoiling.

"What's happening?" Salo asks.

A gleam of understanding appears in the king's eyes. "Your scramblers emit high-pitched sound, do they not?"

"I guess," Salo says. High-pitched noise would be the result of the rapidly shifting kinetic fields necessary to destabilize enchanted cores. "But why does this matter?"

"Ninki nankas have keen senses of hearing. Loud and high-pitched sounds are repulsive to them." A tiny smile moves the king's lips. "Clever man."

On the mirror, Tuk bursts into motion. In the span of one breath he summons a golden blade with a crimson edge and strikes. The lizard's anguished roars come to an abrupt end as Tuk severs its head clean off its toughened neck.

The relief that floods Salo's veins is too intense to be pleasant. "Get out of there, Tuk. Now."

31: Jomo

The Summit

Jomo imagines carving the Crocodile's skin with a knife, how satisfying it would be to hear the man cry and beg, to see his blood seeping from his wounds, but the images do nothing to appease his anger.

His spine is wound up like a spring as he waits on a bench just outside the state room. Some of the headmen and their retinues of brothers, sons, and nephews have already begun to trickle out to the colossus, at the foot of which is the Meeting Place on the Summit. The Buffalo is still inside, though, which is why Jomo is out here. He can't let the man leave until they have his son.

Mother damn the Crocodile, Jomo curses silently. Who the devil does the bastard think he is, starting the Mkutano an hour early?

Granted, it's not an entirely unprecedented thing to do; sometimes the extra hour is necessary, especially if a number of important issues need to be discussed. The Mkutano must end with the rising of the full moon at dusk whether agreement has been reached or not. But there aren't many important issues today. Only one, which eclipses all others with its weight in blood. *Kola Saai knows something is up.*

Jomo goes rigid as he spots the Buffalo strolling out of the state room's large doors with the Rhino and their followers. Forcing down a fit of panic, he lifts his charmed pendant to his lips.

"The Mkutano is about to begin. I have to stop the Buffalo from leaving, or this is all over."

Isa's voice comes an instant later. *"Go ahead. Just . . . delay him, cousin. We'll tell you when it's time."*

"Hurry."

"We're all doing our best. Hang on just a while longer."

And what happens if your best isn't good enough? Jomo asks himself. His feet move before he can think about what he's doing, and he approaches the headmen. "Your Highness," he says, addressing the Buffalo. "If I could have a word with you in private." He tries not to sound too desperate, but he's not certain he's successful.

The Buffalo and the Rhino both stop to stare at him, and so do the men gathered around them. Jomo ignores them all, focusing on his target. "I have something I'm sure you'll want to see."

The Rhino's prominent moongold horn tilts back as he laughs. "Let it never be said that our herald is not persistent." He gives a little bow of his head. "I'll leave you to it, Your Highnesses." He is still snickering as he walks off with his retinue.

Even the Buffalo seems entertained. He's not a tall man, but his horns give him a rather imposing presence. His blue high-necked tunic is simple and minimally embroidered, but his gold-and-diamond chains more than make up for it. With the Yontai's most lucrative diamond mines in his province, he is one of the richest men in the kingdom, which probably explains why he thinks his son should be able to get away with murder. Jomo had hopes to catch him in the act. It makes him sick that he must now help the man get his wish.

"Look here, Herald," the man says. "I know what you're trying to do, but I'll save you the time and effort, all right? Let it go. You'll go mad trying to salvage a battle that can't be won."

Jomo shows his teeth in some semblance of a smile. "I'm quite certain you'll thank me for not letting it go once you've seen what I need to show you."

Unfortunately, the headman is not one to be intimidated. He looks at the men gathered around him and points at the youngest, a boy not yet old enough for the Sentinels. "You, talk to him. I don't have time for this."

"Your Highness." Jomo runs a finger over his heart. "I swear by the Mother and by the blood of my dead parents that if you don't see what I have to show you, you'll regret it for the rest of your life."

The headman's bovine eyes regard Jomo with open hostility. His retinue does much the same. "This better be good, Herald, or you have made an enemy today." He nods at a man who must be his younger brother, and the two of them follow Jomo down the gallery.

Jomo tries to look confident, though in his heart he's frantically praying that Salo and Isa come through to him soon, or this will have all been for nothing.

32: Kamali

Undercity

Kamali and the other prisoner silently follow the girl down a tunnel, up a rickety ladder in a narrow vertical shaft, and through a series of turns in the warrens beneath Northtown. His flimsy slippers quickly become wet with filth.

He's not sure how, but there's a red firefly guiding the girl, and sometimes she talks to herself, as though there is an apparition in the air only she can see.

Along the way they hear shouts and roars and clarions. The other prisoner—Fanaka, was it?—keeps flinching in fear. As for Kamali, his thoughts won't stop spinning around Ayana.

He has already confronted the truth of what she is, what she must be, yet it hardly seems real to him. Those strange markings on her forehead looked like cosmic shards, except they flared white instead of red. And the spells she cast—and those had to be spells—drew not from the moon but from another light.

It shouldn't be, but it is the only thing that makes sense. Not only is she an awoken Faraswa; she is a solar mystic. And both things should be equally impossible. As far as he knows, solar magic is not supposed to work in the Redlands.

He reaches into his pocket to feel the ring. He's still wearing his muting collar, but he can sense power eddying inside the metal, a power unlike any he's ever felt. *Why me, Ayana? And did you know that this breakout was going to happen?*

The farther they go, the clearer it becomes to Kamali that whoever's helping the girl must know what they're doing. By rights, they should have been caught by now and hauled back to the prison. At the least, they should have been feeling the pressure of pursuit. But the girl moves confidently in the tunnels, following the firefly like she knows where she's going.

A sorcerer must be involved. Could it be the Yerezi pilgrim she mentioned? How powerful are they if they can so easily break prisoners out of what should be an impenetrable dungeon?

Light ahead. It spills in from a hole in the tunnel's ceiling, and judging by the ladder hanging halfway down into the tunnel, it's the mouth of a shaft leading up to the surface. The girl stops next to the ladder and nods at the other prisoner. "This is our exit. Go ahead; climb up. A friend of mine's waiting for us on the surface."

The boy looks up into the light, hesitant. "Are . . . are you sure?"

"Time's not on our side, Fawari."

"Fanaka," the boy corrects her. "My name's Fanaka."

The girl's stare clearly conveys she's not the patient sort. It's enough to force Fanaka to hoist himself up the ladder, climbing with his hands first, then with his feet when he's high enough. She makes Kamali follow him.

He looks deep into her eyes, searching them. Then he remembers she's wearing a disguise. "I'll want answers when this is over," he says.

"You'll get them. I promise."

If he still wielded the power of his mistress's Axiom, he might have let himself plunge into those eyes and sift through the truths behind them. As it is, he can only take her at her word.

He climbs up the ladder. The scent of witchwood bark greets him in the courtyard above, a pleasant relief after the rankness of the prison and the sewers. Overhead the skies are sullen, and everything is wet and fresh and alive. A fountain gurgles at the center of the courtyard, beneath the shade of red-flowering witchwood trees.

Kamali immediately recognizes the courtyard as the western Northtown moon shrine, where those too busy to attend sanctuary services go at moonrise to offer prayers of thanks to the Mother and drink from the fountain. The shrines are left alone at all other times, which Kamali supposes is the reason this particular exit was chosen for their escape.

"Well, hello."

Kamali turns and is met with an uncommonly beautiful young woman in foreign face paints, staring at him like he's an intriguing puzzle she'd like to solve.

He approaches her slowly, knowing that his height can be intimidating, but she doesn't appear disconcerted. "Are you the Yerezi pilgrim? Do you know what I made myself forget?"

She tilts her head like he's just gotten even more intriguing. "No to both." Her eyes cut to the other girl as she emerges from the manhole. "So *this* is what I wasn't told about."

The girl in the Mirror disguise doesn't answer her. Moving quickly and confidently, she replaces the metal grille and glances at Fanaka, who's gawking at the two city guards slumped against one of the trees in the courtyard. Whether the guards are dead or unconscious isn't clear.

The girl straightens up, dusting off her hands. "Where's the carriage?"

"Right around the corner," says the new girl.

"We must go."

Kamali and this new girl trade curious stares, each trying to glean answers from the other, and for Kamali, this only breeds more questions.

"Follow me," the girl says at last, then starts leading the way to the courtyard gate.

33: Jomo

The Summit

Jomo lures the Buffalo and his brother into the Ivory Drawing Room near the Summit's private wing, where he knows they can speak freely without the risk of eavesdroppers.

"Please take a seat, Your Highness," he says to the headman, gesturing at a plush armchair with zebra stripes.

Predictably, the man shares an incredulous look with his brother, then looks back at Jomo, the upper lip of his bovine face curling upward in anger. "A seat? You want to serve me tea and sweet cakes while you're at it? Show me whatever the devil it is and be done with it, boy."

Jomo bristles at his tone but keeps a facade of calm. He turns his back on the headman and walks to a credenza by the wall, where there's a crystal bottle of wine sitting next to empty glasses. Surreptitiously, he brings his pendant to his lips.

"Salo? Isa?" he whispers.

"Not yet," Salo says. *"Give us a minute."*

"I don't *have* a minute."

"Think of something. Just keep their attention for a while longer."

Jomo pours himself a glass of wine, leisurely. He can almost sense the Buffalo's rising anger like a wave of heat from across the room. He stretches every word when he speaks. "Your son, Fanaka. He's scheduled for execution in the arena today, is he not?"

The Buffalo emits a low growl. "What of it?"

Jomo dares to face the headman. "I know you hired people to break him free en route to the arena."

"Blackmail? Is that it?" The Buffalo's moongold teeth glisten with contempt. "Boy, if you want to blackmail someone, you've got to have something on them. You have nothing." Anger twists the headman's mask into an expression that almost chills Jomo's blood solid. "You have made a grave mistake, one you will pay for dearly. That is a promise. Come, brother. We have wasted enough time."

The brother sneers before he joins the headman, and Jomo almost wrings his hands as he watches them leave. "Salo, are you seeing this? It's over."

"One second."

"He's left."

"Stall him."

Jomo downs his glass in one gulp, trying to stave off the spell of vertigo threatening to knock him down. "Dear Mother, it's all over, isn't it."

"Now! Show it to him now!"

Breathless, Jomo hobbles after the Buffalo and his brother as fast as his bad leg will allow. The men are practically marching away, so it's almost a minute before he catches up to them in the domed hall outside the state room. "Wait!"

They don't stop.

With trembling hands, he fishes out an oval cipher shell from a pocket in his pants and activates it by pulling down on a lever, unleashing a mirage of Mirror light from its crystals.

"Father?"

The Buffalo stops. Turns around. Sees the vision. His brother gasps.

The face of a haggard young man with dreadlocks takes up much of the vision, and it looks like he's sitting inside a carriage with the curtains drawn. An ornate earring clings to his left ear, and he must be looking straight at the skimmer capturing the vision.

"Father, is that you? They said to tell you I'm all right, that I'm fine."

The Buffalo comes forward. The lines of his body have grown tense, but his mask is impenetrable. "What sorcery is this?"

Jomo takes a deep breath and tries for a confident voice. "This is your son, Your Highness. In *my* custody."

"A conjuring trick."

"Go ahead. Speak to him."

In the vision, the young man fidgets with his earring. *"Father? Is that you? I heard your voice."*

The Buffalo takes another step forward, tentative this time. "Is that really you, my boy?"

The young man's eyes widen with excitement. *"Yes, it's me, Father! I don't know how, but . . . I'm not in prison anymore. I'm alive. Can you see me? They said you could see me."*

The headman stares at the vision, seemingly at a loss, so his brother speaks in his stead. "There's a thin scar on your left shoulder. How did you get it?"

"Uncle, is that you? Oh, it's good to hear your voice!"

"Answer the question, Fanaka."

"The scar is on my right shoulder," Fanaka says. *"You caught me drunk and whipped me silly. Said I should know better than to invite the devil into my body."* His eyes cloud over with pain and regret. *"I guess I should have listened to you."*

"It's him, brother. That's Fanaka. By the Mother I swear it's him."

With the push of a lever Jomo banishes the mirage and pockets the shell. The Buffalo watches the motion of his hand with a dazed and hungry look. "But how?"

"That's not important," Jomo says, hardening his voice. "Your only concern should be what I plan to do with him next. I could keep him hidden, smuggle him out of the city, and hand him over to you at a time and place of your choosing. Or I could save myself the trouble and have him dropped off at the city guard garrison. He's not far from it right now. But what are the chances you'd ever see him alive again? The choice is yours."

The Buffalo takes an angry step forward. "Bastard."

"Your plans would have failed," Jomo says, standing his ground. "If I knew about them, the House of Law probably did too. I saved your son, and this is how you thank me?"

"What do you want?"

Why do they always ask me such an obvious question? "I think you know the answer to that, Your Highness."

"Bastard," he says again, a weak mutter this time, but Jomo knows he's already won, and the wave of relief that rushes over him is almost powerful enough to weaken his knees and bring him crashing to the floor.

34: Kamali

Skytown

Kamali's calloused hands tighten into fists, and he feels the skin stretching across his knuckles. Outside the glazed doors to the balcony of his second-floor guest room, the moon's pockmarked crimson disk is rising exactly above the Red Temple.

The All Axiom.

That is why he killed eight men and erased Mosi's, Ewa's, and then his own memories, ensuring that no one could pry the secret from their minds. He's certain of it now, because nothing else could have made the Pavilion of Discovery behave in the manner the Yerezi mystic has just described.

Kamali feels a knot of dread in his stomach. It's funny. He feared he'd regret his actions once he knew why he'd done what he'd done, but he never considered that he'd regret not having gone even further.

Earlier his rescuers made him wear a Mirror disguise and smuggled him into the emissary's crowded residence. Aside from a much-needed trip to the bathing pool, he's been confined to a vacant bedchamber. He didn't complain or resist, because he wanted his answers.

Now he almost regrets getting them.

He turns around to face the Yerezi mystic, the room's other occupant. "Why?" he says.

The mystic looks at him innocently, the dusky skies reflected on the circular lenses of his spectacles. "Why what?"

Why are you still alive? Why did I not kill you when I would gladly kill a hundred men right now just to keep your secret? "Why did you free me?" Kamali says. "I killed those men. I deserve my punishment."

The mystic hangs his head. "I . . . felt partly responsible for what you did. Perhaps you were too zealous, but you were defending me from the guards. I don't know where I'd be if you hadn't."

He's still wearing his muting collar—he doesn't know how he'll ever free himself of it—but Kamali feels essence rushing up from the moongold cell lodged at the base of his spine and spreading throughout his body. Deadly energy coils around his fists, and a razor edge creeps into his voice as he takes a step closer. "Do you realize the risk you've taken by bringing me here?"

"Of course I do," the mystic says, oblivious to the danger. "If anyone finds out I'm hiding you—"

"I mean the risk of being alone with me," Kamali says, taking another step. "I killed eight men to keep the All Axiom a secret. What makes you think I won't kill you right now? Because I'm struggling to find a reason I didn't do it the first time around."

The mystic gulps but, to his credit, stands his ground. "I'm no threat to you."

Kamali snickers, knowing he looks insane. "I say you're the biggest threat to this kingdom right now!"

"I don't know what you're talking about."

He's been steadily approaching the emissary, whose throat bobs again. The boy's gaze darts to the room's closed exit, but he must realize he'll never get there first, because he starts backing away toward the wall.

Kamali follows him. "What do you know about Ayana?"

"W-who?"

Kamali is—or was—a Blood mystic with the power of hypnosis; he knows a liar when he sees one, and the mystic is lying through his trembling lips. Kamali's voice hardens as he takes another step closer. "Tell me what you know about her."

"She's the Faraswa woman you fought with in the arena," the boy quickly replies. "I've heard she's become a hero to her tribespeople. I don't know much else."

"Are you working with her? You must be."

The boy's back hits the wall, confusion and fear creasing his face. "I've never met the woman in my life."

"You lie."

"It's the truth."

"What do you want from us?"

"From who, Kamali? You're not making sense!"

"From this kingdom! Why are you here?"

His nostrils flare, fear giving way to anger. "I just want to finish my pilgrimage and get the devil out of this city, all right? And I want my people to not have to go to war with yours in the future. Is that a good enough answer for you?"

"I don't know. Is that all you want?"

"Yes."

"Why, when you could have so much more?"

"I don't want more."

Kamali is now close enough to strike. He could lunge forward and snap the boy's neck before he ever knew what was happening. "With the power you wield, you could soak this whole continent in blood. Tell me why I shouldn't kill you right now."

"I'm not defenseless, Kamali." The boy is shaking, but Kamali senses truth in his threat. "I could hurt you. Don't make me. That's not why I freed you."

They watch each other, the tension between them electric and dangerous. Eventually, Kamali allows himself to take a calming breath. He regrets the deaths he caused, but his faith in his own judgment has been restored, for he now knows he had little choice. And if this mystic is still alive, it's because he decided to spare him. He should honor that decision, even if he doesn't remember why he made it.

He backs off slowly, returning to staring out the glazed doors to the balcony. "My apologies. This is all very confusing to me."

Behind him, the mystic lets out a long breath. "I understand. It must have been hard not knowing why you were locked up." When Kamali says nothing for a while, the boy adds, "I saw you fighting in the arena. It was one of the most horrible things I've ever witnessed, but the way you helped save lives was honorable."

Kamali turns to give him an odd look. "I killed eight men, threatened you in your own house, and you call me honorable?"

"I believe you were doing what you thought was right."

"Many atrocities have been committed in the name of what's right."

"True. But the line between right and wrong is always starker in hindsight. We can only do our best with what we know in the moment. I may not completely agree with your actions, but I know I'm probably still alive today because of you. For what it's worth, thank you."

Kamali studies him openly, and what he sees is a well-meaning boy who hasn't yet been corrupted by the immense power he holds, perhaps one who hasn't yet understood it. *Maybe this is why I spared him.*

The temple's giant ruby flashes like a beacon, sweeping the guest room with its strobing light. After six flashes, it dims again. Then a cry comes from below, a man shouting at the top of his voice.

"The Sentinels survive! The Sentinels survive! We're saved! The Sentinels survive!"

Kamali watches how the Yerezi emissary sags against the wall, tilting his head up in obvious relief. He figured out on his way here that the other prisoner was the Buffalo's son. He doesn't know what happened to him, but he suspects he was used in a trade that this emissary facilitated.

"Did you have something to do with this?" he asks, making sure not to sound judgmental. He's simply curious.

The boy lifts one corner of his lips in a smile. "Maybe. Do you not approve?"

"On the contrary, I've often felt that the mystics of my tribe are too removed from the struggles of the people we claim to serve. I'm glad someone did something to stop this genocide nonsense." He adds steel to his voice, looking the boy square in the eyes. "But I will be watching you, honored emissary. I don't know you and I don't quite trust you yet. Should I suspect you have harmful intentions for my people, you will answer to me. Understood?"

The boy nods. "Understood."

35: Musalodi

Midtown

Later that night, upon Alinata's urging, Salo, Ilapara, and Tuk follow her down to the city to partake in the Requiem festivities and to celebrate their victory. They join a long train of people walking along the gold-flecked roads of Skytown, some of whom are braving the outdoors for the first time in weeks.

The Yerezi Plains observe a similar holy day—on the sixth full moon of the year rather than the second—but it is often somber in character. Here the atmosphere is celebratory. People have come out in their numbers, wearing their ancestral masks and holding effigies of deceased loved ones. They swarm the bridges to Midtown, some carrying long sticks that shoot sparks into the river below. They spill out of the music halls, crowd around street musicians and masked dancers on stilts. They gyrate with their bodies pressed closely together, nothing but thin fabric separating their skins.

Colorful explosions light up the night sky, shooting up from parks, courtyards, and rooftops. Incense effuses from pots left burning on windowsills, spreading down the streets like mist. It is the Requiem Moon, so the streetlamps are tinged red, and the people have dressed in their traditional red beads, khangas, and sleeveless tunics. There is so much skin on display for once Salo isn't the least clothed person walking around.

A sonic boom blasts across the skies as a redhawk descends from the heavens, a fiery plume of brilliant light that arcs toward the waterfall.

"Students of the House of Forms are awakening," Tuk shouts as he stares up at the plume. "I reckon we'll be seeing more redhawks tonight than we've ever seen in our whole lives."

Incredibly, four more redhawks descend after that first one, each welcomed by cries of joy as it arrives. The last one circles the city after it lifts off from the base of the waterfall, and Salo shivers with memories of his awakening when it soars directly above him on its four massive wings. Then it envelops itself in flame, and there are gasps as it accelerates into the heavens with a crack of thunder and a lingering rumble.

Laughter and song fill the air. People dance and drink in their terraced gardens while others throw petals and confectionary down at passersby from their windows. Hawkers sell skewered meats and strong drinks from carts at every street corner. Tuk leads the group to one such cart and purchases coconut drinks for all of them, and a bundle of spark-emitting sticks for good measure. They join the flow of people moving through the hazy streets, gorge themselves on sweetmeats thrown at them, dance with the revelers beneath the light of the full moon, and by Ama, Salo wishes this night would never end.

Ilapara wouldn't part with her veil, but she's worn a brassiere of red beads that exposes the piercing on her navel. An endless parade of boys keeps coming to woo her, and they are strung along with coquettish smiles only to be turned away.

Tuk has worn color outside their house for the first time since Salo met him—a red khanga slung low around his hips. Admiring gazes keep raking over his ridiculous physique, and he soaks up the attention, becoming more talkative and flirtatious with each sip from his coconut. He tries to direct those energies toward Alinata, but the girl is aloof and distracted despite being the one who suggested the outing. Eventually

Tuk gives up, and Salo is delightfully scandalized when he trades amorous kisses with a pretty stranger who sticks a rose into his hair. The grin on his face as the girl walks away makes Salo howl with laughter.

Salo himself becomes the subject of attention when a rather strapping youth with a strong jawline shows interest in him, whispering things into his ear that make his cheeks flush. He's about to let the stranger lead him away when he's pulled back by the arm.

"Not tonight," Ilapara says, shaking her head. "You're too drunk." Lifting an eyebrow, she adds, "Besides, what would your ranger think?"

"He's not *my* ranger," Salo protests. "He has no say in what I do here." But Salo comes to his senses anyway and gives his admirer a regretful shrug.

"Come on," Ilapara says, nudging him along.

The full moon arcs over the skies, exciting the city below into a wild state. The air grows charged like a lightning bolt. A fight breaks out in a small Midtown park as Salo and the others wander past. The two belligerents trade blows to the face for a short while, but then they start cackling, embracing like two long-lost friends. They disappear into the crowds with arms intertwined, singing at the tops of their drunken voices.

"That's because of us, you know," Tuk says. He has to shout because there's so much music and laughter coming from everywhere. "It's not just Saires who're relieved tonight. Everyone will be making love, not war, because of what we did."

A primal urge builds up in Salo's chest, and he finds himself climbing onto the base of a street statue and giving a loud whoop. The revelers near him echo him, and suddenly the whole street is whooping and cheering, and for a second Salo feels like he's a king.

At some point he tells the others to wait for him while he takes a piss in a foggy alley, but as he returns, someone pushes him against the wall and surprises him with a firm kiss on the lips.

An enthralling fragrance fills his nostrils as he responds to the kiss, his drunken mind failing to offer a reason to resist. His hands wander over a silken gown, over lush curves and skin as soft as a dream. He falls into the kiss until at last he catches himself, pressing the mysterious woman back so he can look at her.

A goddess. A malaika of the red moon come to bless his mortal eyes. Her scarlet-and-violet gown is so sheer upon her bronzed skin he can see her breasts outlined in tantalizing detail. She stands before him unashamed in her obscenity, a carnal predator in the guise of a woman, and he knows he should run from her, for he has never desired a woman before—he didn't even think he could—but this woman's smile is a challenge he is powerless to escape. It says: *Are you a man? Prove it.*

Salo may be a coward, as he was told many times in the lands of his father, but he is still a man, only a man, flawed, weak, and drunk, and so he falls into the woman.

There, in the smoke-filled alley, beneath the bloody light of the Requiem Moon, he gives in to this strange new desire and loses himself in the woman's flesh, her lips, her skin, her breasts. He becomes so drunk with her touch that when the screams begin all around him, he's too far gone to notice.

36: Ilapara

Midtown

The night is hers, the world nestled in the palms of her hands. She dances with euphoric abandon beneath the moon's crimson light, and all the fears and concerns she once harbored about her future melt away in song and celebration.

She has finally found her place in the world. She has good friends now, people she cares for and who care for her too. Good people. People she would follow to the ends of the world, who she knows without a doubt would do the same for her. She's even grown fond of the Asazi despite her quiet and secretive ways and hopes that they will become better friends in time.

Salo slurs drunkenly about needing to empty his bladder and disappears into an alley. Ilapara dances with Tuk while they wait for him, and even though she knows he has eyes for the Asazi, and even though she usually goes for boys who are at least taller than she is, and even though there's one particular boy who's been on her mind of late, she allows herself to press her skin against Tuk, to let his hands roam her body, to let him kiss her on the lips.

A part of her knows it's a disastrous idea, but she kisses him back. At least until a woman breathes dust into her eyes as she passes by, temporarily blinding her. She coughs, wiping her eyes.

"What the devil do you think you're doing?" she demands, but the woman is already gone, and Ilapara is no longer where she was just seconds ago.

"Tuk?"

The young man isn't anywhere to be seen.

"Alinata? Salo?"

Strangers surround Ilapara. Somehow, between now and the woman blinding her, she has made it to the other side of Midworld Park, though she has no recollection of making the journey.

"Rise, my brothers and sisters of the Wavunaji, we who reap together!"

Confused, she turns around and sees that a mob has gathered within the park, hundreds of angry men and women carrying machetes, sickles, pikes, and knives that glisten viciously in the moonlight. An orator is standing before them, stirring them up into a frenzy.

"Tonight, we reap our vengeance, whether our headmen like it or not! We shall punish their treachery by killing their sons! We shall purge the Saire plague and those who sympathize with the enemy. Reap, Wavunaji!"

The revelers around Ilapara begin to disperse, pushing against her, some shrieking. Ilapara's feet remain rooted to the ground, her gaze fixed upon the mob. What bothers her, even in her inebriated state, is the obvious absence of city guards. A mob this size shouldn't have been able to gather without them intervening.

To her relief, she sees two men in the brown tunics of the city guard approaching the mob, their swords drawn. "Disperse immediately!" one of them shouts. "This is an illegal gathering. Disperse!"

"Your superiors told you to stay away," the orator shouts back. "I suggest you obey your orders!"

The guard spits onto the ground. "I don't take my orders from Wavunaji filth. Disperse!"

Ilapara knows that disobeying the commands of a city guard is punishable by imprisonment, and surely the members of this mob know this, too, yet they make no move to disperse. The air is too heavy with their anger and hatred.

"Kill the sympathizers!" shouts the orator, pointing a finger at the guards. "Kill them all! Begin the reaping! Tonight, the city is ours!"

Ilapara is quietly horrified as the first man rushes the two guards with his machete. He swings carelessly at the shorter of the two men, a move the guard easily evades and counters by hacking him in the neck three times until he falls, clutching uselessly at the gushing spray of blood. The guard probably aims to deter the rest of the mob with this aggressive display of violence, but to Ilapara's dismay, his actions do the opposite.

Five more Wavunaji rush the guards, who stand their ground, back to back, showing decent swordsmanship, hacking and slashing, felling men and women with their blades, but soon they are overwhelmed and are torn apart limb from limb before Ilapara's eyes, their mangled bodies kicked, hacked, and trampled on.

"Reap, Wavunaji! Storm the sanctuaries where the pests are hiding! Kill the sympathizers celebrating on the streets!"

In the ensuing chaos, Ilapara joins the crush of bodies fleeing the park, only to find that there are other armed mobs out on the streets, organized and purposeful, like they were waiting for this moment to come out.

She sees groups of foreigners from the undercity rushing to confront the mobs, joined by Sentinels, Faraswa, and independent mystics, but there are enough armed Wavunaji present to require an army to contain them, and the city guards are nowhere to be found.

Ilapara runs, trying not to fall, not knowing where she's going, her thoughts too muddled for reasoned thought. She didn't think she'd had that much to drink, but she's dizzy and confused. A mystic on the street ahead slings a desperate ball of fire that envelops one man, but the man's comrades continue rushing forward, and the mystic is soon engulfed. Ilapara turns around and flees the other way.

She glimpses a battle outside a grand building with a crimson orb suspended above its cupola—what she knows to be the largest sanctuary to the moon in this part of town. Her heart sinks when she counts only seven Sentinels fighting the mob to protect the entrance. Earlier in the week, many Saires took refuge in the city's sanctuaries, fearful of what would happen when they lost the Sentinels, and even after news of the vote broke, many chose not to leave. Ilapara knows that around two thousand people took refuge in that sanctuary. She can't watch as the mobs overwhelm the Sentinels and rush in through the door.

"Reap, Wavunaji, reap! Storm the sanctuary! Purge the plague!"

A bone-rattling roar fills the night, coming from Northtown. Two Wavunaji chop down a fleeing woman right in front of her. She wants to scream, she wants to fight, but her thoughts are out of control, and her heart is beating too fast.

"You!" With the woman dead, the two Wavunaji who slaughtered her set their eyes on Ilapara. "You have been judged guilty, sympathizer!"

She wants to cry out. She has never been so helpless in her life. The night started so well, but now it is blood and death.

As the Wavunaji run toward her, Ilapara twists her wrist to the left, summoning a stealth field from her wristband. The Wavunaji stop, confused as she vanishes from sight. And then she turns around and runs.

37 : Musalodi

Women crying out in the distance. Sentinels clashing with angry mobs who kill everything in sight. Blood runs thick where revelers danced only a while ago. Bodies float in the river. An arcane beast created for the arena is unleashed upon the streets to rip and tear, and its roars shake the walls of every building in the city.

Salo stumbles through the turmoil in his drunken haze, calling for his friends. The memory of being lost in a woman's flesh has turned to maggots beneath his skin, a violent vision like being swallowed whole by a python, nothing at all like what it felt like at the time. He was drunk before, but now he's in a trance, a waking nightmare soaked in blood.

She did something to me.

"Tuk? Ilapara? Alinata?"

They are nowhere in sight. They were all drunk too.

Salo looks around himself and sees that he's in a part of the city he doesn't recognize, and even though he's trying to move away from them, the roars and wails keep growing louder by the second.

And then, just ahead, the biggest lion he has ever seen turns onto the street. It emerges from the incense mists like a fiend from the underworld, its mouth wet with blood, its thick mane dancing in the air like fire—no, its thick mane *is* fire, angry and crimson like the Requiem Moon.

Two women were running in that direction. They turn around at the sight of the fiery beast, screeching in terror, and one of them collides with Salo as she passes him. The sky spins as he falls to the flagstone road, scraping his arms and getting his spectacles knocked off his face. Without the magic of his lenses correcting his cursed eyesight, brightness blinds his vision immediately.

"Reap your vengeance, Wavunaji! Kill the sympathizers! Wash the city with blood! Justice shall not be denied to us tonight!"

Salo fumbles for his spectacles on the road. His eyes fill with tears. He trembles with so much fear he wants to curl into a ball and weep.

Something powerful blows past him at a gallop, its spines bristling in anger, its roars making the earth tremble as it hurtles toward the fiendish lion.

"Mukuni? Please let that be you!"

It has to be, but a pernicious influence has twisted Salo's mind so he can't feel any of the tethers bound to him.

The scarlet woman. She poisoned me.

When leopard totem clashes with arcane lion on the street, their roars are so terrible the earth shudders from the force of them. Salo keeps pawing the ground for his spectacles, tears flowing down his cheeks like streams.

Then an outline darkens his vision, a presence looming over him, watching him curiously. He crawls back from it, an arm raised defensively, pleading, trembling, but the outline follows.

"You have been judged guilty, sympathizer. Your blood shall water the streets."

Salo squints up at the figure. "Please!"

"Reap, Wavunaji! Reap your vengeance!"

The outline raises something and swings it at Salo's face, and the world goes out.

Interlude: The Lover

Through a breach in the Veil, the Adversary reaches with her mind and becomes a solid presence near a lake of sorrows. There she faces an ancient spirit who feeds on hopelessness and weariness with the world.

"Show me," she says to the spirit.

"Do you not tire of coming here?" the spirit asks. *"You have lived longer than most, yet all you have known is sorrow. Has it not weighed enough on your soul? Would it not be better to finally give yourself the peace you crave?"*

Not for the first time in her many dances with the spirit, the Adversary finds that she is tempted. How liberating would it be to finally let go of her crusade, to simply reject this universe and its injustice, to finally be at peace?

Then she becomes aware of her surroundings and sees that the spirit has pierced through her shield of rage and has coiled one of its thin black tendrils around her neck. Her rage strengthens, shearing the tendril cleanly. The spirit roars in pain while its amputated limb dissipates harmlessly around the Adversary as smoke.

"Show me," she says, and the spirit has no choice but to comply.

This time she lives through the last memories of a lover choking on dust somewhere beneath the rubble of a collapsed mine. He can't feel his right arm, and by the wetness dripping down his side, he's losing blood. He knows he can't have much time left, so he spends his last breath singing the songs he used to sing with him, the man he should not have dared to love.

They were the best of friends until the day they went fishing together, just the two of them, side by side by the lakeshore. It was the day his friend reached for his hand and allowed his face to finally reveal what he truly felt for the lover. Friendship, yes, but something deeper too.

As his blood slowly seeps from his veins, the lover remembers the fear he saw in his friend's eyes that day, as though the fate of the world hinged on how he responded to the silent confession. He remembers how his own heart stopped when he felt the warmth of his friend's hand on his, how his friend smiled tentatively, as if to ask, finally, if the lover felt the same way.

He remembers how his friend lit up when he smiled back, how the sun was like a drop of molten gold sinking into the horizon, clouds set ablaze like tinder in a purple sky. It was an ephemeral light show, a brief window into the soul of a god, as fleeting as it was glorious, as glorious as the kiss he shared with his friend, and the night they spent together, and the songs they sang in the morning.

Then the priests of their village descended upon their homes with fetters and manacles, telling them that their love and songs were sick. Diseased. An offense against the gods themselves. In disgrace they were thrown down separate mines to toil for atonement, as though they had stained themselves and needed to be cleansed.

Here is the lover now, bleeding out in a lonely cavity far beneath the surface of the earth. He will never finish his song, and his body will never be found. No one will ever speak his name again. Just another forgotten victim crushed beneath the cruel boot of an indifferent universe—a universe the gods refuse to fix.

There will be a reckoning for them, and for heaven itself, even if it is the last thing the Adversary will ever do.

PART 4

ISA
*
MUSALODI
*
ILAPARA
*
JOMO

Red steel:

Known only to the reclusive Yerezi tribe, red steel is an essence-transfigured steel variant whose method of production remains a closely guarded secret. Limited study of the material suggests that it is competent both as a receptacle for raw essence and as a medium for storing and processing arcane ciphers, which would make it the only such material known to exist.

Given the apparent low costs of its production and the abundance of its base materials, red steel has the potential to completely replace moongold in the world of enchanting, a development whose positive economic impact across the Redlands would be difficult to overstate. However, concerted efforts to purchase—or steal—the secret of its manufacture from the Yerezi tribe have proved fruitless.

From On Arcane Materials, *an encyclopedia published by the House of Forms*

38: Isa

The Red Temple

Isa slips out of the Void and arrives at the Meeting Place by the Sea with Jomo and Obe on either side of her. She itches to remove the mask-crown but keeps it on as a buffer between the world and her emotions.

Kola Saai is waiting for them by the beach, staring out at the glittering sea while letting the swash of breaking waves wet his bare feet. It's twilight in the construct, and the suns have just set, leaving a wide orange band just above the watery horizon.

Isa suffers a wave of revulsion at the sight of him standing there, looking like a normal human being. Monsters like him should look exactly like what they are.

He's taken off his mask and is holding it in one of his hands, which are clasped behind him. As they approach, he turns around with a sparkle in his eye. "Mother's grace, Your Majesty. It is good to see you again."

"Would that I could say the same," Isa says.

The Crocodile grins at her, then nods at Jomo. "Herald. I have to congratulate you on your success with the Mkutano. Well played. I didn't think you had it in you. Clearly you are your mother's son."

Jomo fumes next to Isa, though he manages to keep himself from shouting. "And you're a murderer. Thousands died that night because of you."

"You're not really blaming me for that, are you?" the Crocodile says. "I had nothing to do with the Wavunaji. They killed some of my own people, you know. I was as shocked as everyone else."

For once, Isa believes the man, though she refrains from admitting it. The true power behind the Bloody Requiem, as it has come to be called, had reach well beyond Kola Saai's means, and though she suspects she knows who this power is, and though this suspicion fills her with so much guilt she weeps herself to sleep every night, she knows she must walk the path set for her, for it is the only way to give her people a hope that will endure.

There's no hope for me. Not in this life. But there can be hope for everyone else.

"Is that what you do to sleep better at night?" Jomo says. "Blame other people for your crimes?"

"I have committed no crimes," the Crocodile says. "In fact, I've heard that a Yerezi sorcerer with designs on this city was behind it all. So it's him you should be glaring at, not me."

"Nonsense," Isa says even as a second wave of guilt washes over her.

"Come now, Your Majesty." The Crocodile gestures at Obe with an open palm. "I have a nephew in the Sentinels. I have no children, so he's second in line to my princedom behind my idiot brother. Do you really think I'd put one of my own heirs at risk? He might be stubborn as a wild bull, but he's blood, and I promised to take care of him when his father passed on." The Crocodile smirks at Obe, who bristles silently. "Looks like I might have done too good a job, though. Look at him. Proud and brave like a true crocodile." The smirk wanes into something that resembles concern. "Whatever happened to your arm, nephew?"

"Murderer," Obe spits between clenched teeth. "I have nothing to say to you."

"You're young and naive, dear Obe. And you're in love. Your judgment is so clouded you couldn't find your own ass if you had to. What young man in love has ever made a good decision?"

Isa decides this has gone on long enough. "Let's come to the point, shall we? My people are still in danger even with the Sentinels preserved. I want your forces to step in and protect them, as you once promised you'd do."

"Is that a command or the start of a negotiation?"

"We're negotiating."

"And what do I get in return?"

"What you've always wanted. Me."

The Crocodile's shrewd gaze scours the three of them for a long while. "I'm not playing this game again, Your Majesty," he finally says. "Your cousin refused to negotiate bride-price in good faith. I must admit, it was an effective stalling tactic."

"This is the negotiation," Isa says. "So what's your offer?"

He makes an amused face. "That's not how this usually goes. In fact, neither of us should be involved."

"I am a king and you are a prince. We can do whatever we want."

"Fair enough." He considers her. "One hundred pieces of moongold."

"Done."

Surprise briefly shows in his expression, as though he expected she'd be more difficult. "Your mask-crown will be destroyed so the Shirika can crown me king. A new totem can be fashioned for your people if you want."

Isa tries to remember why she's doing this. "So long as you put it in writing at the House of Law that the Sentinels will remain obedient to the Saire prince and that no further attempts to disband them will be made for another five hundred years."

"That can be arranged. Another condition: my current wife will remain, but she will become my second wife, and you will be my first."

"Fine, but she will have to move out of the Summit and live in your province and will not come to the city without my permission."

"Acceptable. You will give me a son in our first year of marriage, another in our second, then a daughter in our third."

Silent rage boils off the two boys next to her, and she fears it'll not remain silent for much longer, so she decides to bring the meeting to an end. "I agree to your terms. The wedding shall be two weeks from today."

"One week from today."

The mask conceals Isa's spike of worry. Salo is still recovering. Ten days might not be enough for him to enter the sanctum and return. "Why the hurry?" she says. "I'm not going anywhere."

"The sooner this can be resolved, the better. I'm tired of waiting. The wedding will be in a week, or there will be no wedding at all."

She grits her jaws. "Fine."

He regards her with a critical eye, as if trying to see if there is a trick somewhere in play. "You know, I'm curious why you still want this marriage. You still have the Sentinels to protect your people. You clearly have more sway over the Mkutano than I do. I'd say you've been winning this battle so far. So why go through with this?"

Jomo and Obe asked her the same thing, and if she knew only what they know, she might have agreed with them and put a stop to any talk of marrying her enemy.

But she knows better. The wedding was always going to happen.

"I'm tired of hiding," she says. "And we both know you won't stop until you get what you want. This is the only way to end this conflict without more bloodshed."

The Crocodile must be content with her explanation because he nods. "You are wise beyond your years, Your Majesty. I look forward to seeing you on our wedding day and making you my wife. And who knows, maybe in time you'll come to see that I'm not nearly as bad a person as you think I am."

That will be the day, Isa tells herself, and then she disappears with Jomo and Obe back into the harsh infinity of the Void.

39: Musalodi

Southtown

Brightness. Numbness. The feeling of rising through a thick, endless sea of sludge. The clicking of shoes on a marble floor. The scraping of a steel chair. Voices nearby. Why is death so tedious?

Light assaults Salo's eyes when he blinks them open. He shuts them with a groan. He tries to speak, but it's as if there is a giant rock sitting on his tongue. His body feels numb.

"Good morning, honored emissary. Can you hear me?" A woman's voice, familiar. The whiff of perfume, mingling with the pungent scent of something antiseptic. "I was told you'd be a bit . . . befuddled. Please nod if I'm not talking to myself here."

Salo finds that he can nod, but he feels like there's a cold and solid weight wrapped around his neck.

"Excellent. Now, you may not recognize my voice, so allow me to reintroduce myself. I am Inquisitor Anika Akili of the Prism, arcane investigator of the city guard. I came to your residence seeking to apprehend a list of suspects. Remember?"

Suspects. Saires hiding in his palace. Saires slaughtered on the streets. A scarlet woman. Tuk! Ilapara! Alinata!

He reaches for his mental bond with Tuk, but his mind remains empty. Even his connection to Mukuni is dead.

"I'm sure you're wondering where you are, so perhaps I should start there. You are currently in the intensive care ward of the House of Life in Southtown. You've been here for the better part of a week, ever since the night of the Requiem Moon. You sustained severe head injuries during the Wavunaji riots. Do you remember?"

Salo tries to talk. He needs to know if they made it. Dear Ama . . .

"Please calm down. They said to tell you not to attempt speech. I just need you to listen, all right? Nod if you understand me."

He gasps, feeling like his heart is about to tear his chest open and leap out.

"Calm down, honored emissary. Please, we have much to discuss. Nod if you understand."

It takes a while, but Salo forces his body to go lax; then he nods.

"Good. I'm sure it must be distressing for you, but yes, you've been recovering for the last several days, and this is the first time your healers have allowed you to awaken. In fact, under ordinary circumstances, they would not have allowed it at all, but the circumstances that have brought me here demand exception."

The venom pouring out of her sweet voice scares Salo like nothing has before.

"You see, dire as your situation may be, you are among the more fortunate casualties of the Bloody Requiem. Over four thousand souls perished that night. Many of them butchered in sanctuaries across the city. The Sentinels lost a quarter of their number, the city guard a tenth, and four headmen lost sons to the violence. The entire kingdom is in mourning."

The voice begins to move, shoes clicking on the floor. She must be pacing.

"We knew to expect violence regardless of the outcome of the Mkutano, but the scale of it by far outstripped our expectations given the positive result for the Saire people. The Wavunaji were too organized. They swept across the city too quickly, moved as a unit rather than a loose group of disorderly mobs. It almost looked like they were . . .

responding to the directions of one coherent voice. We had no choice but to launch an inquest. Would you like to know what we found? Please nod if you're still with me."

Salo obeys despite the cold thing gripping his neck. *What is that?*

"Good. Shortly after apprehending all the surviving culprits, we found that each and every one of them exhibited the same symptoms: confusion, headaches, vertigo, hallucination. So we conducted full-body examinations to determine the cause. Lo and behold, they were all suffering from the residual effects of powerful hypnotic suggestion."

The Akili stops. Salo feels her gaze boring into him. "You are probably wondering why I'm telling you this—or perhaps you're not. Either way, honored emissary, the facts tell us that a single malevolent entity is behind the Bloody Requiem, and we have reason to suspect that this malevolence is the same force behind the prison break earlier that day." The Akili's presence draws nearer. "Are you with me, honored emissary?"

Terror grips Salo's being and forces him to nod.

"Excellent. Now, here are the facts as we know them. When you were brought in, your blood was found to contain traces of a stimulant known to enhance hypnotic ability. Then a test of your cosmic shards confirmed that your Axiom is indeed strongly responsive to Blood craft. Additionally, when your healers attempted to sedate you for surgery, they encountered a mental barrier so powerful the only solution was to put you under with near-toxic doses of alchemical opiates. In sum, honored emissary, you're obviously a talented Blood mystic, a fact bolstered by the presence of your cat fiend on the streets that night. We even have eyewitness reports that you continued to direct the beast even after your conveniently nonlethal injury."

What? These are lies! I can't even do Blood craft yet. And none of that proves I had anything to do with the riots. Salo screams the words in his head, but his lips fail to move.

"Over three weeks ago you borrowed several books from the libraries at the House of Forms, among them a treatise on complicated

503

enchantments. A day after the Requiem, we found this in the undercity sewers. You can't see it, so let me tell you what it is: this is an artifact in the form of a venomous skimmer fly. Its power has been drained, but analysis of its cipher core revealed it contains several layers of complex enchantments that in theory should not coexist on something so small. It was clearly enchanted by a talented mystic, using techniques described in the treatise you borrowed."

The Akili's shoes click on the floor as she approaches his bed. "Imagine my surprise when I found records that prove how you, honored emissary, against regulations governing the sale of enchanted artifacts, purchased a cipher shell with a swarm of venomous skimmer flies from a Midtown trinket store. Imagine my further surprise when we discovered that the sting on our little skimmer had been coated with a potent soporific compound, the same compound we suspect was used on the guards during the prison breakout."

Salo trembles where he lies, unable to speak.

"I will be frank with you, honored emissary. The facts do not paint a pretty picture for you. We might not have enough to arrest your associates yet, but I promise that by the time you recover, the only place you will be going is straight to the dungeons to await your trial. In the meantime, as is customary for all mystics suspected of a crime, you've been collared to mute your sorcery. The collar will come off only if you're exonerated of all charges against you."

Salo can't see the Akili, but he feels a spiteful sense of triumph radiating from her. "I warned you, didn't I? You played a dangerous game, and you lost. Now you pay the price."

Her footsteps recede. A door opens. Inside his mind, Salo yells for help.

"Rest now, Emissary Siningwe. We will be seeing each other soon."

40: Ilapara

Outside the imposing entrance to the House of Life in Southtown, Ilapara bunches her eyebrows together as she watches Tuk pace like a caged hound after scenting blood.

It's been seven days since the Requiem Moon, when they last saw Salo on the streets of Midtown. Somehow they all got separated when the killings began, and it was only through her stealth charm that she survived the night, learning the next morning that Salo had been injured and was lying unconscious in the city's main center of medicine.

Ilapara has come here with Tuk every day since they found out, but the receptionists won't let them see him, and the Jasiri guarding the entrance now know not to let them into the building.

"I can't take this anymore," Tuk says. He stops and stares at the entrance, his eyes full of intent. "I'm disguising myself and going in."

"Don't be stupid," Ilapara tells him. "This place is warded, not to mention the Jasiri on duty. You'll only get us in trouble."

He turns around, glaring up at her. "Well, do you have a better idea?"

She bites off a retort and glares back. They've been snappish with each other of late, quick to point out each other's flaws, blaming themselves and each other for letting Salo out of their sight on the Bloody Requiem. As if anyone could have predicted what was coming.

"Let's just be patient," she says. "You know he's alive because your blessing is still active. That means sooner or later, he'll have to come out through those doors. I know you want to see him; so do I. But let's not make things worse by getting ourselves arrested."

Tuk breathes in loudly, but then his shoulders slump. "You're right." He tilts his head up to the sky, tears shining in his eyes. "What the devil happened, Ilapara? Why did things go so wrong?"

She wipes her own eyes. Her core is a pit of anger, dismay, and sorrow. "I don't know."

There has been no acknowledgment of what happened on the night of the Requiem Moon from either the Summit or the Shirika. The city was cleared of bodies, the blood mopped away, the culprits apprehended, and that was that. All Ilapara and Tuk have heard are whispers that someone is being primed to take the fall for all of it. No one's made anything official yet, but they both suspect they know who this someone is, and this suspicion makes Ilapara sick to her stomach.

She also suspects the Asazi knows something. Alinata has been especially quiet since Salo's disappearance, locking herself in her chambers all day long or sitting by the veranda when it rains and staring into space. Like she's guilty of something. If she could, Ilapara would strangle the truth out of her. But she can see that whatever's eating her up will break her.

Let her stew in it.

"You there!" a voice shouts.

Ilapara and Tuk both turn to look and are surprised to see a woman in black robes walking toward them from the building's entrance, accompanied by a pair of angry-looking city guards. She points a long finger in their direction.

"Wait right there! I have questions for you."

Ilapara glances nervously at Tuk. By her moongold jewelry and her manner of dress, this woman is clearly a mystic. Ilapara prepares herself to run if need be, but a subtle headshake from Tuk tells her he's read her intent and decided it's a bad idea.

"Where is he?" the mystic demands, her face twisted with fury.

Tuk frowns at Ilapara, who shrugs in ignorance. "What are you talking about, honored Akili?" he asks her.

"Don't treat me like a fool. Test me, and I will make your lives a living hell. Where have you taken him?"

"Taken whom, honored Akili?" Tuk says, displaying genuine confusion. "We've been standing here all morning. The Jasiri haven't let us in." He registers alarm as he realizes what she's asking. "Are you talking about our mystic? Do you mean to tell us he's not here?"

"Emissary Siningwe was taken from his ward this morning," the mystic says in an accusing voice. "He's no longer in the House of Life. You will tell me where you have taken him this instant."

Shock and anger knock the sense out of Ilapara, and she forgets who she's talking to. "How could you let this happen? How could you just lose someone like that?"

She's annoyed when Tuk raises a placating palm and comes in between her and the mystic. "Forgive her, honored Akili. We're not mystics, and these premises are guarded by Jasiri. We've wanted to see our friend for days now, but they haven't let us in. How could we have snuck past them and stolen him? We don't even know his condition!"

The mystic seems to calm down. "I suppose you couldn't have done it yourselves." Her brow furrows. "But I'll be watching the two of you carefully. Do not attempt to leave the city until further notice."

She starts to walk away, but Ilapara isn't done with her just yet. "What happened to him?" she shouts. "Is he all right? What do you want with him?"

Ilapara makes to follow the damned woman, but Tuk pulls her back, shaking his head. "Not a good idea."

She glowers at him, a harsh remark on the tip of her tongue, but then she sees her own panic in his eyes. "What do we do now?" she says.

He looks toward the entrance to the House of Life, where they'd hoped to see Salo coming out after his recovery. "I don't know, Ilapara," he says. "Maybe we should just go home."

41: Jomo

Red Temple

He looks so weak, Jomo thinks.

As he stands in Salo's room in the citadel's medical wing, watching as a votary raises the incline of his bed so that he's partially sitting up, it strikes Jomo that this is the first time he's ever laid eyes on the Yerezi mystic. It doesn't feel that way, but all their previous meetings have been in the construct, where the mystic always looked dignified and princely despite his unusual manner of dress. Here, with bandages swathing his forehead, a metal collar locked around his neck, and the gauntness of infirmity giving him sunken cheeks, he looks rather vulnerable. And young.

"Can he hear us?" Isa says as she watches him from near his bed. Jomo wants to be here when he wakes up, too, and has chosen to lean against the wall facing the foot of the bed.

"I believe so, Your Majesty," the votary says. "The stimulant should have woken him by now."

"Leave us."

The votary bows. "As you wish."

When he leaves, Isa sits down next to the bed and takes Salo's hand. She has tears in her eyes, which she lets flow. Seeing them makes Jomo ache with sorrow.

"Are you awake, Salo?" she says.

He blinks, and Jomo catches an unsettling glimpse of eyes like the inside of a faceted diamond. The daylight coming in through the windows must be too bright, because he winces and keeps his eyes shut. He nods, which makes Jomo smile.

"Hey, Salo," he says. "You have absolutely no idea how good it is to see you. You had me scared for a while."

Salo begins to breathe in and out rapidly, his face contorting into a grimace. He moves his lips, but no voice comes out.

"I think he wants to know about his friends," Jomo says. "The last thing he remembers was being attacked, so he's probably sick with worry."

Salo nods several times, tears escaping his closed eyes, prompting Isa to wrap his hand tighter with both of hers. "Please, don't despair. Your friends are all right. They're at your residence in Skytown, and they know you're alive. They just don't know where you are right now."

"I'll send them a message later today," Jomo says.

"Your cat familiar, however . . ." Isa continues. "I'm sorry to tell you that he was injured during the encounter with the arena beast. I'm told he stayed by your side after killing it, but when the healers came for you, he hauled himself back to your residence and turned into a metal statue. I'm not sure that's a good thing, but I thought you should know."

By the relief Jomo sees washing over Salo's face, perhaps the cat's fate is not as dire as they thought. "And by the way," Jomo says, "you're in the medical wing of the Red Temple. The high priest had you stolen away from the House of Life this morning."

"You're safe here," Isa tells him in a reassuring voice. "You're among friends, receiving the best care the temple can provide. I don't know if they told you this at the House of Life, but you suffered a head injury during the Wavunaji riots. Do you remember?"

More tears spill from Salo's eyes as he nods, and Jomo's heart breaks for him. Jomo himself spent the Requiem Moon celebrating with Isa and their trusted group of Sentinels in the safety of the temple, so he can only imagine what it must have felt like to be on the streets when the attacks began.

"The riots claimed many lives," Isa tells Salo, "but they would have claimed tens of thousands more had you not . . ." Her voice falters, and she wipes her eyes. "You're still recovering, so let me not burden you with the details. But you do need to know that inquisitors of the city guard are trying to blame you for what happened. I think they know you helped us, Salo, and I think they want to punish you for it."

Salo releases a sob that makes Jomo's own eyes prickle and his heart well with anger on his behalf. The guy doesn't deserve this.

"So we stole you from your ward and brought you here," Isa continues. "I'm sure you noticed the collar around your neck. We haven't managed to take it off yet, but there's someone capable working on the matter. He assures me you won't be wearing it for much longer."

Isa begins to draw idle circles inside Salo's palm. "Look, I need to be honest with you," she says. "We brought you here because this is the safest place for you right now, and I made a promise to help you complete your pilgrimage. But I also need your help. And yes, I know this is terrible of me to ask seeing as you've already helped me so much, but time is not on our side, and if we act quickly, we could do away with these bogus charges that have been laid at your feet. Are you with me, Salo?"

Jomo feels his forehead creasing. He didn't know Isa was going to bring this up now. Why not wait until the guy is on his feet before putting more burdens on his shoulders?

Isa waits for Salo to nod before she goes on. "I've found a solution to the threat Kola Saai poses, a way to strip him of power and remove the lines that divide my people once and for all. Should I succeed, my tribe would never have to go to war with yours, and those who now seek your destruction would be unseated from their thrones. But this solution lies within the inner sanctum of this temple, where I cannot enter. You, on the other hand, are here to complete the Bloodway and could retrieve this solution if you chose."

Jomo isn't sure how he feels about what Isa is doing, but he thinks she means it when she presses a kiss on Salo's hand and speaks in a voice so low he almost misses it. "You're the answer to my prayers, Salo. It's the only thing that makes sense. When I lost everything, I wished with the petals of bloodrose for a malaika to help me, and the Mother sent me you. I won't ask for your answer right now. I only beg that you think about it." She kisses his hand again, wetting it with her tears. "You will be well in just a few days. That is a promise."

And then she leaves the room without saying a word to Jomo. He'd like nothing more than to follow and interrogate her, but he decides to take her place on the chair next to Salo's bed and try to cheer him up with coarse humor and lively gossip.

He even manages to make Salo crack a smile, but Jomo's thoughts remain troubled, and his paranoia grows.

Was what happened to Salo truly an accident or part of Isa's game to get him to do her bidding?

He didn't think she would be capable of such scheming, but she's been keeping secrets from him since the beginning. How much of this is the high priest's doing, and how much is hers?

Mother, do I really know my cousin?

42: Musalodi

Red Temple

Salo blinks as the three figures before him come into startlingly clear focus. He's sitting on a stiff wooden chair in an airy room somewhere above a waterfall, wearing only a white linen loincloth, a slim steel collar around his neck, and layers of gauze around his forehead.

"How do they feel?" the king says. "Can you see? We could get them remade if they're not any good."

Salo pushes his new spectacles up the bridge of his nose. On a superficial level they almost look and feel like his old ones: thin, circular rims; reflective lenses; a frame as light as air. But the frame on these is moongold, not copper, and is enchanted with spells he cannot begin to decipher because of the collar around his neck. Also, the lenses, though dark, don't glaze the world with a smoky sheen—which he didn't even know his old spectacles were doing until now.

Now the colors around him really *pop* to his eyes, and when he aims his gaze at the glowing ruby mounted on the wall across the room, he's able to see the little nicks and blemishes on its many sides.

"They're terrible, aren't they," the king says despondently.

Jomo rolls his eyes at her. "Perhaps we should let him speak for himself." He raises an eyebrow in Salo's direction. "So? Are we still blind as a bat or what?"

Salo chuckles, though the high mystic of the Arc, who is sitting next to Jomo, doesn't appear amused by his playful remark. "Actually, the spectacles are fantastic." Salo looks out the door, which opens to a cloistered walkway with a lawn beyond it. "I haven't seen this well in . . . such a long time."

"The lenses are crystallized with microscopic moongold particles," says the Arc. "They were fashioned at the House of Axles using recently discovered techniques. You're not actually seeing through your eyes."

"I'm not?" Salo says, surprised.

"No. Your eyesight is being suppressed in favor of what the lenses are seeing, which deliver their vision directly to your optic nerve. Even so, the enchantment is efficient enough to draw on ambient essence, just like your last pair, meaning you will never need to worry about charm depletion."

Before he could see, the Arc's cavernous voice gave Salo the impression of grandfatherly patience and a kindly bearing. But such a description could hardly befit the dark-complexioned man sitting across the room in his red-and-cream-colored robes. His head is shaved. A labyrinth of thin scars spans his face in deliberate designs, as if a carver mistook his face for a slab of stone. His stern expression is reminiscent of a bird of prey, like someone for whom the wielding of power is neither joyous nor burdensome but a simple fact of his existence.

And King Isa . . . a slight change occurs in the way Salo sees her, like a subtle shift in the breeze. She's the same person, with the same voice and the same striking features. But now, where he once thought her intelligent but otherwise naive, he discerns the glint of guile in the depths of her amber eyes.

"Thank you," he says. "All of you. You could have left me to rot in—"

"Not another word, Salo," Jomo interjects, lifting a hand to cut him off. "What you've done for us—what you're still doing for us—we could never repay you. These glasses are the least we could do."

"And you'll need them if you're going to keep helping us," Isa adds. "So it's not an entirely selfless gift."

"Thank you anyway."

"You're welcome." The king briefly glances at the old sorcerer, and by the pinched look on her face, she's about to broach an uncomfortable topic. "Not to push you or anything—"

"Your Majesty . . . ," the Arc says in caution.

"I need to ask, Your Worship." Looking back at Salo, she says, "I know you're still recovering, but I need to know when you'll be ready to step into the inner sanctum. My wedding is in four days. I need to have the item with me by then."

Salo settles deeper into his chair, silently berating himself for getting into this mess. His pilgrimage is supposed to be an opportunity to gain wealth for his tribe; now, with the trouble he has brewed for himself in this city, he has no choice but to use his boon to help the KiYonte king instead.

The worst part about all of this is that Tuk and Ilapara warned him not to overreach. Pleaded with him, in fact, not to involve himself in local politics, but he was only thinking about pleasing his queen. And because of the power of his metaform, he fooled himself into thinking he could do anything.

Now look where I am.

He has no choice but to go along with whatever these people want. They're his only hope for leaving this city alive. And when he does eventually leave, he'll be going back home empty handed, proving his detractors right once and for all.

The wound on his left temple has yet to heal, but he feels much better now that they're not keeping him sedated. If only they could take off the damned collar around his neck. "I can go in today, if you want."

The Arc shakes his head in refusal. "The final steps of the Bloodway are treacherous. If you're not at your peak—mentally, emotionally, and physically—you'll never make it."

"We don't have time for him to make a full recovery, Your Worship," Isa says.

"I know, and yet we must spend some time in meditation and prayer before we attempt the journey. Perhaps he will be ready tomorrow."

The way the Arc phrases those words catches Salo's attention. "Will you be coming with me, Your Worship?"

"As high priest, I guide all pilgrims through the first steps of the journey. But you will have to face the innermost sanctum on your own."

"What's in the sanctum, exactly?"

"The Shrouded Pylon."

"Yes, but what is it?"

The Arc's eyes shine with secrets. "If you've never seen it, I cannot tell you what it is."

"What about the item he's supposed to retrieve?" Jomo asks, his gaze wandering between Isa and the high mystic. "You both seem sure it'll help, but you haven't said how."

Isa straightens out the folds of her white dress in her lap. "I trust His Worship's judgment. If he believes it'll help, then I know it will."

"But how will I find it?" Salo asks.

"You need only wish for it, and it will be yours," the Arc says. "It will know that you have need for it and will make itself known to you. I'm sorry, but that is all I can say. Matters of the inner sanctum cannot be spoken of by those who have not set foot within its walls. I'm sure you will understand by this time tomorrow."

Not a satisfying answer, but Salo decides to let his questions go. "I'll be ready whenever you say I'm ready, Your Worship."

"Then it's settled," the Arc says. "Today and tonight, you prepare. At dawn tomorrow, you will step into the inner sanctum."

It rains that night. Thunder ripples across the skies, joining the roaring waterfalls in a dissonant chorus that does away with whatever tranquility Salo gained from meditating all throughout the day. He tosses and turns on his bed until sleep flees his bones entirely.

He stares blankly into the dark. On the night of the Requiem Moon, he left his metaformic amulet in his study before they went out to celebrate. But his extensive use of it established a strong mental tether with the amulet, one whose echo he can still feel even with the collar around his neck. Closing his eyes, he reaches for the tether with his mind, blocking out all his senses, the sound of the rain, the feel of the sheets on his skin. His world becomes nothing but this tether as it grows more solid in his mind's eye; then, after minutes of silent concentration, he pulls.

A white expanse appears all around him, blocks of electrified glass floating in the sky. He sees them as spectral outlines rather than solid objects, however, and even Ziyo's nebula is less a cloud than a smudge of color. He feels the metaform trying to communicate with him, but it's like there's a wall between them.

A bed has materialized in the construct, the same one he's lying on in his chamber. Salo sits down on one corner and rubs his palms together as he waits, his stomach a pit of nerves. Sure enough, a ranger in crimson soon appears, his face the picture of worry. Salo gets up on shaky feet to meet him.

"Where have you been?" Niko says, coming forward like he wants to embrace Salo but thinking twice about it and settling for placing a hand on his shoulder. "I was worried I'd upset you and you didn't want to see me again."

Salo looks fixedly at Niko's chest so he doesn't have to look into his eyes. "I'm not upset with you."

"Then what?" Niko's voice rises an octave as he leans closer to inspect Salo's bandages. "What happened? Were you hurt?"

Salo had forgotten about that, but it's a construct, so he thinks the bandages away to remove the distraction. "It's nothing," he says, rubbing his newly healed temple. "I'm fine."

Niko lets out an exasperated sigh. "Talk to me, Salo."

Looking at the floor, Salo says, "I don't care anymore."

"About what?"

"If you're real. Or not real. If you really feel what you say you feel. If anyone else will know, or what they'll think. I don't care anymore." Finally, Salo forces himself to lift his gaze and look Niko in the eye. "I'm just . . . tired of feeling so alone."

Recognizing the substance of Salo's confession, Niko glances at the bed, then back. His eyes darken with heat, but his voice remains measured. "Are you sure?"

Salo doesn't let himself think about it. He nods, and his heart races like a galloping beast as Niko leans forward to kiss him, slowly, like he thinks Salo might change his mind. Then their lips finally meet, and Salo's expectations of what the kiss of a lover should feel like are rendered completely inaccurate, for Niko's skin is hotter than Salo imagined, the taste of him more complex, not just sweet, as he thought it might be, but also electric and powerful. Forceful. A taste that goes straight down his spine and deep into his soul.

He fought it for so long, but now he gives in to it completely, and they fall onto the bed, the rest of the night melting away in the heat.

Dawn sees him arriving at the entrance to the sanctum with the high priest. It is in the main temple structure at the center of the citadel, down a winding staircase, past a circular pool of rosy water, and down a dim corridor, at the end of which stands a pair of large doors with golden doorknobs. Despite the muting collar on his neck, Salo's cosmic shards tingle unpleasantly as he approaches.

This morning the Arc has a distant, almost unsympathetic look to his eyes, and his red robes are so simple as to be austere. Salo offers him a greeting, but the man wastes no time with idle pleasantries. "Before we begin our journey," he says, "I will give you the same warning I give to all those I guide through the sanctum, the same warning my predecessor gave me when I stood where you now stand. Your mind, soul, and body are about to be tested, and in each test you will learn things that will drastically change the way you see the world. It's quite possible that these changes will be so distressing to you they will plunge you into madness, as they have many others who have gone before you."

Salo's heartbeat quickens. His hands get clammy.

"But you must always remember this, honored emissary. Ignorance is like basking in the suns. It is warm and beautiful, but it is blinding. Step into the sanctum, and your soul will never again taste the warmth of this light. The shadow of knowledge will fall upon you, and you will not escape it, but your eyes will be shielded from the blinding rays, and you will see things you could not have seen before." The Arc's deep-set gaze burns holes into Salo's confidence. "Are you ready?"

Salo gazes at the doors. This is a threshold from which there can be no return, but there is something calling out to him from the other side, and he can't ignore it. "I'm ready, Your Worship."

"Then follow me."

At first, the cavernous chamber beyond the doors is underwhelming. Then Salo realizes that it is a little too cavernous—actually, it *is* a cave, dank, wet and slightly cold, and those reddish-orange icicles hanging from the jagged ceiling are actually stalactites. That glow.

Salo looks back at the doors just as they slam shut, then raises a worried eyebrow at the old sorcerer. The proportions of this cave aren't consistent with the rest of the temple.

The Arc seems to smile without actually moving his lips. It's something he does with his eyes. "The inner sanctum is not what it seems. Come, we must not linger here for long."

Salo follows the Arc toward the group of people huddled around something in the middle of the cave. He's more than a little surprised to see so many people here, and he's about to ask the Arc about them when his eyes bulge at their appalling state.

Filthy and haggard, the five figures are all pulling at their wild hair or chewing on their long nails, crazed eyes fixed on whatever lies in their midst. Tattered rags hang on their bony frames so as to make them appear sexless. A fetid reek swirls around them so thickly Salo can smell it from yards away. He smacks a hand over his mouth and nose in revulsion.

"Step aside," the Arc says to them in a commanding voice. "I won't be long."

The five figures grumble incoherently. One of them rocks their body back and forth and speaks words that come out too fast for Salo to comprehend, words that give him the trace of a headache. He winces and rubs his temples.

"Step aside, or you won't get food tomorrow."

That seems to get their attention. They don't stop mumbling, but they slowly disperse to reveal a stone lectern with a large book sitting upon it. Salo watches them curiously as they hobble to the edges of the cave, where they sit down on the hard floor, each muttering to themselves.

Reluctantly, he pries his eyes off them and follows the Arc to the lectern. The book on top of it is closed. Its cover is black, pitted leather, and it bears no title on the spine or on the front. It doesn't look particularly old, or special, for that matter.

The Arc gives Salo a searching look. "How quick are you with ciphers, Emissary Siningwe? Your life may depend on it."

Salo tries not to gulp. "I think I'm fairly quick."

"We shall soon find out. It will be the difference between enlightenment and a lesser existence. In any event, this book has a name that cannot be known. For our own purposes, we call it the Aina Jina: the Tome of Vanishing Secrets. Inside you will find the deepest truths of our world. It is written in an ancient script similar to ciphers, so I'm confident you'll understand what it says. Go ahead. Take a look."

Salo runs his fingers over the pitted cover, a worried thrill tingling down his spine. *The deepest truths of our world? In one book? Is this a trick?* The Arc is silent as Salo opens the book—

Only for the first page to reveal a secret so shocking it shatters everything Salo thought he knew about the world. There are diagrams, pictures, graphs in bold ink, showing him things so obviously true he wonders why he's only learning about them now.

He gasps. "By Ama! How come—" He falls silent the second he looks up at the Arc, who's still watching him impassively. He was about to ask the old man why no one knows the shocking and yet evident truths in the Aina Jina, but now he's struggling to remember *what* those shocking and yet evident truths are.

He flicks his gaze down at the Tome, only to find that he *does* remember the truths, for there they are, written and drawn on the pages in bold ink. Yet as soon as he looks up at the Arc again, they slip away from his mind like thieves in the night, leaving him floundering for words.

"What's happening?"

"What you are experiencing," the old sorcerer says gravely, "is the curse that brought about the Great Forgetting. History books will tell you it was a single event; it happened, it passed, and then it was over.

But that couldn't be further from the truth. The Great Forgetting is still happening today, and the Aina Jina is proof of it."

The Great Forgetting. The beginning of all human history, when all knowledge that came before was lost in the span of a single night. But how could it still be happening today? Salo's ears ring as he digests this revelation; then a spike of anger takes hold of him. "Why are you keeping this a secret?" he demands. "Why aren't you telling anyone? People have a right to know!"

The Faro's voice remains vexingly calm. "I agree, but the only reason you and I can look upon this Tome and have this conversation is that we have both received helpings of the Mother's blood straight from a redhawk. Had we not, we would not have made it past those doors, and even if we had, we could not have looked at the Tome and remembered it. Knowledge of its existence would have vanished from our minds just as the words in the Tome vanished from yours when you looked away from it."

Light. Twisting webs of golden white, there in the corner.

"I . . . don't understand, Your Worship."

"Someone didn't just want humanity to forget something, honored emissary. They wanted us to be incapable of remembering it. How can you know you've lost something when you can't even remember ever having it or speak its name? How can you know the face of your enemy when she has blinded your eyes? It was the perfect theft of memory."

Webs, twisting and turning. Memories, fading fast.

And now the Arc's voice grows harsher with each word. "That is the insidious power of the Great Forgetting. You and I are by no means immune from the curse, but the Mother blessed us with a chance, just a chance, Emissary Siningwe, to free ourselves of it, if not completely, then enough to see."

Light. Twisting webs of golden white, right in front of him. Memories fading fast.

"My eyes!" Salo cries.

"The curse is strengthening its hold on you, honored emissary. You must confront it. Destroy its patterns before it takes you!"

Salo feels an oppressive weight descending upon his mind. Cobwebs of pure sunlight feather across his vision, moving and twisting in patterns he can't follow. With each passing second, he feels something slip away from his mind, though he can't say what, exactly. He just knows it has something to do with a book.

"Confront the curse, Emissary Siningwe, or this will be the end of you!"

Webs, twisting and turning, growing brighter and stronger. Memories about . . . a book? A voice nearby, shouting at him, telling him about the webs.

He is utterly confused until the webs transform in a pattern he recognizes. Then a segment of the webbing shatters, and he finds that he remembers where he is. What's happening. Why it's happening.

"Confront the curse!" says a distant voice.

But the webs adapt, their transformations become more subtle and frequent, and they begin to thicken again, until Salo loses the thread of why it's so important to resist them.

They are beautiful, like golden fractals or ice crystals. Despite the nagging feeling that something isn't quite right, a part of him is captivated by their movement. He wants to analyze them and know how they work. This is how he comes to shatter another section of webbing, recovering a piece of himself in the process, along with a sense that something profound is at stake, though what, he cannot say.

The webs retreat, self-modify, and reattack, better, faster, even more beautiful than before. It's like a high-speed game of matje against a master, yet it's precisely the thrill of the challenge that keeps him engaged where he would have otherwise let go. Indeed, had the shifting patterns been less interesting, they might have taken him. Instead, he battles for what feels like hours until he shatters through the last bit of webbing and gasps as his memories come rushing back.

"I remember! I remember the Tome of Vanishing Secrets!"

The Arc was gripping one edge of the stone lectern with enough force to cause a crack to appear along its flat surface. The specter of relief crosses his face as he relaxes his grip, but his usual grim expression quickly supplants it. "You did well. How are you feeling?"

Salo lifts his new spectacles and rubs his eyes with a shaking hand. A headache is beginning to drone just behind his left temple, where he was injured. He blinks at the sorcerer. "What the devil was that?"

"You broke a small part of the curse," the Arc explains. "Just enough to remember everything you've learned in this chamber. Everything but the contents of this book." He taps a bony hand on the Tome. "This is the core of the curse. As yet, no one has broken it."

Salo still sees phantoms of the webs whenever he blinks. He rubs his eyes again. "Those webs . . . they felt . . . strange. Were they solar magic?"

A curious light sparks in the Arc's eyes. "That is consistent with what many pilgrims have experienced. But I believe the truth isn't quite so straightforward. Had you been a solar mystic yourself, I believe you would have experienced the curse as fractals of Red magic."

Salo stares at the Arc. "What does that mean?"

"It means this curse was designed to debilitate all of humanity, Emissary Siningwe. All the world's magics were employed in its construction so that no one would be immune. Do not ask me why; I cannot say, but I believe that unearthing the truth of the matter was the original purpose of the Bloodway. It is possible you will learn deeper truths further in the sanctuary. Speaking of which—"

The Arc begins to close the Aina Jina, but Salo stops him by slamming his hand on the pages. He wants one more look, just one more.

His eyes fall upon the Tome, and the secrets he glimpsed therein return to him like a powerful gust of wind, clearing away the thick cobwebs obscuring the truth from him, cobwebs he didn't know existed until today.

"What would happen if I tried to tell others about this book?"

"Unless they had walked this very same path and confronted the curse as you have, they would forget your words as soon as they left your lips. They'd experience a headache, along with the mildly disconcerting feeling of having missed something. We call this sensation arcane dissonance."

Salo almost feels dizzy. He remembers how he couldn't tell Nimara about his awakening, how Tuk and Ilapara got headaches when he tried to recount his communion with the Lightning Bird. Then there was that night in the garden when he tried to tell them about the apparition from the Carving. That was arcane dissonance.

He looks up at the Arc and immediately feels the cobwebs knitting together to cloud his vision once more. "And what would have happened if I'd failed to break the curse?"

The old sorcerer marks the haggard figures by the cave walls with his dour gaze. "I think you know the answer to that question."

Salo nods, steps away from the Tome, and watches in sorrow as the figures rush toward it like thirsty men to a well. They were once pilgrims like him, walking the Bloodway to receive boons for their tribes, but now they're doomed to waste away in here for the rest of their lives.

That could have been me.

"We must continue," the Arc says, and Salo feels a wave of relief.

They leave the cave through a narrow passage that gives access to an even larger cave, this one so vast Salo can't even see where it ends. Scores of luminescent dandelion tufts hang lazily in the air, each one glowing with the brightness of a candle and drifting above an endless, darkly lustrous body of water.

An underground lake.

There is an ivory-colored rowboat waiting by the shore. For some reason its fluid lines make Salo think of burial rafts and sarcophagi, or something else the malaika of death might use as his vehicle of choice. A nervous chill grips Salo as they approach it, and he doesn't think he imagines the rapid drop in temperature.

Clearly unaffected by the boat's deathly aura, the Arc climbs inside and settles down facing the stern, then looks at Salo expectantly. Without further prompting, Salo takes off his sandals, throws them into the boat, and begins to push it into the water while the Arc fits a pair of oars into the oarlocks.

The boat is cold to the touch, even colder than the water, but much lighter than Salo expects. He carefully climbs aboard as soon as it's afloat. "Do you need me to row?"

The old man shakes his head. "What you're about to face will require your full attention." He grunts as he begins to row. In the weak light of the dandelions, he almost looks cadaverous. "I sincerely hope, for both our sakes, that you'll still be with me when I reach the other side of this lake."

Salo doesn't like the sound of those words.

The rowboat continues to cut through the water below with graceful ease. The Arc's bony arms expose their hidden strength with each stroke. For a time, he rows in silence; then he says, "The Shrouded Pylon is one of the world's greatest enigmas and perhaps its best-kept secret. The rest of the world knows of its existence, but only as a curiosity built by mostly harmless if misguided people. What they don't know is that we aren't the ones who built it. This whole temple was here long before the KiYonte were a tribe, even before the rise of the first Ascendancy of the outer world. The Pylon itself almost certainly predates the Great Forgetting."

A tangible pall of gloom settles upon the rowboat as the Arc speaks. Salo pretends not to notice, as if by doing so he could ward it off.

"We don't know who built it," the Arc says. "We don't even know why it was built; this knowledge was lost to the curse a long time ago. But we know at the least that the Pylon is a confluence of time and space. The power flowing within it stretches across the Void and deep into the past. Pilgrims who have made this journey before believe it was built to see into the lives of our ancestors. Others believe it does more than just see; it collects and stores."

Bright lights flare in the gloom directly overhead, taking Salo's breath away when he looks up. He immediately understands that each of those lights is a person of great consequence. They dazzle him with the vibrant lives they lived, humble him with the momentous decisions they made.

"Who are they?" Salo whispers in his awe.

"These, Emissary Siningwe, are some of the most prominent human beings who have ever lived, the heroes of history. They are kings, queens, emperors, and empresses. Leaders and revolutionaries of great influence. Scholars, thinkers, and artists, musicians and people of renowned beauty. They are war heroes and martyrs, people whose legends outlived them, whose deeds echoed across time to shape the future. They are the best of humanity, even if we do not remember them."

"I want to be up there." The words spew from Salo's mouth before he can think to stop them. "I want to matter."

"As do we all," the Arc says. "But why do you look at the brightness above you and ignore the darkness below? Which of the two is greater?"

With almost crippling trepidation, Salo looks into the water and can't help but cry out in dismay at what he sees. If the bright lights above him are stars, then here lies the infinite nothingness that contains them. Here are the faceless multitudes never accounted for, whose lives were given over to misery and injustice.

Inky mists begin to rise from the lake and surround the boat, blotting out the fragile light of the dandelions and plunging the cavern into blackness, leaving nothing but the creaking of the Arc's moving oars.

"Ready yourself, Emissary Siningwe."

"For what?" Salo asks desperately. But he doesn't have to wonder long because a great horror emerges from the mists, a deformed spirit with long, tangled limbs, one of which slams Salo in the chest, toppling him backward so that he almost tumbles out of the boat. Before he can lift himself back up, another limb snakes around his throat and squeezes, stifling his screams.

As the apparition looms above him, choking the life from him, Salo realizes that he knows this spirit, that he has seen it before, though never in such a form.

Its name is Sorrow.

Trapped in its breathless embrace, he's powerless to stop the innumerable slivers of past lives that plunge into his mind like daggers and *explode.*

Here he is now, a boy stolen forcefully from the arms of his grandmother. The men who take him say he must fight. They put a weapon in his hands and send him to the front lines with other frightened boys wrenched from loving arms.

He doesn't know why he must fight, only that if he doesn't, the men who took him will beat him until they cripple him. So he marches into the trenches with the other boys, a long, solemn line crawling through the jungles like a giant millipede beneath the yellow moon's light.

Like the other boys, he knows he's going to die, for the enemies are strong and have weapons that spit deadly flames and go off in vicious explosions. He survives long enough to have nightmares when he sleeps, memories of boys screaming after their limbs have been blown off their bodies. But he, too, succumbs one cloudy morning, death taking him after he steps onto an explosive trap in a field of blood.

Later, his bones are buried in a mass grave with the bones of all the other boys who died on that field. No one will mourn their deaths or remember their names.

A nameless child soldier, forgotten, and not the only one in this lake. There are countless more, and their last moments are each delivered to Salo's mind in horrendous detail.

"Stop!" he cries.

But Sorrow isn't done with him.

Here he is now, a young woman hiding with her son in the small cupboard of their hut while her drunk husband shouts in rage outside.

She was young when she was married off—she is still young. She had dreams for herself, but she had to give them up to become a proper wife. It was less than she'd hoped for, but in this world, girls like her are never given a choice, so she accepted her lot and tried to make the best of it.

Her husband is far older. He smiled at her on the day of their wedding, and she thought that perhaps he would be kind to her. But as she lay next to him later that night, her skin marked with bruises, her cheeks stained with tears, she knew she had been condemned to a lifetime of sorrow.

The days wore on, the light in her eyes dimming a little each time she suffered her husband's wrath, until she began to feel like a ghost in her own body, waiting for the day he'd strike her so hard she'd never get up.

But then her son came into her life.

He was a ray of light in the gloom, a reason to get up in the morning.

She's been saving the little she gets from selling her crafts at the market so she can send him to that new school up the road when he's old enough. She wants him to grow up to be strong and kind and caring. The kind of man who won't strike his wife, who will protect his daughter the way her father never protected her.

He will be everything his father is not.

The cupboard is flung open, and a snarling face leers down at her, eyes full of drunken violence. Her two-year-old son starts wailing despite her efforts to keep him silent. She pleads with his father, begging him to be merciful, to forgive her for whatever wrong he thinks she has committed.

But the man is too far gone in his rage, and today is the day she always knew would come.

She will never watch her son grow.

A nameless victim of a universe that cares not for the powerless, and just one of a multitude.

How many such stories since the dawn of history? What would they look like if they gathered in one place? And if they could speak, what would they say?

In the cavern's infinite blackness, Sorrow seeps into Salo's being and coils around his soul. He becomes each and every nameless ghost entombed in the lake, not all at once but each one separately, alone, as they lived and died. The true face of humanity.

He tries to wrestle with the spirit of Sorrow, to deny what it has shown him, but the voices of the nameless drown out his protests, and he sees through their eyes, over and over again, how evil continuously prevails over good in this universe. And how could it not, when pain is mightier than pleasure? Would the anguished cries of one hell not eclipse the laughter of a thousand heavens?

Evil and sorrow are the net sums of humanity, he sees, and as he begins to accept this horrid truth, his soul yields to Sorrow's embrace and its promise of quiet relief, of permanent freedom from an unjust universe.

"Let go," the spirit says to him. *"Let me free you from this wicked plain and give you eternal peace."*

In front of Salo, the Arc has wrapped himself in a gray shield of dispassion. The spirit's inky mists flow harmlessly around the shield, failing to break through. There are no notions of just or unjust within the shield's structure, no good or evil, no right or wrong. The nameless are a simple fact of life upon which the Arc looks with detachment.

Salo tries to do the same. He tries to distance himself from the child soldier who died alone, from the young mother who broke beneath her husband's rage, from all the other countless victims with similar stories. It doesn't work. The spirit roots itself deeper within him like a cancerous growth, unsympathetic to his muffled screams.

The warmth of being starts to recede, until it is a faint memory, a candle flickering somewhere far away.

Then a tiny voice rings within him like a bubble rising to the surface from a sinking ship. It says, *"But what if . . ."*

"Hush now. It's almost over."

"What if I lived my life to stop others from becoming nameless? Would that not be a worthy reason to keep on living?"

"Naive child. No action of yours could ever redress the evils committed by the rest of your species."

"But I can't give up. I have to at least try. I want that chance."

"Let go. It is the only way you will lessen the suffering humanity has wrought."

"I . . . I choose to stay."

The mists try to pull him deeper into their embrace, but his resolve strengthens into a steady blaze that blooms outward from his core. It becomes a shield of light that wraps itself around him and pushes the spirit away, brighter than the Arc's shield but noticeably weaker.

"I choose to stay," he shouts, pulling off the limb that was strangling him and sitting up. "You will not take me!"

The spirit doesn't give up. It pushes and probes his shield with its inky-black tendrils, occasionally slipping in and sapping his resolve. But he knows he can defeat it now, and this knowledge is power.

Eventually the mists swirl into an angry whirlwind before dissipating with a hiss; then the glowing dandelions return, almost like they never left.

The Arc continues to row the boat in silence and helps Salo pull it to shore when they reach the other side. They don't speak.

When the boat is beached, Salo tries to follow the old man toward the tunnel up ahead, but his wobbly legs almost give out beneath him.

A crushing vise grips his chest. He can't breathe. He turns away from the Arc's unsympathetic gaze, gripping the rowboat and using it for balance as he makes his way around it. On the other side, he crouches down to the ground in a childish attempt to hide himself.

It starts as a sob; then he's weeping as hard as he wept when Monti died. But even as he weeps, he knows no tears can ever be enough. Nothing ever will be. Not for the nameless.

The lakeshore funnels into a dingy tunnel, at the end of which stands a large double door. Salo follows the Arc toward it in silence.

His chest feels lighter. He wept until his eyes went dry, and then he wept some more, but there's only so much grief the human heart can pour out before there's nothing left.

And that's exactly the problem, isn't it? The nameless deserve lifetimes of mourning, but a half hour was all his body could give. Even now a part of him is already telling itself that things will be better; he's already begun to forget.

"The lake of the nameless has claimed many who have tried to cross it," the Arc says as they come to the doors. "It is never an easy task to justify human existence when faced with its most frightful consequences."

Salo looks at him unhappily. "How do you do it? How can you see all of that and . . . not care?"

"Of course I care, but only for those things in my power to control. I have accepted that the universe owes me nothing. I expect no more of it than what I can take from it, and I am always wary of what it might take from me. Worrying about anything else is an exercise in futility."

"I suppose that's a pragmatic way of looking at things."

"*Pragmatic* is probably the kindest word you could use." They both fall silent and stare at the doors next to them. "And so here we are. Your mind has prevailed, and so has your soul. Now your body must take you to the end of your journey. Unfortunately, this is where we must part ways. When I open these doors, I will return to where we began. When you open them, you will face your last challenge before you reach the innermost sanctum. I can tell you nothing about it save to say that if you hesitate, you will surely die."

Salo nods, though he has many questions the man probably can't answer. "What about the artifact I'm supposed to retrieve?"

"Your desire to find it should point you toward it," the Arc says. "I'm sure you'll understand once you get there."

Staring at the doors, Salo takes an uneven breath. A trial of the body. What horrible truth will it show him? Will he survive it, or will it be too much? "Do I go first?"

"It matters not."

Salo's hands are shaking as he reaches for the doorknob. Light floods the tunnel when he pulls the door toward him. There's so much light he can barely see what lies beyond. He swallows, glancing nervously at the Arc, who nods. With one more heavy breath, Salo steels himself and walks across the threshold.

And into a great desert landscape. Ancient ruins rise in every direction, bearing witness to a glorious past that ended suddenly in a blaze of fire.

Morsels of knowledge seep into Salo's mind directly from the environment. It dawns on him that the desert was once the seat of an empire that spanned the heavens above it. Now it's the abode of misshapen creatures that have long since forgotten they were once human. Their eyes burn with white fire, and they roam restlessly across the landscape, searching for life force to consume, even though the last life force was drained from this desert many eons ago.

Salo's blood chills in his veins.

In the distance, the pillars of the Shrouded Pylon rise like two columns of red light among the ruins. The Paragon is a strobing star whose rays are calling out to him. As soon as Salo sees it, the tikoloshe roaming the desert come to a dead stop, and all at once, they turn their white, burning eyes toward him.

A breeze whistles by.

"If you hesitate," the Arc said, "you will surely die."

Salo breaks into a run. He was a cowherd of the Yerezi Plains, so he can be light footed when he needs to, but the tikoloshe leap into motion as well, converging upon him from all directions, their monstrous cries thundering across the sands like the flight of a redhawk.

He reaches what could have been a marketplace once, now a crumbling ruin of pillars. Symbols are carved onto the ancient stone, inviting closer scrutiny so he might know what secrets they hold, but he doesn't give in to the temptation.

Something bursts out of the sands behind him, and when he looks, he sees the largest fiend yet, what looks like the abominable offspring of a skeletal human and a giant spider. It skitters on its eight legs up a fallen pillar in the ruined market before leaping down, racing after him.

He keeps running. The Pylon grows larger as he gets closer. It's a gateway he must reach if he is to leave here alive, and it radiates power like nothing he's ever felt. *I'm almost there.*

There's a lanky figure waiting for him on the other side of the gateway, just behind a curtain of light. Fear and excitement fill his bones; he can even make out a face cut from lapis lazuli, bright blue like the blue at the heart of the New Year's Comet.

Along a scarlet road, past a gateway beneath a red star. It shines far beyond your horizons.

Here's the gateway now, beneath a gemstone whose brilliance is like starlight.

Salo powers himself into the final sprint. The steps to the Pylon are now in sight. He draws up every ounce of strength left in his body, pushes his muscles to the point of tearing, almost there now, can almost touch it, but the arachnid tikoloshe lunges forward from behind him to grab his ankle with a skeletal hand.

He tumbles to the ground just shy of the steps, bruising his knees and elbows. Instinctively, he kicks at the creature with his free leg, yelling as he does so because this will not be his end. He will not fall here. Not before he sees what's on the other side of that gateway.

The tikoloshe pulls him with enough force to break his leg, but he catches the rusty railings on the steps before it can carry him away. The wails of a billion redhawks assault his ears. The demon horde is a cloud of bones and dust seeking to engulf him, but for some reason it appears they can't come any closer to the Pylon.

With sheer willpower he inches his way up the steps. The tikoloshe gripping his leg pulls harder, and Salo feels something crack.

He screams at the tremendous pain, but he is no stranger to pain. He will see what is beyond that gate even if getting there kills him. He pulls himself farther up the steps. The entity behind the shimmering curtain of light watches him with interest but makes no move to help.

No matter. Salo pulls himself up one last time. The instant he touches the curtain, a shock wave of red energy ripples outward from the Pylon and blasts the tikoloshe away.

"The Veil is falling, prince of the leopard," the tikoloshe hiss at him. "History shall be rectified. This is inevitable."

Then a second shock wave blasts the landscape away.

When Salo opens his eyes, he finds that he's lying prone on the reddest earth he's ever seen. Gone is the ruined city engulfed by the deserts and fell creatures of the underworld; now a rocky and barren plain of crimson soil stretches away from where he lies in every direction.

His leg doesn't hurt anymore, so he sits up and fixes his spectacles upon the bridge of his nose. There's no firmament above him, no clouds, only the yawning vault of the deep black, which twinkles with more stars than he's ever seen. His mouth falls open when he spots the blue-and-green crescent adorning one side of the empty sky. The twin suns glare down at him from almost directly behind this crescent, which he realizes must be a waxing moon.

No. Not a moon. A world.

It is I who's on the moon.

43: Isa

Red Temple

Isa waits in the temple's forecourt when Tuliza's rented carriage arrives to deposit her. They beam at each other as she alights; then she looks about herself with clear interest.

"Everything is so big!" she exclaims.

Isa approaches her, and they embrace. "Tuliza. It's good to see you."

Tuliza's eyes shine brightly as they separate. "You too, Your Majesty. How have you been?"

"Well, all things considered." Their smiles become tinged with sadness as they remember what's transpired since the night they descended to the depths of the undercity and discovered its secrets.

They walk the temple's cloisters together, trading stories about the night of the Requiem Moon. "I never told a soul, but somehow word got out that it was you who infused the other Eternity Crystal with Engai's light."

"Eternity Crystal?" Isa asks, puzzled, and Tuliza gives her a slanted grin.

"That's what they're calling the torches we carried during the rite. It turns out Engai blessed them so fiercely they will not deplete for thousands of years. The undercity never has to worry about running out of power."

"That's good news," Isa says, to which Tuliza snorts.

"You underestimate what this means, Your Majesty. Because of you, there can be more machinery operating in the undercity. More air recyclers. Lighting. Hot water. The lives of the people down there are already improving in ways that weren't possible before, and they know they have you to thank."

They come to a stop next to a pond teeming with colorful minnows, and Tuliza's gaze becomes distant as she stares down into the water. "On the night of the Requiem Moon, every able-bodied man and woman of the undercity went out to face the Wavunaji. The bastards were well armed, and so many of our people got hurt, but the Wavunaji didn't expect so many to rise against them." Tuliza looks at Isa, eyes full of conviction. "You inspired the undercity, Your Majesty, and because of it, many lives were saved."

Isa looks away and tugs the other woman by the arm to get them moving again. "Don't credit me alone, Tuliza. I wouldn't have managed without you."

"I only followed where you led, Your Majesty," Tuliza demurs.

"You convinced your father to allow me the rite. And I'm not sure I'd have stepped through that portal if you weren't there."

They reminisce at length about their time in the undercity, the things they saw, snippets of life from a distant past. All the while, Isa steers them toward what has become her favorite prayer room in the citadel.

Past the doors, they sit together on the steps to the pulpit beneath the stained glass mural.

"I need to tell you something," she says, getting to the reason she asked Tuliza to visit her. An upswell of emotions threatens to overwhelm her and rob her of speech, but she plows on. "I need to tell you why I'll be marrying the Crocodile in three days."

Tuliza listens attentively as Isa spills all the secrets she's been keeping since the day the high priest took her into the citadel's main temple and revealed his plans for her. She leaves nothing out, unable to stop once she starts, the truth pouring out of her heart without reservation. By the time she's done, her hands are shaking and her vision is unfocused.

For the longest time, Tuliza's expression is unreadable. "Why did you tell me all this?" she asks.

Isa wipes her eyes, looking up at the ceiling to repress more tears. "Because I hate who I've become, Tuliza. I've had to keep secrets from the people I love, to lie to my friends and imperil their lives. I thought that if I told someone, if someone understood . . ." Words fail her, and she looks down into the hands on her lap. "I don't know." She risks a glance at Tuliza and finds her frowning in thought. "If you were in my shoes, what would you do?"

Tuliza shakes her head, not looking Isa in the eye. "Your Majesty, I cannot tell you what to do. The position you've been put in, I'm not sure how you've managed to keep sane for so long. I wouldn't wish it on anyone."

"I'm asking for your advice," Isa says almost desperately.

"I'm not sure there's anything useful I could say to make things better for you, Your Majesty. You're in an impossible place."

Isa nods, wiping her eyes as her resolve hardens. "But you at least see that I have no choice."

"There's always a choice, Your Majesty," Tuliza says. "It's only a matter of deciding which consequences you're willing to live with."

Put that way, the choice seems straightforward. "This is something that must be done."

"Then you have made your decision. If it's my approval you seek . . ."

"No, but I have a favor to ask you."

Tuliza looks up. The cheer that shone in her eyes when she arrived has been displaced by pity and sorrow. "I'm listening."

Touched by her empathy, Isa finds the courage to reveal her last secret. "When I looked into the Dazzling Light, I acquired certain . . .

knowledge I didn't possess before, and I saw—not a way out, exactly, but a way to finish this on my own terms. Your priests wield the power to call upon the soul of a recently departed person and . . . delay its entrance into the great beyond, do they not?"

Tuliza blinks, seeming at a loss for what to say. It's likely such a secret is known only to the innermost circle of her sanctuary's membership. "I have heard that they do," she hedges.

"I know they do, Tuliza. And now with the power of the crystals, it should be easier. In fact, I believe this is precisely why they were given to us. I asked the spirit of Engai for hope, and he showed me a way and gave me the means to walk it. How else would I know that it's possible? I would not lie about such a thing."

Tuliza heaves a sigh. "I know," she says and stares intently at the floor for a long minute, weighing her options. "What would you have of me?" she says.

"I'd like you to call upon a soul for me," Isa tells her. "And I'd like you to convince your father to do it on the day of my wedding."

44: Musalodi

Elsewhere

"Dear Ama," he breathes, not wanting to believe. "I am on the moon!"

"And here you are, at last."

Salo looks up from where he's seated on the ground. The entity he first met in the Carving, then at his awakening, now stands before him in a loincloth of hide. He balances a long spear of blue metal in one hand, blue like his skin, blue like a pendant on a friend's necklace, a stark counterpoint to the harsh crimson landscape. He looks down at Salo with faceted eyes that catch the unfiltered sunlight like diamonds one moment and then sapphires the next.

Terrified because he suspects he now knows who this entity is, that he is in all likelihood in the presence of divinity, Salo averts his gaze and moves to kneel with his head bowed.

"Great one. What's happening?"

The entity speaks without ever moving his lips, and though his voice is a whisper like the icy breeze of a winter's morning, it seems to reach every nook and cranny on this barren moon.

"You are standing near a permanent breach in the Veil, and our minds are in communion on the moon. You brought me here during your awakening, though I could not speak to you until you had broken enough of the curse on your memory to understand me. I have been waiting for you."

"Who are you, great one? Are you the Star of Vigilance?" *Are you Ama Vaziishe's beloved brother? Am I really talking to a god right now?*

"My true name has not been spoken in ages, but what you call the Star of Vigilance was once my seat of power. From its halls I presided over eons of peace and blessed those who sought my wisdom." The facets of the god's eyes shift from ice blue to crystal clear. *"You may call me Vigilance, if you wish."*

Even though he suspected this, Salo is nearly struck speechless. "You honor me, great one. But I still don't understand why I'm here."

"You are here to help me restore what was lost. But first you must understand how we got here and what is at stake. Rise. Let us walk."

Salo obeys, and they start to walk together, though he can't for the life of him figure out exactly where they're going, since there's nothing in the vicinity but a barren moonscape. Then the god stops and waves a hand throbbing with a blue-white glow, and the empty black skies ahead come alive with lights.

At first Salo thinks that the stars are getting brighter for some reason, but then he sees an oval shape moving among the lights, surrounded by a halo of blue flame. Its surface seems to be spangled with enchanted crystals.

A vessel, some corner of his mind supplies. *And so are all the other lights.*

They are an immense convoy of enclosed ships meant to sail—not the waters of the earth but the heavens above it. In his wonder, Salo finds himself reminded of the visions he saw during his communion with the Lightning Bird of Lake Zivatuanu: a convoy fleeing to a great princess of the stars.

"What are they?" he asks.

The deity's eyes reflect the lights as he tilts his head upward. *"You are witnessing humanity's arrival to your world, thousands of years ago."*

Salo feels like his head is spinning. "I don't understand."

"I come from a time when humanity had achieved its pinnacle. We had breached the gates of heaven itself, a dimension outside this universe in which a soul could ascend through the infinite ranks of godhood. The Ascent, we called it. You know it as the Infinite Path."

Beneath the great convoy, the moonscape begins to move, the deity's words coming to life in front of Salo as visions of light and red sand. He sees an endless path spreading out before him, and though he can tell that it is immensely glorious, he knows that his capacity to comprehend its glory is inadequate.

"Life after life lived," Vigilance says, *"each one successively more transcendent than the previous, though to what end, we never understood. Not even the beings we found already walking the path could tell us why it was there, and there were many such beings, some vastly older than humanity, some so far along the Ascent they could only be perceived by the echoes of their footsteps, like the faint twinkle of distant stars."*

The visions transform to show a dazzling pantheon of transcendent beings, spirits, and malaikas, some nearly as marvelous as Vigilance, others even more so. *Ascendants,* a voice whispers to Salo. *Beings who have touched infinity and survived.*

"For eons we had worshipped at the altars of unseen gods," says Vigilance. *"But the Ascent opened our eyes to the truth: not only was godhood achievable—it was simply a relative notion describing an imbalance of power. God was that which was above us, that which we had yet to become. You call me a god, for I am more transcendent. The spirits that roam your world, though shadows of what they once were, were also venerated as gods. But there are beings immeasurably godlier than us all, and beings even godlier than those beings, and so on. God is a never-ending journey upward. The Infinite Path itself."*

The skies seem to catch fire as a new vision replaces the convoy: a milky spiral of stars like the vanes of a turbine with a core as bright as a sun. Salo recognizes this constellation as the Devil's Eye of the southern hemisphere, whose center marks the south pole, but he has never seen it in such detail.

A new word explodes into his mind right then, a staggering concept that stuns him with its cosmic scale: *galaxy*.

"Behold humanity's empire at the peak of our might. The age of the Ascent was one unlike any ever seen. It gave us magic. It gave us the heavens. We held the stars in the palms of our hands, our immortality assured."

Salo lifts an open palm to stop Vigilance from going any further. He feels like his mind is being broken. "Surely none of this is literal," he says. "It must be all symbolic."

Gemstone eyes regard him curiously. *"You already know the truth."*

Even in the lake of the nameless, he glimpsed visions of worlds with one sun, of worlds with rings in their skies, some with impossibly tall cities and machines. But how could any of them be real? "It's too much, great one!" he cries. "Other worlds? What happened to them?"

Vigilance gazes at the unnatural star field, a profound aura of loneliness engulfing him. At the same time a corrupting mist begins to spread from one arm of the Devil's Eye to the rest of the spiral. Some of the stars go out in brilliant explosions, and though at first it seems there's an opposing force resisting the encroachment of the mists, they eventually reach every corner of the constellation.

"In some far-flung recess of our imperium, a formerly human entity achieved transcendence without touching the Infinite Path. Hers was a different sort of power, born of machines and the endless hunger that rages around collapsed stars. She had been denied the Ascent, for she had lived a life full of malice. But instead of repenting, upon achieving her corrupted transcendence, she was filled with hate and the thirst for revenge. She waged war against the rest of her species in her wrath, seeking to destroy the gates of heaven. For eon after eon she pressed us in a war of attrition, learning our weaknesses, until at last she conceived of the Scourge, a curse that turned humanity against itself."

The vision shifts to show balls of fire raining down on city after city, on world after world, unleashing hordes of disfigured humanoid creatures whose only desire was to kill and destroy.

The desert landscape, barren and desolate. Hordes of tikoloshe roaming restlessly. Salo is both shocked and saddened when he makes the connection.

They were once human.

"You cannot imagine the scale of destruction she wrought, the multitudes who fell to her curse, the Ascendants who sacrificed themselves to save what was left of humanity. In a desperate attempt to escape the onslaught, my fellow surviving Ascendants and I gathered the remnants of our imperium and fled to the nearest ocean of stars, a place named after a princess from a world so ancient not even we Ascendants knew its location."

The convoy reappears above the moon, and this time Salo is struck with a sense of the distance they traversed to get here, the centuries spent in flight with the hopes of finding a new home.

"But she whom you call Arante gave chase when we fled, and though it took her a time to arrive at our new world, she had agents embedded among us. Of the Ascendants who remained, only four of us were powerful enough to stop her from completing her work, but we were betrayed, and in the end, we could do little more than delay the inevitable. We hid the gates of heaven and threw up a barrier between this world and the metadimension in which Arante and her forces reside."

"The Veil," Salo whispers with awe, and Vigilance nods. "Is *that* what caused the Great Forgetting?"

"Arante used its power against us as we cast it, a vengeful and calculated strike to ensure the world would forget her and thus be unprepared when the Veil lost its strength. But I refused to let her win. Even with the Veil cutting me off from the world, I found ways to make humanity remember her in their myths and fireside tales. I found paths to communicate and send messages, to prepare them for what is coming."

"Is that why I'm here?" Salo asks, his throat feeling dry.

"*There have been others before you,*" Vigilance says. "*Red mystics I groomed for the All Axiom so they would come here and see what you've seen. But without my presence, without my guidance, they misunderstood what was presented to them and went on to drench the world in blood, believing that a world cowed beneath the heel of a single empire was what was needed to stop the coming threat. They were wrong.*"

Salo's mouth falls open as he makes another connection. "You speak of the Hegemons of the Ascendancy. That's why they called it that, isn't it? Because of the Ascent. Because of you. *You* were the force behind the Hegemons."

The deity's eyes shine with resolve. "*Now I shall be the force behind you.*"

Salo takes a step away from this god who would have him do terrible things. "I cannot, great one. Even if I wanted to help you, I do not wield such power."

Vigilance remains fixed, his glittering gaze unyielding. "*But you do. The Axiom you built, the one I took great pains to put into your mother's hands; it is a key. The instant you walked into the sanctum, it unlocked an ancient relic that will give you the power of the Hegemons when you claim it.*"

Salo almost doesn't want to know. "What is this power, great one?"

"*The power of the ancestral talents. All of them, even those lost to time. To wield and bestow or take away from others as you please. She whom you call Mother of Sovereigns governed her realms as strict meritocracies; the All Axiom was her ultimate test of worthiness. With its power in your hands, you will be the moon's vicar on earth.*"

Nausea bubbles up in Salo's stomach. This is far beyond insane. "To what end?"

"*Do you not already see? I am the last of the four great Ascendants. The others sacrificed themselves to strengthen the Veil. I was left behind so that their sacrifices would not be in vain.*"

"Are you saying Ama is . . ." An ache fills Salo's chest. "You're wrong," he says. "I have felt her power. She can't be . . . *gone*." He can hardly even speak the word.

"The source of her power is alive," Vigilance says. *"The same is true for the sources that reside in the suns. But the Ascendants who ruled over them are no more, though I am certain their souls remain on your side of the Veil. That is why I need you. You must help me revive them, if possible, and restore them to their thrones. It is the only way to survive the fall of the Veil. But first you must take the mantle I have offered you. You must complete the pledge you began at your awakening."*

The pledge. Salo had forgotten about it, how he failed to complete it because the words wouldn't come to him. Because there was a curse upon his mind. "I pledge myself to these fires," he said that night, "which warmed the faces of my forgotten ancestors. I pledge myself to these soils, which hold their bones." He stopped there.

The rest of the pledge comes to him now. All he needs to do is speak it.

He hesitates.

"But why do you weave untruths, old friend?"

At the sound of this new voice, Salo turns around and almost screams as a phantom of black mists begins to take shape before him, settling vaguely into the shape of a woman. No single vision of her will settle in his mind; one moment he sees a face as lovely as a blooming rose, and the next he catches a glimpse of monstrously sharp teeth. Her presence is terrible, chilling, like rage that has distilled over eons into hatred most pure.

"Surprised?" she says to Vigilance. "I set foot here long before you did." While Vigilance speaks like a glacial wind, this entity's voice is a metallic harmony.

Vigilance rearranges the panels of his face into a frown. *"The stench of your corruption is hard to miss."* He points at the visitor, his eyes gleaming coldly at Salo. *"Gaze upon the face of your enemy, she who would destroy your world to become god of all things."*

Salo remains immobile as the woman saunters closer, her eyes fixed on him. *Arante, in the flesh.*

"He would paint me the devil," she says, "a mindless evil bent on destruction, yet he cowers behind half truths and omissions. What does that tell you?"

"I have not lied," Vigilance hisses. *"You* do *seek to destroy his world."*

"Because you have given me no choice. And we both know *I* am not the one who seeks godhood. If anything, I seek the opposite. I seek justice."

Salo can only gape, not believing his eyes. *Am I really standing in the presence of the Star of Vigilance and the devil herself?*

"He told you about the war I waged on humanity," she says to him, impossibly. "All true. What he lied about is why."

"Do not listen to her. She is the devil. None other in history has deserved the name more than she."

The devil points a clawed finger at Vigilance, addressing Salo. "Ask him how many stars he consumed to become what he is."

"A tired argument," Vigilance declares. *"Unlike yours, my transcendence left no victims."*

"No victims?" scoffs the devil. "Your journey up the ranks of godhood devoured stars that would have shone for ages, giving rise to new life. Instead they became fuel for your vanity. And that's the truth about heaven," the devil says to Salo. "It devours universes to feed the greed of its gods. Stars, worlds, everything turned to ash. But why? Why, when that power could be harnessed to fix this universe and make it better? All those people you saw in that lake. All that sorrow. The gates of heaven hold the power to rectify those wrongs. *You* could help me do that, and those people you saw could live again. This cruel universe could be transformed into a more just place, a haven where they wouldn't have to suffer."

She's the devil, a deceiver, mother of the underworld, and Salo knows this, but he can't help looking at Vigilance, hoping to hear a denial. "Is she right, great one? Can those people . . . the nameless . . . can they be saved?"

A gentle light enters the god's jeweled eyes. *"We cannot change the past, Musalodi. Only learn from it. What was done cannot be undone. The consequences of attempting to do so would be catastrophic."*

It's not a denial.

Salo's fear had subsided, but now it rushes back with a force. He begins to feel like he can't breathe, like this moon is turning against him.

"I can't do this," he says. "I will not. Not me. Find someone else."

He turns around and runs. If his mind was projected here, he should be able to draw himself out. Behind him, Vigilance calls his name, but he doesn't listen. He concentrates, imagining his hands gripping a tether tied to his mind, and then he yanks.

Still waters press against his body. He can't say how long he's been here, only that he is suddenly aware of his presence in the water, like waking up in a nightmare and realizing that it's not a dream at all.

He kicks until his head breaches the surface, gasping in a lungful of air. The high noon suns shine down on him from directly above. He sees that he is in a pool in the middle of a courtyard and quickly swims to the nearest edge. The spires of the Shrouded Pylon stand motionless on either side of the pool, but the space around them seems to tremble slightly, as if the Pylon won't decide how big it wants to be.

Salo stumbles out of the water on weak legs. The Pylon is supposed to be large enough to tower over the city, and yet here in the courtyard it appears no more than two pillars several yards tall with a head-size ruby floating between them. He fails to discern which is the lie: the giant structure seen from outside or this almost unremarkable gateway.

Perhaps both are lies. At this point, Salo wouldn't be surprised. He can't be sure that anything he knows is true anymore.

Two marble pedestals stand at one end of the courtyard, in front of a set of stairs that leads up to a large double door. On each pedestal sits an artifact of power hidden away here during a different age. Salo instantly knows that those artifacts are the boons he has earned in the sanctum, one of them because he desired it, the other because it was forced upon him.

The artifact to his right is a large yellow crystal set on a golden chain. It is cold to the touch as he lifts it gently off its pedestal and is possibly the prettiest thing ever made. He may not know what it is or why such a thing would help the king accomplish her goal of ending the clans of her tribe, but he knows in his gut that this is the item she sent him here to retrieve.

He also now knows instinctively that no one else could have retrieved it for her, that no one else, in fact, would have been given a choice in what boon to receive, and this raises questions about how she knew he could do this in the first place.

Does she know about my Axiom? But how?

He shivers as he moves to the second pedestal. The item sitting on top of it is a crown. Surprisingly simple. A circlet, really. Interwoven bands of gold, copper, and moongold like twisting vines. He could almost swear it was made to fit on his head.

Nothing happens when he picks it up. The circlet gleams in the sunlight as he inspects it, and he feels shudders running down his spine. Vigilance and the devil both want him to claim this thing so he can do their bidding.

But he won't. He can't. Not when he doesn't know who's telling the truth.

He studies the crown for a moment longer before he walks up the stairs and makes for the doors. And then he steps out into a new world.

45: Jomo

Red Temple

Salo is gone for two days.

Jomo spends most of that time pacing outside the main temple while Odari and Kito smoke their pipes and play board games by a nearby bench. He keeps waiting for the temple doors to open and for Salo to step outside glowing like the suns and looking smug as a Faro, or something equally dramatic. So when Salo does come out, finally, and he's shivering and hugging himself while his teeth chatter—quite frankly, looking as pathetic as a newborn lamb—Jomo is disappointed.

And greatly relieved.

He rushes to the guy just as the doors to the temple shut behind him with a loud thud. Salo looks like he's about to keel over, so Jomo reaches for his shoulders to steady him. "Hey there, friend. Are you all right? By the Mother, did you take a dip in ice or something? You're freezing!"

Salo stares at him like he's trying to remember where he is; then he lets out a pitiful laugh. He's still wearing that damned muting collar around his neck. "It's good to see you too, Jomo."

"Come, let us step into the sunlight." Jomo pulls Salo away from the temple and is grateful when his Sentinels vacate their bench without prompting. It's noon on a sunny day, so there's no reason for anyone to be freezing to death, but as Salo sits down on the bench, he's shivering like he's trapped in a frostbox.

Jomo looks to the side, where the pipe-smoking Sentinels are staring at Salo skeptically. The two are even more suspicious of sorcerers than Jomo is, remaining wary of the Yerezi mystic. "Do you mind getting him a blanket?" Jomo says.

"And something to eat, please," Salo adds.

"Yes, that too. And please notify Her Majesty of his return."

Odari throws Salo another suspicious glance before he tugs his comrade away. They bicker about who'll do what as they go; Jomo makes sure they're out of hearing range before he sits down next to Salo and leans in to whisper, "So did you get it? The thing?"

He hasn't failed to notice the crown Salo is clutching in one hand, a band of precious metals interwoven like a wreath, one of which must be moongold, since it seems to burn with cold fire in the sunlight. Jomo can't help his burgeoning disappointment, because even if this crown is magical, how could it possibly end the interclan hostilities of his tribe?

Then Salo unfurls his other hand, and Jomo is instantly entranced by the yellow gemstone sitting there in the shape of a teardrop. Sunlight throbs along the edges of its facets. It would probably cost all the riches of a small kingdom, but it's still just a gemstone. "That's . . . that's the prize?" he hears himself say, his voice full of bitterness and defeat. "All this effort for a piece of jewelry? Are you sure you took the right thing?"

Salo turns his head up toward the suns and soaks up their warmth. "When I emerged from beyond the Pylon, I stepped into a courtyard with many wonders hidden there. I knew which one I wanted, and it was delivered to me." He looks at Jomo. "I was told I'd know when I saw it. I'm quite certain this is it."

Jomo takes another good look at the guy. Judging from his sorry state, he must have gone to the pits and back. *And here I am giving him a hard time.* Jomo sighs, sitting back into the bench. "Forgive my impatience. I guess I expected . . . more. I mean, how is a necklace supposed to solve our problems?"

A shadow crosses Salo's face, and for a moment he looks like he's going to tell Jomo what's on his mind, but then he palms the diamond and hugs himself, turning his face away. "I don't know, but I don't like this diamond. I sense power inside it, and it feels . . . wild and uncontrollable. Let's hope the high priest will know what to do with it."

And Jomo doesn't like the sound of that at all.

46: Isa

Red Temple

Isa finds Salo sitting on a bench close to the citadel's main temple, chewing on a piece of flatbread while Jomo and his two Sentinels try hard not to stare at him. The weather is warm, but he's hunched up with a blanket draped over his shoulders. Isa falters when she sees the faraway look on his face.

Does he now know the games I've played with him? Does he know that I might as well have put that collar on his neck myself?

His Worship said he wouldn't know, but Isa isn't so sure. How could he not? How could he step through those doors and not have the universe laid bare before him?

Walking next to her, Obe Saai notices her hesitation. "Is something wrong?"

He can be too perceptive sometimes. "Nothing. It's just . . . I've been told that the sanctum weighs heavily on the soul and that some who enter it never make it out. I guess it's just hitting me that there was a chance he might not have returned."

Obe studies her, his forehead creasing. "You care for him."

Isa spent her morning getting her hair plaited for her wedding tomorrow. It now falls over her left shoulder in a single braid. She lets an idle hand wander and pull at it. "More people would have died that night if he hadn't helped us," Isa says, then looks Obe in the eye. "You're not jealous, are you?"

"Of him? No. But I sense he means more to you than you're letting on. His presence here, the way he helped you; none of it's a coincidence, is it? You've had your eye on him since he came to the city. I guess I'm wondering why."

Isa doesn't have the heart to lie to Obe, but she knows she can't tell him the truth either. She looks away. "I needed an ally who could act where the high priest couldn't, and it was the high priest who brought him to my attention. If I care for him, it's because he went over and beyond what I hoped he would do for me."

The truth, though not all of it. Obe probably sees this, but he decides to keep his own counsel.

When Salo sees them coming, he scoffs down the rest of his flat-bread and tries to get up, but Jomo puts a hand on his shoulders to keep him seated. "How about we stay off our feet until we can stand without swooning, huh?"

Salo wipes the crumbs off his face and manages a sheepish grin. "Your Majesty," he says in greeting.

Isa smiles back, wondering if he can see through her act, then almost jumps out of her skin when she spots the necklace sitting next to him on the bench, inside a circlet of precious metals. The Covenant Diamond.

Her heart sinks to the floor, and only now does she realize that a part of her was hoping Salo would fail to retrieve the gem. *Dear Mother, how could I be so selfish?*

"Hello, Salo. Mother be praised that you made it back safely." She frowns when she notices the spot of brown staining his bandage. "How's your head?"

"It's fine. Why?" He seems confused for a second, like he's forgotten about his head injury. "Oh. This?" He prods his left temple briefly. "It's all right, I suppose. I don't feel anything."

Jomo leans closer, as if noticing the stain for the first time. "Looks like it bled, though. Maybe we should summon one of the physicians."

"Maybe later." Salo's spectacles shimmer at Isa in a way that makes her shiver. "Your Majesty, might I have a word with you in private?"

He knows. He's seen through my ploys and knows I'm not his friend.

"Of course." Isa sweeps her gaze at the other boys. "Perhaps you should excuse us so the emissary can remain seated."

Jomo sniffs, clearly displeased to be excluded, but he gets up from the bench and ushers the Sentinels away. Isa takes his place on the bench next to Salo and doesn't look at him when she says, "I take it you were successful."

"I was."

Silence falls between them, and Isa decides she won't be the one to break it. After a while, Salo picks up the Diamond and holds it out in his palm. "I don't know how you intend to use this, it's none of my business as far as I'm concerned, but please do be careful with it."

Isa risks another look at the artifact, and her breath turns to frost inside her chest. She didn't expect such a cursed thing to be so pretty.

"I can't explain it," Salo says. "Maybe I'd know more if I didn't have this collar around my neck, but this gemstone feels incredibly wrong to me. I'd hate to see you hurt. Promise me you'll be careful."

He doesn't know.

A wave of relief washes over Isa at first, but it quickly turns to bile in her throat when she realizes she'll have to keep lying to him, playing games. At least if he knew, if he saw what she had done to him, then the lies would end. Now she must keep the ruse alive. "I promise," she says and can't look him in the eye as she does so.

He offers her the Diamond. "Then I believe this belongs to you."

Isa's gaze slips beyond the offered gemstone to the twinkling circlet still sitting on the bench, and she feels an overwhelming urge to tell him to run. She looks up and sees a pair of Jasiri walking down a cloistered walkway just a stone's throw away from the bench. Another pair is standing guard on a second-floor balcony with a good view of the temple entrance.

She isn't sure when the tears started streaming down her face. She hasn't shed tears like this since the night her family was taken from her, but they pour out of her now, and she can't stop them. She quickly wipes her cheeks and accepts the necklace, wrapping her fingers around the stone. It's so cold she suffers a spasm as it touches her skin. "Thank you, Salo. You don't know how much this means to me. You have given my people hope, and for that, you have my eternal gratitude."

By the way he unexpectedly reaches out to squeeze her hand with affection, he must not recognize that her tears are born of guilt. "I don't know if this will help, but I'm terrified, too, Your Majesty. I'm in over my head, and I feel like I can't breathe. I wish someone would take my hand like this and assure me that everything will be fine, but I'll settle for taking your hand and telling you that you're not alone. I won't abandon you."

Isa's tears flow faster. She wants to tell him she won't abandon him, either, but that would be a lie, and she can't find it in her heart to lie right now. So she tells him something true. "You've been a good friend to me, Salo. Thank you."

He nods, squeezing her hand one more time before he lets go and shrinks into his blanket like a man five times his age.

Something broke him inside of the sanctum, even if he's trying not to show it.

As night falls on the eve of the biggest wedding in the kingdom's history, Isa draws Obe Saai into her private chambers for one last moment of intimacy before she has to break his heart.

She knows she shouldn't, that she'd be doing him a service if she pushed him away and made him hate her. But she gives herself over to him in a way she has not before, and they reach new heights of ecstasy.

"I love you," he whispers as he holds her in his arms. His prosthesis is cool against her skin. Their hearts are pressed close together, and for a treacherous moment Isa entertains a notion of escaping with him. They could ride north along the Artery to new tribelands. Start a new life where no one knows them, where the marks on their necks would be nothing more than curiosities.

Tears threaten to spill out of her eyes, so she nestles deeper into Obe, resting her head on his chest. "Is your mother in the city?"

"No," Obe says, and Isa can hear the frown in his voice. "She left for the province a while back. Why?"

"I was just curious," Isa says, doing her best to hide her relief. "I have a request to make of you."

"Anything."

"I need you to keep my cousin away from the wedding," she says. "Go drinking with him if you like. Just keep him away from the Summit."

"He's your only living relative," Obe says. "Why would he stay away from your wedding?"

"I don't want him watching while I marry the man who took everything from him." Isa lifts her head to look at Obe. "I don't want you there either."

Obe reaches out to caress her cheek. "We are grown men, Isa. You don't have to coddle us."

"It's less about you and more about me. I don't think I could go through with it with both of you there. It would hurt too much." She closes her eyes and lets herself enjoy the sensation of Obe's touch. "Just promise me you won't be there." When he remains silent, she opens her eyes and searches his face.

He's watching her with a contemplative look.

"Please," she says.

He leans over to kiss her on the temple. "I'll make sure your cousin stays away," he says.

"Thank you," Isa says, finding that she can breathe easier, and lets him pull her back into his arms, where she stays for the rest of the night.

On her wedding day, they dress her in a strapless gown of shimmering yellow and gold, the color of fertility and bountiful harvests. An elegant affair, the gown, hugging the curves of her body as is the fashion, though its long train will flow behind her as she walks.

They weave yellow wildflowers into her braided hair and paint her shoulders, arms, and hands with white bridal body paint. She is about to be a queen, but she's still the King of Chains, so they adorn her shoulders with the golden chains of her forefathers and hide her face behind the elephant mask-crown.

Her servants gush at her beauty when they're done. They bring a full-length mirror to her so she can see herself, and when she looks into it, a flash of sunlight catches her eye.

There, dangling between the curves of her bosom, is an absurdly pretty yellow diamond.

She hasn't left the temple in weeks, not since the night she descended to the depths of the undercity. It had begun to feel like a prison, but now, as she rides away from it in her royal cavalcade, accompanied by mounted Sentinels, she feels a shiver of dread.

She was safe in the temple. It was familiar. The city below is anything but. It is supposed to be the seat of her throne, but this is no longer the city she remembers. It has seen death and sorrow while she was locked up safe behind an impenetrable barrier. Its people have seen and done things she can only imagine in her worst nightmares.

It's her wedding day, so her people have lined the road. They cheer as her open-top carriage rolls by. They throw petals into the air, sing for her, beat drums, pretend that their souls aren't bleeding inside, that they can't still hear the screams that pierced the air on that bloody night such a short time ago.

She gives them what they want. She waves at them, complicit in the lies they're telling themselves, but this isn't a difficult thing to do.

It's her wedding day, but servants dressed her and painted her body, not her mother and the women of her family. Hers was the largest bride-price ever paid in the kingdom, but her cousin accepted it, not her father and uncles. She rides up to the Summit escorted by nervous Sentinels, rather than to her groom's clanlands with her brothers.

The streets are yellow and gold, like her dress, or like daisies in bloom. Golden streamers ripple in the breeze, yellow petals strewed on the roads. The citizens of Yonte Saire have worn yellow too. Yellow robes, boubous, khangas, beads, flowers.

Yellow is the color of joy and hope, of birth and good things to come, and right now Isa is the single ray of hope shining on the city. She understands that her people seek a new beginning after the horrors they've seen, that they need to celebrate.

Their cheers and songs harden her resolve. They remind her of her duty. A new beginning is what they need, so a new beginning is exactly what she will give them. Her gift to her people, her last act as king.

47: Ilapara

Skytown

Ilapara broods by her bedroom window as morning falls over the Jungle City like a golden veil. The sight of a rainbow arching over the eastern rock face and above the Red Temple like a ramp into the heavens should be soothing to her, but she's given herself over to restless thoughts and feelings of impotence of late.

Why in the pits has Salo not returned from that damned temple? And where the devil is Alinata? Ilapara didn't worry on the first night the Asazi failed to return to the residence, figuring the young woman could take care of herself. But three more nights have elapsed without any sign of her, and she hasn't made any attempt to contact either Tuk or Ilapara.

She's probably not in danger, which only makes her absence all the more galling to Ilapara. Could she not have waited for Salo to return before going missing herself? It's not like they don't have enough to worry about.

Seeking clarity of mind, Ilapara goes down to Salo's study. She has searched it many times this week but can't keep herself from doing so again this morning. Maybe there's a clue somewhere about why everything went to shit on the night of the Requiem Moon. Maybe there's a way she can reach out to Salo to see if he's all right.

She opens a drawer on his desk and caresses the metaformic crystal sitting inside. He left it here when they went out into the city on the night of the Requiem Moon. A pity, because without it there isn't a way he can communicate with them, since Tuk still can't reach out to him through their mental bond. The blessing remains alive in his bones, however, so there's reason to be optimistic. Salo is still alive.

Ilapara picks up one of the papers on his desk and smiles at the note he wrote in his barely legible handwriting reminding himself to buy more smoking herbs in the city. Then a pang of sorrow hits her when she remembers he's still missing and there's nothing she can do about it.

She ventures to the cipher shell sitting on the table across the study. Salo won't be in the construct since he doesn't have his amulet, but that hasn't stopped Ilapara from checking it before, so it doesn't stop her now. She sits in front of the shell and opens her mind. When she crosses the walkway from the Storm craft porch to the central pavilion, she's not surprised to find the place empty.

An array of floating mirrors on ornate frames reflects her a dozen times over, seeming to magnify her loneliness. She sighs. "What did you expect?"

She's about to pull her mind out of the construct when a familiar voice echoes out from one of the mirrors.

"Is someone there?"

Ilapara's eyes widen. "Alinata?"

"Oh, thank Ama. Ilapara, is that you?"

There's no visual mirage on the mirror, since there aren't any more skimmers flying around, but the voice is perfectly clear. She must be speaking into one of Salo's enchanted earrings.

"Where have you been?" Ilapara asks, her initial surprise giving over to simmering indignation. "You've been missing for three days! Are you all right?"

"Never mind me. Where are you?"

"Where do you think? Home."

"You need to get out of there, Ilapara. Right now. Get Tuksaad and get out."

Ilapara stares at the mirrors floating in front of her, perplexed. "Alinata, what's going on?"

"I can't say more. I never meant for any of this to happen." There's a pause before Alinata speaks again. *"I'm sorry."*

A wail pulls Ilapara out of the construct. Her heart is pumping rapidly as she rushes out of the study and toward the source, only to freeze when she sees, at the other end of the adjacent hallway, a man in a horned mask and crimson robes running through one of the house servants with his sword.

The blade pulses with red sparks when he pulls it out of his shocked victim, and it's just as the servant crumples to the floor that the reality hits Ilapara with the force of a boulder rolling down a steep hill.

We're under attack. And, by Ama, that man is a Jasiri.

48: Musalodi

Red Temple

He gives up sleep just as dawn begins to spill through the open shutters of his private cell, where he spent the night tossing and turning, dreaming of gods, devils, and distant worlds long since destroyed.

Never has he felt so small, so insignificant. What is he to a universe so frightfully large? He's no more than a mote on a pebble. No matter how tremendous the labors of his life, the brutal march of history will one day crush his memory and disperse it to the four winds, leaving the universe no different than it was before.

A repressed memory from his childhood has taken new significance: *His mother, approaching with a vial of acid that she would pour into his eyes, telling him she had seen visions of the future. "I have looked to the edge of time, and I know what awaits there, the great and terrible things that will one day part the skies and shatter the world. It is why I must do this."*

Somehow Vigilance had gotten to her, and she knew about the All Axiom and the power it would give her in the inner sanctum. She knew about the power of the Hegemons.

I finally understand why you were willing to go as far as you did, Salo thinks, but this doesn't bring him the peace of mind he thought it would. Though he now knows his mother wasn't a mindless monster, that she was tormented by what she knew was coming to her world, a part of him hates her for casting that burden onto him. Better if she had just gone through with it herself.

A knock comes. He slants his eyes away from the vaulted ceiling and blinks at the door.

"Just a second," he calls.

Something tells him he knows who's there, so he rises from his bed, splashes water onto his face by the washbasin, and changes into a presentable loincloth before he pads barefoot to open the door.

An oppressive aura rushes in to meet him. He senses it even with his muted shards. "Your Worship. It's good to see you."

"I would have come sooner, but I thought you deserved your rest." The Arc wears a grand crimson robe with one sleeveless arm. He regards Salo curiously from the other side of the threshold. "May I come in?" he says, and Salo knows he doesn't have a choice but to accept.

"Of course." He steps aside and lets the old man come in, closing the door behind him. The cell is a small room, and the Arc's presence makes it feel smaller.

A nagging question has been tweaking Salo's anxiety all night. How was it that this man knew that Salo could retrieve the yellow gemstone from the sanctum? Did he know about the All Axiom? And if he did, who would have told him? Certainly not Kamali Jasiri, who went as far as tampering with his own memory to wipe the secret from his mind.

So how did the Arc know? And more worryingly, why didn't he mention it?

Salo moves to pick up the wooden chair in the room and places it next to the Arc. "Please take a seat, Your Worship. I would offer you something to drink, but I have nothing here, I'm afraid."

He waits for the man to sit down before he settles down on his bed, facing him. The Arc watches him for so long Salo squirms and is forced to break the silence.

"I was wondering if you've figured out how to get this collar off me," he says, clutching at the damned thing. "It chafes when I sleep."

The Arc smiles—actually smiles—and Salo knows he's made a dreadful mistake. "Let us drop the pretenses, shall we?"

He starts to rub his hands, praying silently that his ears have played a trick on him. "I . . . don't understand."

"By the fear reeking off you, it's obvious you now know I am your enemy." The high priest's cosmic shards begin to glow, eight rings coiled around his naked arm. Worse, a crimson light starts to bleed out of the corners of his deep-set eyes. "What gave me away, if I may ask?"

49: Isa

The Summit

Her groom's family is all there to welcome her, decked in lovely shades of yellow and motifs of the Crocodile. They sing and dance by the roadside as her cavalcade enters the palace grounds. "Welcome home," they sing with great cheer. "Our bride has come home."

Beautiful though it may be, their song is an insult to her ears. It's meant for a bride who has left the lands of her father, now arriving at the lands of her husband-to-be, which will be her new home.

But these grounds have been her home since the day of her birth. These revelers are the strangers here, not her. They have no right to welcome her.

Yet she waves at them with one hand while the other clings to a bouquet of yellow roses, hoping they'll interpret her unease as the nervousness of a young bride forced into marriage by circumstance.

When her carriage comes to a stop, a young man opens the door for her, a warrior dressed in a smart green tunic with the crest of the Crocodile on his breast. She almost screams when she catches sight of his shiny prosthetic arm, but she forces her mask-crown to show nothing. "You promised," she whispers.

"Heaven is no heaven without you in it, Your Majesty," he says. "You have made your choice, and so have I." He offers his hand to her. "Come, let us walk to your new husband together."

He knows what she's about to do. He must have seen it in her eyes when he held her last night, must have figured it out somehow. But he's not here to stop her. He is here to offer support.

He once told her he would storm the gates of heaven and raze its walls to the ground for her. At the time she thought they were lofty promises that carried no weight, words of lustful worship. She never expected he might be telling her the simple truth.

Her heart breaks, because hell would be more bearable for her if he were in heaven. And yet his presence fills her with strength she didn't know she needed.

Reluctantly, she takes the warrior's hand and lets him walk her to her husband-to-be.

50: Ilapara

Skytown

Standing over his victim's corpse, the masked Jasiri lifts his head and spots Ilapara by the door to Salo's study. Another shout comes from elsewhere in the house, pots rattling as they fall to the ground, glass shattering. Another attacker? Ilapara doesn't wait to find out.

She runs for the drawing room across the study, intending to escape through the open glass doors and out into the garden, but a flash of red lightning arcs in front of her accompanied by the loud clap of thunder, and suddenly the Jasiri is blocking her way forward.

By reflex she slaps down hard on her bangle's largest carnelian crystal, and a suit of spectral armor erupts all around her. In her desperation she veers to an ornamental longsword adorning the nearest wall and pulls it into her grasp. The blade is blunt and was probably never meant for actual combat, but she holds it up with both hands in a defensive stance.

The masked Jasiri tilts his head, amused.

"We're under attack!" she roars.

He surges forward, and their blades meet in a union of sparks and cling. She almost screams at the force on her wrists, but the longsword does not shatter, and she has enough speed and strength in her bones to swing for his head.

He doesn't dodge. He lets the cutting edge of Ilapara's blunt sword hit his mask, and she realizes why as soon as the blade connects. She cries out as a painful shock ripples down the metal sword into her arm and throughout the rest of her body. While the Jasiri suffers not even a dent to his mask, Ilapara's wrist loosens, letting the blade fall. Then she follows it to the ground in a fit of shudders.

She is vacantly aware of the Jasiri moving closer to finish her off. But a figure appears in the periphery of her vision in a blur of black garments. He springs off a low seat with a single flashbrand drawn and leaps at the Jasiri, who pivots to face him, his sword ready to cleave him in half. But then the figure disappears—

Only for the real Tuk to appear behind the Jasiri just a split second before sinking his blade into the Jasiri's back. The warrior howls like a dog at the full moon. There's a clap of thunder and a bolt of lightning that arcs out the doors, taking him with it.

After making sure that the attacker is truly gone, Tuk walks toward Ilapara with eyes wide as plates, his flashbrand still active in his hand. "Are you all right? What the devil is going on? That was a Jasiri, for Ama's sake!"

Ilapara forces herself to stop shaking and accepts Tuk's hand when he offers to help her get up. "Alinata warned me just minutes ago," she says. "We have to leave."

Tuk gapes at her. "How the devil did she know?"

"No idea, Tuk." Ilapara almost jumps when Kamali enters the room through a side door, also carrying an ornamental blade. He was somewhat aloof when she first met him, and every time she's spoken to him since they rescued him from the undercity prisons, she's felt like he was constantly calculating how fast he could kill her and everyone else in sight if he needed to. "Why did one of your friends just attack us?" she demands. "Is this about you?"

"Those were the Arc's Jasiri," Kamali says, a mad light in his eyes. "I'm only alive because the one I fought didn't expect to see me here.

He was surprised, wasn't sure how to proceed. They'll be back. We must leave."

"Where to?" Tuk says. "I'm not leaving this city until we find Salo."

Kamali shakes his head. "We may not have a choice. Your friend is in the Red Temple, and the high priest just sent his Jasiri to kill us. I'm sorry, but this doesn't bode well for him."

Tuk blinks up at the much-taller Kamali, looking younger than usual and utterly lost. "So what do we do?"

Alinata knew the high priest was sending Jasiri to kill us, Ilapara realizes, which raises a thousand questions, but she pushes them aside because they need somewhere to go right now.

But who can we trust?

"The Valau embassy," she says as the answer comes to her. "It's not far from here, and the ambassador seemed to like Salo. She might give us asylum if we explain what's happening."

Tense silence grips the drawing room; then Kamali breaks it. "It's a plan. Gather your things. We need to be out of here in the next five minutes. We'll use your enchanted invisibility amulets and jump over the back wall to elude anyone who might have eyes on the house."

"What about our mounts?" Tuk asks. "We can't just leave them here."

"Riding out the gates isn't an option," says Kamali. "We'll be safer on foot."

A shudder rocks the entire house right then, toppling an ornamental vase that shatters as it hits the ground. Glass breaks somewhere upstairs.

Ilapara looks to the others to make sure she hasn't lost her mind. "Was that another earthquake?"

"It doesn't matter," Kamali says. "Let's get going."

51: Musalodi

Red Temple

It all happens within the span of a split second: Salo leaps from his bed, intent on reaching the door before the seated high mystic, but the old man reacts with the speed of a viper, unleashing a spell that lifts Salo off the floor and slams him against the wall back first.

Salo cries out as his head wound reopens beneath its layers of dressing, his vision almost blackening from the pain. Restraints of lightning quickly bind his neck and all four of his limbs, keeping him pinned against the wall, shocks rippling along his muscles every time he resists.

"This doesn't have to be painful," says the Arc in a conversational tone. "Stop struggling."

Salo goes slack, letting the arcane restraints take his weight. He blinks his eyes open and sees the high mystic through a film of tears. "I'm not your enemy, Your Worship," he pleads. "All I want is to go back home."

The Arc is watching him from across the room, hands clasped behind him. Something akin to regret crosses his stern features. "Not long ago you asked me if I care for nothing in this universe. Do you remember what I said?"

Salo struggles to speak against the restraint nearly choking him. "That you care only for those things in your power to control."

"A half truth," the Arc confesses. "You thought it was dispassion you saw protecting me from the spirit of Sorrow, but what you really saw was my resolve. I *do* care about the world I live in. I, too, am sickened by the injustices I see around me. The tribalism. The slavery, xenophobia, ritual sacrifice . . . I look at the decadence and indifference of the orthodoxy in this kingdom, and it blinds me with rage. But I accept the universe as it is, for I have no power over its nature. What I can control is *my* place in the order of things, and I refuse to simply lie down and submit to the forces of entropy without fighting back."

The Arc must notice Salo's shortness of breath, because he waves a glowing arm, and the neck restraint disappears. Salo coughs, wheezing. The Arc remains silent until Salo's breathing has stabilized.

"When I first crossed the lake of the nameless as a lowly Akili, I vowed that for as long as I lived, I would strive toward power and use it to carve as big a slice of goodness in this merciless universe as I could. That I would erase as much injustice as I could, no matter the cost." The Arc tilts his head, seeming to appraise his bound victim. "I saw you make a similar vow. Very commendable. What you failed to understand, however, is that the pursuit of power *must* be the first step toward fulfilling your vow. Without power, you are chaff in the wind. How can you expect to impose your will upon the world when you cannot prevail over its forces? How can you cow the warlords, rapists, and murderers into submission if you cannot strike fear into their hearts?"

Salo finally sees the high mystic for what he is. "You want to be Hegemon."

The old man's eyes flash. "I see that you have been enlightened. Perhaps now you will understand why I have been cautious with you. But no. I do not seek to be Hegemon. That is what you would have become if I had let you. And like your predecessors, you would have inflicted even more injustice upon the world."

"The Hegemons were misguided," Salo argues. "They misinterpreted what they saw in the inner sanctum. They didn't get the full story."

The Arc lifts a skeptical eyebrow. "And I suppose you think you know better?"

"I do, but it doesn't matter. I refused the role. I'm no threat to you. Take the damned crown if you want it. It's inside the drawer next to the bed. Take it and let me go."

"You would freely give up the power of a Hegemon?" the Arc says, his eyebrow climbing farther upward. "You are not tempted even in the least?"

Salo doesn't have to lie. "Knowing what I know, I want *nothing* to do with it."

Troubled thoughts seem to cloud the Arc's expression for a moment; then he brings a finger to his chin. "I suppose the inner sanctum would have revealed more to you than it did to me. I hardly remember what I saw myself; it has been a long time. But I came out understanding that a great threat was coming and I could not afford to be powerless when it arrived. Would you say I am misguided?"

Salo almost nods, then figures the old man will know if he is being deceptive. He gulps and shakes his head. "Not exactly, but it's a little more complicated than that."

"It always is," the Arc says, sounding vindicated. "There is always a deeper layer of complexity beneath the truth, but we must work with what we know, for we can never unravel all the mysteries of the universe. Even you, who saw more than I did in the sanctum, are filled with doubt. I can sense it in you, the turmoil and disquiet, the questions. There are things you do not know about what was shown to you, are there not?"

Salo remains quiet, and the Arc nods, taking the silence as agreement.

"I hold you in the highest regard, Emissary Siningwe. What you achieved with the All Axiom is nothing short of brilliant, and if it were possible, I would let you go. But I have a vow to fulfill, and the Hegemon's crown will answer to no one else so long as you continue to draw breath."

Desperation fills Salo with courage. "The crown was forged in the sanctum for me and me alone. It won't answer to you even if you kill me."

"You are not the first Hegemon to have his power taken from him," the Arc says, unconcerned. "Preparations to part you from your crown began on the night of the Bloody Requiem. The carnage that transpired beneath the midnight full moon filled the city's holy shrines with the necessary blood essence. The ritual will take place tonight."

Salo gazes at the high mystic in horror. "*You* orchestrated the Bloody Requiem?"

The man isn't ashamed. "Interclan violence was inevitable. I gave it a limited, controlled outlet while making sure the bloodshed would not be in vain. You might think me callous, but my actions prevented many more deaths."

Another realization stabs Salo in the chest. "The collar on my neck was deliberate. You knew I wouldn't be able to claim the crown even if I wanted to."

"I would have never let you step into the sanctum without a collar," the Arc says without hesitating.

"You targeted me from the start," Salo says, beginning to understand. "You lured me in with the amulet. You . . . you used the king to get to me. You've been manipulating me this whole time. But how did you know about me?"

The Arc sighs. "Does it matter in the end?"

"I'd like to know."

"Your queen did not send you here to be a diplomat. She sent you into my hands to realize a vision we share for this continent."

Salo blinks as the world around him stops making sense. *The queen betrayed me. Did Alinata know? Did King Isa?*

"She and I became acquainted at a royal wedding in Shevuland over fifteen comets ago," the Arc says. "We discussed the state of the continent and realized we shared similar aspirations for what we could become if only we seized our forgotten heritage with both hands. When she found out about you and that you did not understand what you held, she realized you were an opportunity to enact our vision. Except we could not risk you becoming Hegemon. You needed to be handled deftly."

Salo sees it all now. The queen's shock when she found out about his Axiom. Then she left the kraal for weeks while he recovered from his awakening, and the next thing he knew, he was on a mission to the Red Temple, only to find it closed to him unless he did the king's bidding.

I've been such a fool. Kamali's violent reaction to finding out about his Axiom should have been a clue; instead he tried his best to forget. "I'll go away," he pleads. "I'll disappear. You won't ever hear from me again."

The Arc shakes his head, and though there's no malice in his eyes, his shards brighten, and a needle-thin dagger of pure red lightning forms in one hand. "I'm truly sorry that this is necessary."

He surges forward on the currents of a lightning bolt, plunging his arcane dagger deep into Salo's heart. The ensuing burst of pain that spreads from Salo's chest to the rest of his body isn't the worst pain he's endured. In fact, it's not nearly as painful as he might have expected.

But as he dies staring into the high priest's deep-set eyes—cold eyes that feel next to nothing for him—a freezing chill more profound than any he's ever known washes over him and holds his hand as it ushers him into a still, silent night.

52: Isa

The Summit

She is a king about to give up her mask-crown, the first in her people's history to ever relinquish her power. It is therefore only appropriate that her wedding vows be spoken where the first king was crowned, that place at the foot of a colossus, where a young man's ashes were buried after he was sacrificed so that his father and all who succeeded him could straddle the center of the world and rule its beating heart.

For some time now she has wondered what the young man must have thought as the fires flayed and consumed his body, if he cursed his father or forgave him, if he screamed for mercy or bore his torment silently. Now, as she walks to her husband-to-be, arm in arm with her lover, she wonders if someone will speculate about what *she* was thinking at this moment. She prays they don't curse her name.

Her husband-to-be is waiting for her with a victorious smile, dressed handsomely in princely green robes and a ceremonial blade by his hip. The colossus rises behind him, so lifelike she feels it might move at any time and crush her with its foot to punish her for the sins of his father, whose blood flows in her veins. She's not entirely sure she wouldn't deserve it.

She wanted the guest list to be as short as possible. She forbade her Sentinels from lingering, ordering all of them back to their barracks as soon as they delivered her. But important people from all over the kingdom wrangled their way into the wedding despite her wishes. Here they are now, lining the aisle to the altar, throwing fragrant yellow petals at her feet. She wishes none of them were here, that she didn't have to pretend for them, but there's nothing she can do about it now. Her steps remain steady as she draws strength from the warrior next to her.

The more important guests are closer to the end of the aisle. She counts among them all ten totem masks and six of the seven moongold half masks, all of them looking up to her at this historic moment. She's not surprised that the seventh half mask is absent, and she doubts anyone else has paused to wonder why its wearer has not appeared. After all, he's known to be contrary.

She stops somewhere halfway toward the altar and looks around. Her well-dressed guests stop singing as her pause stretches. She sees people looking to each other in confusion, perhaps wondering if she's about to change her mind and jilt her groom at the last minute.

Isa removes her mask, and the warrior next to her doesn't hesitate to accept it when she offers it to him. "Before we begin," she shouts, "I have something to say."

Brides do not generally make speeches on their way to the matrimonial altar, so her announcement pricks every ear around her. A whisper of anxiety makes her shiver when she realizes that she hasn't spoken to such a large gathering in her capacity as king before, but she forges ahead.

"Centuries ago," she says to her rapt audience, "on this hill by some accounts, eleven people were tortured with fire before they were allowed to die, all so their tormentors could rule over princedoms sealed in blood."

Her groom gives her a long-suffering smile, crocodile teeth glistening in the suns. Everyone else regards her with shock, for this isn't a subject ever spoken about in public.

She continues. "I stand here because one of those tormentors was my forebear, and though this made me king many centuries later, I am here to say this to all those present today: I am ashamed! It shames me deeply to be descended from such a vile man, for what he and his collaborators perpetrated that day was a crime of monstrous proportions. Not only because of the unspeakable horror they caused those they sacrificed, but also because they took a united people and divided them without their consent."

Her audience watches, stunned. They came for a wedding and are now witness to scandal.

"Marks appeared on our necks, and we were forced to bow to those who had inflicted them on us," Isa says. "We fell prey to the whims of greedy, power-hungry princes who stoked hatred where there was none, imposed difference where there was oneness, jealousy where there was empathy. Just look at what happened on the Bloody Requiem! Look at how tribesmen slaughtered each other with wanton glee, and for what? What was gained on that night but pain and sorrow?"

Isa's groom isn't smiling anymore. "What do you think you're doing, Your Majesty? Stop this nonsense. You're embarrassing yourself."

She looks to the warrior next to her for reassurance. She finds it in his eyes, so she removes her yellow diamond necklace and holds it up to the sunlight. A brilliant white glow flowers at its center, and she immediately feels it growing warmer to the touch. Some of her guests gasp when they see the gemstone.

"Today will be the day those divisions end," she shouts. "Just as eleven innocent victims gave their lives so that a united people would be divided into eleven princedoms, today, eleven princes shall give their lives so that a divided people are united."

Murmurs rise as the guests begin to figure out what she's holding. "Impossible," says a woman in a half mask.

"It's the Covenant Diamond!" shouts another. "Kill her!"

A man similarly masked draws magic into his shards and begins to transform into a giant bat. The woman next to him summons a wind that begins to billow around her robes and lift her upward. Isa's groom draws his sword and points at her.

But it's too late. She knows the words she must speak. She raises the glowing Diamond as high as she can and shouts: "May what was writ in blood be erased by blood. I declare all clans dissolved."

The Diamond becomes a sun in her hands, concentrated into a single point. Strong arms surround her and hold her against a solid chest as a wave of devouring heat explodes across the Summit. Then all becomes light.

53: Jomo

Midtown

In a midtown teahouse, Jomo feels his chair shudder beneath him just as he hears a rumble, followed quickly by a commotion from outside.

He shares glances with Odari and Kito, his guards turned closest friends, and wordlessly they rise from their table and walk out of the teahouse to investigate. At first, all he sees are people screaming and yelling as though the world were ending.

"What is it?" he asks a woman trembling on the sidewalk with a hand covering her mouth. She points, and Jomo follows her gaze northwest, to the hole that has been torn into the sky.

The colossus is gone. In its stead, an eerie storm of fire and light.

"Obe was right!" Odari cries, and Jomo grips his arm so hard he would have broken it if he were strong enough.

"What was he right about? Tell me, damn it!"

"My uncle!" Kito cries as he stares up at the firestorm in shock. "My uncle is up there!"

Guilt and fear reflect in Odari's watery eyes. He opens his mouth to speak, but then he gasps, pointing at Jomo's neck.

"By the Mother, your mark!" he cries. "Yours too, Kito! They're gone!"

Jomo looks at Odari, then at Kito. They were each born with a different clan mark laying claim to their necks. The marks have vanished.

People on the streets realize the same thing. And suddenly Jomo knows what Odari was going to tell him, and he crumbles to the ground with a sorrowful howl.

Epilogue: The Apprentice

Red Temple

When light blooms at the foot of the colossus and the shock wave from the explosion hurtles down the hill, an apprentice watches from her perch next to a queen and a high mystic, at the top of the Red Temple's tallest tower.

The apprentice has wound the Void's indifference tightly around her heart like a cocoon to shield it from the troublesome emotions that have haunted her of late, the debilitating guilt, the soul-rending sorrow. They snuck up on her like creeping vines, and she didn't see them until they held her solidly in their clutch.

When did I become so weak?

"I can't believe she did it," the queen says, looking toward the storm of light above Skytown with uncharacteristically expressive eyes. She arrived earlier this morning on the wings of her ravens to witness the culmination of the high mystic's victory; given the look on her face, she must have thought his plans unlikely to succeed.

The high mystic folds his arms with grim satisfaction. "It is why I chose her for the task," he says. "She was the youngest of Mweneugo's children but stood out to me where I found her brothers wanting. It takes a unique strength of character to stand at the edge of the abyss, to see it for what it is, and still leap over the precipice for the greater good. Isa was courageous enough that when I planted the idea in her mind, she did not hesitate to leap even when she understood what it would cost her."

The queen's copper crown of spiked feathers glints as she tilts her head. "I must admit, Your Worship, I was worried you were overreaching. I would have preferred to keep our dealings simple. But not only have you delivered the Hegemon's crown; you have also destroyed all your enemies in one fell swoop, clearing the path to your ascension. I'm impressed."

"A new dawn has risen over the Yontai today," the high mystic agrees. "Now the divisions that have plagued my people can begin to heal." He inclines his head respectfully to the queen. "Of course, I couldn't have done it without you or your apprentice." His deep-set eyes slide to the apprentice, and she shivers. "Things went according to plan in no small part because of her contributions."

"She's very capable," says the queen. "I couldn't have made a better choice."

This is supposed to make the apprentice happy, but the words make her feel like she has taken a dip in a pool of blood.

She shakes it off. *I am because we are,* she tells herself. *That is the Yerezi way. The fate of our people is more important than one life.*

"But I wonder if you're not being too optimistic," the queen says. "After all, clans can still exist even without marks. People hardly need visual distinctions to be divided."

The high mystic looks out at the city below, an emperor surveying his new domain. "That is true, and I suspect that even with the marks gone, my people will cling to old prejudices if left to their own devices. But I have every intention of guiding them away from those impulses. Indeed, I will forbid the use and display of all clan symbols and unify the legions into a homogenous army. As for the orthodoxy, its apathy and sectarian ways will be no more. I will build a new merit-based hierarchy of mystics to actively serve the people, and all who have the mettle to learn magic will be welcome. The marks ultimately limited the number of mystics we could induct into our covens; that is now a thing of the past."

"It seems you will be busy over the coming years," the queen says thoughtfully.

"This will be a lifelong project, Your Majesty," the high mystic says. "Change does not have to come overnight, but it *must* come eventually. Those of us who commune regularly with the spirits of the earth sense a great evil amassing beyond the horizon. I cannot say when it will rear its head, but I know that we must be prepared when it does. Once our empires are established—you in the south, I in the north, and our foreign ally beyond the Jalama—we will bring an age of strength and prosperity to this continent unlike any ever seen before, and the Mother will be pleased. Is this not why we are here?"

The apprentice almost gapes like a fool in her shock. Did the high mystic just casually offer *all* the Redlands south of the Yontai to her queen? But how could he completely misunderstand the queen's intentions? She didn't send a tribesman here to die so the Yerezi could become an empire! And the apprentice certainly didn't betray someone she came to consider a friend just so her people could go to war.

All of this, coming to the city, lying, scheming, it was meant to avoid a war, not find the excuse for one.

The apprentice expects her queen to explain this to the high mystic. Except the queen's expression loosens with satisfaction, and she nods in agreement. "Indeed," she says.

And the apprentice feels sick.

ACKNOWLEDGMENTS

This book was a blast to write, and I want to thank you, dear reader, for coming along for the ride. You make writing worth it.

Many thanks to the reviewers and bloggers and Twitter personalities who spread the word about the first book. As a newcomer to the industry, I've found that your contributions make all the difference.

Another thank-you to Adrienne Procaccini at 47North for running the show in the publication of this series. Yet another thank-you to Clarence Haynes, my developmental editor, who helped me turn an unwieldy tome into a tighter and stronger story.

To Laura Barrett, Riam Griswold, and Stephanie Chou: you have demonstrated to me just how underrated copyeditors and proofreaders are in general. I'm amazed by your work ethic and your attention to detail. You probably know my world just as well as I do, if not better. Thank you for the shine you've added to my work.

Thank you as well to Kristin Lunghamer, Megan Beatie, and the PR and marketing team at 47North and all your efforts behind the scenes to get my name out there.

I also want to thank Julie Crisp, my agent, for her continued support of me as an author.

And last but definitely not least, I want to thank my family, who continue to be a tireless source of motivation for me not just as a writer but as a person. I am blessed to have you all in my life.

ABOUT THE AUTHOR

Debut author C. T. Rwizi was born in Zimbabwe, grew up in Swaziland, finished high school in Costa Rica, and got a BA in government at Dartmouth College in the United States. He currently lives in South Africa with his family and enjoys playing video games, taking long runs, and spending way too much time lurking on Reddit. He is a self-professed lover of synthwave.